Philip Verrill Mighels

As It Was in the Beginning

C000164514

Philip Verrill Mighels

As It Was in the Beginning

1st Edition | ISBN: 978-3-75241-141-6

Place of Publication: Frankfurt am Main, Germany

Year of Publication: 2020

Outlook Verlag GmbH, Germany.

Reproduction of the original.

AS IT WAS

IN THE

BEGINNING

BY

PHILIP VERRILL MIGHELS

CHAPTER I

A TRUSTED MESSENGER

Grenville was not the type to be readily excited, yet a glow of exceptional brilliance shone in his eyes as he met the searching gaze of his friend, and wondered if Fenton could be jesting.

That he had made no reply whatsoever to Fenton's proposition he failed to realize till Gerald spoke again.

"Well, Sid," demanded that impetuous lieutenant of finance, "gone dumb? Perhaps I haven't made it plain," and he particularized on his fingers. "You get an ocean trip of eight or ten weeks' duration, tropic sun at its best, leisurely business without a fleck of bother, absolute rest, good provender, thorough recuperation, your entire expenses cheerfully paid, vast service rendered to me, no time lost on your equilibrator, time for countless new inventions to sprout in your fertile brain—and the unutterable joy of escaping this abominable climate, practically at once!"

Grenville's smile, still brightly boyish, despite the many reverses and hardships of his six and twenty years, came creeping to his eyes. His wan face suggested a tint of color.

"Don't wake me up for a moment, Fen," he answered. "I haven't dreamed anything like it for years."

"Dreamed?" repeated Fenton, resuming his interrupted pacing up and down the rug, where the firelight reddened his profile. "Does that mean you like it?—you'll go?"

"Would Cinderella go to a ball?" replied the still incredulous Grenville, half seriously. "What's the joker, old chap? What is the worst that could happen at the midnight stroke of twelve?"

Fenton came at once and laid his hands on the broad, bony shoulders of his friend.

"Have I ever played a joker with you yet?" said he. "Never mind the apology. I forgive you. I understand the compliment. Proposal sounds too good to be true, and all that sort of rubbish. The fact is, old man, I want you to go to Canton, China, and bring home my affianced bride. That's absolutely all there is to the business. You need the change and voyage; I haven't the time to go out there and fetch her myself. Elaine is alone in that heathenish country, miserably heartsick over her uncle's sudden death. She wishes to return at once. I can't let the poor girl come alone. I've no one in the world but you I'd care to send—and there you are."

The glow departed from Grenville's eyes. His doubts of any proposition with a woman in the case lurked deep in his level gaze. His face became once more the rugged mask with which he had so long confronted a world persistently gray. The smile he summoned to his lips was more quizzical than mirthful.

"It sounds perfectly simple," he replied. "But—you know there are several tales, recorded in prose and verse, of kings who have sent a trusted messenger on precisely such an errand. The joker somehow managed to get into play."

"Just so," agreed Fenton, readily. "Three or four times in a thousand cases the girl and the—er—messenger rather thoughtlessly—well, a complication arises. The percentage, however, is excessively low. We'll consider that a negligible possibility. You see, I know both you and Elaine, and I am not a king. The question is—will you go?"

Grenville was always amused by Fenton's arguments.

"I have seen no statistics on the subject," he admitted. "In this particular instance you think there is not the slightest danger?"

"Of finding in old Sid a modern Launcelot?" Fenton turned his friend about till both of them faced down the length of the room. "Well," he added, "to be sure——"

Grenville's quick glance had sped to the massive mirror, ten feet away, where both himself and Fenton were reflected from heels to crown. He comprehended in a glance the ill-clothed, thin, ungainly figure he presented: his big hands hanging loosely down, his face too ruggedly modeled, too sallow for attractiveness, his hair too rebellious for order.

A Launcelot indeed! The irony of the situation struck home to his sense of humor.

"Have a look," continued Fenton, his nervous glance indifferent to his own athletic fitness, the perfect grooming of his person, the grace and elegance of his tailoring. "Do you discern anything of the disloyal ambassador in that hard-worked friend and comrade of my happiest years?" His eyes gleamed irresistibly. "You see, old chap, you have trusted an invention of perhaps incalculable worth to my honor, and must leave both your fame and possible fortune in my keeping while you are long away."

"Yes, but——"

"I know, exactly. This is the sort of thing you and I have always done by one another. I had no thought of refusing your trust in me, and so—I have booked your passage for Wednesday."

He turned again to the mantel and began to fill his pipe.

Grenville pivoted slowly and rubbed the corner of his jaw.

"You have—booked my passage—for Wednesday?"

Fenton nodded. "Elaine is quite desolate and lonely. You need immediate sunshine and warmth, and can do no good remaining here. Fine day all round for starting, Wednesday, and no boat sailing sooner. There are one thousand dollars in that wad by the statue of Anubis, for your outfit and incidental cash."

Grenville glanced mechanically at the dog-headed god of the ancient Egyptians, apparently guarding the money towards which Fenton had waved a careless gesture.

"One thou——"

"If it isn't enough, draw on my bankers for more," interrupted Fenton, puffing at his calabash industriously. "I have written Elaine so fully you'll have nothing to explain."

"By George!" said Grenville, more aggressively, "I like your nerve—the way you'd plunge me into trouble! Do you think I'm a mere senseless rack of wires and bones because I'm not my usual self? What's to prevent me from falling head over heels—— What's the rest of her name—Elaine what? And you probably have her photograph somewhere among your possessions."

"Her full name," Fenton answered, moving to the desk beside the mirror, "is Elaine Lytton—twenty-one this month. We've known each other seven years." He returned, extending a small-sized photograph. "Fine girl. That's her picture. Good likeness—sent me last winter from China."

Grenville studied the photograph superficially. He used it to tap on the table as he once more faced his host.

"About as I expected," he announced with his customary candor. "Nice-looking girl—nothing extra, perhaps, but nice enough. Now tell me how any healthy male friend of yours can guarantee not to fall in love with Elaine, on a long, lazy trip through the tropics," and he cast the picture from him towards

4

the lamp.

Fenton relighted his pipe. "Well, suppose he did commit the folly you describe, what then?"

"What then?" echoed Grenville, incredulously. "By the long, curved lashes of Juno's eyes, if I were the man you'd certainly see what then!"

"All right," said the imperturbable Fenton. "I accept your conditions, fully, and about your outfit I'd suggest——"

"Hold on!" interrupted Grenville. "I haven't accepted your commission, much as the trip——"

"The trip!" said Fenton. "Ah! that's the point! I insist on your making the trip, you see, and taking the rest. Fetching Elaine from China is merely incidental—only don't forget her completely and come back here empty-handed." He sat down to wrestle with his pipe.

Grenville looked at him amusedly.

"Now, see here," he said, "don't you make the slightest mistake, you confident old idiot. If I should just happen to fancy Elaine, I wouldn't give you twenty cents in Mexican money for your chances at the wedding bells and trimmings."

"Then you'll go!" Fenton suddenly exploded, springing to his feet. "Come on, that's settled—shake."

But Grenville retreated from the outstretched hand, a queer smile playing on his features.

"Hang your infernal self-conceit," he answered; "you don't think I could win her if I tried."

"I don't believe you'll try."

"That isn't the point. I might. If I loved her I would, you can bet your final shoe peg! Your proposition isn't fair—subjecting a man, and a friend at that, to possible temptation, all kinds of treachery, and a war between love and duty. Rot that kind of duty! I want you to know that if I take the trip and happen to fall in this muddle with your girl, I'm going to pitch your infernal old duty game overboard in less than two seconds and go in and win her, if I can!"

"Well, what's all the row about, after that?" inquired Fenton as before. "Haven't I said I accept your challenge? Go out there and fetch her, that's all. As for the rest—win her, if you can!"

"I don't say I'll try to win the girl. I may not like her for a cent."

5

"Then why all this futile argument and waste of valuable time?"

"But I may—confound your egotistic nerve, and your insistence! And I warn you, Fen, I mean every word, in case——"

"I understand—I understand you fully, without repetition," Fenton once more interrupted. "For Heaven's sake, give me your hand, old man, and cease firing."

"You meant it, then—no strings on the proposition?"

"Not a string—absolutely not a string."

A strange new thrill of pleasure crept into Grenville's being, warming his thin, anæmic pulses suddenly, as he met Fenton's gaze and once more permitted his thoughts to dwell on all the proposal embraced. Since Fenton refused to be worried concerning himself and the girl who supplied the motive for the trip, then why should he consider it further? Elaine was, in fact, swiftly fading from his reflections.

All his nature yearned towards the tropic seas. All his overwrought frame and substance ached for the long, lazy days of indolence, rest, and recuperation that alone could restore him to himself. He had always longed for precisely this excursion to the far-off edge of the sphere. His faculties leaped to the new-made possibility of a contact with the ancient world, heretofore so wholly inaccessible.

Already new color had come to his face and a new blaze of fire to his eyes. Privations and toil, those two unsparing allies that had made such inroads on his health and strength, seemed fading harmlessly away. The prospect was far too alluring to be resisted. There was no good reason in the world for refusing this favor to a friend.

The brightness of face that had ever made him so lovable, came unbidden, there in the glow.

"I suppose I'll have to go," he presently admitted, "if it's only to win your girl."

"Shake," said Fenton; and they shook.

CHAPTER II

AN UNEXPECTED OUTBURST

The sea is an ancient worker of miracles in amazing transformation, but rarely does it bring about a more complete or startling metamorphosis than that which was wrought upon Grenville—trusted messenger for afriend.

Long before the shores of Cathay loomed welcomely upon his vision he had lost all sense of weariness or depression, and likewise all that worn and gaunt appearance of a large, thin frame inhabited by a dogged but thoroughly exhausted spirit.

He was once more his strong, bold, interested self, merry of speech, bright-eyed, untamed in his buoyant nature, lovable, thoughtful of those about him, impetuous, and never to be repressed. He had flirted uninterruptedly with all the old women and the children on the outward voyage, and was now as cheerfully repeating this gay performance on the steamship "Inca," homeward bound, on which he was certainly the favorite of the crew and his fellow-passengers.

The fortnight passed with Elaine upon the sea had been wholly uneventful, save for the vast commotion astir in Grenville's being. The worst that could happen, he told himself, had happened. His daily deportment towards his charge had baffled, piqued, and amused that young lady alternately, and convinced her that here was a brand-new specimen of the genus man with which she had never had a genuine experience.

She found him boyish, unexpected, apparently indifferent, and even unaware, at times, of her existence on the vessel, then fairly effervescent with deviltry that left her all but gasping. He was not to be classified, fixed, or calculated, save in certain traits of fearlessness, generosity, and kindness to those most needful of a helping smile, a merry word, or a spell of relief from daily cares.

He commanded a certain admiration from the puzzled girl, but as yet her actual feelings towards him were quite unanalyzed. She was constantly finding herself astonished at the scope and variety of his information; she was glad to listen when he talked; she was frequently touched to the very heart by his tender care of one or two frail little beings on the ship to whom much of his time was devoted.

There they were, with the situation between them apparently commonplace to dullness—till this one particular day.

It was not a common day on the ocean. Despite the fact he was neither mariner nor meteorologist, Grenville felt some vast disturbance impending in all the lifeless air, regardless of the fact the barometer was steady and the calm, rainless spell had been exceptionally prolonged. It was not precisely a premonition that addressed itself to his senses; it was something he could not explain.

A wave of heat passed swiftly through his body, leaving a strange excitement in its train, as he paused for a second to wonder if the "symptoms" he sensed were concerned not at all with sea or weather, but wholly with Elaine.

He admitted the love—the wild, free, passionate love that had swept him away, past all safe anchorage, with her entry into his existence. He had made no effort to conceal it from himself, to deny its overwhelming force. He had cursed Gerald Fenton most heartily and consistently for casting him into this maelstrom of conflicting emotions, and daily and nightly he had waged mighty war with that fortunately absent individual, who had calmly accepted his challenge.

The trouble had come unbidden. Elaine was so wholly different from the girl represented by Fenton's photograph! The picture had seemed so lifeless— and she was so gloriously alive! That one fact alone seemed sufficient excuse to Grenville for all that had happened to him since. He had not been fully informed, he argued, respecting her wondrous charms.

The two weeks mentioned, with Elaine at his side, had certainly accomplished the world-old complication once more, despite all his hard and honest struggling. When the fight had ceased he did not even know. What Elaine's private attitude was towards himself he had taken no time to inquire. That part mattered less than nothing at all—at least as concerned the present. He had warned old Fenton what to expect, but now—by the gods—how deeply he was mired in the quandary!

He was certainly mighty hard hit, he confessed, but meantime was equally positive that the singular something he plainly felt, invading the air and telling its message to some faint, imperfect sense of his being, had nothing whatsoever to do with this business of passionate emotions. Yet not a sign of uneasiness on the part of officers and crew could his keenest wit discover, in any quarter of the iron craft plowing steadily on across the sea.

He had climbed to the topmost deck of the ship, where he and a carpenter, who was hewing out a boat thwart with a gleaming adze, were temporarily alone. It was not Grenville's manner of wooing to hover beside Elaine throughout the day or evening. He had done no wooing, as a matter of fact, beyond assuming a somewhat bold but unoffending guardianship, which she might have found refreshing had it not so frequently taken her breath with its very matter-of-factness.

At the present moment, as Grenville was well aware, she was somewhere down on the shaded portion of the promenade, where the erstwhile stir of tropic air had ebbed to utter sluggishness and finally expired. One of the purser's young assistants, dressed in wrinkled white duck, was dumbly adoring at her side.

Impatiently banishing Fenton from his thoughts, Grenville gazed idly at the sultry sky, and as idly at the carpenter, wielding the polished adze. When a deckhand presently called this workman away, Grenville took up the implement left behind, felt he would like to swing it just once at the root of the complication now arisen between himself and his distant friend—on whose money he was voyaging—and whose sweetheart his nature demanded for a mate—and, replacing the tool on the weathered planks, he thrust both hands in his pockets and paced to and fro, beside a pair of inverted lifeboats and a raft, that occupied most of the deck.

He finally flung himself down on a hatch, in the shade of a white-painted funnel, and plunged his warring faculties into concentrated study of a problem in mechanics involved in a new invention. On the back of a letter, drawn from an inside pocket, he drew black hieroglyphics, that to him were wheels and levers that relieved his state of mind.

Absorption claimed him for its own. The swift, weird changes of the sky and atmosphere escaped his engrossed attention. He was not even aware of her presence till Elaine had been standing for fully five minutes, a few feet only from his side.

When he looked up at last and beheld once more that singular glow and beauty in the depths of her luminous eyes, and felt the subtle flattery involved in the fact she had come to the place to find him, seek him out, a flood of tidal passion surged to his outermost veins.

It was just the one straw too much, this unforeseen encounter, with the smile upon her lips. His sturdy resolutions all went down in utter confusion before the wild gladness of his heart. Yet he made no outward sign for Elaine to read.

Calmly, to all appearances, he placed the letter in his pocket.

"I hope," said Elaine, "I haven't disrupted anything important."

He arose and gazed at her oddly.

"You have, Elaine," he answered, in a voice he strove hard to control. "You've not only disrupted everything heretofore moving along its accustomed path of order, law, and calm, but you've also upset all sorts of established institutions and raised some merry Hades."

A spirit of the lively old Nick was infusing with his youthful blood as he stood there gazing upon her. Elaine, however, either failed to detect its presence, or she failed to understand.

"I?" she said, "Mr. Grenville. I'm sorry. What have I done?"

He could not have done the conventional thing, the deliberate, calm, or expected thing, to save his immortal soul. His nature was far too honest, too unabashed. He came a step nearer—and then she knew, but she could not have moved at the moment had death been the oncoming penalty for remaining where she stood. She had never been so startled in her life.

They two were absolutely alone and unobserved. Of this the impulsive Grenville was aware—and the knowledge had fired a certain madness in his being he was powerless to quell.

"Elaine," he said, as he suddenly caught her unresisting hands, "you've put old Fenton entirely out of the game. You're going to marry me."

She was dimly conscious of pain in her hands, where he crushed them in his ardor. But her shocked surprise was uppermost, as she faced him with blazing eyes.

"Mr. Grenville!" she said. "Mr. Grenville—you—— To say—to speak ——"

"Elaine," he interrupted gayly, bright devils dancing in his boyish eyes, "it simply couldn't be helped. We were intended to meet—and were cut out for one another. So the hour must come when you'll pitch old Gerald's ring in the sea by order of the very Fates themselves!"

She snatched away her hands in indignation.

"For shame!" she cried in rising anger, her whole womanly being aflame with resistance to all his growing madness. "You haven't the slightest right in the world——"

"Right?" he repeated. "Right? I love you, Elaine! I love you! Haven't I said——"

"Oh, the treachery—the treachery to Gerald!" she cut in, with swiftly increasing emotion. "To say such things when your honor——"

"Wait!" he interrupted, eagerly. "I told him what he might expect from any such arrangement. I warned him precisely what might happen. He understood —accepted my conditions—made it a challenge—declared if I tried I couldn't win! And now——"

"You can't—you can't!—you can't!" she cried at him, angrily. "To think that Gerald—to think you'd dare——"

He suddenly caught her in his arms and crushed her against his breast. He kissed her on the mouth, despite her struggles.

"Elaine," he said, "you are mine—all mine—my sweetheart—my comrade —my mate!"

She finally planted her fists against his throat and thrust him from her in fury.

"You brute!" she answered, sobbing in her anger. "I hate you—I loathe you—despise you utterly! I wish I might never see your face again!"

"I'll make you love me, Elaine," he answered, white at last with intensity and deep-going passion. "I'll make you love me, as I love you—as madly—as wholly—as wondrously—before ever we two get home."

Already Elaine was retreating from the place.

"Never!" she answered, wildly. "Never, never, never!—do you hear?—not if it takes this boat a hundred years!" And gropingly, almost blinded by her sense of shame and rage, she fled from the deck and down the stairs, leaving him shaken where he stood.

CHAPTER III

A MIDNIGHT TRAGEDY

Not the slightest alarm had invaded the ship, when Grenville finally urged his senses back to the normal, notwithstanding the unaccustomed suddenness with which the aspect of the day had been reversed.

The storm broke at last, about one in the afternoon, with a deluge of rain and an onslaught of wind that seemed for a time refreshing. The huge steel leviathan appeared to elevate her nose, give her shoulders a shake that settled her firmly in the gray disorder of the elements, and then to accept the rude old contest with a certain indifference, born of well-established prowess.

By two o'clock there was nothing refreshing suggested. A dull, stubborn struggle was waging in the drab of a wild and narrow field of commotion. Chill, musty billows of air, made thick by something that was neither scud nor mist, pounced heavily upon the laboring "Inca" in a manner chaotic and irregular. The sea was rising sullenly, its waves, like tumultuous cohorts, with ragged white banners, ceaselessly advancing.

With an easy, monotonous assurance the great device of steam and iron plugged steadily onward. It could ride out a sea of tremendously greater violence. It knew from long experience every crest and every abyss of these mountains of air and water. It met huge impacts majestically, with a prow that cleaved them through, while its huge, wet bulk plowed up its mileage with a barely diminished speed.

Few of the passengers were actually alarmed. A storm evolved so suddenly, they were confidently informed, would expend itself in one brief spasm of impotent fury and subside almost as it had come. It was all some mere local disturbance that the spell of dry, calm weather had accumulated too swiftly for any save a violent discharge.

Discomfort increased to a certain pitch; locomotion about the saloon became impracticable. The crew alone remained upon their legs. It seemed like the climax to the storm. But another stage swiftly developed.

It might have been somewhat after three P.M. when a shroud of darkness settled from the heavens, its substance foreign both to cloud and sea. It was thicker than before, and decidedly more musty. As black as night, but unrelated to all ordinary essences of darkness, it wrapped the stormy universe in Stygian folds with a suddenness strangely disquieting.

The cataclysm followed almost instantly, as if from behind a concealing curtain. It came in dimensions incredible, a prodigious wall of rumpled water, like a mobile mountain chain. It towered forbiddingly above the quivering vessel for one terrible moment of threat, then confusion, utter and seemingly eternal, plunged roaringly over and under the helpless ocean toy of steel, submerging the very sea itself in Niagaras of sound and weight and motion.

A hideous shudder quivered through the feeble plaything of the elements. Strange, muffled thunderings, sensations of oblivion sweeping miles deep across the ocean, and a horrible conviction of the ship's insignificance, impressed themselves pellmell upon the senses, while ebon blackness closed instantly down, like annihilation's swift accompaniment, and the hull seemed sinking countless fathoms.

Such a moment expands to an æon. Doom seemed an old acquaintance when a complex gyration, a sense of being flung through space, and a reassertion of the engine's throb preceded the struggle to the surface. Yet it seemed as if no miracle of buoyancy and might could survive till the great steel body rose once more to the air. Men held their breath as if they must drown if the top were not immediately achieved.

A stupendous lurch, an incredible list to starboard, another streaming by of immeasurable torrents, and the steamer wallowed pantingly out into daylight once again, to flounder like a thing exhausted till she steadied once more to the roll and pitch of the former storm-driven sea.

There had been no time for any man to act till the monstrous thing had come and gone its way. As helplessly as all the others, Grenville had clutched at the table, there beside Elaine, while death passed and roared in their faces. He had gone to her chiefly for appearances, yet quite as if nothing had happened, despite their scene above, while Elaine had issued from her stateroom in terror of the storm. It was not till new, sharp sounds of activity broke on his senses, from above, that Sid left her side and went to inquire concerning the sum of their damage.

His face had lost a shade only of its usual cheerfulness, when he finally returned. The ship was rolling heavily, fairly in the trough.

"Our rudder is gone, with six of the lifeboats and as many men," he told his charge, whose courage he had previously gauged. "The worst is undoubtedly over. We can steer with the screws, sufficiently to make the nearest port."

"Our rudder!—half a dozen men," Elaine faintly echoed, her brown eyes ablaze with dread and sympathy, as she steadied from the shock of Grenville's news. "What was it? How did it happen?"

"A tidal wave. There must have been a huge volcanic disturbance, doubtless under the sea. Or it may have been an earthquake, tremendously violent. Nothing else, according to the Captain, could account for a storm so sudden, or for all this strange thickness of the air. He is confident now of our safety. The storm may subside in an hour."

There was not the slightest cessation of the storm, however, till eight o'clock in the evening. Even then the night continued thick and wild.

Fortunately the sea was vast and deep. There was nothing known in two hundred miles on which the ship could blunder. Hour after hour the crippled "Inca" limped erratically onward, buffeted helplessly here and there, and scalloping angry abysses of darkness and water, as first one screw and then the other was driven full speed, or slowed to half, or reversed altogether, to hold her nose to the altered course that would finally fetch them to a port for highly essential repairs.

The rage of the elements, abating at last a trifle, had far exceeded the Captain's expectations. And when at length the center was passed, and comparative ease had supervened, the wind was still a considerable gale, while the sea would run high till nearly morning.

The passengers, however, were sufficiently assured to retire at a fairly early hour. Elaine had readily responded to Grenville's matter-of-fact instructions, and, long before midnight, was fitfully sleeping, although she had not undressed.

When eight bells struck from the bridge somewhere above him, Grenville still sat on the edge of his berth, rumpling his hair with one vigorous hand, while the other prisoned a book on his knee with a piece of white paper upon it. The paper was literally covered with mechanical designs and hieroglyphics, involved in his latest problem.

He arose at last, removed his coat, and began to fumble with his tie. His eyes were fixed upon his paper. The problem's spell was cast again upon him. He sank, as before, to his inconvenient seat, and drew yet another design.

How long he remained there, tranced by the lines that represented levers, gears, and eccentrics, the man could never have stated. He was dimly subconscious it was time to go to bed, and from time to time one hand would return to his collar. As a matter of fact, the hour was past one of the morning.

Then, of a sudden, apparently beneath his very feet, the frightful *thing* occurred.

It came all together—the grinding crunch, the colossal upheaval of the ship's great belly full of vitals, the scream of iron ripped from iron, the roar of steam from broken pipes, and the tremor of death-throes, shuddering thus promptly down to the canted bow and stern from the wedge-shaped split amidships.

They had struck on a rock, upheaved by the earthquake, where a hundred fathoms of crystal brine had existed the previous noon!

The hideous conviction of doom and horror sped as swiftly as the shiver of destruction to the farthest confines of the vessel. Screams far and near, hoarse bellowing, a shrill, high pæan of mortal fright, and sounds of disordered scurrying followed with a promptness fairly appalling.

Grenville waited for nothing. As well as the most experienced officer on board, he realized the significance of the impact, the ship's awful buckling, and the quiver stilling the creature's heart—the engines that had ceased at once to throb.

His door had been flung widely open. Before he could reach the turning of the corridor, the one electric bulb, left glowing for the night, abruptly blackened. But he knew the way to Elaine.

He seemed to be plunging through a torture hall, so hurtling full was the darkness of fearful cries and confusion. The broken hulk of the steamer slightly lurched, as the plates broke yet farther apart. Sidney was flung against a cabin wall, but he righted and pitched more rapidly down the already canted passage.

"Elaine!" he called. "Elaine!"

"Yes!" she answered. "Yes! I can't get out!" She was not at all in a panic.

Someone, a man, rushed headlong by and nearly bowled Grenville over. He was spilling golf clubs from a bag and calling for the steward.

Grenville caught at the knob of Elaine's hard-fastened door and threw his weight upon it. A stubborn resistance met his effort. The frame had been distorted by the splitting of plates and ribs. The wedging was complete.

"Stand back!" he called out sharply. "I must break it in at once!"

He knew they were late already—that swarms of beings, nearer the exits, were wildly pouring from the ship's interior, to be first to the boats, so fatally reduced in numbers.

With all his might he hurled his shoulder against the door, that merely creaked at his impotent assault. The hall was narrow. He could gain no momentum for his blow. The second and third attack made no impression.

A clammy sweat exuded from his forehead. That the sea was tumbling torrentially into the helpless vessel he knew by countless indications. Elaine must perish helplessly in her trap, could he not immediately force the barrier. He suddenly got down, full length, upon the floor, braced his shoulders against the opposite cabin, and, with knees slightly raised, placed both his feet against the door. Then he strained with superhuman strength. The door remained immovable, but its paneling slightly cracked.

Meantime the shrieks, the shouts, the roaring of steam, and the terrible chaos of destruction had increased to a horrifying chorus. The corridor was filling with hot, moist vapor from the burst pipes. A dozen stokers had perished. Fire had attacked a portion of the vessel abaft the midships section.

Once more, with a wild, fanatic conjuring of energy, Grenville spent himself upon the door—and a panel snapped out, flinging little splinters on Elaine. In a fury of desperate activity the man on the floor beat out more with his driving feet.

"It's large enough! It's large enough!" cried the girl as the orifice widened. "Don't wait to break it larger!"

She was now fully dressed, having swiftly prepared for any sort of emergency. A candle, provided from her bag, was glowing in her hand.

This she thrust forth for Grenville to take, and then, with deliberate care, she wormed her way out through the jagged hole with the confident skill of a child.

"Not there!" called Grenville, as she hastened ahead to gain the forward companionway. "Everybody's there, all fighting for their lives!"

He caught her actively about the waist, as a further lurch and settling of the "Inca" would have hurled her to the floor. Down through a shorter passage and up a strangely tilted stair he drew her rapidly, his heart assailed by a sickening fear of what their delay might have cost them. Yet less than five minutes had actually passed since the first vast shock of disaster.

They emerged to a portion of the slanted deck that seemed to be utterly deserted. A gust of wind blew out the candle. The sky was clear. An uneven fragment of the aging moon shone dully on the broken ship, whence fearful sounds continued to arise.

Only one of the boats had been dropped to the tide—to be instantly whirled *inside* the parting steamer, on the torrent filling her mighty belly, where the latest lurch had laid her widely open.

Grenville ran to the starboard rail for a glance towards the struggle farther forward. There, about the impotent crew, laboring hotly with people, boats and davits no longer adjusted to normal working order, the wildest confusion existed.

A boat that hung out above the sea was filled with screaming beings. Some madman arose and slashed with maniacal fury at the rope of the blocks, to hasten the craft's descent. Of a sudden its bow shot perpendicularly downward, its stern still high in the air. Its cargo dropped out like leaden weights, while the empty shell, like a pendulum, swayed to and fro above the smothered cries.

To join such a throng would be but to choose a larger company in which to perish. Grenville saw that the steamer must presently drop from her rock and sound illimitable depths. This could hardly be delayed for more than ten minutes longer.

A sickening qualm assailed his vitals at the thought of Elaine, doomed to drown thus helplessly, along with himself and the others. He knew that not only were the boats insufficient, but there was no time left to load and launch them!

Then, at length, he remembered the life-raft on the roof. Once more, with his arm supporting Elaine, he clambered up a tilted stairway. The place was deserted. The raft was there—but securely fastened to the planking, fore and aft and at the sides! The ropes that bound it down were thick and doubled!

With his knife the man attacked them desperately. The blade broke out of the handle when one strand only had been severed. His second blade was small and useless for such a labor.

He groaned, for a ghastly tremor was seizing the "Inca" as she hung above some crumbling abyss for a final plunge to the bottom. Then the moonlight gleamed on the carpenter's adze, which had slid down the deck to the railing. He darted upon it like an animal, and, hastening back, swung it with swift and savage blows that severed the ropes like cheese.

"Quick! Quick!" he shouted to Elaine, as he flung the implement from him; and, catching her roughly about the waist, he bore her face downward beside himself, full length upon the raft.

It was already slightly in motion, where the ship was toppling to her grave!

CHAPTER IV

THE NIGHT—AND MORNING

With a rattle and scraping along the deck, the device with the two prone figures desperately clinging to its surface, was halted and tilted nearly level as it struck a spar and partially mounted upon it.

A sudden glare lit up the scene where the fire had burst through shattered windows. Screams yet more appalling than those already piercing the gale arose with the movement of the vessel. A picture grotesque and monstrous was for one awful moment presented. The huge iron entrails of the vessel heaved up into sight with her breaking. Her funnels, masts, and superstructure pointed outward, strangely horizontal. Innumerable loose things rattled down the decks. She belched forth flame and clouds of steam, against which one huge iron rib, rudely torn on its end to the semblance of a giant finger, seemed pointing the way to inscrutable eternity.

The lantern, up at the "Inca's" masthead, describing an arc as it swept across the heavens, was the last thing Grenville noted. He thought how insignificantly it would sizzle in the sea! Then he and Elaine, with raft and all, were flung far out, by the suddenly accelerated velocity of the doomed leviathan, turning keel upwards as it sank. When they struck, their puny float dived under like a crockery platter, shied from some Titanic hand.

With all his strength the man clung fast to Elaine and the lattice-like planking of their deck. It seemed to Grenville, still submerged, he could never resist the force of the waves to wash them backwards to death. It appeared, moreover, the raft would never return to the top. A million bubbles broke about his ears. He felt they were diving to deeps illimitable.

With a rush of waters drumming on their senses, it shot precipitately upward at last, till air and spray greeted them together. Then, sucked deep under, anew, and backward, by the gurgling vortex where the ship had gone, and swirling about, pivoting wildly, as the raft now threatened to plunge edge downward to the nethermost caverns of the hungry sea, they met a counter-violence that forced it once more towards the surface.

The boilers had burst in the steamer's hold, with confusion to all those tides of suction. Erratically diving here and there, a helpless prey to chaotic cross currents in all directions, the float swung giddily in the mid abyss, while the water walls baffled one another.

Elaine, even more than Grenville, was bursting with explosive breath when, at length, the raft came twisting once more to the chill, sweet region of the gale. And even then strong currents drew it fiercely in their wake before it rode freely on the waters.

Dripping and gasping, Grenville half rose to scan the troubled billows for companions in distress. Not a sound could he hear, save the swash of the waves. Not a light appeared in all that void, save the distant, indifferent stars.

Elaine, too, stirred, and raised herself up to a posture half sitting. She was hatless. Her hair was streaming down across her face and shoulders in strands too wet for the wind to ravel. Her eyes were blazing wildly.

"The ship?" she said. "What happened?"

"Sunk." He stood up. Their platform was steadying buoyantly as it drifted in the breeze. "I can't even see the spot," he added, presently. "We couldn't propel this raft to the place, no matter who might be floating."

"It's terrible!" she whispered, faintly, as one afraid to accuse the Fates aloud. "Couldn't we even—— You think they are all—all gone?"

"I'll shout," said Grenville, merely to humor the pity in her breast. His long, loud "Halloo" rolled weirdly out across the wolf-like pack of waves, three—four—a half dozen times.

There was not the feeblest murmur of response. Yet he felt that, perhaps, one boatload at least might have sped away in safety.

"God help them!" he said, when the silence became once more insupportable. "He only knows where any of us are!"

"After all we'd been through!" she shivered in awe. "If only we two were really saved—— Oh, there must be land, somewhere about, if the Captain was trying to reach a port! But, of course, this isn't even a boat, and, perhaps, it will finally sink!"

He tried to summon an accent of hope to his voice.

"Oh, no; it will float indefinitely. It's sure to turn up somewhere in the end."

"We haven't food—or even water," she answered him, understandingly. "What shall we do to-morrow?"

"We are drifting rapidly northward. We may arrive somewhere by to-morrow…. You'd better sit down. It taxes your strength to stand."

"God help us all!" she suddenly prayed in a broken voice, and, sinking lower where she sat, was shaken by one convulsion of sobbing, in pity for all she had seen. She had no thoughts left for their earlier, personal encounter.

For a time Grenville stood there, braced to take the motion of the raft. The wind continued brisk and undiminished. Aided by tides, which had turned an hour earlier, to flow in its general direction, it drove the raft steadily onward over miles of gray, unresting sea.

The water slopped up between the slats whereon Elaine was sitting. She was cold, despite the tropic latitude. She was hopeful, only because she wished to contribute no unnecessary worry to the man.

Grenville at length sat down at her side, but they made no effort to converse. Elaine was exhausted by the sickening strain and the shock of that tragic end. For an hour or more she sat there limply, being constantly wet by the waves. She attempted, finally, to curl herself down and make a pillow of her arm, and there she sank into something akin to sleep.

Gently Grenville thrust out his foot and lifted her head upon the cushion of flesh above his ankle. The night wore slowly on. Three o'clock came grayly over the world-edge, where the waves made a scalloped horizon.

Slowly the watery universe expanded, as the dawn-light palely increased. By four Grenville's gaze could search all the round of the ocean, but nothing broke either sky or sea.

Five o'clock developed merely color on the water, but no sign of a sail or a funnel. Elaine still slept, while Grenville, cramped almost beyond endurance, refused to move, and thereby disturb her slumber.

But at six, as he turned for the fiftieth time to scan the limited horizon, he started so unwittingly, at sight of a tree and headland, flatly erected, like a bit of sawed-out stage scenery, above the waste of billows, that Elaine sat up at once.

"It's land!" he said. "We're drifting to some sort of land!"

She was still too hazy in her mind, and puzzled by their surroundings, to grasp the situation promptly.

"Land?" she repeated. "Oh!" and a rush of hideous memories swept confusedly upon her till she shivered, gazing at the water.

Grenville had risen to his feet, and Elaine now rose beside him. Somewhat more of the flat, wide protrusion from the sea became thus visible to both. It still appeared of insignificant extent, a blue and featureless patch against the sky, with one half-stripped tree upon its summit.

"I should say it's an island," Grenville added, quietly, restraining an exultation that might prove premature. "It is still some miles away."

"There must be someone there," Elaine replied, with an eagerness that betrayed her anxious state of mind. "Almost anyone would certainly help us a little."

What doubts he entertained of some of the island inhabitants in this particular section of the world, Sidney chose to keep to himself.

"It's land!" he said, as he had before. "That means everything!"

"Do you know of any island that ought to be in this locality?"

"I haven't the remotest notion where we are—except we are somewhere, broadly speaking, in the neighborhood of the Malay peninsula. The steamer must have drifted tremendously out of her course after we lost our rudder."

"Have you been awake for long?"

"I haven't slept."

"Have you seen or heard anything of any of the others?"

"Not a sign.... We may find some of them, landed on this island."

He had no such hope, and this she felt. She summoned a heart full of courage to meet the situation, however, and gazed off afar at the misty terra incognita enlarging imperceptibly as they drifted deliberately onward.

20

"It's fortunate," she said, "the steamers pass this way."

"Yes," he said, unwilling to shake this solitary hope that brightened her uncertain prospect, but he knew they were leagues from the nearest track that the ocean steamers plowed. "And I trust we'll find it entirely comfortable while we're waiting," he added. "We're sure to get dry and find something fit to eat."

She was silent for a moment. A sense of constraint was returning at last for their scene of the previous day. "It seems to be rather far away," was all she said.

"About another hour—if the breeze and tide continue favorable."

It was nearer an hour and a half, however, before they were finally abreast the headland with the tree, and swinging and turning slowly by the island's coast on the surface of a complicated tide.

The features of the land had developed practically everything usual to this latitude except habitations of men. That it was entirely surrounded by water was convincingly established. Indeed, it was not an extensive outcrop of some ocean-buried range, and, despite the luxuriance of its various patches of greenery and jungle, it was decidedly rugged in formation.

The edge past which the raft was leisurely floating was a broken and cavern-pitted wall of rock affording no promise of a landing. Above this loomed the solitary tree that Grenville had seen from a distance. Nothing suggestive of hearth smoke arose against the sky from one end of the place to the other.

This one vital fact, in her excitement, Elaine entirely overlooked. She likewise failed to note the look of concern that Grenville could not have banished from his eyes. The prospect of reaching a dry, firm soil outweighed her immediate worries.

"Couldn't we paddle in closer?" she said. "Where do you mean to land?"

"Where the Fates shall please," he answered, grimly. "Without even a line for me to take ashore we must not be over fastidious."

"We could swim—if we have to," she told him, bravely. "We seem to be floating farther out."

They were, at that particular moment. The powerful current carried them swiftly seaward a considerable distance, till at length the raft was drawn to a species of whirlpool, some two hundred yards in diameter, the inner rim of which was depositing weed at the edge of something like an estuary, indenting the shore of the island.

On the huge circumference of this whirlpool they were finally rounding towards the one bit of beach that Grenville had been able to discover. Yet when they approached within almost touching distance of this sunlit strand, the current failed, permitting the breeze to waft them again towards the center.

"Stand by to go ashore," said Grenville, resolving suddenly on his course, and overboard he slipped, at the float's outer edge, and, using his legs like a powerful frog, he pushed at the raft with sufficient force to overcome the action of the wind.

For a moment his efforts seemed in vain—and then the clumsy affair nosed reluctantly shoreward an inch, and was once more assisted by the tide. Ten feet out he found the water shallow and, planting his feet on the solid sand, drove the raft at once to the estuary's edge, where Elaine leaped lightly ashore.

Some startled creature slipped abruptly into the pool that the tiny harbor formed. This escaped Elaine's attention. A moment later the raft rode scrapingly over a bar that all but locked the inlet, and Grenville stood dripping on the sand.

"Welcome to our city," said he, an irrepressible emotion of joyousness and relief possessing him completely at the moment, and, going at once to the near-by growth, where a long stout limb had been broken from a tree, he dragged this severed member forth to the beach and across the estuary's mouth, where it effectually blocked the channel against the raft's escape. Then he folded a couple of large-sized leaves with his hands, secured each with a slender twig, and, giving one to Elaine for a cap, placed the other upon his head.

Elaine was no less relieved than he, so elastic and buoyant is youth.

"The villages must be on the farther side," she said. "What language do you suppose the natives speak?"

"Well—doubtless some Simian, in any case," he answered, having fancied one movement half seen in the trees beyond was made by an ape or a monkey. "I'd suggest you recall your fondness for fruit for breakfast."

She comprehended his meaning with amazing promptness. Her face took on its serious expression.

"You don't believe we shall find the island inhabited? We shall have only fruit this morning?"

"I am sure we shall find some fruit," he said, "and we must certainly look for water."

A sense of helplessness and despair attacked Elaine momentarily. She began to wonder, with alarm, how long they might be stranded on the place—and what attitude Grenville might assume. She had thoroughly comprehended the passion of his nature in the outburst she had seen. A sense of distrust she dared not show came creeping to her mind.

"We must make the best of it, of course," she said, as calmly as possible. "We can't even light a fire, I suppose."

"I certainly have no matches," he answered, cheerfully. "All I had were in my coat. Suppose we explore the island first and leave despair till after breakfast."

She met his gaze with fearless eyes that set his heart to pounding.

"I shall never despair," she answered, more bravely than she felt,—"at least, I shall try to do my part, till we are taken off."

He understood the challenge in her attitude.

"I felt that from the first," he answered, easily. "Perhaps we'd better begin by climbing up to the headland."

He caught up a short, heavy stick and turned about to force a way up through the rocks and tangled growth between the shore and summit.

And what a figure he presented—even to the frightened girl, whose anger still lingered in her veins—stripped, as he was, to his shirtsleeves, a powerful, active being, masterful and unafraid. With a strange, dreadful sense of isolation and the primitive, aye, even primal, conditions in which they had been cast, she followed helplessly at his heels for their first real look at the island.

CHAPTER V

THE ISLAND

The ascent was steep and difficult, so unbroken was the undergrowth, except where jagged and pitted rocks rose grayly on the slope. Bananas, nut palms, and mangoes Grenville promptly noted. Indeed, every tropical tree, shrub, and fruit of which he had ever learned was represented in the thicket, together with long, snake-like creepers, huge ferns, and many plants with which he had no acquaintance.

There was abundant life in all directions. Here, with a grunt, and beyond with a bound of startled surprise, some animal scuttled to cover in alarm at their approach. A small flock of parrots abruptly arose, flashing their brilliant plumage in the sunlight and screaming raucously. Half a dozen leeches, clinging firmly to the fat, green leaves next the ground, where all was moist and shaded, attracted Grenville's notice as they lifted their heads and groped about for flesh upon which to fasten.

Here and there in the tree tops a monkey obscured a patch of sky for a moment and chattered or squeaked a warning to his kind. Grenville, almost wholly convinced that man seldom or never visited the place, and puzzled to account for a fact so extraordinary, now emerged at the edge of a natural clearing and promptly discovered a small patch of sugar cane, reared above the grass and vines. He was certain that man had brought it to the island.

A half minute later he underwent a decidedly complex set of emotions. He was barely five feet ahead of Elaine, who was following blindly in his trail, a prey to new dreads of all the sounds about them, when he halted in a tense and rigid attitude of alertness. Elaine glanced quickly ahead.

Apparently a patch of orange sunlight was lifting from the grass. Then Elaine, too, saw the black, irregular stripes, the huge, topaz eyes, and the lazy movement of a mighty shoulder muscle, as the beast before them arose and blocked their path.

It was not the fact that he had rarely if ever seen a tiger so large that most impressed the man, thus unexpectedly confronted by this unfrightened monarch of the island—*the brute bore a collar about his neck, gleaming with gold and the facets of some sort of jewels*!

He had obviously once been a captive! He knew the form of man, if not his nature!

For a moment or more there was absolute stillness in that grassy arena, where two world-old enemies stood face to face in their first, preliminary contest of courage. A certain arrogance, a contempt of all possible adversaries, here in his undisputed realm, shone unmistakably in the eyes of the motionless brute. His paunch was rounded significantly. He had recently dined.

Grenville could think of but one thing to do, unarmed as he was, and unwilling to compromise an encounter so vitally important.

He let out a shout such as a demon might have uttered, and, rushing madly forward, with his club upraised, yelled again and again, his aspect one to strike terror to the heart of a giant. He was almost upon the astonished tiger when the brute abruptly fled. The roar the great beast delivered, as he bounded from sight in the jungle, was the sullen note of a creature that obeys, reluctantly, the command of one superior to himself.

"Now, then, a little discretionary haste," said Grenville, quickly returning to Elaine. "I prefer the top of the rocks."

But she did not move, so helpless was her will and so rigid all her being. Once more, with his arm about her waist, Sidney firmly urged her forward, on a beaten trail he took no time to study.

It led in a tortuous manner up the last steep acclivity, where, with every rod, the growth became less luxuriant, and the rocks more thickly strewn. Thus they presently came upon a second natural clearing, a sort of uneven terrace, some fifty feet lower than the dominating headland crowned by the solitary tree.

The trail to this final eminence was plainly scored along a narrow, crumbling ledge, where the volcanic tufa, comprising the ancient upheaval, had for years disintegrated in a honeycomb fashion that left all the bowlders and even the walls deeply pitted.

When they turned about together on this dominating mount, the island lay mapped irregularly beneath them in the purple sea, revealed well-nigh in its entirety.

In all its expanse there was not a sign of a human habitation.

They knew, without a word of argument, they were absolutely alone on this tropic crumb of empire, sole survivors of the frightful wreck, completely ignorant of their whereabouts, and surrounded not only by savage and inimical jungle brutes, but also by some mystery that was not to be understood.

"Well," said Grenville, presently, "such as it is, it's ours."

"Ours," said Elaine. A cold little shiver ran along her nerves, at thoughts of her plight between the man she had called a brute, and the still more savage creatures of the jungle. "Where are you going?" she added, as Grenville moved away.

"To look about for a moment," he replied, "and then I must pick some breakfast."

The examination of the hilltop was promptly concluded. It proved to be a flat, uneven plateau of small dimensions, with precipitous walls on every side, except where the trail led downward. Much loose rock was scattered on its surface. Three-quarters of its boundary rose perpendicularly out of the sea. The remainder plunged down into jungle greenery, and the natural clearing that lay between two dense, rank growths on either side. Not far from the center of the table-rock a fair-sized cave, that bore unmistakable signs of former occupancy and fires once ignited on its floor, afforded a highly acceptable shelter, both from the sun and the elements. It occupied, of course, a position that could be readily and easily defended.

There were other, smaller caverns close at hand, but none with a whole or unpierced roof. Fragments of broken clay utensils lay scattered about, together with the whitening bones of small-sized animals that had one time served some denizens for food. There was nothing in or about the principal cave of which Grenville could make the slightest use.

The view of the island from this point of vantage was not particularly encouraging. Midway of its rugged bulk, that jutted from the azure tides, and on the side directly opposite the estuary, another wall of rock loomed, gray and barren, above the tops of the trees. Behind this, at the island's farthest, left-hand extremity, a third "intrusion" of volcanic stuff rose to a height only barely lower than this whereon the raftmates stood. It was not, however, flat.

A portion only of the estuary was visible—the outer bay, where the raft was plainly floating. Save for areas covered with rock and brush together, the remaining surface of the island appeared to be thickly grown to jungle, the forest comprising foliage of infinite variety.

With Elaine walking silently at his side, afraid to be with him, yet more afraid to be alone, Grenville passed from this hasty examination of the island's general topography to a closer inspection of the perpendicular scarp of the terrace. On the seaward side it rose about one hundred feet above the mark of high water. Its right front appeared to overhang its base, a reassuring distance above the highest tree. Across its entire bulk at this place the cliff had once been cracked, and a "slip" had formed a ragged shelf. Then came the slope where the trail was worn, beyond which forty feet or more of unscalable tufa was reared above a section of the jungle once devastated by fire.

In the midst of this section, being rapidly reclaimed by vines and creepers, stood the shell of a huge old tree, the heart of which had been consumed, from the roots to its blackened top, leaving walls still thick and solid.

"Well," said Sidney, returning again to the principal cave, which he reinspected critically, "it doesn't take long to overlook our possessions. You'd better begin to make yourself at home, while I go below for fodder," and, taking up his club from a ledge where he had let it fall, he went at once down the long-abandoned trail and out across the clearing.

Elaine had followed to the scarp, where she watched till he disappeared. How helpless she was in the hands of this man, whose declaration and deeds had so aroused her indignation and hatred, she thoroughly understood. A sickening conviction that days might elapse before she could hope to escape, increased her sense, not only of alarm, but also of distrust in Grenville. His action in taking up his stick had not escaped her attention. Strangely enough, a horrible pang went straight to her breast as she suddenly thought of that tiger again—and of what it might mean if Grenville never returned. Whatever else might happen, nothing could be so terrible as to perish here alone. She tried to assure herself, however, that Grenville was thoroughly competent to cope with the dangers of the place.

Yet the silence of the jungle where she had seen him disappear, oppressed her unendurably. Not even a tree was shaken, to indicate where he had gone. Summoning all her resolution, she returned to the cavern, alone.

A slab of rock, once doubtless employed for a table, lay with one end resting on the earth, while the other leaned upon a second rock, against the wall of the cave. She lifted this slab to a second prop, then blew the last fragment of dust and sand from its surface, by way of preparing it for breakfast. She looked about, longing for further employment, but, inasmuch as two rude fragments of the rock already reposed beside her table for seats, there was absolutely nothing more she could add, either by way of utensils or furnishings, from the boulders scattered loosely on the terrace.

When she thought of leaves, whereon to serve what fruits the jungle might surrender, she started briskly for the trail—but halted at its summit. A horror of unknown things that might be lurking at the thicket's edge impressed itself upon her. Nevertheless, she shook it off, and, descending rapidly, soon filled her arms with large, clean "platters" from a rankly growing plant of the "elephant's ear" variety, then clambered back to her aerie.

Two of the leaves she dropped at the bend of the trail and left them there in the sun. Twice after that she returned to the edge, to search all the greenery for Grenville. Her uneasiness respecting his long absence was rapidly increasing when she turned once more toward the cave. He emerged at that moment from the farther thicket of the clearing, came unobserved to the winding trail, and discovered the leaves she had abandoned.

He was amazingly "loaded" with similar leaves for breakfast purposes, as well as with fruits, and a singular bowl of water, yet he paused, with a smile upon his lips, to discard every leaf he had provided, in order that Elaine's thoughtful effort at assistance might not be in the least belittled.

She met him just as he came to the top, and began to take a portion of his burden.

"Oh," she said, "you've found water—or is it the juice of the melon?"

"Water," he answered, moving towards the cave. "The bowl is half of a paw-paw, which, next to that spring itself, is the welcomest thing I've discovered."

She was glad to note bananas among his several fruits, but she made no further observations. More and more her sense of constraint increased, as she clearly foresaw her dependence upon and intimate association with this man, who had overstepped the bounds of honor to his friend, and to whom she had spoken in such anger.

Breakfast was soon begun. Elaine consumed all she could relish of the fruits, although neither the loco (loquet, a yellowish sort of plum), the guava —green and full of seeds—nor the custard apple, which was somewhat sickishly sweet, appealed irresistibly to her fancy.

She drank from a leaf, curled up to form a cup, and found the water decidedly refreshing and agreeable, despite the fact it was slightly flavored by the juices of the paw-paw shell in which it had been served.

Grenville leaned back, when his appetite was thoroughly appeased, and began to empty his pockets. He produced the remains of his broken knife, a few loose coins, a ring of keys, a pig-skin purse with several pieces of gold as its contents, the stub of a pencil, and his watch, which, by great good fortune, was waterproof, and still in good running condition, despite its several immersions.

Elaine was watching his movements, puzzled to guess his intent.

"Taking stock," he said, presently, "by way of facing the situation and formulating plans…. These trifling chattels are all I possess in the world—our world, at least—with which to begin certain labors. You probably haven't even hairpins."

Elaine had coiled her hair upon a twig. She shook her head, and faintly resented his allusion to the island as a sort of partnership property.

Grenville began to segregate his belongings.

"Money, keys, pencil, and watch—all mere encumbrances, absolutely worthless. One broken knife—invaluable. We shall require, as soon as possible, water-jugs, basins, cooking utensils, something to make a fire, implements to chop our fuel, some primitive weapons, and tools with which to fashion a boat. I must lose no time in exploring beyond the spring. I have found nothing yet that will especially lend itself to our uses."

Elaine's brown eyes were very wide. "You expect to remain here long enough to build a boat, when the raft—— I know it can't be rowed, of course, but—couldn't you try a sail?"

"We couldn't sail it in its present form," he answered, "even if we knew which direction to take when we started. With a small, swift boat we might venture a few explorations from the island as a base."

She was silent for a moment, and grave.

"You haven't much faith, then, in hailing some passing steamer?"

"I think it wiser to prepare against a probable wait that may be rather long." He read and understood her impatience with the situation—a situation rendered infinitely more complicated and delicate by what he had dared to say and do the previous afternoon.

Once more black dreads that she dared not permit to reveal themselves completely arose to engulf her mind. She could not doubt that Grenville knew, far better than herself, how meager were their hopes of immediate rescue or escape from this exile in the sea. More than anything else, however, she wished to be worthy of and loyal to the man to whom her plighted word had been given. That she owed so much to Grenville already was an added irritation. A braver, finer spirit than she summoned to her needs never rose in a woman's breast.

Her eyes met his with a cold look of resolution in their depths.

"I know you will show me how to help. I must do my share in everything. Can you tell how long it must have been since anyone was here?"

Grenville had never thought her finer—never loved her so madly before. Yet he quelled the merry demons of his nature.

"No," he replied, as he took in his hand a bit of bone, bleached cleanly white. "I can't even understand why an island so abundantly supplied with fruits and game, to say nothing of useful woods and the like, should be so utterly abandoned. There seems to be nothing wrong with the place, and much that is quite in its favor."

"Perhaps that tiger," she suggested.

Sidney shook his head. "It's something that goes a bit deeper—at least, there may once have been something sinister. The natives of all this part of the world are rather accustomed to tigers."

Her sense of divination was exceedingly keen.

"You think there is something worse? You haven't already encountered something more——"

"Nothing," he hastened to interrupt. "The problem of our daily existence affords our greatest present cause for concern—and I frankly admit I considerably relish the prospect of proving we are equal to all that our situation may demand."

She was not to be satisfied so readily.

"But there may be something wrong with the island?"

"Possibly—from a native's point of view."

"But—you are almost certain to meet that tiger again."

"All the more reason for getting to work at once." He arose in his quick, active manner, and once more surveyed their camp.

"A few rocks piled in your doorway," he continued, "and your cave will meet your requirements admirably. I should say mine would better be this small retreat, the roof of which I can readily restore. It is close enough to be neighborly, and is nearer the head of the trail."

The smaller cave thus indicated occupied a position suggestive of a sentry's box, before precincts to be guarded. Its opening faced the gateway of the trail, while its size was sufficient for the needs of any primitive man.

Elaine, who had mechanically followed Grenville from the shelter, looked resignedly about. She had failed till now to think, concretely, of actually remaining, perhaps night after night, in such a place.

"It was terrible!" she said, "—the accident—everything!—terrible!" She suddenly thought of the threat he had made—to compel her to love him as he loved her, before they should reach their home—and shivered anew at the unforeseen predicament in which she was plunged, and hated him more than before.

"Bad business," he answered, briefly, "but at present the task before us is to cut a lot of grass and strew it about on the rocks to dry."

He opened the stubby blade of his knife, glanced at it ruefully, and, selecting a bit of stone, began to whet its edge. But he halted the action abruptly.

A low, weird sound, like a human wail, came from somewhere over behind them.

CHAPTER VI

VARIOUS DISCOVERIES

The sound had no sooner died on the air than a second, far louder, and far more uncanny in its suggestiveness of someone in mortal pain, followed piercingly, up around the rock, and rang in their startled ears.

The third sound more resembled a scream. It was immediately succeeded by a chorus of hideous cries and moans, singularly distressing. They rose to a pitch incredible; they seemed to involve every accent of human grief and torture, and to wrap the rock escarpment completely in an agonizing appeal.

This chorus sank, but a haunting solo of wailing arose as before, to be followed again by the air-splitting scream, and at length once more by the mingling of many dreadful voices.

The island exiles glanced at one another inquiringly, Elaine blanched white with awe.

"By Heavens!—it can't be human," Grenville muttered, as the programme recommenced with only a slight variation.

To Elaine's dismay he started for the cliff.

"Mr. Grenville!" she cried, and helplessly followed where he went.

The wail was dying, in a horrid series of feebler repetitions, when Grenville came to the edge of the wall and peered down below at the water.

There was absolutely nothing to be seen in any direction. The direful sounds, fast progressing once more to that nerve-destroying climax, appeared to issue from a natural cove, a little along to the left.

Grenville continued around the edge, to a point directly above them. But here, as before, there was nothing in all the sea suggestive of boats or beings. The tide, Grenville thought, ran in and out with particular force, reversing at a certain point, and performing singular movements in a basin of hollowed stone.

Elaine had paused behind him, a rod or more from the brink. He waited deliberately for all the cycle of sounds to be repeated, then turned away with a smile.

"I think we have come upon the explanation of the island's uninhabited condition," he informed the girl, as he came once more to her side. "Those noises are made by the sea, forcing air to some cavern in the cliffs. It is doubtless repeated twice a day at a certain stage of the tide."

"It's horrible!" Elaine replied in dread, as a feebler rehearsal of the chorus filled all that tropic breeze, "simply horrible!"

"It may be our greatest bit of good fortune," Grenville informed her, sagely. "I much prefer those sirens to a colony of Dyaks who might otherwise live on the place."

"We shall have to endure it twice a day?"

"Possibly not. I may be entirely mistaken, concerning that. I can only be certain it is caused by the tide, and is, therefore, not to be dreaded."

For fully ten minutes, however, the tidal conditions were favorable to the sound's continuance. It subsided by degrees, the last moaning notes possibly more suggestive than the first of beings perishing miserably.

Meantime Grenville had gone indifferently about the business of cutting huge armfuls of the tall grass and ferns abundantly supplied in the clearing. This moist and not unfragrant material Elaine in silent helpfulness carried to the top of the terrace, where she spread it about on the rocks. She was certain Grenville was providing far more than they could use in reason, yet although his stubby knife-blade was a poor tool, indeed, for the business, he toiled away unsparingly, blithesomely whistling at his task.

"You may be glad by nightfall to burrow into a stack of this hay," he told Elaine as he brought the last load up the trail. "If you wouldn't mind turning it over from time to time I think I'll look about again to get an idea of the island."

Elaine had as little inclination to remain on the terrace alone, with all manner of worries respecting Grenville's safety, as she had to follow where he would lead through the shades and thickets of the jungle. She was aware, however, her presence at his side would be more of a care than assistance; while the necessity for his explorations addressed itself clearly to her mind. She made no confession of her natural wish to see him returning promptly.

He departed, with his club in hand, quite certain he should not be gone above an hour. He had not, however, reckoned with the jungle.

Despite the fact he had set his mind on the region about and beyond the spring, the flow of which formed the estuary, some wonder respecting the area once blackened and cleared by fire attracted his attention immediately upon his descent from the hill.

Through a fringe of scrub he forced his way to this region close under the walls, discovering old, charred stumps, many dead saplings, and quantities of half-consumed branches, affording a large supply of fuel. There could be no doubt the fire had raged within the previous year. Human visitors of some complexion had come, left this scar, and departed.

Hopeful of some enlightening sign as to who or what they might have been, he searched the earth about and between the shrubs and grasses with considerable care. Not so much as a bone, however, rewarded his scrutinizing gaze. He came to the tree trunk left hollow by the flames, and paused to marvel at its size. Above his head it was four feet through, while the base was certainly eight. An arch had been formed in its substance, near the ground, and into this he curiously peered.

Kneeling thus on the earth, he was readily enabled to look straight up through and out at the top. The hollow in the stout old jungle champion was fully two feet in diameter, and almost perfectly round. There was nothing else of interest to be found about the place, save a huge, smooth log, lying with one end resting on a rock, and long enough to make a splendid boat.

Attempting the passage of the jungle from this point across to the midway wall of tufa, Grenville expended fully fifteen minutes of the toughest sort of effort, and was then obliged to retreat once more to the trail. He encountered here the first wild animal discovered since his meeting with the tiger.

It was a porcupine, bristling with trouble for any attacking beast. Grenville could have slain it with his club. He was fairly on the point of providing this much meat for the sadly empty larder, when the fact that he could ignite no fire deterred his ready weapon. He thought, in that extremity, of his watch, the crystal of which might serve to give him a white-hot spark from the sun.

Trusting the porcupine might await the result of his quick experiment, he lost no time in submitting the glass to a trial. It formed a ring of brilliant light on the back of his hand, but the rays would not come to a focus.

"Go thy ways," he said to the porcupine, and he continued at once on his own.

Observing the trail more closely than he had on his earlier excursion, he presently discovered a divergence to the left that led towards the central wall of stone. Here he frightened a considerable troop of monkeys that swung in a panic of activity through the avenues of foliage overhead. There were likewise sounds of heavier beasts that escaped observation on the moist and thickly cumbered earth.

The trail under foot was rather well worn, and not, the man was certain, by the hoofs or feet of brutes. The explanation was presently forthcoming, at least in part, for the path emerged at a clay pit that lay against the frowning tower of stone.

Grenville could have shouted for joy as he took a bit of the smooth, sticky substance in his hand, and began thus promptly, in his fancy, making pots and jugs innumerable to meet their every need. The deposit had been previously worked. The evidence of this was unmistakable. But none of the tools employed by former craftsmen had been left for Grenville to discover.

He spent some time investigating all the mute signs of former activity expended at the pit, and finally glancing up at the cliff above, abandoned all thought of conquering its summit, and retraced his steps along the trail.

Where the path to the spring made a second fork, he continued straight on through the jungle. One glance only of the estuary, tortuously penetrating the waist of the island, was vouchsafed him through the thicket. Beyond this point, in swampy ground, flourished a forest of giant bamboo. The creepers and vines in that immediate section were particularly varied and abundant. The bird life was equally impressive. Hundreds of swallows were skimming in the air, a number of argus pheasants wildly fled from the visitor's presence, parrots screamed and wheeled in huge flocks above the light green bamboo foliage, and several fine flamingoes made shift to find concealment in the reeds.

"It's a haunted paradise," Grenville muttered to himself, his thought having gone for a moment to the wails and moans that had startled himself and Elaine.

Regretting that his broken knife was a wholly inadequate implement with which to assail such a bamboo stem as he would gladly have taken to the camp, he was once more making his way from the thicket when his foot crashed audibly through something brittle, on the earth.

He parted the shrubbery and uttered a low exclamation. He had stepped upon a human skeleton, white and suggestively huddled, every fragment of it perfect—except that it lacked a head.

In a certain sort of anxiety Grenville searched about to find the missing member. The skull was not to be discovered. Persuading himself this might be accounted for by many natural explanations, and resolving to keep his discovery entirely to himself, he forced his way around this grewsome inhabitant—and came upon another.

This one he did not strike with either foot. It lay outstretched before him, in company with scattered and broken bits of rock—and, like its neighbor, it was headless.

Had some monstrous head-hunter written "Dyaks" on all the empty lattice of those human ribs, Grenville could not have been more convinced of what this business meant. He returned to the trail accompanied by a sense of dread that all but sent him back to Elaine. His thought was entirely of her, and of their helplessness, cast thus alone upon this unpeopled island, clean stripped of weapons and of all things else save their wits and bodily strength.

"We've got to escape," he told himself in a new, swift fever of impatience. "There is not an hour to lose!"

He continued on through the jungle towards the hill at the farther end.

CHAPTER VII

A GREWSOME GUARDIAN

Apparently the trail, that had once been formed through the axis of the island, had been found of little use. It was overgrown by all manner of plants well-nigh to extinction.

The region hereabout was obviously the final retreat of many beasts, both timid and bold. Grenville found signs of at least one Malay bear and of many wild hogs in the thickets. He fancied he saw one flash of moving orange, where either his tiger or another of his ilk moved silently through the growth behind him. Of the monkeys there appeared to be no end; and the snakes were amply represented.

He was glad for every clearing that he came upon and crossed, and felt a decided sense of relief on achieving his hill at last. This worn old eminence of rock and substances volcanic was far more steep and rugged than the one where he had left Elaine. It possessed no caves, and no particular flatness at the summit.

Grenville explored it rapidly, considerably disappointed to find nothing of special utility upon its broken surface. He had hoped for some hard and useful stone at least, if not for actual flints. Completing its round in a haste that the rapidly increasing heat of the day considerably accelerated, he presently came upon an unusual ledge protruding from the slope's unpromising surface.

Here he halted in idle curiosity. The ledge was of sulphur—a blow-out from the hill's once molten interior, lying untouched and useless in the sun for the elements to wear away and sluice at last to the sea. With no particular purpose in view, he broke away a fragment, dropped it carelessly into his pocket, and continued on his way.

His gaze returned with a certain steadfast eagerness to the hill and camp beyond. He was not precisely disappointed on failing to discover Elaine, who might have been waiting to wave him a signal from the heights; he was somewhat concerned to know if all was well upon her rock. She was not to be seen at all about the place. He clambered to the top of a broken bowlder for a view more comprehensive.

This, too, appeared a wasted effort, at least as concerned Elaine. The island map, however, was laid out before him in a manner to complete his former survey of the place. There were several clearings thus revealed that could never be seen from the farther point of vantage.

Acknowledging each of these in turn, Grenville was once more about to direct his footsteps homeward when one of the smaller, near-by breaks in the jungle, quite at the top of a species of rift in the island's ruggedness, down upon his left, attracted a second glance.

For a moment he fancied some colossal remains, as of an animal long since extinct, were lying there in the clinging embrace of the creepers. He decided, then, it was a boat, but dismissed this notion as preposterous, so high above the water's edge, and so near the island's center, did it lie. About ready to conclude that certain giant shadows contributed much to round out a half-imagined form, his gaze encountered a bowsprit thrust through all the foliage, its identity not to be mistaken. The hull of a ship was undoubtedly there. He hastened down, expectantly, to make its better acquaintance.

The wonder when he came there was—how it came to be stranded so high and far above the water. As for the vessel itself, it was merely a rotted old shell, with its cargo bursting through its ribs.

So far as Grenville could judge from its fast-decaying remains, it had been an inferior type of the old-fashioned barque, and of very modest dimensions. Its masts, however, were gone, together with every accessible piece of metal that eager hands could remove. Its moldy and slimy old cabin had partially collapsed. Without effecting an entrance through the treacherous deck, Sidney could discover nothing respecting its interior.

He could peer through the ribs at several places along the hull, and even near the keel, by stooping low, but the most he could determine by such a superficial examination was that there was nothing even here that he could use. The cargo he thought for a moment to be chalk, or lime. He scraped a clean sample from the weathered heap, and rubbed it in his palm. Its crystalline structure was not that of either lime or chalk. When he placed a particle on his tongue, he dropped all he held with no further interest.

The stuff was common saltpeter. That the vessel had been westward bound, perhaps from Borneo, with this mineral common to so much of that tropical section, he understood at once. But to find her stranded thus so loftily was amazing. He scraped at the soil with the toe of his boot to dig below the surface.

As he had rather expected, seashells and pebbles of a former beach were readily brought to view. Some old upheaval had undoubtedly lifted beach, vessel, and all to this altitude above the tides, and left it there to decay.

Considerably disappointed to find the hulk so completely stripped of the metal furnishings of which he might have wrought some sort of tools or weapons, Grenville hesitated between an impulse to continue home to Elaine without greater delay, and a strong desire to investigate the cabin of the barque. The latter temptation was not to be resisted.

He grasped the branch of an overhanging tree and, by dint of much active scrambling, clawing, and thrusting his toes into various chinks, at length gained the planks of the slanted deck and broke his way into the one-time sanctum of the captain and his mates.

This, too, had been pillaged with exceptional thoroughness. There was, however, a passageway leading to another apartment beyond, where a door, half open, was revealed by sunlight streaming through the broken roof. Thither Grenville made his way—to behold an extraordinary sight.

The place was a room, partitioned off from considerably larger quarters. It contained one object only—a form, half mummy, half skeleton, that had once been a powerful man. *And this was chained to the wall!*

It was sitting propped against the lintel of a second door, a panel of which was raggedly broken out. It had never been robbed of its head. A strong, black beard still remained upon the emaciated face, and the eye-sockets stared straight forward at the door by which the visitor had entered.

Grenville was not to be easily dismayed, yet the attitude of this grewsome thing was very far from being pleasant. The being had been almost naked when he perished here alone with a heavy iron band about his waist. All this his visitor swiftly discerned while inclined to turn about and flee the place. He discovered, then, an additional mystery.

The skin, in a patch fully six inches square, had disappeared from the helpless being's breast. That it had not wasted away by a natural process was, moreover, perfectly obvious, since the square-cut edges of parchment, which the remainder of his cuticle had become by the mummifying process, were distinctly to be seen. It had been removed with a knife. It appeared to Grenville that the captive had been propped artificially where he sat, as if to guard the passage. A trickle of water, saturated with saltpeter, had served to embalm both his flesh and skin, in part.

That the cabin beyond had likewise been despoiled of its treasure was almost a foregone conclusion. However, Sidney stepped closer to the silent form and peered through the broken panel.

The room into which he was gazing was dimly lighted by the rays of daylight filtering through a number of cracks which the weather had opened in its ceiling. When his sight grew accustomed to the darkness, he saw that the place had evidently served not only as quarters for the former crew, but likewise as a storage hold for ropes, paints, extra furnishings, and, doubtless, victuals.

Its contents lay scattered about in confusion and decay, yet promised more "treasure" for Grenville's needs than all the rest of the vessel. He drove his shoulder against the door, and its lock broke the rotted woodwork away with a suddenness the man had not expected. He passed the mummified guardian at the portal somewhat hurriedly, as he lurched inside the chamber; and he nearly fell across a box that had spilled out a dozen old pieces of brass.

Upon these he pounced with avidity, despite the fact they were greenly incrusted with "rust." Among other articles of plunder thus provided to his hand were several row-locks, a broken turnbuckle, a dozen at least of useless hinges, and a hatful of screws more or less cemented together.

With vague ideas of employing the metal somehow, he filled his pockets with the smaller articles and looked about for possible tools. From a broken locker in a corner much similar scrap stuff had fallen. Here was a large brass porthole rim, parts of a broken binnacle, half of the brazen cap from a towing-bit, two heavy bronze handles of swords now fallen to pieces with decay, an old brass lantern with a useless lamp, a large coil of excellent copper wire, a ball of lead, and remains of several iron marlinespikes, mere effigies now in flaky rust.

From beneath a heap of rotted cordage a greenish cylinder protruded. Grenville drew it forth. It proved to be a small brass cannon, unmounted, and apparently filled with mud. Near by he discovered the rapidly disintegrating remnants of an old-time flintlock musket. This was a priceless treasure, for the flint, which was still intact. He likewise saved a bit of the steel that the cordage had protected.

The thin and wasted skeleton of a hand-saw hung upon a hook. When he took the blade between his fingers it fell apart like paper, charred, but still holding its original form. Not an object he found of iron was worth removing to the camp. Resolved to return at an early date, to annex the old cannon and such other heavy bric-à-brac as he could not conveniently carry away to-day, Grenville finally left the mysterious dead man still sitting in chains beside the door, and once more regained the wholesome earth.

He finally glanced at his watch. The time was nearly twelve! He had been for at least three hours away from Elaine, who was waiting alone upon the hill! Back to the trail, and then along its sinuous windings through the jungle, he strode at his swiftest pace.

When he came to the final clearing before the towering rock, he was all but paralyzed with dread at a bit of drama being there enacted.

At the edge of the jungle stood Elaine, her arms and jacket filled with fruits she had gathered against his coming. By the foot of the trail that ascended to their camp, posed in a waiting attitude, his long tail only in motion, gracefully sweeping his great tawny side, was the tiger that wore the golden collar.

Not a sound escaped from Elaine's white lips, as she turned to glance across at Sidney. Then she limberly sank on the earth.

CHAPTER VIII

PRIMITIVE CONDITIONS

A short, sharp cry was the only note that Grenville uttered.

The tiger had turned his blazing eyes on the man he but partially feared. Sidney was coming less at him than towards the helpless, prostrate form that lay upon the grass.

The man had forgotten his danger in his greater concern for Elaine. He reached her side before he confronted the jungle beast, who still remained undecided. Slowly then, deliberately, the malignant animal, superb not only in his strength and splendid proportions, but also in his arrogance, his indifference to man, the master butcher of the world, ran out his tongue to lick his chops, stretched his terrible mouth in a fang-revealing yawn, and trod his way into the thicket.

The fruits she had gathered were scattered all about as Grenville lifted Elaine in his arms and carried her up the steep ascent. Not having actually swooned, she had fairly begun to revive once more before he reached the cave.

When he placed her down on a heap of half-dried grass she had thrown together while awaiting his return, a faint tinge of color was returning to her face, and her eyes dimly focused upon him.

"You've worked too much, that's what it means," he said. "You see you're tired."

"I'm—sorry," she faltered, faintly. "I really—didn't mean to be—so weak."

"Never mind," he said. "I'll kill the brute. His skin is certainly a beauty." With the utmost apparent indifference to Elaine's recovery, he went at once to the clearing for the bits of old junk he had dropped.

When he returned, his mind was still on the tiger.

"We've got to live—move about—and not be annoyed," he said. "If I had a single rifle! But I'll get him somehow, soon!"

Elaine still remained upon the hay.

"If he doesn't get us sooner," she replied, a little grimly, but not as one in fear.

"I shall wall up the trail," mused Grenville, aloud, looking about at the quantity of rock so readily afforded. "That much I can do this afternoon."

She sat up a bit more sturdily.

"I dropped our luncheon, I suppose.... I hope to do better, later on, when I get more used to conditions." She was mortified to think he had been thus

40

promptly obliged to carry her "home" in his arms.

"You are doing fairly well," he said, in his off-hand manner. "We shall soon be all right. It's a fine and tight little island."

Her one idea was to get away as soon as possible.

"Shouldn't we put up a flag, or something, in case a steamer should happen to be passing?"

"As soon as I can cut a long bamboo. I must have both tools and fire as promptly as possible."

"You must be hungry," she remarked, arising rather weakly and going to the end of her cave, where all the water that remained in the half of the paw-paw shell had been carefully stored, in Grenville's absence. Then, emerging with her burden, she added, "I meant to have your luncheon ready, but we have almost nothing left."

"All that you gathered was left by the tiger," he answered, cheerfully. "The beast prefers more solid diet." Once more descending the trail, he presently returned with the fruits that had fallen from her arms.

They ate, as before, in the shade of her cave, for the sun on the rocks was becoming hot.

"The wall this afternoon," said Grenville, as he finally concluded his simple repast with a drink of tepid water. "Then our mast and signal of distress must be erected. I shall try for fire directly. I must make a bow and some arrows. A clay pit I found will provide us with earthenware utensils, and then—if only I could manage to melt some brass—— You see, the worst of it is, no stone I've discovered on the place is fit to use for a tool."

Elaine avoided the boyish gleaming of his gaze. "Are we thrust so far back as the stone age, then? It's really as bad as that?"

"Bad?" he said. "It's tremendously diverting. I've got to begin, as it were, with my naked hands. But fortunately, I believe, for us, the bronze and stone ages lap," and he drew from his pockets some bits of the heterogeneous collection he had brought from the rotting barque.

"You have found some metal?" Elaine inquired, excitedly. "But where?"

"In a wreck that must have arrived here years ago." He related as much as he thought advisable and undisturbing to the thoroughly wondering girl.

She could see no possible use for all the rusted bronze and brass he had earned away from the wreck so strangely discovered, but she made no discouraging comments to dampen an ardor which to her was not precisely

41

comprehensible.

"I hope I can help," she told him, as she had before. "I'm afraid I'm not very clever."

"We'll see," he answered, cheerfully. "Necessity is rather a strict instructor."

But she could not assist him with the wall, at which he was presently perspiring. The stones he rolled and carried to the narrowest shelf or ledge that was scaled by the trail were far too heavy for her delicate hands and muscles.

"Can't I do something else?" she begged, eager for any employment. "There must be some work I could do."

"You might plait a basket of some sort," he said. "We shall need some presently."

He thereupon went below again, cut all he could carry of tough and limber creepers, and, fetching them up to the shade of her cave, instructed Elaine in such of the rudiments of basket-weaving as he himself could readily invent, and left her busily employed.

The wall he required to prevent any possible night attack on the part of the beast that was already inclined to stalk either one of them, or both, was not of any considerable length, owing to the narrowness of the pass he had chosen to block with bowlders. He had, however, to make it thick and high. By taking advantage of three large blocks, which he rolled down hill to the place selected, he secured a substantial foundation with comparative ease. After that it became a matter merely of carrying stone after stone, from their inexhaustible supply on the summit, to lodge in rough, uneven tiers to the height desired.

He had left a narrow gateway next the natural wall that made his structure complete. This he could block with a heavy log, or even more stones, for the night.

For fully three hours he wrought prodigiously, returning from time to time to Elaine, to guide and assist her with her basket. Between them they managed to produce from their rough material a crude, misshapen receptacle, coarse of mesh and clumsy, yet strong and not to be despised. Grenville expected to use it to fetch his clay from the pit.

It was not until this product of their combined ingenuity was fairly complete that Grenville discovered he could split the bark of the creepers readily, and tear out a smooth white core, like a withe, far more suitable to their uses. He then not only stripped out several full-length cores, but he also found that the bark or covering thus removed was constructed of numerous thread-like strands amazingly tough and long. These fibers were not so readily separated as the core had been from the covering with which they were incorporated, although their recovery was not a difficult operation. His inventive mind saw ample employment for them later.

The wall was not entirely finished when, at length, he left it for the day. He was weary in all his bone and sinew, despite the prodding of his will. He had made no attempt at kindling fire, and none towards procuring a mast to erect for a flag of distress. These were tasks that must wait for the morrow, with the others he was eager to attack.

The dinner at sundown was necessarily a repetition of the previous meals of the day. It could not be followed by the cheer and comfort of a fire, and the darkness, that drew on rapidly, brought a sense of chill and depression to Elaine, notwithstanding her bravery of spirit.

The wind had ceased, except for the merest intermittent puffs of breath that floated upward from the sea. Not even the lapping of the tide against the wall arose to break the silence. The stillness was painfully profound, though Elaine's imagination depicted a hundred nocturnal brutes of the jungle, prowling in every trail and clearing, in a savage quest for blood.

As a matter of fact, the nightly tragedies were already well begun. But it was not until some victim shrilly voiced its animal fear and agony, just beneath the towering wall, that Elaine had a realizing sense of her nearness to these creatures of the darkness, or the working of life's inexorable laws.

Her mind reverted, by natural process, to all the terrible occurrences crowded into her life within the last couple of days—occurrences that seemed so needlessly tragic, and all the alarms excited in her breast, not only by the frightful accident to the "Inca," but likewise by the almost unknown man upon whom she was now dependent.

She recalled with singular vividness every accent, every gesture, look, and deed that had accompanied Grenville's declaration. She burned again, with shame and indignation, to think of the things he had dared to say and do—the treachery done to his friend—the indignity done to herself.

She hated him now more intensely than before, since he seemed, by some enormity of purpose, to have been in some manner responsible for the fate that had brought her here in his company, absolutely at his mercy. That his promptness of action had saved her life she willingly and justly conceded—but to fetch her here, all by herself, to an island unpeopled and awful, far from the track of ocean-going steamers—with his threat to compel her love still ringing in her ears—this seemed to outweigh any possible service he had done or could ever accomplish.

What would he do, she wondered, on the morrow? When would he speak of his passion again? What means, in this situation, might he presently adopt to coerce the love she knew she should never bestow?

There could be no answer to her questions—least of all from the man himself. He, too, had fallen into silence, and a study of the vast and merciless problems, not only of existence till their escape could be effected, but likewise as to how that escape could be attempted, in safety, and where they must steer their ocean course to come to a land which should not prove inhospitable.

He seemed, for the time, to have quite forgotten the presence of the girl at the cave. This she finally observed. She wondered, then, what sinister outcome his brooding might presage.

Keyed to a pitch of nervous sensibility she had never experienced before, she retired at length within her shelter like a child thrust alone in the dark. Much as she felt she disliked the man, she found herself most reluctant to move very far from his presence, or refuse his protecting care. She was certain her dread of all it meant to be hopelessly cast upon this island, with one doubtful human being only for comfort and companionship, would haunt her to sleeplessness throughout the night. Yet she fell into slumber almost at once, and only dreamed she was still awake and worried.

It was still quite early in the evening. Elaine was finally approaching a thoroughly restful oblivion, when a low, moaning wail, and then shrill screams, abruptly ushered once more into play that hideous chorus of the morning, produced by some phenomenon of the tides.

"Sidney! Sidney!" came an answering cry; and Grenville arose, to see Elaine running wildly towards him from her cave.

CHAPTER IX

THE MOTHER OF INVENTION

It was not until the entire cycle of haunting sounds had been repeated for its final time that Elaine could consent to return to her pallet of grasses. And even when she had once more knelt upon this improvised bed, she could not consent to resign herself to the mercies of the night without one more glance towards Grenville's cavern.

She returned, unseen, to her door, and peered forth through the starlit night, discerning his dimly outlined figure, as he sat before his door.

He even arose as she paused there, uncertainly. She noted his listening attitude, the alertness of his pose. Then he sat once more upon the stone at his threshold, where she knew his club lay ready to his hand.

A sense of security, despite her bitterness of feeling, came slowly stealing upon her. She went back to her couch and slept.

Sidney, for his part, sat there alone, while hour after hour went silently by, and the constellations hung in higher arches. A thousand ramifications of thought he pursued in his active brain. But through them all, like an ever recurrent *motif*, stole a troubled reminder of the tiger, twice encountered in the day.

To slay this contemptuous, savage beast that already drooled about the jaws at thoughts of a human morsel, was the one imperative business to be promptly executed. Elaine and himself could live on fruits, and neglect all else, without serious results, for a week, or even a month, but this affair was not to be delayed.

He thought of pitfalls, giant traps, and automatic engines of destruction by the score, each deadly device absurdly impracticable and beyond all power of his achievement. His mind, accustomed to civilized ways, ran in higher ingenuities that were absolutely useless in this primal state of their existence.

When at length he leaned back against his wall and began to wonder if, in the end, he must arm himself with primitive man's crude bow and arrow, and thus engage the master prowler of the jungle, he was ready for Nature's claims. He slept there, too utterly exhausted to drag himself in to his bed. And there Elaine found him in the morning.

That day was a long one, of varied and wearying employments. The wall was finished across the trail, Elaine's too widely opened cavern was partially blocked up with stone, and, at length, in addition to searching the jungle for something particularly downy and inflammable for tinder, to use in making fire, Grenville went with his basket down to the clay pit and fetched sufficient of this moist and plastic material to mould a number of vessels.

This last useful art was not, however, immediately attempted. Unfired jugs and basins were absolutely useless—and as yet they had no fire. The search for tinder had resulted only in producing a silken, fluffy material that grew in a fat green pod. It was moist, when found, with the natural juices of the plant.

While it dried in the sun, under Elaine's supervision, Grenville worked at a stout, elastic tree-branch to taper out a bow. His stub of a knife-blade served indifferently against the close-grained wood, which, nevertheless, was obliged to yield to his persevering efforts.

At noon the weapon, save for the cord, was rudely finished. No arrows had been as yet provided. Obliged at this hour to replenish the camp supply of water, Grenville once more visited the spring. So fresh were the tracks of the tiger here, in the mire about the trickling stream, that he felt they must almost be warm. The brute was undoubtedly near at hand, but, perhaps, well fed, as before.

"There is nothing quite so important now as fire," was Grenville's remark, as he once more rejoined Elaine. "Without it we are practically helpless. With it—there is almost nothing we may not hope to achieve."

He had thought of a number of extraordinary and highly important implements and arts that only flame and glowing heat could render possible.

Elaine brought the fluff she had thoroughly dried, while Grenville cleaned his flint and steel. For an hour, then, he strove in vain to ignite his bit of tinder. It was not at all an easy matter to strike a spark from the stone. What few brilliant specks of incandescence sped occasionally downward like vigor transmuted into swiftly fading stars from Grenville's varied and over-eager strokes, either died on the air or missed their mark or struck it and found it uncongenial.

"This must be a vegetable asbestos," he finally declared. "If I had just a pinch of powder, this flint might recognize—— By Jove!" and he started at once to his feet. "I'm the greatest fool on legs!"

"What seems to be the trouble?" said Elaine, who could not possibly comprehend his meaning. "Have you made some sort of mistake?"

"I've been asleep—my brain defunct! Excuse me half a minute!"

He started madly down the trail, running like a boy. Before Elaine could do more than stare in wonder at his antics, he had reached the bottom of the wall, darted across the clearing, and disappeared in the jungle growth beyond.

He smashed his way hotly to the wrecked old barque, and, pawing deeply beneath the surface of the wasting saltpeter, that had been for long somewhat protected in the hold, promptly filled two pockets with the mineral, and went racing back as he had come.

But beyond the clearing he altered his course to enter the region once blackened by fire. Here he went directly to the hollow tree he had once before examined, and, wriggling inside, through the ample orifice burned out by the flames, he attacked the charred interior with his knife as if his very life depended on his haste.

In the briefest time he had chipped off more than a double handful of crisp, but inferior, charcoal. Retreating no less promptly than he had entered, he gathered this carefully in a giant leaf, and hastily rejoined Elaine.

"Powder!" he said, belatedly explaining. "Everything lying here and ready, and my brain a howling blank!"

To Elaine this was not precisely clear.

"There is gunpowder here on the island?"

"No! The ingredients merely. But any child—— Ah! here's my bit of sulphur! There's a ton of it ready to be gathered. Powder? I can make enough to blow a dozen tigers into ribbons! The wreck is full of niter and, once we have a fire, I can burn all the jungle into charcoal!"

The mystery had not entirely lifted for Elaine, but this she hardly expected.

"How can I help?" she asked him, quietly. "There must be something I can do."

"It's a matter of grinding these materials," he answered, more calmly, depositing sulphur, saltpeter, and charcoal on a rock before them. "It's a simple composition, after all."

Barely less feverishly than before he began a search for suitable stones to employ as mortars and pestles. There were many small bowlders slightly hollowed by the elements, but a number of these had surfaces ready to crumble, and were, therefore, reluctantly discarded. In throwing about some loosely huddled fragments, to liberate a smooth, hard slab of stone that was dished from its edges to its center, Grenville was doubly rewarded by coming upon a large, thick seashell, practically perfect.

With this and the basin of harder rock, he returned at once to the shade. He was soon reducing the charcoal, while Elaine no less industriously attacked the lump of sulphur.

"We need a little only for a trial," he said, as he presently sifted out his powdered product, and began to grind the niter. "I wish I remembered the proportions."

In his haste to obtain results as soon as possible, he finally shook up and ground together a large-sized pinch from each of the three materials, producing thereby a grayish, unpromising mixture, decidedly too rich in both the charcoal and sulphur.

This he placed on a rock, a safe distance away, and attacked with his flint and steel. Elaine had ceased her grinding operations, to stand at his side and watch. He struck, perhaps, a dozen times before he produced a shower of sparks—and nothing occurred. He looked at the stuff for a moment, helplessly, discouragement swiftly lodging in his bosom. Half-heartedly he struck the steel again.

A single spark flew hotly from the flint. It seemed to curve to the outside edge of the powder. Instantly, however, the mixture was ignited.

It did not burn in a quick, fierce flash, but more with a sputtering, imperfect combustion, productive of stifling fumes. Grenville's hand was slightly scorched—but his joy in the triumph was complete.

"We're kings!" he cried, sublimely indifferent to genders. "We're monarchs of all we survey!" He leaped up, waving his flint about his head, his face outbeaming the sun.

Elaine was vaguely glad of his results.

"I'm afraid I don't understand it in the least."

"Not at all necessary," he informed her, candidly. "It's the very worst powder ever made. My charcoal is poor and my proportions wrong, and I only half ground it all together. But it burned! That's enough for me—it burned! It assures us a fire, and I'll make a new batch, that will go off like a Spanish revolution!"

He went below at once to gather twigs and fuel, bits of dried grass, and other kindling, and brought a large bundle to the terrace. More carefully, then, he mixed and ground his succeeding sample of the powder. Recalling more clearly the accepted formula, he increased the proportion of saltpeter to something nearer seventy-five per cent. of the whole, approximating thus the standard long since established.

Aware that, when he finally came to manufacture an explosive of higher efficiency, he would do much better to wet the ingredients and later dry the finished product, he now proceeded, as before, merely to try for a fire.

Thus he presently laid a train of his grayish mixture from one small heap to another, in a place selected for his trial. Over one of the powder pyramids he arranged his combustible straws, twigs, and branches with the nicest care. And when, at length, he struck a white-hot star, divinely potential, into the midst of the second heap, a hissing snake of incandescence and smoke darted swiftly along the surface of rock—and his fire leaped into being.

On the towering rock, as on an altar, the flames that meant life to the exiled pair rose goldenly bright and clear.

A strange exultation in Grenville's prowess possessed Elaine, as she stood by in wonder, looking on his face.

"It shall never go out," he told her, presently, "not if I can prevent it."

CHAPTER X

THE MASTER POACHER

There were woods in abundance about the base of the tufa cliff that would burn almost as slowly and retain their glow about as long as the hardest of anthracite coal.

Yet it was not on these that Grenville depended, that particular night, to maintain the fire he had conjured from flint and steel. All those long dark hours he served his altar flame with fuel gathered for the purpose. An easier method for its preservation, by means of the woods that were promptly discovered, he adopted, however, very soon.

Each day that was ushered in and closed by the island's haunting wails and chorus, now beheld some new development in the plans that Grenville was laying. Elaine, less disturbed by the hideous sounds, might have learned more promptly to accept them as part of the ordeal of living in this extraordinary fashion, had they always come at stated hours. But, born of the tides, they came with the tides, which, all the world over, shift with each day till every hour of the twenty-four has had its visitation. Like a horrid reminder of the brevity of life, the thing was fore-ordered to rise unexpectedly, fret forgetful senses, and linger longest, apparently, in the deadest hours of the night. Concerning her companion, her mind was far more calm. Her distrust and dislike were unabated, but he gave her no cause for added worry.

By the third day after his fire had been accomplished, Grenville had considerably altered their aspects and prospects of living. Their bamboo flagpole stood in a crevice of the highest rock, with "rags" of banana leaves idly flapping out a signal of distress; a number of pipkins, large and small, were grayly drying in the sun, to be subsequently fired; his bow was strung, beside three unfeathered arrows, crudely tipped with points that Sidney had pounded out of screws; charcoal was burning, down in the blackened clearing; a number of traps and dead-falls were nearing completion; and several basket loads both of sulphur and saltpeter were stored in caverns, which the man had roofed to protect them from the rain.

Much toil had been involved in these achievements. The bamboo pole, for instance, had been most laboriously burned off, close to its base. To accomplish this end, the man had carried coals of fire to the estuary swamp, created a blaze, and repeatedly heated his longest piece of brass, which had slowly charred a channel through the wood when smartly applied to its surface.

The cord that secured the "flag" upon this serviceable mast, had been made, like the string for the bow, by twisting together innumerable threads of the fiber imbedded in the bark of the creepers. This had then been "waxed" with the glutinous ooze from the nearest rubber tree, with which the jungle abounded. He had also found wild sisal in the rocky places of the island. This plant had a leaf like a bayonet, sometimes six feet long, and readily split into fibers of most astonishing strength, especially when three were braided into a cord.

Considerably to Grenville's amazement, the molding of jugs, some crucibles, and other essential vessels suggested by the presence of the clay, was not at all a simple matter. His material, which at first was mixed too soft, was readily stiffened to a workable consistency, and the bases and first six inches or more of flaring walls of his pipkins had been fashioned as a child would fashion "pies." It was when he undertook to crimp and contract this flaring rim that the craftsmanship known to the potter required once again to be evolved.

For a time the longer he wrought at the stubborn material the more completely Grenville was defeated by the clay. He discovered at last, as similar workmen in every age and clime have ultimately discovered, that potteries thus constructed by hand must be built up in rings, one ring at a time, especially where the walls draw in to an ever narrowing diameter.

When, at length, this simple fact had been established—the first success having come to Elaine, whose feminine wit had been nimbler far than the man's—a highly respectable family of jugs and useful receptacles had rapidly come into being.

Mid-afternoon of this busy day found Grenville engrossed with his labors. Despite the fact they had not yet dined on anything but fruit, he was preparing salt for meat. The shell he had found was full of water from the sea, evaporating rapidly in a bed of hot ashes and coals. This, however, was resigned to Elaine's efficient vigilance, while Sidney worked absorbingly to complete a number of small clay molds designed for the casting of tools.

When, at length, the last of these was done and set aside to dry with the jugs and assorted vessels, he glanced briefly up at the sun. There were several hours of this blazing light remaining. Resolved in one moment to hasten to the jungle with his bow and the unfeathered arrows, which might be relied upon at easy range to fly sufficiently straight for all his purposes, Grenville determined in the next to make them a bit more certain.

A branch and leaf from a freshly despoiled banana plant had suggested "feathers" for his shafts. It was the work of a moment only to cut out and trim a slender bit of the fibrous branch from which the leaf substance projected. The leaf part itself, which was rather tough, and considerably like a stiffened cloth in texture, he cut to shape no less quickly. Then, binding on each of the arrows a trio of these improvised "rudders," he took up his club, informed Elaine he might be absent half an hour, and descended at once to the clearing.

His porcupine, seen no less than half a dozen times when his arms had been burdened, or his club was not at hand, was not to be found for all his elaborate searching, now that he was desirable for dinner. Naturally, Grenville had no particular preference for porcupine where pheasants were not impossible. But the fact that the bristling hedgehog is not to be despised, he knew from past experience. Moreover, he had fondly hoped this somewhat stupid quarry might be readily found and taken.

Notwithstanding the fact that for three days past not a sign had been vouchsafed him of the tiger, Grenville took to himself no fulsome sense of security as he made his way slowly through the jungle, towards the estuary swamp. The island was small; the brute was always near—and some day the contest between they two must be waged to a definite conclusion.

The axiom is old that the most game is seen when the huntsman has no weapon. It seemed to Grenville, slipping as noiselessly as possible down towards the water, where birds and beasts had always been encountered, that the island had been suddenly deserted. He saw not a thing, beyond the vaguest movements in the trees, perhaps for the very fact he moved so cautiously, and thereby assumed an aspect that was crafty, sinister, or suspicious.

Some reptile glided to the water, starting a ripple on the surface, but not even its head was visible to the watchful eyes of the man. An arrow was notched upon his bow, and, while the practice in which he had indulged had been far too brief to develop the skill he knew he might finally acquire, Sidney was certain that up to a range of five or ten yards his shaft would prove fairly deadly.

He had heretofore seen no game at all that was not, in fact, almost under his very feet. Of the pheasants, flushed before on at least three separate occasions, he detected not so much as a hint. The monkeys were silent. Not even the noisy parrots flew out with their usual disturbance. All about the growth of bamboo he trod, wherever a space was open, but in vain.

Reflecting that the pheasants might have gone beyond, to a section where rocks and shrubbery doubtless afforded the seeds or berries on which they would probably feed, he started more briskly towards the trail that would take him past the wreck.

He had not entirely cleared the bamboo growth when, abruptly, there in the open space before him, hardly fifteen feet away, a wild hog paused, fairly startled to inaction where it had entered the clearing from the jungle. It had turned its head to stare at the man inquiringly. Its two little eyes, maliciously gleaming, increased its threatening aspect as the bristles slowly rose on its back.

Without making the slightest unnecessary movement, Grenville raised his bow. He drew the arrow fairly to the head. A sharp twang followed instantly. A streak of gray sped swiftly and obliquely towards the earth. Then, for a second, Grenville saw the stout shaft quiver where it was buried in the base of the creature's neck.

One challenging grunt the wild hog uttered, starting as if to charge. But the arrow had shattered the nerves that make for rage and courage, cleaving to the seat of life itself.

The boar staggered blindly, instinctively, back to the dense, concealing jungle.

Grenville heard it grunt once savagely, as it broke its way past interfering branches of the growth. He realized it was escaping, that it might reach a hole or other concealment before it fell, and cheat him of his dinner.

He dropped his bow, as a useless impediment in such a tangle, and plunged in a reckless manner through the shrubbery and vines where his quarry was no longer in sight.

The hog must have stumbled forward with considerable speed. A vibrating palm, ten feet ahead of his position, urged Sidney impulsively forward. He was baffled and retarded in a most exasperating fashion by the creepers woven through the thicket.

Obliged to make a slight detour, he smashed a path between two stout banana palms—and came upon a hidden clearing. There was one unexpectedly violent movement of the growth just opposite, and there he thought his hog was dying.

Instantly upon his startled vision impinged a blot of yellow color. The full active form of the tiger was immediately revealed, as the brute leaped forth and sank his teeth in the neck of the sinking boar.

There was one shrill mort cry only as the hog became inert. Half raising the limber form in his massive jaws, the while his eyes wildly blazed his challenge to and defiance of the man who had halted in the clearing, the great supple creature, with the studded gold band about his neck, slowly strode once more within the jungle.

With a horribly disquieting comprehension of the fact he had doubtless been stalked for the past half hour, which fully accounted for the absence of game along the trails, Grenville retreated from the place. Why he had not been leaped upon and instantly slain was too much to understand—unless the unknown beings who had placed a collar, like a badge of inferiority, upon the animal's neck, had so impressed him with a dread of man that he dared not make an attack.

All zest for the hunt had departed from his being when Sidney recovered his bow. Anger and exasperation took its place as he reflected on the ease with which this insolent, fearless beast could continue to rob him of his quarry. And one day, he knew, the animal's boldness would increase to a point where a treacherous leap would restore his undisputed mastery of all this bit of land.

"I'll kill him!" said Grenville, unexcitedly. "I'll blow him clean out of his skin!"

He went boldly down to the rotting wreck, climbed eagerly up to the slanted cabin, and saluted the dead man, sitting there in chains.

"Brother, I've come for the cannon," he said. "There's little else left for you to guard."

Although the small bit of ordnance would make a load of fully fifty pounds, Grenville determined, then and there, to make a clean sweep of all the old hulk's remaining bits of brass and bronze not appropriated earlier. He, therefore, heaved the cannon out through a gap in the rotting planks, and began a hurried overhauling of everything left in the lockers.

He had drawn out coil upon coil of ancient cordage, that broke like wetted paper in his hands, before the largest and last of the lockers had been emptied of its junk. This was a deep and comparatively sound sort of box beneath a former bunk. Its interior was absolutely dark.

Unwilling to overlook the slightest metal object, Grenville got down on his hands and knees, to peer to the farthest corner. There seemed to be nothing remaining in the place. Nevertheless, he reached well inside and swept his hand about the walls, till it came to a slight obstruction.

This was a screw-head, so far as he could determine, in the planking just to the left of the door, in one of the nearest corners. He pressed rather heavily against the moldy woodwork, and his fist went through, breaking away a decayed square of wood that had once been a tiny door.

Convinced at once that a small and, heretofore, undiscovered locker, of insignificant dimensions, had been made between the walls of two of the usual compartments, he conceived it to be a secret hiding-place, and strained the full length of his reaching arm, blindly to explore its interior.

He could not touch its wall at the rear without crawling fully inside the larger locker, and for this he felt but little relish. With a plan worth two of that discomfiting scheme, he arose and kicked out the paneling from the front of the narrow box.

Once more he knelt, and thrust his arm to the end of the place. His fingers came gropingly upon a round, metallic object, wedged tightly down between two supports of wood. He broke it out in his vigorous way, and drew it to the light.

CHAPTER XI

A MYSTERY

With an odd sensation tingling in his veins, Grenville examined his find.

It was merely a cylinder, made of brass, fully three inches in diameter, and, perhaps, eight inches long. Its cap was rusted so firmly in place that he could not possibly remove it. He gave the tube a shake. There was something inside, but its weight was exceedingly light.

Once more he knelt before the secret locker to examine all its walls. But although his fingers finally played upon every square inch of the sides and ceiling, there was nothing further to be found. Apparently the only "treasure" the place had concealed was contained within the tube.

He thought of a score of documents the one-time captain of the barque might have thus desired to preserve, but the sun was rapidly nearing its purple horizon, and the old ship's hold was growing dark. Grenville gathered the last of the metal spoils he had found in an empty box, half rotted, on the floor. The tube he thrust firmly in his pocket.

What with the cannon balanced on his shoulder, his box of rusted metal hugged beneath his arm, and his bow, club, and arrows clutched tightly in his hand, he presented a singular figure as he finally made his way along the darkening trail, and came at length to the clearing, to be hailed from the heights by Elaine.

"Just for the sake of variety," he said, when he came to the terrace with his burdens, "we'll eat one more dinner of fruit."

"I couldn't think what you had killed," said Elaine, "when I saw you coming with this," and she placed her foot on the cannon he had gladly dropped to the ground. "What is it, anyway?"

"A pop-gun," he said, "to tickle my friend the tiger."

She was instantly apprehensive. "You have met him again?"

He had no intention of arousing her alarm.

"The brute is still about the island. I should like his skin for a rug."

"You could really shoot him with this?"

"Well—I shall mount it, in any case, though I have my doubts of his standing while I blow a few rocks through his person."

When he went for a fresh supply of fruits he brought up a log some four or five feet in length, with a burned-off prong at its end. This he intended to prepare as a "carriage" for the gun. He placed the pronged end down in his fire, to burn out a niche for the little brass piece, which he cleaned of its mud then and there.

His preliminary work on the bit of ordnance was soon concluded. When his log had burned to a moderate depth, he removed it to a near-by rock and gouged the charred portions away. Into the hollow thus rudely formed, the breach of the gun loosely fitted, ready to be firmly bound in place.

But the day was done, and Elaine had spread their "table," to which Sidney was glad to repair.

He had mentioned nothing of the tube still fatly bulging his pocket. Until he should first determine what the cylinder contained, he meant to arouse no unnecessary speculations in the breast of his companion. How much she might yet have to know of the barque and the mummy chained in its cabin he could not determine to-night. That something sinister lurked behind the mystery which this and the two headless skeletons involved was his constantly growing conviction.

It was not until night was heavily down, and Elaine had crept gladly to the comfort of her cave, that Grenville produced the brass cylinder, and stirred up new flames of his fire.

Then, sitting alone in the ruddy glow, with a rock for a stool, and another before him for an anvil, he scraped all he could of the greenish oxidation from the cover of the tube, and tried, as before, to wrench it off. The stubborn parts remained solidly rusted together.

This he had apparently expected. For he took up a rock of convenient size and, gently beating the cylinder just below its union with the cover, he bent it slightly inward about its entire circumference, meanwhile pausing from time to time to thrust his knife between the cemented pieces and force them a little apart.

The tube was considerably mangled by this process, while the cover still adhered. In a final burst of impatience, Grenville thrust the battered cap in the crevice between two bowlders and wrenched it roughly away.

Then he turned the hollow tube to the light, revealing, within, the edge of some document, thick and loosely rolled. This he readily removed and straightened in his hands, placing the tube beneath his arm.

For a moment the parchment seemed, despite the firelight upon it, a mere blank square, of leathery texture and weight. Then he fancied he saw upon its surface some manner of writing, or signs.

He resumed his seat and held the thing to the fullest light of the flames. It was yellowish tan in color, a trifle stiff, and inclined to curl to the shape it had held so long. Grenville turned it over, so dim were the characters it bore. There was nothing, however, on its outer side, wherefore he bent more closely towards his wavering light above such signs as he could finally discern.

Perhaps the fact that he began by expecting to find some ordinary map, or printed or written characters, for a short time baffled his wits. Howbeit, he began at length to discover the fact that a few large signs or hieroglyphics had been rudely sketched upon the parchment. When this discovery was finally confirmed, he had still considerable difficulty in tracing the lines that comprised these singular designs.

The firelight cast dark shadows in certain crease-like traceries that folds in the substance had formed. It was not until he presently managed to discriminate between these mere wrinkles and the "writing," that he made the slightest progress. His eyes at last became more keen to follow the artist's meaning. With his stub of a pencil, on a whittled bit of wood, he began to copy what he "read."

The result was, crudely, this:

It was not a map; it could hardly be a message—unless expressed in some short-hand system heretofore unknown—yet it must at some time or other have been accounted important to have been so elaborately preserved.

Grenville turned it upside down, compared his copy with the original repeatedly, and then examined the parchment with most minute particularity in search of some smaller writing to explain these mysterious signs.

There was nothing further to be seen—at least by the light of his fire. Two of the symbols only did he recognize as ever having come to his attention before. These were, first, the lines like a series of M's, and second the oval, about a human figure. This last suggested unmistakably an ancient Egyptian cartouch—the name or title of a king. But containing one sign only, and that apparently representing a mummy, it puzzled the inventor no less than the pyramids and curves.

That some either crude or crafty mind had combined this mixture of Egyptian and nondescript hieroglyphics with intent to reveal some secret message or information to other initiated beings, while concealing its import from all accidental beholders of the script, seemed to Grenville perfectly obvious.

He sat for three hours replenishing the fire and goading his brain for a key to the puzzle, before it occurred to his mind at last the tube might contain the explanation.

All this while he had held it beneath his arm, hard pressed against his body. As he peered down its dark interior once more, he likewise thrust in his fingers. It was they that discovered and fastened upon another sheet of something he had missed.

This clung so close to the tube's metal walls he wetted his finger to remove it. The light then shone opaquely through its substance. It was ordinary foolscap paper, the half of a sheet, gone yellowish with age, but otherwise very well preserved.

It was covered with roughly scrawled characters.

Grenville glanced it through—and irrelevantly longed for a pipe. He felt he should like some good tobacco to assist in the puzzle's solution.

He felt convinced, however, that a crude example of the simplest, most primitive cipher was contained upon the sheet. Should the words later prove to be in English he could finally read it all. He began to compare the recurrence of the various symbols at once, discovering that the sign in the form of a cross had been used no less than fourteen times, and was therefore almost certainly E. The next in importance was the figure 3, which he felt might be either A, or N, or S, since these, after E, are among the characters in English spelling most frequently employed.

On another clean chip of whittled wood he jotted down a few of the "words" with E's in each instance substituted for the crosses, and then began attempting to make clear sense by substituting A's, N's, and S's for the figure three, the figure one, and open squares, which, he found, had been often represented.

It was a blind and tedious business. His fire burned low, in his absorption, and the midnight constellations marched past the zenith of the heavens before he finally realized the folly of his quest.

"It's not a bit of good in the world, if I knew all about it," he finally confessed, "no matter what it means."

He went to bed. But he did not sleep. Those singular pyramids and the cipher still lingered before his inner vision. What was the mystery hidden behind the dead man chained in the rotting barque, the headless skeletons lying near the swamp, and now these documents, found in the tube and so carefully concealed?

"I give it up," he told himself at last, in an effort to dismiss it all and compose his active brain. "I wish I had a stouter tube to make a good bomb for the tiger."

He thought perhaps he could use the oxidized cylinder as it was, and began thereupon to wonder how he should make a fuse by which its powder contents might be ignited. Thus he drowsed off at last, with fantastic dreams swiftly solving the sum of his problems.

CHAPTER XII

AMBITIOUS PLANS

Grenville awoke with a brilliant idea, born in his brain as he slept.

It was not concerned with the documents found in the old brass receptacle, but entirely with the tiger. He knew how to fashion a fuse.

The creepers had answered this latest need, with their bark so readily hollowed. He had burned up yards of the drying stuff with the core removed, all of it shrunk and twisted tight, like long coils of vegetable tubing. He had only to fill it with his powder while green, and then let it dry in the sun.

He could likewise fill the useless cylinder, wrap it about to increase its resistance to the powder—and thereby render its explosion far more violent. If, after that, a chance were presented to ignite it under the tiger——

It was possible always, he confessed, the tiger might prove unwilling. However, both the cannon and bomb should be immediately prepared. There could be no peace upon the island while the brute remained alive.

All thoughts of the cipher were postponed for evening recreation. The day's work began after breakfast in preparing large quantities of powder.

At this Elaine assisted. She was glad of any employment. No less in her veins than in Grenville's the promptings of being in the primitive were daily surging stronger. Like himself, she was hungry for meat; and while she had no thoughts of turning Amazon herself, she felt an increasing interest in all that Grenville was attempting in his task of coping with nature.

Meanwhile Sidney was daily assuming a wild and unkempt aspect that he could not possibly avoid. His beard was an unbecoming stubble that he was powerless to shave; his hair was uncombed and a trifle long; his clothing was not without its rents. But what an active, muscular being he appeared, as he moved about at his work! He seemed so thoroughly fearless, so competent and at home with naked Nature. His thoughtfulness, moreover, had no limits, and neither had his cheer. He had made no further disquieting advances, but seemed rather to have forgotten, utterly, the lawless emotions to which he had one day given way.

This day it was he started the fires to bake his vessels of clay. They were all sufficiently dry for the purpose, and, huddled together, a bit removed, in a rudely constructed furnace made of rock, were piled about with abundant fuel to provide an even heat.

The morning was sped between the various duties. Some ten or more pounds of powder Grenville finally stored in his cave. The labor of grinding and mixing had undergone many interruptions while he attended the fire about his jugs. He finally fetched some creepers from the growth and, stripping out the pliable cores, poured powder in several of the hollow coverings, bound them together, here and there, with fibers, and placed them out on the rocks to dry.

With the withes thus provided to his hand, the cannon was bound upon the log he had hollowed a bit to receive it. This he knew to be crude and, perhaps, even quite insufficient, but the gun was, in any event, far too unwieldy for use against the tiger, unless the brute should deliberately pose as a target, in the clearing down below.

That mid-day the porcupine once more volunteered for dinner. His services were accepted. Grenville dispatched him with a club—and skinned him in the thicket. He was far too considerate of a woman's sensibilities to fetch the creature into camp, with his arsenal of spears still upon him. But the task of removing the hedgehog's hide was amazingly difficult.

Aware of two important facts—namely, that meat too freshly cooked is certain to be tough, while even fresh meat for three hours wrapped in paw-paw leaves becomes incredibly tender, Grenville lost no time, when the skinning was done, in thoroughly swaddling his "game." He had carved it up for more convenient handling. When he finally brought it for Elaine to see, it looked decidedly attractive.

"I shall save some scraps for bait," he said. "To-morrow we'll try for fish."

What with carving a number of tough, wooden hooks, preparing some line from various fibers, and supplying new fuel to the flames that were firing his needed potteries, his remaining hours were full.

At length, in preparation for their dinner of meat, he went below, dug a hole somewhat laboriously in the sand and earth of the clearing, and started another brisk fire in the hollow thus created, Elaine tossing down a few glowing twigs for the purpose.

And how brave she looked, he paused to note, as she came to the brink to be of this much assistance! How beautiful she was—and how delicate she seemed, to be cast into such conditions! Despite her sturdiness of heart and limb, she had always been tenderly reared. How far might she go, enduring this life, reduced to savagery?

These were thoughts that had come and been banished from his mind innumerable times. There was nothing he could do to alter or even greatly alleviate the hardships by which she was surrounded. Her aloofness from personal contact with himself, even her constant suspicions of his motives, and her lingering indignation for what he had done, he felt every hour of the day. But he could not have begged her forgiveness if he would—and would not have done so if he could.

How long would it last, he asked himself—and what would be the end? Would no ship ever come—or how long might it be till succor finally arrived? Would a search be made for the missing boat that had gone to the bottom of the sea? Or, before this could happen, would smaller craft arrive—the strange, swift craft of these eastern waters, manned by fanatical outlaws, pirates, or even the wild, head-hunting Dyaks, who had probably been here before?

When he finally placed his meat in the pit, where the fire had burned down to glowing embers, his mind was filled with the many plans he was impatient to materialize without another half hour's delay. He covered the leaf-and-clay-wrapped dinner, first with portions of the coals and heated ashes, and then with all the sand he had dug to make his natural oven, after which he returned to the terrace.

Neither the process of cooking, nor that of firing his earthenware could be hastened now by Grenville's presence.. He saw that his pottery furnace was properly supplied with fuel, and then sat down where Elaine was busily plaiting a flat sort of mat with withes she had somehow split to half their former size, and there he began to carve at some slender branches of wood he had brought from down below.

"What are you making?" he presently asked, as he watched her nimble fingers at their task.

"A platter for the meat," she told him, briefly. "And what are your sticks to become?"

"Forks for the same. I hope we shall need no knives.... I must soon find time to dig about and, perhaps, unearth some yams. They are not so good as potatoes, but they answer at a pinch."

"You have planned so many things to accomplish," she said. "Do you think you shall ever have the time?"

"Can't tell, but meantime I thoroughly enjoy this wresting an existence from more or less stubborn conditions. Just as soon as I eliminate the tiger I shall melt up my pieces of metal to make a number of tools."

Elaine looked up at the man in wonder, but not incredulously.

"What perfect confidence you seem to have in your ability to accomplish difficult things."

His utterance sank a tone lower as he answered:

"What I say I'll do—I'll do. What I say I'll have—I'll have."

It was the first word he had spoken since their coming to the island that might have been construed as a survival of the feelings he had demonstrated on the steamer.

Elaine felt her whole being suddenly burn with strange excitement. She felt the underlying significance of his speech, and her soul was instantly bristling with defiance.

His words went too deep and were uttered too gravely for any mere idle boasting. She had already seen, and partially acknowledged, the power that lay in this strong man's hands to compel his desired ends. She felt this potency emanating from him now—and resented the fact that she herself had been as much selected as the tiger for his ultimate conquering.

She was angry again on the instant, ready to fight like a very little demon, should he dare so much as lay a finger on her hand. She resolved anew that, though a hundred years should pass before they two escaped this island exile, not the tiniest bud of answering love should ever sprout in her breast.

For the past few days she had felt a new sense of security and ease. The man with whom she was working out this singular and intimate existence had made no sign of renewing his advances, had seemed to forget he had ever broached the subject of his passion, and had been a most agreeable companion, cheerful, resourceful, and courageous to the last degree.

Now that she knew what unworthy thoughts still lingered beneath the surface of his calm, indifferent demeanor, not even their earlier friendship seemed to her possible again—and for this she was disappointed and annoyed.

Her glance had fallen instantly back to her work. That her color burned up, to the tips of her ears for Grenville to see and, perhaps, enjoy, she felt with added irritation. But she would not confess, by word or deed, she understood the meaning of his speech.

When she spoke she employed a quiet and common-place tone of voice, and returned to impersonal subjects.

"I can understand," she said, "how you might possibly shoot the tiger, but I thought one needed furnaces, tall chimneys, and things, to melt up bronze and brass."

"Dead right," he answered, readily. "You see, you've got such a grasp on things that I never cease to be surprised—and delighted. I've engaged quite a chimney already."

She forced herself to continue the conversation, if only by way of ignoring the personal element of his answer.

"Engaged a chimney?"

"You'll see about that, later. If getting the tiger were only half as easy as some of the other things I expect to accomplish, I'd certainly be tickled clean to death."

She felt—she almost knew, indeed—that she and her love were classified among the things he expected to "accomplish" so easily at last, and her hot resentment burned hotter. She was tempted to flash out her wildest cry of the loathing—the bitter, eternal loathing—his words had begotten in her bosom. She was tempted again to a desperate wish that the tiger might rend him in pieces—as *she* would do if ever he touched her again. But she dared not trust herself to speak, or even to show, by the slightest sign, that his threat was comprehended. She clung in desperation to the subject she felt to be safe.

"Then—you do think the tiger dangerous—hard, at least, to kill?"

"Well, I wouldn't call him exactly plum pudding and gravy."

"Your cannon would kill him, though, of course?"

"If he'd pose in front of the muzzle, a rod or so away."

A cold chill crept along her nerves at thoughts of the savage animal she herself had twice encountered. She wondered just what Grenville's method would be—in overcoming some of the things he had vowed to conquer.

"You hardly expect to shoot the creature, then, after all?"

He held up the fork he was carving, for critical examination.

"I'm rather inclined to favor the plan of leaving a bait in the jungle, and letting go a bomb when he comes to dine."

Her natural concern for the man's own safety could not be long expelled.

"How shall you know when he comes?" she inquired, and she dared look up as before.

Grenville continued to bend his gaze on his labor.

"I expect to hang around and see."

A sudden fear and sinking of the vitals seized her, unaware.

"But—doesn't a tiger usually feed at night?"

"His club hours are usually rather late, I believe."

"And you'll wait around for him to come in the dark?"

"What else can I do? Can't expect him to 'phone me he's arrived."

"Oh!" she said, impulsively, "couldn't we build a wall of stone around enough of the fruit for just ourselves? I could help at that. I'd do so gladly!"

If an exquisite thrill shot directly to the deeps of Grenville's nature—a thrill aroused by her courage, her generous spirit, her honest and helpful sympathy—he permitted himself to make no sign. Also, he took no fulsome flattery to his soul. But he pictured her forth, with bleeding hands, and torn and grimy garments, as she rolled and carried great stones to the brink, to supply him with blocks for a wall; and his spirit was wondrously glad to think he had made no error of judgment in appraising her character.

That all she could do she would do, as mere assistance—do for anyone else in a similar situation, he comprehended fully. But he felt not a whit less exultant for the knowledge of the fact. She was never for a moment a mere useless dependent. She was daily, aye, hourly, assisting in his wholly unequal combat for their lives, and this was a joy to his heart.

But he spoke with his usual bluntness, and without a single hint of sympathy in all she had eagerly suggested.

"Wholly impractical scheme. I've thought of a dozen just as poor."

Elaine was instantly sorry she had proffered him her help. She placed a withe between her teeth, bit through it neatly, and began to divide it with her fingers.

"Here, don't do that. You'll spoil your teeth," said Grenville, brusquely. "I'll split you enough for half a day."

She made no reply as he went at the withes and split them with skillful ease, but she hoped he could feel, through some sensitive chord, how intensely she disliked him.

He could not. "I've been thinking," he said, "I may be obliged to make a loom to weave these fibers into some sort of cloth for garments. May need them before we get away."

Elaine once more responded, in her honest, impulsive manner.

"I could knit some things, I'm sure, if you'd cut me a pair of needles."

"Cut 'em to-night," he answered. "That meat must be done, and my potteries need attention."

He dropped in her lap the forks he had roughly completed, and strode away to his fire.

CHAPTER XIII

A MIDNIGHT VISITOR

The porcupine dinner was good. In its ball of clay, Grenville brought it to the cave in the basket that he used for heavy burdens.

It was far too hot to be handled carelessly. And when he broke away the earthy covering and leaves, and arranged the steaming pieces on the platter Elaine had prepared, it was perfectly cooked, as tender as quail, and of a flavor surprisingly fine.

The banquet, however, would have been immeasurably improved by the commonest of bread and potatoes. To provide some palatable substitute for these essential commonplaces of civilization became another of Grenville's problems, which, he told himself, he must tackle—after the tiger.

Everything was after the tiger, or else over-fraught with danger. The thought of this made Grenville fret more than anything demanding his attention. That night, when Elaine had finally retired, he went to his fuses, broke off a length, and returned to light it at his fire. It was still too damp, from the juices of the plant, to burn efficiently. His bomb he, therefore, would not make until the following afternoon.

The fire about his potteries he was now permitting to die. It could not be altogether abandoned, since a too sudden cooling of the vessels would crack and ruin every one. Therefore, from time to time, he went to the furnace to regulate the heat. He had leveled a rock for a table, at the fireplace near his cave, and on this he finally spread the mysterious paper and parchment recovered from the tube.

They had been all day neglected. Grenville had thoroughly intended a daylight examination of the parchment, concerning the nature of which he was considerably in doubt.

A new supply of whittled wooden "tablets" on which to write lay ready to his hand. Scratching at his head with his pencil, he studied the hieroglyphics for an hour or more before he returned to the written sheet with the scrawl spelled out in cipher.

As a matter of fact, his mind refused the task on which he was endeavoring to focus his attention. Despite his utmost efforts, his thoughts would return to Elaine. He would have given almost his hope of eternity to secure her absolute comfort and freedom from anxiety. And, inasmuch as the tiger was responsible for much of her worry, his mind was made up that a trial should be made to slay the brute without another day's delay.... It is always so easy to plan!

He was finally staring straight into the fire, though his hand still rested on the parchment and the paper. The flames sank lower and lower, wavering finally like dull red spear-heads among the glowing embers.

At some fancied sound he turned sharply about, to peer through the darkness of the trail. All appeared as silent and calm as the grave. He wondered if, perhaps, Elaine had arisen to come to her door.

She was not to be seen at the indistinct entrance of her cave. He turned once more to stir his fire—then wheeled like one on a pivot.

His senses had not been deceived. Beyond, in the darkness, a few feet only from the cavern occupied by Elaine, two blazing coals had been fixed like twin stars by his movement.

A sudden recollection that he had failed to close the gap in the wall swept hotly and accusingly through him. Some beast of the jungle had passed the barrier, perhaps to enter the very cave that the wall had been built to protect!

With a note that broke the stillness abruptly, Grenville caught up a flaming branch of wood from the mass of embers in the fire, and sprang to the path to the cavern.

The prowling animal stood for a moment undecided, then started as if to spring before the oncoming man to the shelter of Elaine's rock retreat, doubtless to turn there in desperation for a mad encounter in the dark.

But, perhaps by a yard, the man was there before him. The brute, even then, refused to retreat towards the trail by which it had come. It leaped towards the place where Grenville made his bed—a shadowy form that he knew at last was not the arrogant tiger.

It turned for a moment in the mouth of the cave, as if aware this smaller retreat was too shallow for adequate shelter. But before the man could crack his fiery brand upon the creature's head, it leaped wildly past him, growling a savage protest, and reluctantly retreated towards the trail.

One more attempt it made, even then, to escape by Grenville's active form, and regain the larger cavern. But his fierce, hot rushes were not to be withstood. It finally turned with another sort of bellow, and cowered uncertainly upon the downward path.

After it no less desperately than before, Sidney plunged along the steep descent, his firebrand brightly glowing in the wind. A whine of fear escaped the jungle creature as he slunk at last through Grenville's gate to the outer precincts of the wall.

Almost immediately followed a frightful din of growls and wauling. There were certain deep gutturals and mouthings that Grenville was sure his tiger only could produce. There were sounds of a conflict, fierce and bloody, retreating down the trail. Like a battle of cats, enormously exaggerated, with screams and roars intermingled, the disturbance rose on the air. But Grenville had blocked his gate with logs and bowlders, and calmly returned to his place.

Elaine was crouching by the fire when he came once more to the terrace. She had called him in vain, and was visibly trembling as his form appeared within the glow.

"What was it?" she cried. "What has happened?"

"Why—it sounds like a couple of jungle politicians engaged in a tariff argument."

"You weren't down there?"

"I strolled to the wall, to make sure it was closed for the night."

"There was nothing—up here? I dreamed there was something—fighting with you—some terrible creature—like that."

She waved her hand towards the hideous sounds, retreating swiftly in the darkness.

"Can't understand such a dream," he said. "We've had no corned beef and cabbage. You'd better go back and try again."

He started at once for his pottery fire, in his brusque, indifferent manner.

Elaine stood there, watching his figure, retreating in the darkness, and made no move to retire. Like a dim silhouette of Vulcan, projected against the reddened glare of his furnace, he presently appeared, from the place where she eagerly kept him in her vision. She felt she could not bear to creep away until he should return.

She saw him stand for a little time observing his waning heaps of embers before he faced about to return once more to his seat. Then, slowly, as she heard his footsteps approaching, she glided silently back to her shelter, and so at length within the door. Even then she lingered eagerly, to make certain he was not far away. Until he sat down, and stirred up the flames, she did not return to her couch.

"To be so perfectly fearless!" she murmured, half aloud, and so crept away to her dark, uncomfortable cave.

Grenville pocketed the documents, still lying face up on his rock. He finally slept beside the fire, to finish his plans in dreams.

These plans, which were vague enough that night, matured fairly early in the morning. He had resolved to try for the tiger at the spring.

Fully expecting to encounter abundant signs of the animal conflict of the midnight hours, he descended the trail before Elaine had appeared, intent upon removing such evidence of trouble as might be found disturbingly near their tower.

There was nothing at all along the trail to show that a fight had taken place. Where the grass and shrubbery began in the clearing below the walls, there was one mere tuft of hair upon a twig. But a rod removed from this there was at least a hint as to what might have caused the engagement.

This was a trampled and slightly reddened ring where something had been eaten—some quarry doubtless captured by the smaller of the prowlers, who had found himself suddenly attacked and driven from the feast by the master hunter of the jungle, on whose sacred preserves he had probably dared to poach.

Grenville proceeded to the spring, not only to fetch a fresh supply of water, but as well to indulge in a vigorous washing of his hands and face, and to make some observations.

He found that by breaking several limbs a none too comfortable seat in the branches of a rubber tree might be prepared, provided he could climb to the perch. With a very long fuse attached to his bomb he might be enabled to execute a coup upon the tiger, under cover of the night. Could he only slay some animal—another wild hog, for instance—and place it here as a lure, his chances of securing the tiger's attendance would be infinitely increased.

A number of things were essential to his plan. The first, a rope ladder, was the simplest of the lot. That he could fashion with ease. His greatest problem was the fire with which to ignite his fuse, should he wish to explode his bomb. The wood he had found, that so amazingly retained its glow, might answer his needs for, perhaps, two hours, as he sat high up in the tree. It was all he possessed, and upon it he must needs rely. But how he should manage to discern his beast, in the darkness, when the prowler came at last to drink, was more than he could determine.

"A dead-fall might do for the brute," he soliloquized aloud, as the business revolved in his mind. "But I couldn't get one ready by to-night."

For several reasons a dead-fall was impracticable. The thought was, therefore, abandoned, while the details of loading and placing the bomb were elaborately planned. So vivid was Grenville's imagination that already he pictured himself high in the tree, heard the tiger come to lap the water, lighted his fuse—and ended that trouble forever.

CHAPTER XIV

TRUANTS OUT OF SCHOOL

He returned to the terrace, lightly whistling. The morning was perfect, a delightfully refreshing zephyr lightly stirring in the trees. Elaine beheld him approaching, and nodded from the cliff.

"The jugs look beautiful!" she called, enthusiastically. "The fire is barely warm."

He had brought their supply of water in the sea-shell, so variously employed. Before providing fruits for their breakfast, he went to his furnace with Elaine. The firing was complete, though the vessels were not yet cool. A few were cracked, slightly, despite the care that Grenville had exercised, and one was hopelessly ruined. However, he felt the product as a whole was surprisingly satisfactory, especially some of his molds and the crucibles meant for his foundry.

"At noon we'll fill a jug with water," he said, "and you'll find it will keep surprisingly cool. The clay is slightly porous. The water oozes through, evaporates on the surface, and thereby chills the contents. They use nothing else in Egypt, and, I think, in Mexico.

"If it weren't for the tiger," said Elaine, "I could often go to the spring."

"Right ho!" said Grenville, cheerily, believing he understood a wish that lay beneath her speech. "That reminds me. I believe I could manage to deepen a basin I saw in the rock on our lowermost shelf above the sea, back yonder, and easily fill it by dipping salt water with a jug on the end of a rope. Any nymph should enjoy such a pool."

"Oh!" said Elaine, delighted by the thought; "do you really think you could make it?"

"Well—I've thought of it, you see, on an empty stomach. After breakfast —— There's quite a bit to do, by the way, after breakfast."

With the fruits now presently gathered, he brought a fresh supply of creepers and leaves of the sisal, for labors soon to begin. And while Elaine prepared what was left of the meat, and the other things afforded by their larder, he went to the shelf of rock so completely protected by its wall, and made up his mind that, with one good tool, plus a hammer, he could hew out a bath with amazingly little trouble.

"Meant to go fishing this morning!" he confessed, as the sight of the clear, limpid tide below aroused new desires in his being. "There must be oysters and many good fish, if I had the time to get them."

Fish-lines and other "diversions" were again postponed when the breakfast was concluded, while Grenville braided fibers and tied stout rungs along their length, to form a rude sort of ladder. This he carried to the spring at length, and hung across the limb of his tree by lifting its end on a pole.

Once in the tree, he labored diligently, breaking or cutting away a number of interfering branches, and arranging a makeshift for a seat, on which to rest as he waited. The bomb would be better prepared in the afternoon.

On his way, returning to the camp, he gathered a bundle of the special wood that he used to retain his fire. It was while he was thus engaged, in an unexplored part of the thicket, that he came upon a fallen tree, fairly brittle with resin. He snapped off branch after branch of this, till his load was too heavy to carry. With all he could take he climbed the trail.

A piece that he tried at the embers of his fire blazed promptly enough, producing a volume of thick, black smoke, and a flame that burned slowly down the wood, as he held the lighted end aloft.

"If we happen to need a torch," he said to Elaine, who, as usual, was watching results, "this will always be stored here, ready." He placed the fagots in a near-by hollow of the rocks, against possible future need.

There was nothing further to be done at the spring until the hour of sunset. The jugs and vessels from the furnace were found to be sufficiently cool for handling, and were brought to the rear of his shelter.

The molds he had made excited anew his various ambitions.

"To-morrow I shall start operations on the smelter," he told his companion. "No tools means no boat—and no boat means no escape."

Elaine felt a bound of excitement in her veins at the mere suggestion of escape. She inquired: "How long will it take to build your boat?"

"Can't tell," said Grenville, briefly. "Never built one on a toolless island before."

"I only meant about how long," Elaine explained. "It will take at least a week, I suppose."

"More likely two," he answered, as before. "Meantime I'm going fishing. Want to come?"

Elaine had little liking for any such off-hand invitation.

"Not at present, thank you." She turned away from him, coldly.

"It's an art and a sport you ought to cultivate," he informed her, cheerfully. "Might sometime keep you from starving." He gathered up the necessary paraphernalia, adding, "I hope the fish will bite," and started on his way.

He had fully two hundred feet of the line he had braided from fibers. It was thoroughly "waxed" with juices from the rubber tree, and although it was frequently knotted along its length, it was strong as a wire, and not inclined to kink.

His wooden hook was clumsy, but tough as steel, while its point and its barb were exceedingly sharp. Also, the bait he thrust upon it concealed it well, except where the line was stoutly attached. With one of his old rusted hinges for a sinker, it was presently ready for use.

He had chosen that protected shelf of rock whereon he meant to hew out a bath for Elaine, since this was the nearest possible approach he could make to the water from the cliff. There, alas! at the very first cast attempted, his line was atrociously tangled, while the hook remained suspended some ten feet up from the tide.

In patience he sat himself down on the ledge to restore the line to order. Elaine, who had doubtless pondered wisely on his observation, anent fishing as an art to be acquired, came half reluctantly wandering over to his side, while Grenville was still engrossed with his mess of tangles. She watched him in silence for a time, then, finally, sank to the bench of rock and began to lend her assistance. He made not the slightest comment, and even failed to thank her when the task was finally concluded.

Once again, at last, he swung the line for a cast far out in the waters. It seemed to Elaine the hook and sinker would never cease sailing outward. Yet they fell and sank, much closer in than even Grenville had expected.

He began to pull it back at once, since there might be rocks on which the hook would foul, and his labor be wholly lost. The sinker, and then the bait, emerged from the crystal depths of brine without so much as a nibble. Again Grenville sent them full length out, and again drew in with no results, save a possible inquiry, far below, where he fancied he saw a gleam of silver.

The third cast fared no better than the others. But the fourth was no more than started homeward when a sharp, heavy strike was briskly reported on the line, and Grenville's jerk responded.

"Oh! you've got one!—you've got one!" cried Elaine, with all the true pleasure of a sportsman. "Please, please don't let it get away!"

Grenville was taking no chances on slack in the line, with his simple wooden hook. He hauled in, hand over fist, while his catch fought madly to escape. With a wild inward dash and a mighty flop, the silvery captive on the barb leaped entirely out of the water.

Grenville's answering maneuver with the line, snatching up fully a yard of its length, and instantly stooping to clutch it low again, was all that saved the situation. His fish barely touched the surface, after that, then was swiftly sailing up in air.

He was a beautiful specimen of his kind, but the species was new to his captor.

"What's the use of going to school?" was Grenville's query, his eyes as bright as a boy's. "The next one may be a whale."

The next one, however, was a long time coming. When it was hooked, the wise fisherman knew it was small, and, most unexpectedly, he delivered the line to Elaine.

"Now, then, give him the dickens!" he instructed. "You want to make him think he's struck by lightning."

Surprised as she was, and unprepared for this particular favor, Elaine did her best, and hauled in valiantly, but the captive got away.

Five or six casts were made after that before the hook was once more nibbled. Grenville was rather inclined to change for a spot more popular with the purple water's tribe. Yet he made another of his longest throws, and had drawn in much of the dripping line when a clean young tortoise so deeply swallowed the hook that he could not have spat it out to save him.

The fight he offered was tremendous. He dived and skittered through the crystal tides like some giant saucer of dynamics. Whole lines of the brightest silver bubbles arose as he visibly flapped about and scuttled towards the bottom. The line raced wildly here and there, cutting the waves with the sound of something hot and sizzling.

But it held for a full half hour of fighting. It was strong enough for the weight of a man, as Grenville afterward declared. It conquered the tortoise finally, and drew him up, but not before he had wearied the fisherman's muscles and greatly fatigued Elaine, who was panting with sheer excitement.

"There you are," said Grenville, boyishly exultant, "he's wash basin, comb, a few hairpins, and what-not, all in one, not to mention turtle soup."

There was no more fishing done that afternoon, nor were knitting needles carved. What with his turtle, his fish, the digging of several yams, and the making of his bomb, Grenville was amply employed.

Elaine was at length made acquainted with his programme for the night. She made no effort to dissuade him from his purpose, but excitement rose in her bosom. She feared for what the tiger might by mischance accomplish, and, also, she felt that in some occult way her own fate and the animal's were alike, if not related—that if such a brute must helplessly succumb to the man's superior prowess, there was no chance at all for anything as feeble as herself.

A wild, unreasoning hope was in her breast that the tiger might escape, or die in some different manner—do something, almost anything, rather than contribute one more testimony to Sidney Grenville's might. She could not wish the creature to live, nor yet to injure this bold, audacious man. She only knew that some dread of the being who could dare engage or attack this savage monster of the jungle was once more assailing her quaking heart and stirring her nature to rebellion.

In a manner that was largely automatic, she assisted in providing an early evening meal. It was dusk, however, when Grenville was finally ready to leave her on the hill.

She followed him down to the gate against the wall, in the way of a child who fears long hours alone.

"Good-night," he said to her, cheerily. "If you hear my little imitation of Bunker Hill—you might drop one tear for the departed."

Her dread of the night, and the outcome of his excursion, had suddenly increased. "If you kill him," she said, "you'll come home?"

He nodded. "Tickled to death and bragging like a pirate."

Then he placed the logs and rocks against the barrier, and once more bade her good-night. She waited till his final footsteps died away in the gloom, then hastened once more to the brink above for a final glimpse of his form.

He had passed, however, across the clearing, and not even the spark that he bore to the gathering darkness threw her back a dull red ray.

He had lost little time after leaving the foot of the trail. The jungle was wrapped in somber shadows as he made his way to the spring.

Some nimble little creature leaped lightly away when he came to the place. Otherwise there was not a sign or a sound to disturb the ringing silence. His bomb he placed beside the ebon water, where a ledge of rock would throw its violence outward. The fuse, which he carefully uncoiled and laid upon the grass, was amply long to meet his needs.

At length, with his fire-stick held between his teeth, he ascended the ladder to his perch. The end of the fuse he now brought to the limb, conveniently near for lighting. Then he settled himself to wait.

Once he blew on the coal slowly eating his brand, to clean the incandescent cone. Of a sudden, then, he heard the sound of something directly beneath him, rudely brushing the foliage aside.

His heart for a second stood still.

CHAPTER XV

A NIGHT IN THE JUNGLE

It was not the tiger Grenville heard above the pounding of his heart.

The squealing of some little insignificant beast, apparently more in sport than apprehension, betrayed very soon the fact that no sinister visitor was even prowling near. So heavy a sound as the little brute had made would doubtless be avoided when the master of the jungle should arrive.

All the excitement unduly engendered in Grenville's system rapidly subsided. He listened as intently as before, and peered below in an effort to pierce the densest shadows, but could not detect the form or whereabouts of his early visitor. He doubted if this small creature drank, since the pool of the spring was still quite clearly visible, like a surface half of ebony and half of tarnished silver.

At length the absolute silence prevailed as it had before. Save for the lightest of zephyrs, that barely sufficed to fan the topmost foliage, not even the slightest stir could be detected. The darkness below became absolute, where shadows, tree-trunks, and thicket all blended into one. A portion only of the pool was now discernible, and in this, clearly mirrored, were two bright stars, that burned dull gold in the ebon.

Grenville sat back in his lumpy perch and blew, as before, on his coal. Its slender wreath of invisible smoke ascended pungently. The hour was still very early for nocturnal business to begin. The tiger might not come till midnight. Sidney reflected that the brute would doubtless eat before a drink would be desired.

He regretted, vainly, that no bait had finally been provided. Even the fish they had only partially eaten for dinner might have been attractive to the tiger. Any price now would be cheap enough to rid themselves of this terror.

His reflections ran the gamut of their island world, and sped far over seas. He thought of that day with Fenton, and of what this friend would think. Had they heard the news, in that far-away home, of the steamer gone down with every soul?

He thought of the morning he had greeted Elaine—and the something that had happened to his nature. He remembered in detail every hour of every day they had spent together on the steamer. Then the hideous details of all that last experience, in the storm and night, paraded by for his review.

One after another the swiftly moving procession of events brought him back to this present hour. He was, then, confronted once again by the questions—how long would it last?—how might it end? The island's mystery impinged once more on his varied cogitations, making him wish he might have had a torch, by which to study the documents reposing in his pocket.

Mentally picturing forth the signs on the leathery piece of parchment, he busied himself for above an hour for a clew as to what they could mean. They suggested nothing to his mind that made the slightest sense. He tried to recall the characters on the "explanatory" sheet. But this was a hopeless task.

Aware of the value of deduction, he began on a reasoning line. Anything to occupy his thoughts and time till the hour when the tiger might have fed, and would come for his evening drink, was highly welcome.

He began by a natural presumption that both the documents, found together in the tube, and so carefully concealed, related to this particular island. Did they not, then of what possible value would be their final decipherment and solution?

Granting this premise, then what should follow next? Certainly some mention of the island—with its name—in the written message, at least. There would naturally be, in these circumstances, some word in the cipher spelling "Island"—but what would the place be called?

Such places, he knew, were frequently named quite unofficially, by wandering sailors, adventurers, and drifters on the sea. Attempting to level his state of mind to that of such human beings, he wondered what he, if left to himself, would christen this bit of rock and jungle.

So often, he reflected, a place was named for its appearance. This one, for instance, might aptly be called "Three Rocks," "Three Walls," or "Three Towers." He remembered, finally, the abominable sounds produced by the tides twice daily—sounds he had thought might have frightened the natives away. The cognomen, "Haunted Island," might not seem wholly inappropriate to a superstitious mind.

The more he reflected, the more certain he felt that some one of the names suggested to his mind might also have occurred to those of others. Considerably aroused in his centers of curiosity, and convinced that even by the dull cherry glow of his firebrand he might be enabled to confirm or confute his theory, he moved sufficiently to draw from his pocket the closely folded documents, and held them up to his torch.

The one with the inexplicable signs he promptly returned as of no immediate avail. At that instant his attention was arrested, by a sound below him on the earth.

Something, he thought, was lapping at the water!

He leaned far forward, tense and rigid on the limb, shielding his spark in one of his hands, while he peered about the pool.

There was nothing he could possibly discern—no form of a head projected out to obliterate his stars. Yet the sounds at the edge of the silent basin rose distinctly to his ears.

All but ready to bend to the end of his fuse, and touch his fire upon it, he paused, looked closer, saw ripples move to disturb his mirrored planets—and then beheld some form darkly limned on the waters.

For a moment he was certain his insolent tiger was there. Some huge blunt muzzle seemed inkily contrasted with the dull gray surface of the spring. Then the muzzle suddenly detached itself from the imagined form behind. The entire figure of some little beast was seen as it waded the pool.

Once more, disgustedly, Grenville reclined and relaxed the strain on his nerves. It was some time, then, before he thought to return to his quest of the cipher. He remembered, finally, he had meant to count the characters in some of the words to see if the number of signs thus used might not correspond with the number employed in "Island," "Three," "Haunted," "Wall," or "Tower."

A dull red glow, of most unsatisfactory dimensions and illuminative capacity, was the most he could procure from his brand. It barely sufficed to present the "writing" to his vision. For a moment, indeed, he despaired of discriminating clearly between the ending of one word and the beginning of the next. Fortunately, however, the writer had used large periods between his every word.

Considerably to Grenville's satisfaction, the third word thus denoted he was almost convinced was "Three." Not only had it the proper number of letters, or signs, but the two final characters were exactly alike, and both were the crosses he had previously selected as probably representing E.

The next word along, he was equally certain, was either "Wall" or "Hill." Its two final characters were the same particular sign repeated, while its meaning, in conjunction with the preceding word "Three," fulfilled his logical deduction.

A word of two characters followed this, and then, to Grenville's intense delight, occurred a word of seven letters, which not only met the numerical requirements of "Haunted," but, also, in proper sequence, employed the various letter-signs already somewhat proved by the word he felt certain was "Three."

This was more than sufficient evidence on which to base a test of the message's sense, if it were not, indeed, enough of a key with which to decipher the entire inscription.

Eagerly fumbling in his pocket for his pencil, with the intention of attempting a bit of substitution of letters for the signs contained upon the sheet, Grenville shifted his position—and the paper fell from his fingers, fluttering obliquely from his sight.

He leaned quickly forward, as if to follow the flight of the missive through the darkness so densely spread beneath him. But it disappeared almost instantly—with its mystery still unsolved.

On the point of descending, at whatever cost, to recover the important bit of foolscap, Sidney was halted in movement and impulse by some new arrival at the spring.

As a matter of fact, two animals were there, as he presently discovered. That neither was his tiger he was presently persuaded, but that one or both were fairly large seemed equally assured.

It was certainly not a time to leave the tree. And while the reflection that, perhaps, the silent visitors were leopards was presented to Grenville's mind, and a momentary thought of slaying the pair by igniting his fuse became a strong temptation, he contented himself by staring more or less blindly down upon the place where they seemed to be, and bided his time as before.

At nine o'clock it seemed, to the cramped and impatient hunter in the tree, that ages had passed since he bade good-night to Elaine and came to this lonely vigil. There were sounds in abundance about him now, arising from time to time. Some were the cries of the lesser beasts, in the clutches or jaws of their captors; some were sounds of munching. All of them indicated rather grimly the tiger's absence from the scene. There would be no petty murderers thereabout when the arch brute came for his drink.

Leaning back once more, and long since weary of his fruitless adventure, Grenville stared at the glowing cone of fire slowly eating away his brand. It was lasting far longer than he had believed would be possible—yet certainly less than one hour more could the consuming substance serve to give him a spark.

He could almost fancy he saw a face, in the film of ash upon its surface. He was sure the face was developing a likeness to Elaine. Even the soft clear radiance of her cheek—— How eagerly she had asked concerning his coming "home"—but how far it seemed away.... He could hear her saying "You'll come home ... come home ... come back...."

He awoke with a start, for something had burned him on the wrist.

The firebrand, all but consumed in his relaxing fingers, had dropped and deposited a blister. In his sudden move to rid himself of the torture to his flesh, he threw off the red-hot candle of wood, and it fell straight downward, sizzling once where it struck in a trickle of the water.

Reviling himself for a stupid blunderer, and arousing vividly to a sense of where he was, and why, he began to question the expediency of returning at once to the terrace. He was still debating the wisdom of the move, when the question was decided by the tiger.

That belated midnight reveler—the old roué of the jungle—was ushered in with questionable pomp—the panic of lesser brutes in flight. And when he drank, beside the useless bomb, there was no mistaking his presence. He presently paused, half satisfied, and lifted his head, against the shudder of the water, to sniff at the jungle breeze.

The wind had betrayed the presence of the man, and the great brute voiced his satisfaction.

CHAPTER XVI

A DEAD MAN'S SECRET

That was a long, weird night in the jungle.

What hour it was the tiger finally departed was more than Grenville could have told. And whether the daylight, finally approaching, or a royal disgust, or some easily captured morsel, had served to urge the brute upon his way, was equally unknown.

Grenville descended from his perch at last, when the palms and ferns had darkly emerged from the velvety blackness of the thicket. He took up his club, left the bomb in its place, and, searching about, recovered the sheet of parchment dropped in the darkness. Aware that the silently moving enemy might still be lurking by the pathway, he made his way no less boldly from the shadows, and came duly to the hill.

His chagrin was complete when he told Elaine that his night had been spent in vain. She had scarcely slept, as he could see, for her face was still pale with worry, while her eyes showed her lack of rest.

"I shall try again to-night," he said, but from that he was dissuaded.

The strain was too great upon Elaine, if not upon himself. He presently promised to wait a day, and see what might develop. He could not subject his companion to another such session of agonizing worry as Elaine had undergone until he felt more certain of results.

But to wait a day in idleness, while he felt that every hour that passed might bring new dangers upon them, could scarcely accord with his intentions.

He declared the tiger an arrant coward, who dared not confront him in the day.

"We have faced far greater perils than this," he told her, as they ate their simple breakfast, "and we may be called upon to face the like again. We're enormously fortunate to have nothing more than this striped beast to limit our freedom on the island."

Elaine could have thought of countless other animals, including snakes, that would amply curtail her roaming inclinations, but she was not in the least in the habit of rehearsing her many dreads.

Grenville went promptly to work, after breakfast, fetching clay in the basket from the pit. It was not brought up to the terrace, but dumped in a heap beside the hollow tree, in the burned space under the walls. This tree, he at last explained to Elaine, he intended to use as a smelter.

"It's a natural chimney I've annexed," was the way he presented the problem. "If I built a fire in it now, however, it would burn, and be destroyed. I intend to line it with clay—plaster it on, inside, some eight or ten feet high. Then when this fire-resisting substance dries, I can smelt my metal and run it in the molds. The draught will make a prodigious heat—far more than brass requires."

"I see," said Elaine. "Meantime I am utterly idle."

"I'll cut you those needles. You can knit," he said, "unless you prefer to go fishing."

He had come to the camp for one of the jugs in which to carry water for the clay. This task was temporarily abandoned while he sat in the shade, beside Elaine, and carved out the promised tools. These were made of wood, instead of bone, since the latter material was far too hard for his fragment of a blade, and one of the woods provided by the jungle was so straightly grained and elastic, that even a slender splinter would bend like steel before it broke.

For a short time after they were finished, he sat there to watch the craft displayed by Elaine's nimble fingers, as a slender bit of the fiber stuff began to accumulate in stitches.

"You were made for a home-builder's mate," he said, and arose and left her to her thoughts, and to certain inflammable emotions.

He carried his jug down the trail and to the spring, resuming the business in hand. The sight of the pool not only served to arouse his disgust anew, but he was likewise reminded of the documents, reposing still unread in his pocket. The bomb, he knew, should be carried back to camp, lest the fuse become dampened in the thicket. With this and his jug full of water, he hastened back to the foot of the trail—and forgot them both forthwith.

The half sheet of paper, readable at last, had enslaved him then and there.

He sat on a rock, with the paper on his knee, and was lost to all things else.

For a moment he thought, perhaps, he had dreamed of obtaining the key to the hidden message. But one hurried glance at the words he had read convinced him the trick had been done.

On the back of the sheet he began at once to jot down the signs of which he felt most certain. The results, as he made them, were these:

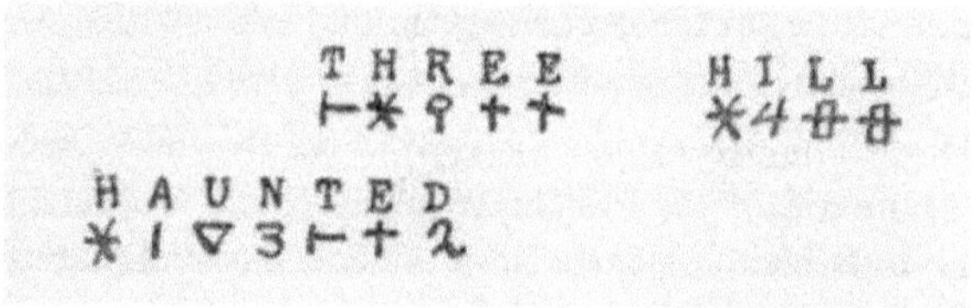

```
T H R E E          H I L L
⊢✳♀†✝          ✳4♉♉

H A U N T E D
✳ I ▽ 3 ⊢ † 2
```

The next word, according to his deductions, should be "Island." This, he felt, was indisputably confirmed by the fact it contained precisely the required number of "letters," with the sign for L, A, and D, already discovered, occupying their proper positions. He, therefore, added:

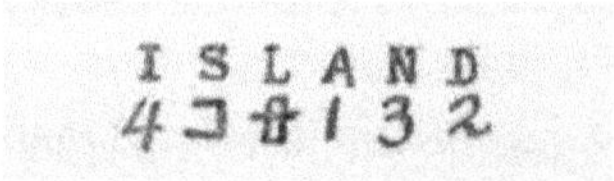

```
I S L A N D
4 ⊐ ♉ I 3 2
```

to his growing collection of letters, and promptly produced the following results by the process of substitution:

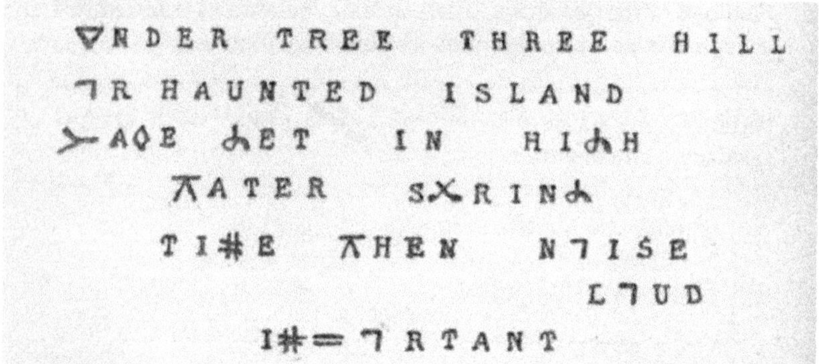

```
▽R D E R    T R E E    T H R E E    H I L L

⊓R  H A U N T E D    I S L A N D

≻A◊E  ⅃E T    I N    H I ⅃ H

𝘼A T E R    S⤬R I N⅃

T I # E    𝘼H E N    N⊓I S E

                              L⊓U D

          I # = ⊓R T A N T

#A�養E    N⊓    #I S T A�養E    #A=

·⊓N    ⴷL I    S H⊓𝘼 S    S A#E
```

There could be so little doubt, after that, concerning such words as "Under," "High," "Important," and "Water," which supplied the characters, U, G, M, P, W, and O, which was also suggested in "Or," before "Haunted," that a bit of additional substitution very promptly cleared the entire affair.

Grenville jotted it down, to make sense, in the following fashion:

"Under tree, Three-Hill, or Haunted Island, Cave. Get in (during) high water (in) Spring time when noise loud. Important. Make no mistake. Map on Buli shows same."

The one word which he felt to be doubtful was "Buli," which, he confessed, might as readily be "Zuli," "Juli," or "Quli," but this was of no significance, one way or another. Its meaning was still obscure.

There were several things in the message or statement, however, that confirmed his earlier uneasiness. The principal of these was the statement that it was important for the possible seekers of some cavern under the greater wall of rock to visit the island only during the time when the hideously haunting sounds were at their height. This argued, he thought, that the sounds would finally subside, or altogether cease, when complications—doubtless in the form of visitors—might be expected to develop.

That the visitors would be natives and, probably, Dyaks, Grenville could have no doubt. As to what there was in the cave beneath the rock, he had small curiosity only, since it was hardly likely such tools as he desired would be so concealed from a prying world, and tools alone had value for him now.

He could not doubt, however, that something there was in the cave here described, for which men had risked their lives. He thought of the headless skeletons, and then of the mummy in chains.

Suddenly, at thought of that guardian of the barque, his heart gave an added leap. He snatched from his pocket the parchment referred to as a map. He could instantly see, by the light of day, that the leathery substance was leather, indeed, of the most grewsomely repellent description! It was simply *tanned human skin!*

And abruptly he understood that phrase—"Map on Buli shows same." The pyramids represented the island's three great hills, and other signs the cave. The pole with a knob, on the tallest hill, was the tree so near his camp.

Aye, the thing was a map in very truth—and once it had been ON Buli! For Buli was he who sat in the barque, chained fast to prevent his escape!

This map he had borne, tattooed on his breast, from which it had finally been stripped!

CHAPTER XVII

FEVERISH EMPLOYMENTS HALTED

A species of horror attacked the man on whom the truth had flashed. What abominable cruelties and crimes lay back of the business thus finally to some extent revealed, he could only faintly imagine.

He felt quite certain of one or two things, that were not to be told to Elaine. First, he could not for a moment doubt that the barque had been brought to the island with the sole intent and purpose of looting the cave of treasure. He was equally convinced its crew had been foully slaughtered—and their heads removed. This smacked of Dyak atrocities. Finally, there was ample evidence that men of some sort had visited the island long since the wreck was stranded, and probably within the year.

He had not required the warning made "important" on the sheet to urge him to haste in preparing a boat with which to attempt an escape. To learn that the haunting sounds of the tide would at length subside was a new and disquieting addition to what he had previously deduced. He had accurately hit upon the natives' superstitious awe of the sounds to account for the island's desertion.

How long these invaluable shrieks and moans might be counted upon to continue became a vital question. Could they only last till a boat could be completed, launched, provisioned, and directed away to a safer retreat, he would ask for nothing more.

He returned again to an inspection of the "map"—now singularly plain. The island was graphically represented by the three conventional "hills," with the sign for water inscribed at either end. The tree, so conspicuous upon the tallest wall of rock, was no less vividly portrayed.

Below this identifying picture of the place the hill with the tree was repeated, with the cave and design for water, while just to the right the detail of the cavern, with more water signs, indicating both high and low tide, was depicted somewhat enlarged. The cartouch was not so readily comprehended. Grenville was inclined to believe it spelled some crude king's name, while the scarab, or beetle, was, of course, an old Egyptian symbol concerned with life and death.

It would hardly have been human of Grenville not to wonder about the cave or to contemplate a visit there—just to have the merest look about the place. He even went so far as to wonder if its entrance might not be effected from the upper brink, by means of a longer rope ladder than the one he had already made.

He did not, however, seriously contemplate delaying affairs more important to gratify this whim. Indeed, he was fired with new impatience to work night and day against the hour of escape. The thought put him back on his feet, then and there, with the documents stored away. There was no time to lose—not a moment—not even to fool with the tiger!

He left his bomb and its fuse upon the rocks, and carried the water to his clay. To line his hollow-tree furnace as promptly as possible must be his first concern. No boat could be made without suitable tools, and—— He wondered how he should make it, even then.

The log he had found on the day they arrived was such a huge affair to attack with the implements his limited craft made possible, despite all the bronze he could melt. And yet, without it, he was helpless. The raft was far too clumsy for propulsion. It afforded practically nothing transformable into a boat, as he had no nails, no saw, no anything with which it might be first dismembered, and finally reconstructed.

"By Jove!" he exclaimed to himself, aloud, as a new thought crept subtly to his brain. "I can hollow the log with fire!"

He went at once to the straight and ample tree-trunk, lying propped upon a rock. Its ends had already been partially consumed, and thereby rounded, in the flames that had ravaged the place. How he could cover such parts as he must not burn with a plaster of his clay, Grenville instantly conceived. And there was the log already lifted away from the earth, for the fire to be kindled beneath!

The wisdom of starting this process at once, even before his tools were made, was immediately apparent. Back to his clay heap he hastened eagerly, and, pawing it over to form a hollow pyramid, he poured in the water to soak through the mass, and so make it soft enough to use.

A new, unsparing spasm of labor seized the man in that hour, and he worked unremittingly. He felt he had loafed away his time which important requirements demanded.

The task of digging the clay from the pit and fetching it up to his hollow tree in the basket, made of creepers, was interminable. The sticks and wooden "spades" he had managed to fashion, not only broke from over-use and straining, but they were dull and heavy and awkward. The basket was scarcely more convenient than the implements in fulfilling its simple function. He could manage to carry its weight upon his head, but at this he had meager skill.

For three days he worked to get the clay, or to work it up and apply it with his hands. A considerable portion of the fallen log was thus quite promptly covered. He had then to wait for the clay to dry before his fire could be ignited.

The supply of clay he had managed to amass was clearly insufficient. He paused, on one of those warm and breathless afternoons, to set a number of traps in the animal pathways, and construct an awning for Elaine. This was merely a structure before her cave, to support a roof of leaves and grasses. It afforded a shade, however, that was exceedingly grateful.

There were numerous interruptions, also, for procuring meat and fruits. Grenville had brought down a pheasant with the last of his two remaining arrows. And not even a quill, supplied by the wings, had blown away from his "store." He had cut new shafts by his evening fire, and tipped them with points of sharpened wood. Elaine had feathered them skillfully, after once being properly directed.

Not a sign, all this time, had Grenville seen of the tiger, still haunting the jungle. He had been too industriously engrossed, either to wonder or to care where the brute had recently been lurking.

On the fourth warm morning of his toil about the furnace, the reminder came home with a jolt. Some few yards away from the clay pit's edge lay the master murderer's kill. It was part of a freshly eaten boar.

Grenville was neither revolted nor angered by the sight. He was suddenly excited with a new hope of getting a certain robe to lay at the feet of Elaine. It never occurred to his eager mind that the brute who bore it might be lying near, in a mood to resent his intrusion here, where the kingly banquet had been left for a sitting again that night.

His first concern was to keep away, as far as possible, lest the smell of his boots offend the lordly brute when he finally returned. Meantime such preparations as the scene made possible must not be unduly delayed.

The trees above the reddened spot afforded more choice for his necessary perch than he had found on the previous occasion. He rapidly sketched his plans for the night with mental notes and observations. Where the bomb could lie, to prove most efficacious, and still at the same time offer no great menace to himself, was readily determined. The ladder required for ascending to his stand would better be hung on the side most removed from the trail, for which he must a little clear the thicket.

His club, without which the visit here at sunset was not to be undertaken, could lean on the tree-trunk while he sat above, since there, should any need arise, he could find it in the dark.

He abandoned all thought of treading back and forth from the clay pit to his smelter, and carried his basket away. The ladder he brought at once from the spring, and, expending an hour in more careful preparation for his comfort than had even been possible before, he finally departed from the site of the tiger's gory refreshment, well satisfied with all he had been able to accomplish.

He returned to the camp, made a careful examination of the bomb and its fuse, and selected the wood to be finally used in preserving his essential spark of fire. Then, willing at last to turn his attention again to his daily occupation, he once more descended to his clay-covered log and found the plaster sufficiently dry upon it for the first of the burning to be started. He called to Elaine, who threw him down some glowing embers, from the fire always burning near his shelter.

All day he found abundant employment, working with flame and clay. The eating away of the log in a manner to leave a hollow shell, could not, he found, be accomplished as swiftly as he had hoped. Moreover, the fires required his constant attention, lest they burn too deeply to right or left, and thus destroy, or considerably impair, the walls he desired to protect.

In the afternoon he permitted this fire to die. Until more clay could be plastered about and the blackly charred portions of the wood removed with a tool, the process must be halted. He had still a small section inside his natural smelter to cover before he could undertake the melting of his metal, but his heap of clay was gone.

Once more, as he had on the previous occasion, he informed Elaine in the late afternoon of his intentions for the night. Her look of alarm was the only sign that escaped her resolute being. She had silently noted his earlier activity with the bomb and his fire-preserving wood; she was not surprised by his plans.

"I shall not be down at the spring," he said, "but over there nearer the clay pit. I have found a place where I rather expect our friend to arrive at a decently early hour."

Her eyes were startled and wide.

"Do you mean he sleeps where you have been walking every day?" "No—

certainly not. But I'm sure he was there last night—and I hope he'll come again."

She was quick to divine the unpleasant truth that Grenville was striving to avoid.

"You mean—he's been eating there—and left some awful——"

"Good pork," he agreed, as he took up his bomb; "a fine wild boar— enough to have done us for a week."

She resumed her work of knitting, on a small, round basket-like affair.

"I hope there are more of those hogs for him to get," she told him, quietly. "I hope they are easy prey."

"Right ho! But I trust he'll not be off with the old pig before he is on with the new. I want him to come to the party there to-night."

Elaine looked up for a moment, and thrilled to the look in his eyes.

"Yes," she said, "I suppose you do."

CHAPTER XVIII

AT THE TIGER'S KILL

The island twilight was brief. When the sun departed from that speck of verdure in the purple sea, the covetous darkness seemed to form like a presence that had crouched to bide its time.

Grenville was early on the scene of the tiger's previous feast. He had no idea how soon after sundown the jungle monarch might appear. It was not such a place as inspired hilarious joy in the heart, in any circumstances. Moreover, one last examination of the bomb and fuse, and one clear impression of the features beneath and about his tree, seemed to Sidney a wise precaution.

The day had, therefore, barely ended when he climbed aloft to his perch. The end of the fuse was tied to a limb a little removed from his feet. He closed his eyes and found it with his hand, by way of making certain it should not be missed in the dark. The larger and denser of the forms below, created by shadows and growing plants, he noted in their relation to the kill. The latter was not to be clearly seen, since a screen of leaves he had purposely left to conceal his presence from the banqueter, served to shield it from his view.

Finally, closing his eyes again, he practiced retreating behind the trunk itself, as he knew he must do when nothing could be seen and his fuse was finally lighted. This was rather a delicate operation to manage in the dark. He made up his mind it must be calmly done, for ample time would be provided by the generous length of fuse.

This length, by the way, was considerably less than he had formerly employed. The bomb was, therefore, nearer to his stand. Yet the bulk of the tree-trunk was, he thought, an entirely adequate protection should he have the delight of hearing his powder explode.

Through the lattice of leaves he presently beheld the last of the day's dying splendor. The army of shadows, already on the march, was taking rapid possession of all the jungle deeps. The same impatience he had felt before, the same vague dread and loneliness previously experienced, and the same slow drag of time impressed themselves upon his senses.

He wondered how long his brand would last, although it was longer than the other. He wondered about Elaine, on the hill, and how tedious the hours would seem to her. But the constant, underlying worry was—when would the tiger arrive?

Elaine's suggestion was a bother. Might there not be hogs so plentiful, quarry so readily captured, that the overdisdainful monarch would prefer warm meat to cold?

There was no mysterious cipher to be studied here to-night. There was nothing, in fact, with which to pass the time. Not even a new speculation concerning the cave and the rotting barque arose to give him entertainment. The haunting, suggestive stillness engulfed him where he sat. The world below had merged in one featureless gloom. Except for a few fringed patches of sky between the leaves and branches, there was nothing but velvety blackness to be seen above or below.

He waited and waited, a time that seemed eternal. His resting-place was hard and uneven. One of his legs was cramped. To shift about and make no noise was not an easy matter.

Without the slightest warning, suddenly down below him something leaped and crashed through the thicket with a most unexpected sound. Whatever it was, it went bounding off, recklessly parting the jungle. Some creature in fright it undoubtedly was—and Grenville was instantly rigid and alert for the next development.

He was certain the tiger, coming to his feast, had thrown some timid creature into a panic of blind and desperate fear. He listened, with all his powers of concentration, for the sounds that should presently succeed.

But save for another plunging, far beyond, there was absolute silence as before. For fully half an hour after that the stillness was well-nigh insupportable, so fraught was it all with the tragic sense of noiseless life where both hunted and hunters moved about with the cushioned feet of shadows.

Far off towards the spring, or the estuary, a disturbance finally arose. It was neither loud nor clear. It seemed to interpret some struggle for life, or pursuit of the weak by the strong. It approached for a time, then ceased for nearly half a minute, only to break into clearer accents of some brute's agony, poignant but mercifully brief.

At this the discouragement in Grenville's breast was unavoidably increased. He was certain the tiger had taken fresher prey, and would now ignore his former kill. So intent were his senses on that far-off bit of jungle drama that he failed to detect a nearer sound repeated beneath his feet.

When his sharp ears abruptly warned him that something was moving down below, an extraordinary climax to his adventure was swiftly coming to a focus.

Some creature had come to the tiger's kill—of that there could be no doubt. It was lapping, or chewing at the meat!

Unable to distinguish the slightest thing in all that Stygian darkness, Grenville paused, with his brand slightly shielded from the creature's possible notice, waiting a moment to confirm the fact that a banqueter was present before he touched the fuse.

A tremendous roar instantly startled the silence, a few feet beyond the boar's remains. Before the man could move a hand, either to light the ready fuse or steady himself in the branches, some heavy form was hurled against the tree in which he sat—*and that something was climbing madly upward!*

Only a tremor had shivered through the trunk, but the limbs were bent and the foliage stirred as if from a breath of heavy wind. That the creature might run against himself and turn to fight, in its double fear and desperation, Grenville was keenly aware.

Subconsciously, also, he was equally sure the tiger was below. The catlike thing in the tree with himself had undoubtedly dared to sit down at the huge brute's kill, to flee for its life a moment later.

Instinctively turning to protect himself and thoroughly disturbed by this unforeseen complication, Grenville heard his unwelcome companion utter one sudden whine, of surprise and added terror, as it came abreast him in the branches.

It dared not retreat, and, therefore in a wilder panic, clawed its way higher up the tree. The limbs continued to shake their leaves for another protracted moment. Then the beast found a place to halt above his head, and doubtless glared down upon the unknown peril which man supplies to all the brutes.

Grenville recovered his wits as best he might. He had no particular dread of the animal crouched somewhere in his neighborhood, but neither did he relish its presence. What effect the affair would have on the creature he had come there to engage he could not, of course, determine.

He bent to listen for sounds from the space below. Not the faintest suggestion of a moving or feeding animal could his focused senses detect. He thought perhaps the tiger might have smelled him or seen him in the tree. It occurred to him, also, the brute might be waiting for the catlike thief to descend and be slain at the kill.

But a far more likely supposition was that the tiger, having sniffed the taint of some beast without caste, now left on the meat that was sacred to himself, had disdained to touch it, and had gone away, to return to the place no more.

Ready to curse the despicable animal now sharing the tree's security with himself, Sidney was all but resigned to another long night, spent in vain and in utter discomfort, when once again a lapping sound came crisply to his attention.

His brute was at the feast!

With heart abruptly pounding and senses suddenly tense, Grenville leaned down, with his glowing brand, to complete his work for the night.

His hand felt blindly along the limb, to pick up the end of the fuse. But someway the place was lost. More eagerly then, and telling off each twig like a sign that blazed the trail, he explored the branch anew.

He found the fiber that had held the fuse—but the fuse itself was gone! The panic-stricken creature that had climbed the tree had clawed or broken it down!

A bitterer disappointment to Grenville could scarcely have been planned. He was sickened all through by disgust, and a sense of the utter uselessness of all he had striven to accomplish. With fire in hand, the bomb all laid, and the tiger actually present—he was helpless, after all!

It was futile to rage at the cowering beast, above him somewhere in the darkness. He glanced up once and saw its eyes—two blazing coals of fear and malice, like near-by sinister stars!

"By Heavens! I'll not be cheated!" he murmured to himself. A mad new thought had possessed him.

The fuse had been drawn about the tree before it could be fastened near his perch. Had it fallen straight down, when torn from its hold, it would still lie close at hand.

His ladder was hidden from the tiger's position by the tree. Any sounds he must make might be thought to be those of the cat. There was no particular danger in descending to the ground—with the ladder near with which to regain a safe position.

Noiselessly, yet not without excitement, he began his retreat from the branches. With every step he paused for a bit, to listen to the sounds of the tiger.

The brute was seemingly quite engrossed in the business of filling his belly. But, despite his utmost efforts at silence, the leaves of one of the branches loudly rustled as Grenville's weight was intrusted to the ladder.

He halted and held his breath. The tiger continued his eating. Holding his firebrand firmly in his teeth, Grenville slowly and cautiously descended, with the furtive alertness of a thief.

When he reached the earth, he was certain his heart would betray his presence with its pounding. He leaned there, heavily, against the tree, to still the mad leap of his pulses. Then, at length, he began to feel about for the fuse that should be at his feet.

It was not to be found—and he moved a little outward. His hand came in contact with a long, slender thing—but it proved to be a creeper.

Further and further out he moved, blindly groping with his fingers. He encountered a shrub, and, fumbling between it and the tree, bethought him to feel about its crest. There he found one end of the fuse he sought—but it proved that the length had been broken! He held the useless end!

One despair after another had seized him within an endless minute. More recklessly, in a burning fever of impatience, he pawed about and moved even closer to the tiger—whose sounds were horribly near.

He could almost have uttered a cry of joy when the severed fuse was discovered. He waited for nothing, but immediately pressed his brand against the sun-dried substance.

There was no powder there. It had spilled when it broke, and it harmlessly smoked as it burned.

Why a groan did not escape him, Sidney could never have told. He broke off the tough, resisting substance six inches further along and again applied his spark.

It seemed as if in all its length there could be no powder remaining. He was savagely grasping the fuse once more, to break it at a fresher place, when a fiery-red line, some four feet away, seemed creeping like a snake out beyond him.

The spark that was racing along to the bomb had been started while still he was sweating there with baffled and excited impatience.

He took no time for further caution, but sprang away to the shelter of the tree and caught at a lungful of breath.

There was not a sound in all the place. This much he knew in that second, as he hugged up close to the trunk. The tiger had ceased to lap at the meat, and perhaps was poised for a spring.

It seemed to Grenville, waiting there, that nothing would ever happen. A thousand doubts went darting through his brain. The fuse had failed! It was broken again. Or, perhaps——

A low growl broke the stillness. There was a sound of something moving towards the tree!

Instantly a frightful red-and-yellow glare leaped upward from the earth. A deafening, crashing detonation rent the intimate universe and shook down incredible stars. The air was filled to overcrowding with rushing billows of concussion that rocked the trees as in a storm.

Grenville went down, dazed and helpless, unable to think, so jarred to chaos were his senses. But, beyond being stunned for a moment, he was totally unhurt.

He leaped to his feet, aware of some mighty disturbance in the curdled, heavy darkness that had followed.

The tiger it was, in some extravagant activity, moving towards Grenville and the thicket. He was almost upon the staggering man before he could move to escape. Then Grenville stumbled towards the ladder.

The jar to the limb, as he tugged at a rung, brought something down from above. This was the creature that had hidden in the tree. It had partially fallen, earlier stunned by the huge concussion. It dropped upon Grenville leadenly—and down he went in a heap.

The three sworn enemies—tiger, man, and jungle-cat—were embroiled on the earth together. Before the man could sufficiently recover to stagger from his knees to his feet and grasp his club, the tiger flung out a mighty paw, that struck him a blow upon the chin.

Without a sound he sank limberly down, inert and helplessly unconscious.

CHAPTER XIX

GRENVILLE'S RADIANT STAR

Even had sleep overcome Elaine, the explosion must have startled her awake like a wildly fluttering bird.

All her life she had known the sound of guns, but never before had her ears received such an air-splitting shock as this.

Her alarm could know no bounds. It had come so suddenly and unexpectedly; it had been such a cataclysmic destruction of the island's haunting calm! She was certain some hideous blunder had occurred—that Grenville, too, had perished by the thing he had fearlessly dared to create.

She had seen for an instant that fan-like glare, as she gazed far out across the jungle. And now, as she stood there, rigid with fears and fixedly staring at the formless gloom—why did she hear no sound?

"Oh, he might—he might call!" she said, and she tried to halloo, but in vain.

She waited a time that seemed endless for some little sign from the jungle. He had promised before that, if all went well, he would hasten home at once. Surely this promise held good to-night—especially after that explosion!

Perhaps it was not yet time; perhaps it was farther away than she had thought. The glare had seemed near, but he had no torch, and must walk but slowly through the thicket. How dark it must be along the trails, in that tangle growth, with nothing for a light! How could he possibly hasten?

She was standing out on the brink of the wall, staring down at the gloom of the clearing, convinced that her ears, if not her eyes, would detect the first sign of his coming. Just the merest red gleam from the firebrand was all she would ask of the darkness—just that dull little star in the firmament of black!

But the ebon remained unbroken. That he might be lost occurred to her mind, but again she thought it was yet too soon for his return. She stumbled swiftly to the fire again, to stir it to brighter refulgence. It would seem to him a beacon against the sky to guide his footsteps home!

She thought of a blazing brand she could carry to the brink of the wall. With the largest limb afforded by the fire she returned, in haste and eagerness, to wave him a signal of welcome. And still nothing came from the clearing.

"Sidney!" she cried through the stillness, at last. "Sidney! Are you there?"

The night surrendered no response, save some animal cry far off where the barque was rotting.

"If he's dead!" she moaned. "If he's dead!"

But he might be wounded and helpless, she thought, with no one to come to his side. He might not be hurt unto death itself—if aid could reach him now!

If he died—if he left her thus alone—— A thousand times she preferred to die beside him!

"Sidney!" she cried, as before.

With a strange dry note, choked back between her lips, she fled once more to the fire.

Meantime the man by the tiger's kill continued to lie without motion on the earth. Not even the glow of his cheering brand remained like a sign of life in that silent theater.

The jungle cat, smitten and addled in its brain, had dragged itself painfully away to the cover of the thicket, its instinct feebly alive. There was not a sound in all the place, where crash and roar had been so tremendously expended for one prodigious second.

A vague, weird dream came finally creeping intangibly through Grenville's brain, resuming an intermittent function. When at length it began a little to clear, he dreamed he was trying his utmost to rise, but something held him down.

Consciousness poured a trickle through his being, and he felt he was partially awake. Then a flood, a cataract of surging life, rushing back to its centers, brought confusion and tumult to his thoughts. He was still only partially aroused.

His eyes at length were opened. The darkness which their gaze encountered seemed more complete than that of his region of dreams. He attempted to rise, but his muscles and nerves refused their customary obedience to his will. He tried to remember what had happened, but the glancing blow sustained on his chin had blotted him out, temporarily, like a stroke of death itself. And, had the stroke been more direct, his jaw or his neck must have broken.

When he raised his head a bit from the ground and propped himself up on his elbow, the sense of dullness and leadlike weight in both his feet and legs continued unabated. He was battling to retain his consciousness.

He began to remember, slowly. The process was only well started, however, when it was singularly interrupted. He was staring blankly through the jungle, which he partially recollected. It was funny, he thought, how a star should fall and wander through all those aisles of trees.

It was a star, he was fully convinced, coming haltingly through the gloom. Its course was erratic. He lost it at times, but still it persisted in approaching. How beautiful it was—the largest star he had ever known—with its flames divinely ascending.

He sat up stiffly, his will momentarily gaining strength to resume the sway of his body. Some mantle partially fell from his brain, to accompany his physical rousing. Then he knew, not only what had happened, but also what was happening.

"Elaine!" he tried to call aloud, vainly striving to rise or regain the use of his limbs, then once more he sank in oblivion.

A strange, wild note broke from her lips as Elaine came plunging along the trail with a torch redly blazing in her hand, held well above her face.

She saw, before she could reach his side, that the tiger lay lifeless upon him. She feared the man was dead, but, with wits exceptionally clear and ordered, she thrust her torch-end firmly in the earth, laid hold of the huge, limber beast she so fearfully dreaded, and tugged and dragged it feverishly off with all her fine young strength.

The face of the inert man beside the tree was redly smeared with blood. He lay horribly loose and still upon the grass. She knelt at his side and placed her hands upon him, feeling above his heart.

"Sidney!" she said to him. "Sidney! You cannot—you shall not die! I never meant the things I said—or thought—or anything! Oh, please, please don't—don't look like that! You've got to come back—you've got to!"

She tore at the band about his neck and lifted his head on her knee. She wiped the red from his pallid face with the hem of her briar-torn skirt.

"I'll find the spring!" she told him eagerly, starting as if to rise, but the still form moved, and, dully at first, the two heavy eyes were opened.

"Oh!" she said. "Oh, you're hurt. Don't try to do anything but rest…. You didn't come—you didn't come home!"

Despite her entreaty, Grenville weakly raised his head and propped himself, half sitting. The weight being gone from his outstretched legs, his normal circulation was returning. He regained his strength with characteristic swiftness.

"Hurt?" he said. "No—I don't believe—— I must have got a knockout blow. The tiger? Did I get the tiger?"

He sat up uncertainly and, glancing about, saw the huge striped form where Elaine had dragged it from his body. She still remained on her knees, fixedly gazing on his face. Her strength was ebbing rapidly, as Grenville's now returned.

"You didn't come home," she repeated, by way of explaining her presence at his side. "I couldn't live here alone."

Grenville arose and assisted her weakly to her feet. She stumbled to and leaned against the tree.

"By George!" he said, "I'll bet a hat you could!"

He knew what courage had come to her aid before she could make her excursion. "I went down like a dub," he added, in his customary manner. "No good excuse, but I do apologize. Better get out of this, I'm thinking."

He took up the torch she had planted in the earth, to examine the tiger, dead and mangled in the grass, One of the creature's great front paws had been rudely torn from his body. He could only have escaped instantaneous death by having moved from the bomb at the moment of its explosion.

"Your robe looks mussed," Grenville continued, with a gesture towards the animal's motionless body. "But I think it can be washed."

Elaine slightly shivered at sight of the frame now done with life.

"You've killed him," she said. "I'm glad!"

He took her firmly by the arm and led her away through the thicket.

When they reached the camp, Elaine was not yet fully convinced that Grenville was uninjured. She brought him a rag she had torn from some of her clothing and begged him to wash his reddened jaw. Even the restoration of his former stubbled complexion could not suffice to bring her that sense of certainty and calm essential before she could sleep.

She remained beside him at their fire till long past the midnight hour. Indeed, she had made no move to retire when at length the weird, unwelcome disturbance made by the tide had begun its uncanny chorus. Perhaps she had waited for the conclusion of this added feature of the night's long ritual of nerve-attacking events, for she seemed to be considerably cheered when its final wail had died upon the air.

"It seems to me that doesn't continue quite as long as it did at first," she said to Grenville, as she rose at last to go alone to her cavern.... "I think you ought to rest. I wish you would."

"I will," said Sidney. "Good-night."

But, for some time after she had gone, he sat there wondering if those abominable but protective cries, that haunted the island's solitude, were actually on the wane.

"God help us if they are!" he said, to himself, but he went to bed and slept.

CHAPTER XX

A GIRDLE OF GOLD

Elaine had not yet appeared on the scene when Grenville went down to the jungle. The morning hour was still decidedly early, but plans and impatience to be up and at work had prodded the man from his rest. The lassitude that should have followed his night of excitement had not yet laid its weight upon him.

Apparently nothing had come to the jungle scene where the tiger had met his end. The great form lay there, torn and rigid, but no sign of the cat could be discovered.

Grenville passed his trophy, presently, to examine the space beyond. The spot where the bomb had exploded was a gaping hole in the earth. This was not the place where Grenville had placed the deadly tube, which he knew must therefore have been moved—doubtless when the fuse was pulled and broken by the creature taking refuge in the tree.

All about the spot where the kill had been the shrubbery was shredded. The boar's remains had been blown away when the gap was made in the sod. The trail, Grenville saw, must be repaired or a new one must be made about the place.

He returned to the tiger, and was suddenly elated to behold the metal collar, half-hidden by the fur about his neck. He had quite forgotten this bauble, thus singularly employed, and, kneeling down to inspect it closely, not only found it was massive gold and set with costly jewels, but also discovered he must break or force a heavy link to take it from the creature.

It was not until he had brought two sharp-edged rocks to his needs that the collar was finally freed. Its weight and worth then amazed him. The band was fully two inches in width, with the edges curved up and turned under, in a simple and hammer-marked finish. It was all hand-wrought, each blow that the smith had struck with his tool being faintly recorded in the metal. The jewels—three sapphires, three rubies, and one diamond—were simply and solidly set with bands that barely clasped their bases. The rubies only were cabochon cut, the other stones gleaming with facets.

There was not a mark upon the collar's outer surface to show what was meant by its presence here in such extraordinary keeping. But Grenville presently bethought him to glance at the inner circumference. He was not in the least astonished, but he was a bit concerned, to discover a number of those mystic symbols, deeply graved in the gold, that had once been tattooed on the man sitting dead in the barque.

Here were the three hills, bounded by the water, and one with the tree on its summit, while on either side the cartouch appeared, bounded by crude drawings of the tiger. That the brute had been liberated here upon the island as a sort of sacred guardian of the cave that was mentioned by the writing found secreted with the map, Grenville could not, or did not, doubt. There was nothing more to be found engraved on the gold.

He finally slipped the heavy band about his own smooth, sun-tanned neck and went at the task of securing Elaine's promised robe. This toil was far more difficult than even his lack of proper appliances had led him to anticipate. Although he had sharpened his stub of a knife-blade to a very respectable cutting-edge, it was far too small for the business.

His doggedness and application were the assets on which he had most to count, and without them here he must have failed. As it was, he remained so long away that Elaine, who was up, was alarmed. And, when at last he appeared below with the heavy, striped skin across his shoulder, she started abruptly, till she saw he was not another tiger.

"I thought you might like to see the size of his hide," he said, as he brought it to the terrace, "before I take it down by the shore for tanning. I shall soak it a while in a mixture of brine and saltpeter. Both are highly preservative—and the best the island affords."

"He was simply tremendous!" Elaine replied, when the skin had been spread on the rocks. "What have you got about your neck?"

"Oh, this?" said Grenville, removing the golden collar. "This is a symbol of royalty that his Bengal highness wore—your property now, as a trophy of the hunt."

She took it a little uncertainly as he held it forth in his hand.

"Why—it's gold!" she said. "These jewels—— The tiger was wearing this?"

"About his kingly neck."

"But how—unless someone put it on?"

"Undoubtedly someone did. He must have been a captive once, and probably escaped."

It could serve no good end to acquaint her with his actual suspicions, which might be ill-founded, after all.

"It's beautiful," she continued, gazing in admiration on the collar's simple massiveness. "But it's not for me, I'm sure." She held it out for him to take. But he bent above the skin.

"Then pitch it away," he instructed, laconically. "Toss it into the sea."

She colored, looking at him strangely. She could not throw away his property—anything of such great intrinsic value. She was baffled again, as he managed so frequently. Her hand and the golden circlet fell at her side. She could think of no appropriate speech of final rejection. A whimsical notion only arose to her groping mind.

"Fancy me wearing this priceless band of splendor," she said, "and eating with a stick!"

"It will just about fit around your waist," he conjectured, taking it from her as he rose. With easy strength he bent it in his hands, to make it more snugly conform to her slender and graceful little body.

Why should he not bend it thus, she thought, who had wrenched it from a tiger? She felt how weak and inadequate was her own diminishing struggle. But to wear this band—a symbol, almost, of Grenville's ownership—— A hot recurrence of her former pride came surging to her bosom.

"It's too heavy to wear," she told him, a trifle coldly. She once more accepted the girdle, however, despite herself, from his hand. "The tiger that wore it," she concluded, "met with a lot of trouble."

"You've met with some yourself," he answered, candidly, and he shouldered the skin and started off for the estuary's mouth.

Elaine burned suddenly scarlet, interpreting his speech in some manner of her own. Helplessly she carried the girdle to her cave, and left it there in a hollow of the rock.

The incident concerned with the tiger was practically closed. A new, bright era of security and liberty thereupon commenced, particularly for Elaine. She could not take immediate advantage of the comfort thus vouchsafed in moving about the island, but at least her worry was lessened when Grenville was obliged to venture in the jungle.

His return to the work so frequently interrupted was delayed but the briefest time. So eager did he constantly feel to accomplish his boat's completion that he had grudged every hour the tiger had cost him from his labors.

With no thought of sparing his tireless strength, he promptly resumed the task of digging and fetching the clay. Elaine might have joined him in the clearing now had not some task she was eager to complete engrossed her attentions at the shelter.

That day the remaining surface of his prostrate log was plastered by Grenville's eager hands. He likewise mixed sufficient clay to finish his furnace in the morning. The fire that was helping to hollow his log was once again ignited. Much of the old charred substance, left from previous operations, Grenville knocked away with an improvised tool of brass, in order to daub more clay inside the shell before the flames could continue removing the wood as he required.

On the following day, while the walls in his smelter were drying, Sidney wove a two-piece door of wattle—framework of creepers, plastered with clay —to fit across the orifice at the bottom of his tree. With this he felt he could regulate the draught and protect himself while removing his crucibles of metal. The top door only would be tossed aside to accomplish this latter purpose.

He likewise plastered the edges and sides of the hole that pierced his smelter. He knew the heat, when he came to melt the brass, would spread at once to all unprotected wood. After that he had still to contrive a clay-covered implement for lifting out his crucibles, and a tripod affair to be placed inside the furnace to support these crucibles upon.

What with more work done upon the boat-to-be, and a goodly portion of the afternoon expended in killing and preparing another of the pheasants for their dinner, Grenville's hours sped swiftly away.

A weary but elated craftsman he was that day-end when at length he returned for the final time to the terrace. He had been to the shore, where the tiger-hide was curing in a strong solution of brine and saltpeter, mixed in a hollow in the sand, and, having there turned it over, had washed himself to a fresh and ruddy color.

Notwithstanding the unbecoming growth of beard upon his face, he appeared to Elaine the most commanding figure she had ever taken time to inspect. He looked every inch a master of the island, if not also of his fate and her own. But she was more than usually excited that evening, as she disappeared within her shelter.

She presently emerged with such an air of uncertainty and diffidence about her as had never before appeared since their coming to the island. But she did not hesitate in the task she had set herself to perform.

"I have finished my first bit of knitting," she said, "and there it is."

To Grenville's thorough amazement, the clean, new article held in her hand, and shyly offered for his acceptance, was a cap she had made for his head. It was not unlike a golf-cap in shape, but the visor was considerably wider, to protect his eyes from the sun.

She had woven this of finely divided creeper-core on a frame neatly made of the same. Its meshes had then been filled by fibers, snugly and neatly plaited back and forth to make it opaque to the light. The frame was firmly knitted to the cap.

"Pretty good," said Grenville, busied with several arrows. "Thanks;" and, placing it carelessly on his head, continued with his employment.

Elaine, who had conjured all her resolution to make of the presentation the merest commonplace affair, was wholly confounded in her thoughts by the man's unheard-of conduct, after all she had recently undergone before she could make him such a gift.

She had feared some demonstration of the passion shown on the ship—or at least some disturbing outburst she had armed herself to quench. But this— such scant courtesy or gratitude as this—left her absolutely impotent and baffled.

She was piqued, disappointed, chagrined. It was horrid of anyone, she was sure, to be so outrageously unfeeling. There was nothing, however, she could do, and nothing she could say. Standing there, mortified, almost angry, and conscious she was burning guiltily red with various emotions that he did not even notice, was such a footless and irritating proceeding, with the situation robbed of its point.

She turned away, fairly ready to cry with vexation, and pretended to make herself busy with things already well prepared for their evening meal. But the new rebellion of her nature, partially begotten by the uncontrolled and uncontrollable impulses loosed in the jungle the previous night, when Grenville lay helplessly stunned, with his head loosely pillowed on her knee, was not to be longer contained. She presently fled from before the cavern, across, through the shadows of the terrace, to the hidden shelf where

Grenville had angled for fish.

There she suddenly sank to her knees on the rocks and covered her face with her hands.

"I hate him!" she said, in a hot and passionate utterance, suggestive of a sob. "I hate him! I hate him! I hate every man that ever lived—and you, Gerald Fenton, as much as all the others!"

She snatched off the ring from her finger. It was Fenton's ring, with a single stone that gleamed in the failing light. It seemed to her to represent the man far absent from her side.

"It was you who brought it all about!" she continued, in her fiercely waging conflict, and, overwrought, she cast it down on the ledge as if it burned her palm.

It bounded lightly where it struck and, clearing the shelf, fell swiftly downward to the water. A gasp and a moan escaped her lips together. Vividly, of a sudden, she remembered Grenville's prediction that she would throw it away in the sea.

"Oh, Gerald, I didn't mean to!" she moaned. "I didn't! You've got to believe me!" She sank farther forward on the ledge, her face closely hidden in the curve of her loose brown arm. She wept and wept there, bitterly, in a mood of mixed emotions.

"I hate him! I hate him!" she said, as before. "It's not my fault in the least!"

And after a time, as Grenville did not come, she returned to the camp alone.

CHAPTER XXI

MOLTEN METAL AND HOPES

The following day was calmer for Elaine, and vastly interesting, since Grenville's smelting operations were begun. She told herself that interest only laid its hold upon her nature, and, being a woman, she knew.

The clay that lined his hollow tree was sufficiently dry at last for Grenville's fire. The other accessories, all more thinly coated, were likewise ready for his use. He began in the morning to heat his natural chimney against the actual needs of afternoon. The small fire kindled upon its hearth established at once the efficiency of the draught.

Not without a certain boyish eagerness in the culmination of his labors, Sidney began the assemblage of his various paraphernalia an hour at least before noon. His molds and crucibles he carefully brought from the summit of the terrace, disposing them as conveniently as his crude conditions permitted. All his rusted scraps and useless bits of brass and bronze were divided into parcels, while salt, some powdered charcoal, and an over-abundant supply of saltpeter were provided to be used as flux, according as the smelting might demand. He could not be certain of which he should use till experiment should determine which, if any, rendered good results.

The principal difficulty, he soon discovered, would be adding the fuel to his flames. His smelter-door was not well arranged for this essential business. He expected, however, to heap a considerable quantity of wood inside before the chimney should become too hot. Later he thought a lot of short material could be readily introduced, and against this need he gathered an impressive heap of branches, which he broke to a workable length.

Elaine was with him when at last the work began. She was far more excited than Grenville seemed, since it appeared to her no less than a miracle that any man, in a place like this, should dare assume such a mastery over Jovian metals and flame. She had never before seen anything of smelting. This intimate acquaintance with its mysteries seemed to her a privilege, greatly enhanced by the fact that the lord of it all pretended she was actually helpful.

She assisted when he bound the sections of his clay-made molds together. She handed him fuel when the furnace-door was opened and gushes of heat came voluminously forth.

The fire, which for a time had loudly roared, was now more intense and quiet. The volumes of smoke, which the "chimney" had belched, had likewise finally ceased. Only a quiver of superheated air and a greenish bit of gas and fume now ascended to the sky.

From time to time, Grenville opened the top of the door to peer within. He wrinkled his features, in the waves of heat, and held his hand before his face. At length he adjusted his "tongs" about a crucible and drew it entirely forth.

It was white with heat, its surface sparkling with a hundred tiny stars that died on its glowing surface.

"Just toss in some of that stuff there on the leaf," he quietly instructed

Elaine. "It will soon be ready to pour."

The "stuff" was flux, and Elaine obeyed directions like the stanch assistant that she was. She wondered what was coming next.

It came very soon. She was certain no ruddier figure of Vulcan, employing mighty flame, had ever been presented than now when Grenville made ready for the climax of his work.

He removed the door as he had not previously done, and set it aside from his path. He thrust in his tongs, while flame and heat came pouring out to paint him a deep and glowing color. Then, seemingly hotter than ever before, and smoking goldenly above its blinding incandescence, the first of the crucibles, itself fairly dripping, where some of the flux had trickled down its surface, was supported over to the molds, to be quickly and vigorously skimmed of its oxidized matter.

But the molten brass, indescribably beautiful, with ruby and gold and silver gleams imbedded and breaking in its substance, was the wonder of it all. Elaine stood entranced, to see it flow and fill the hollows of the molds.

The second was hastily drawn from the flame, and then the third and last. But not till all lay finally empty and smoking on the earth, their surfaces rapidly dulling, did Grenville pause to look at Elaine and smile.

"Can't even tell what we've done," he said, "till the molds are cooled and opened."

"Must you wait very long till you know?"

"I couldn't wait long," Grenville answered. "I'm too much of a curious kid."

As a matter of fact, brass poured in a mold begins to harden at once. In less than fifteen minutes, Grenville was gingerly untwisting the hot copper wire that bound each mold together. Soon after that the first of his tools, a heavy and serviceable chisel, lay uncovered to the air.

It was still glowing hot, although no longer red. It was darker, less brassy in appearance than Elaine had expected to see, but it seemed to her a wonderful thing to be made of those useless bits of metal.

The tool next in importance was much like a butcher's cleaver—an implement intended for cutting or hacking wood or branches, either to clear a path in the jungle or to rough out anything of timber. The edge of this casting was imperfect, where the metal had failed to flow. Both it and the chisel had a thin fringe of brass along those sections where the halves of the mold had come together, but this would be readily broken away and was quite to be expected.

Smaller chisels, a blade that Sidney expected to notch along its edge to make a species of saw, and a number of smaller implements were contained in the other sets of molds. None of these was perfect, and one or two merely served to instruct the master-molder in the way to go to work another time. But the net results were highly satisfactory, and seemed to Elaine a veritable triumph.

The poorness of their quality as tools with which to accomplish swift results developed the following day. Grenville had melted a part of his lead and cast the head of a hammer. With this and the largest of his chisels he attacked the log chosen for a boat.

So long as his gouging was confined to the portions charred by the fire, the tool held well to the labor. Its edge soon went to pieces, however, when the solider substance was encountered. It was sharpened repeatedly. He early foresaw that, work as he might, the business of conjuring forth a boat from material so raw was certain to be slow, if not exhausting.

Indeed, at this time a tedious period began. There were days and days of dull, stupid repetition ahead like the ones that were presently past. Fire after fire he maintained beneath the log, which must always be newly plastered with the clay. Hour after hour he chiseled off the black and dusty flakes that the flames would leave behind, since it hastened the work to present a new surface to the heat. It seemed as if the task could never have an end.

But, if this was a season of dogged application to an uncongenial business, it was likewise the one long era of peace vouchsafed to the exiled pair. There was nothing to rouse a sense of alarm in any near portion of the jungle. And, if those fast succeeding days brought no welcome sign of a steamer approaching on the distant blue horizon, neither did their lengthening hours develop those craft upon the sea for which Grenville was constantly and apprehensively watching. They were happy days, as well as peaceful. Concerning the ring she had lost in the sea, Elaine could not force herself to worry. Grenville never, by any chance, gave her occasion for alarm.

There were many full afternoon vacations from his work when the fire was left to hollow out his log that Sidney spent at her side. He wove her a hammock of the creeper withes and built a shady bower by the shore. He had sawed her a comb from the tortoiseshell, bent hairpins of the copper wire, and made her a comfortable couch. Her tiger-skin robe he had worked with his hands to a soft and pliant finish. The skin of a cheeta he had killed he used to supplement his rapidly vanishing shirt. Sewing was strongly, if not prettily, accomplished with such needles and thread as his ready ingenuity provided.

They were busy days that were doomed, however, to pall. Elaine was assisting with a loom to weave a sail, while between times Grenville chipped out the stone for the bath he had promised on the ledge. He became a skillful marksman with his bow, and knew every animal trail the island afforded. In many of these his traps did deadly service. Their larder rarely lacked for meat, made tender by paw-paw leaves. Elaine caught many a silver fish that they roasted together in the sand.

But her gaze more frequently roved afar, for the ship that did not come. The days were growing sultrier, and constantly more monotonous.

The new moon had come and waxed to the full and was once more waning in the heavens. They were marvelous nights the old orb made upon the island, but always weird and exciting a sense, in Elaine at least, of loneliness and aloofness from the world. On their cliff above the murmurous tides, she and Grenville frequently sat for hours at a time without exchanging a word.

Such times were fraught with strangely exciting moments; and subtle tinglings came unbidden to her nature, giving her pleasures wildly lawless and precious beyond expression. Yet she feared them also when they came, and refused to give them meaning.

But to-night a new wistfulness burned in her eyes as she turned to her silent companion.

"I wonder," she said, "if we couldn't put a fresher flag on our pole to-morrow."

"Sure shot," said Sid, "the freshest flag that ever grew."

She was silent again for several moments. Then she said:

"What should we do if a year went by—two years, perhaps, or even more —and a ship should never come?"

"Do?" said Grenville. "Sail away."

"I know. But I mean, supposing we found no place to go—and had to come back every time."

"H'm!" said Grenville, rubbing the corner of his jaw, "you probably also mean to suppose we were always unmolested."

"Why, yes, of course. Who could come to molest us here?"

"Molesters," he said, "if anyone. But perhaps they never would."

He had given no answer to her question, which she hardly cared to repeat. It was one of the times, which frequently came, when she could not prevent herself from wondering if this strong, primal man she had once called a brute could have utterly forgotten the passionate declaration made on the steamship "Inca" the day before the wreck.

She wondered also, had he meant it at the time? Or had one of his many inscrutable moods possessed him, barely for the moment? She had never dared recently confess to herself what feelings might instantly invade her tingling nature should she learn he had only pretended, perhaps on some wager with Gerald, as a test of her faithfulness and love.

It was womanlike, merely, on her part, to desire to know his mind. No woman may long resent being loved by a strong and masterful man. And Elaine was delightfully typical of all her delightful sex.

"Well," she presently said, "we've been here now much longer than we ever expected that day when we arrived."

His gaze, which had been averted, now swung to a meeting with her own. She had never seemed lovelier, braver, more sweetly disposed than now. The moonlight deepened her luminous eyes till the man fairly held his breath.

"Elaine," he said, finally, glancing once more towards the silvered sea, "what is your notion of love?"

The shock of the word threw all her wits into confusion.

"My notion?" she stammered, helplessly, feeling the hot flames leap like floods of his molten metal to her neck, her face, and her bosom. "I don't believe—I have—any notions."

"Your convictions, then?" he amended. "Or, if you like, your principles?"

"My—my principles of—of all that—are—just about like—everyone else's, I suppose," she managed to answer, fragmentarily, "—being honest—and true—and faithful—unto death."

"To the one that you *really* love?"

"Why—certainly—of course." The heat in her face increased, so significant had she felt his words with that low even tone of emphasis.

He stared so long at the sea after that she began to suspect he had not even heard her reply. After a time she was tempted to play, just a trifle, with the fire. She added, "Why did you ask?"

"Wanted to know." Once more he fell dumb, and again she waited, afraid he would, and more afraid he would not, continue the delicate topic. Once again, also, she was tempted.

"And what," she inquired, "is your—notion?"

He did not turn. "Of love or crocodiles?" "Of—

of love—was what you asked me."

"I believe I did," he responded. "Oh, about the same as yours!"

Elaine had received but scanty satisfaction. After another long silence she ventured to say:

"We might have to be here a year—or even longer."

He turned to her directly. "Do you like it here, Elaine?"

She would not reply, and therefore demanded, "Do you?"

"I'm a savage," he admitted. "This sort of thing appeals to something in my blood."

"I know," she answered, understandingly, "—building up an empire with your naked hands, unaided—conquering metals and elements—wresting the island's dominion from the brutes. Naturally you love it!"

He reddened. "I can't make an apple dumpling and make it right! This island's dominion? Great Cæsar's frying-pan—this is a regular picnic-ground, with everything on earth provided!"

She smiled. "And things all made and ready, including tools and powder, not to mention a tiger-skin rug.... You refuse to admit you like it for itself?"

"Like it or not," he answered, "we must get away—and home."

"Home," she repeated, oddly. "Home.... I wonder if home will ever seem —— It certainly would be wonderful, a miracle, I think, to see a steamer really coming—and to go on board and have it take us back to—everything— somewhere home—— But we'd sometimes think of this—a little?"

"Probably."

To save his life, he could not banish thoughts of Fenton.

"I'm sure we would," murmured Elaine. She gazed away, to the jungle's softened shadows. She wanted to cry out abruptly that she loved it to-night, with a love that could never die. She wanted the comfort of something, she hardly dared wonder what. After another long silence, she finally said, with eyes averted and excitement throbbing in her veins:

"I know the name of this little place—do you?"

"No," he said, wondering what she might have discovered. "What do you think it is called?"

It seemed to Elaine her heart pounded out her reply.

"The Isle of Shalimar."

If Grenville knew the Indian name for Garden, he made no sign that she could read. He made no reply whatsoever, but gazed as before at the sea.

He was turning at last when a low, but distinctly briefer, recurrence of the island's haunting wails arose to disturb the wondrous calm—as well as his peace of mind. There could be no doubt the tidal phenomenon was gradually but steadily failing.

What might occur when it altogether ceased was more than the man could divine. He felt a vague dread of that approaching hour and of what it might develop.

"It must be after midnight," he said, at last, "—time for night's ordinary dreams."

Yet, when he was finally stretched on his bed, he did not lose himself in slumber. Instead he lay thinking of the island's haunting sounds and the cave somewhere underneath the headland.

He had meant to attempt an inspection of this place, if only to gratify a natural curiosity. The thought occurred to him now that, in case of dire necessity, it might afford such a shelter as was not to be found on any other portion of the island. It was not a thing to be neglected. He made up his mind that the following day he would make an exploration.

CHAPTER XXII

A TOMB OF STONE

The ladder that Grenville constructed in the morning was not entirely new. He had found upon testing the original contrivance, made for his séance with the tiger, that, although the creepers had become quite dry, they were neither weak nor brittle.

He fortified the older section with additional material, however, to make absolutely certain it would not abruptly part and drop him into the sea. All morning he worked, while his smoldering fires continued to eat out the hollow for his boat, securing new length to the rungs already provided, since the distance down from the brink of the cliff was fully one hundred feet.

To Elaine he explained that he thought perhaps a cave might exist in the rock. The wailing sounds, it was easy to argue, would indicate some such cavity, which he felt it important to examine. If she somewhat divined the further fact that he hoped to discover a possible retreat, should unforeseen dangers threaten, she made no revelation of her thought.

It was not without considerable anxiety, however, that she finally discovered precisely what he meant to attempt. His ladder, she was certain, was far too frail for any such business as climbing down, above that boiling tide. One careless step, or a parting of the strands, and nothing on earth could save the man from death on the jutting rocks below. She had glanced at the waters under the cliff, and their crystal depths were not at all reassuring.

The thorough precautions against a mishap that Grenville finally completed considerably lessened her fears, yet she had no wish to watch him descend when at length he slipped over the edge. She was gazing with fixed and wide-open eyes at the heap of rocks in which he had fastened the ladder.

The matter to Grenville seemed simple enough. The brink overhung the wall itself, in consequence of which the ladder swung quite free, down the face of the scarp, till it touched at a jutting ledge below. It swayed to and fro and sagged a bit loosely at some of the rungs, but it could not be broken by his weight.

He made no attempt at a rapid descent, neither did he pause to enjoy the scenery. When the ledge was reached he rested, made certain no sharp-edged stone could impinge upon and perhaps cut into his twisted creepers, and again proceeded downward.

His course for a matter of two or three fathoms was rendered rather more difficult by the fact the ladder lay closely bent against the wall, instead of hanging free. The rock face was pitted and exceedingly rough, its indentations ill-arranged for footholds and far too treacherous for any such employment.

Grenville was nearly at the lower lip of this projection before he attempted a look below to determine what he was approaching. He discovered then it was undercut again—and likewise that his ladder was considerably short. Its lower end dangled about with irregular gyrations as he shifted his weight from rung to rung. It was fully two yards above the water. There was nothing in sight on which to plant his feet, so far as he could discern from the point then occupied.

He continued down the ledge. When he reached its base, his suspicions were immediately confirmed. It overhung a cavern, which was not, however, the cave. To the final rung but one of his ladder he descended, and there he rested to have a look about.

He was hanging directly before a massive pot-hole in the cliff—a huge, roughly rounded sort of chamber, the roof of which was arched. On the left, it shared its pitted wall with a second and smaller chamber. On the right, its edge was jaggedly broken against a yawning hole. This hole was undoubtedly the cave-mouth described by the documents found in the hidden tube.

From this point only, as Grenville could see, would its mouth be readily discovered. Thick curtains of greenery, draped from its neighboring walls of rock, would shield it from view from passing boats, unless they should nose to its portals. This, with a swirling and dangerous tide, no craft would be likely to attempt.

The shrubbery, hanging so thickly from the ledge, afforded Grenville a puzzle. He knew it could not be a seaweed, since the tide never rose to such a level. He presently realized it was simply an air plant of unusually luxuriant growth. Its roots had found lodgment in a crevice, where nothing would be likely to disturb it in its possession.

Concerning the possible contents of the cave, its extent, or immediate surroundings, there was nothing to be discovered from his ladder, twist as he might or crane his neck to stare in the cavern's mouth.

He had practically determined to return to the top, shift his ladder along, and once more make the descent, when he realized his effort would be wasted. A thick, broken shelf of the pitted tufa jutted many feet out above the cave, and even beyond the growing weed. Should he hang his ladder directly before the opening, he would find himself, when he came to its end, swung helplessly over the water.

He could see distinctly where the final base of the wall projected into the tideway. It would certainly be no less than ten feet removed from the nearest point he could possibly reach by this particular method.

It occurred to his mind he could lengthen his strands, drop himself off the ladder-end, and swim to the edge of the cave. But, even as he turned to examine the physical features afforded to a swimmer, a huge dark form loafed like a shadow through the crystal tide, to rise beyond and cut the sparkling surface with a blackish dorsal fin. There was no mistaking Mr. Shark.

Grenville nodded, grimly. "Thanks for the timely suggestion," he said, as the monster once more sank. He presently added, "It's a boat or no explorations." Somewhat disappointedly, he returned up the ladder to the top.

"The cave is there," he told Elaine, who promptly sat down, in sheer relief, when she saw him finally safe, "but it has to be entered from the water."

"Oh!" said Elaine. "But why does it have to be entered?"

"Well," said Sidney, at a loss for a better argument, "it might be full of treasure;" and he smiled.

Elaine was no less ready with her answer. "Treasure is certainly indispensable to us here. No wonder we've felt that something was strangely lacking."

"There you are," he rejoined. "I think I can paddle the raft about the cliff, for the tide could never be better."

She was certain that Grenville attached some unusual importance to an inspection of the cave.

"Couldn't I help?" she asked him. "What was the fault of the ladder?"

"Fully six feet too short. Perhaps you'd better watch for passing steamers. If we missed one—whom should we blame?"

They had slowly returned to the shelter, where the table was attractively spread.

"What a luncheon!" said Grenville, enthusiastically. "I'll eat in a rush and be back before you know I've gone." He certainly ate with lively promise.

But, after the raft was launched on the tide, he lost all sense of time. He had left his shoes and stockings on the shore. He had brought a torch, lighted, which he lashed in an upright position on the raft. Wading and paddling, punting, pulling, and at times even pushing his craft along the beach, he warmed to his work in the briefest space, since the tide could hardly have been more favorable to his needs.

The pole he had brought had a hook at the end, bound firmly in place with copper wire. This was an excellent provision, especially when he came to the cliff, where wading was out of the question. He was thus enabled to catch at a ledge, or any open crevice, and draw his unwieldy float along, while fending it off from various rocks on which it might otherwise have pounded.

His work was hard and slow. The distance was not discouraging, however, and with some of the swirls to assist, here and there, he finally came to a broken sort of cape, from which he readily saw his dangling ladder. After that a hot bit of fighting was required to maintain his position near the wall. The tide was uneasy—a hungry, ugly swirl that alternately came and subsided.

When he passed it at last his task was done, for the cave was a stone's toss away. It was not even then to be seen, and its presence in the cliff would scarcely have been suspected. But Grenville knew the luxuriant plant that grew across a portion of its entrance. When he presently moored his raft to a rock fairly under the shadow of the weed, the cave was just above him.

Under his feet the ledge was rough and sloping. It was pitted so completely as to form a rude natural stairway to the opening under the overhanging shelf. This mouth to the cavern was hardly six feet wide and not more than four in height. Its access was comparatively easy.

Grenville, with his torch in hand, was presently gazing within. Obliged to stoop, and beholding nothing but absolute darkness ahead of his light, he stumbled against a lumpy vein of rock—and nearly met with disaster. He barely halted at the edge of a pool of ebon water.

After all his effort to gain the cave, it appeared to be filled with this inklike accumulation. The pool was absolutely still. Not a ripple disturbed its shining surface. How deep it was and how far it extended from the ledge that held it from flowing into the sea, could not be gauged by Grenville's torch, as he held it aloft to stare at the wall of velvet gloom.

He sounded a note that rolled about and reverberated weirdly. But he could not determine from the echoes how far the waves had traveled.

Casting his dull-red illumination to the left, and lower down, he proceeded a little along the ledge, till it merged in an upright wall. There was nothing at all to be seen in this direction save water and rock, that faded away into Stygian darkness beyond.

He retraced his steps and explored the ledge on the right. This led him considerably further than the first had done before it was similarly ended. He was then aware the cavern was of no inconsiderable dimensions, at least with regard to its width. He raised his eyes towards the ceiling, where nothing was to be seen.

At length he bethought him of another test—that of throwing lumps of rock against the walls. There were fragments in plenty scattered loosely at his feet. The first one he threw went straight out ahead—and presently thumped on something solid. He reckoned the distance some sixty feet away, but admitted it might have been eighty.

Every missile he cast right, left, or at an angle promptly reported a wall; and some plumped back into water. The cave was not gigantic, but all its floor was apparently flooded. His hand, which he thrust in the water where he stood, groped blindly and found no bottom. He rolled up his sleeve and tried again, without more definite results. The water, however, was warm.

"Good place for a swim, in any case," he told himself, aloud; and, planting his torch with a sudden determination that he would not retreat with information so utterly meager, he stripped off his clothing at once. He let himself into the ebon depths, with his torch held well above the water. He had rather expected to be able to wade, but he sank to his neck without sounding to the bottom.

Swimming almost perpendicularly, employing one hand only, he presently lost all sight of the walls and was out in an unknown pool of blackness. Save for a slight sensation of its weirdness, the experience was decidedly pleasant. He tasted the water as he swam and found that it was fresh. He turned to look out at the opening, but could barely see light through the weeds.

Some twenty or thirty feet from the ledge, his feet encountered a ridge. It was stone, and across it he waded to a greater depth beyond. Yet once again he was soon enabled to stand erect and walk along the bottom. The broken, uneven surface that he felt with his feet made his progress slow and careful.

He had presently crossed the underground pond, up the sloping bank of which he was soon making rapid progress. He emerged on a dry ledge beyond. Even then the walls were not to be seen till he walked a rod straight onward.

The briefest examination sufficed to establish the fact he had come to a sort of natural antechamber to the larger cavern he had crossed. Also, apparently, the entire place was as empty as a last year's bird's-nest.

Vaguely disappointed, though he hardly knew why, the man surveyed the place anew, by the light that entered at the opening as well as by that of his torch. He saw at once that, could it be drained, the place would afford a retreat of amazing security for anyone needful of shelter. He was also certain he could drain it in a day by blasting through the ledge of rock that blocked the entrance from the sea and so retained the pool.

With one more brief and cursory examination of the rocky structure about him, he was turning away when something foreign about a slab of stone, that seemed a fragment of the solid wall, attracted his attention.

He laid his hand upon its top as if to pull it down. It came away so readily it all but fell on his feet. Behind it the crudest sort of masonry walled up a natural door.

Ten minutes later, standing on the heap of blocks he had tumbled rapidly down in forming a gap through four feet at least of this bulkhead, Grenville thrust his torch within a nichelike chamber of the cavern.

A low exclamation of astonishment burst from his lips at the vision thus suddenly encountered.

The place was a tomb for dead kings' gold and precious stones that threw back the gleams from his torch!

CHAPTER XXIII

A DESPERATE CHANCE

For fully a minute Grenville was motionless, there in the gap, surveying the treasure crypt.

The more his eyes became accustomed to the yellowish light and inky shadows, the more extensive became his estimate of the wealth the cave contained.

The symbols and trinkets of solid metal and glistening stones were arranged not only on rudely-hewn shelves about the cavern's walls, but likewise in several stone receptacles, like sarcophagi in miniature, cut from the tufa of the island. It was partially because of this feature of the hidden niche that Grenville concluded the property here had once belonged to either Indian or African native chiefs and that this was a mortuary house of guarded treasure.

There was, however, further confirmation of his theory. This was a crude inscription on the wall above the shelves and caskets. It was simply that same cartouch he had found on the map or parchment—once part of a living being —with the figure of a mummy in the oval. On either side of this the beetle or scarab was repeated.

The utter inutility of gold and gleaming jewels was momentarily forgotten as Grenville stared in from the wall. The island, its perils—everything save an underlying current of thought that wove about Elaine—had ceased for the moment to impress his newly dazzled senses. He withdrew his arm to plant his torch in the stones already removed. Then lustily heaving out stone after stone, like some naked god of the underworld, half revealed in the smoky glare, he began to demolish the barrier so carefully erected in the cave.

He had torn down nearly half the bulk of this uncemented wall, filling the larger cavern weirdly full of the crashing and thudding noises, when one of the fragments, tossed unthinkingly behind him, bounded from another rock and struck down his torch and its light.

Utter darkness instantly descended. He tried to grope his way quickly forward, thinking the torch might be recovered and blown to a flame again. But he stumbled, fell down upon his knees, and was bruised on the stones about his feet. When he finally found the torch with his hand, a rock lay squarely upon it; the last of its fire was gone.

Thoroughly disgusted with his carelessness, he stood undecidedly above the unseen ruin he had wrought. To attempt further work of removing the wall by the faint diffusion of light that entered from the outside world, was out of the question. To enter the crypt before the aperture could be considerably enlarged was equally impossible. Moreover, the treasure was safe, as he presently admitted.

As a matter of fact, he began to realize at last how futile had been his labor. He remembered, abruptly, where he was, the details of his helpless situation. Except as something to show Elaine, or to load her with as presents, the stuff in the cave was as worthless as so much dross.

There was nothing to do but retreat as he had come. This he presently did, reluctantly turning from the half-uncovered cavern and wading into the pool.

Without his torch, and swimming towards the light, he was now enabled, to some extent, to discern the limits of the cave. He could see a portion of the ceiling and a bit of the wall on his left. Both were featureless, to all appearances. The water's surface presented a more extensive aspect with the light thus spread before him, but its farther limits could not be descried, where its inkiness blended with the gloom.

When he came at length to the ledge that formed a natural dam across the entrance, thereby impounding the water, he looked it over with greater care than when he had first trod upon it, to determine where would be the likeliest spot for a blast to break it down.

There could be no debate upon this subject. Over against the upright wall, on the left-hand side looking out, the ledge not only narrowed down, where a pot-hole pitted it deeply, but a tiny crevice extended so nearly through the remaining substance that a trickle of water already oozed downward towards the sea. The perpendicular wall here also was broken, a number of fragments of exceptional size appearing so loose as to threaten toppling over.

Grenville was leisurely in all this examination. He was either obliged to permit his body to dry in the air or dress while dripping wet. Yet at length he was once more clothed and ready to depart. He remained for a moment, taking a final survey of the place and planning the details of his blasting operations, then stooped and made his exit from the place.

The brilliant light of outer day bewildered him momentarily. He stared below, however, as if he felt he might be blind. The raft was not where he had left it.

Hastily scrambling down the incline of the ledge, he promptly arrived at its base. His view was limited, even then, to a segment of the open, purple sea. But the worst of his fears was confirmed. The raft had floated away. It was nowhere to be seen!

The tide had run out with amazing swiftness. Its level was such that the ceaseless swells ran under his ledge, instead of up about it. The creeper-cord, which he had utilized to moor his craft to the bowlders, hung uselessly over the edge. It had parted at once when the ponderous raft had been caught in the swirl of an eddy.

This eddy was running intermittently, as Grenville soon discovered. Disgust with himself for his carelessness, and a vague disquiet concerning his helpless situation, addressed his comprehension together. He was bounded by huge overhanging walls and a water abounding in sharks. If only by boat could the cavern be reached, then only by boat——

He thought of his ladder, dangling in air where he had left it, and believed for a second he could hook it in with his pole, still lying on the rocks. But no sooner had he climbed a little up the ledge, to a point from which the ladder could be seen, than he realized the folly of his hope. It was twenty feet off at the least, and fully eight above the water.

The fact that the tide was continuing to fall, that the raft had doubtless departed the island forever, and that night might find him here, a helpless prisoner, was no great motive for alarm. But Grenville was not slow to realize that escape from his predicament would be no more readily accomplished on the morrow than it could to-day—that high tide and low tide were alike of no avail to return him to the terrace and Elaine.

The thought of Elaine and the fears she must certainly experience, did he fail to return that night, aroused a new impatience in his blood. He could almost have made up his mind to slip overboard at once and take his chances of swimming about the base of the wall, despite its treacherous currents, had he not remembered the sharks.

"It's the ladder—or night," he murmured, paraphrasing Wellington's utterance at Waterloo, somewhat grimly, and again he went down to the edge of the shelf of rock left dripping by the tide.

"Elaine!" he called, with a lusty breath, yet without an accent of distress. "Elaine! ... Elaine! ... Are you there?"

There was no response, save the swashing of the waves, which he knew were constantly retreating, leaving the ladder yet more high above the heaving surface.

Once more he shouted as before, perhaps a trifle louder. And again he heard no reply. He began to fear the shelf of rock that projected out above him might send the sound waves too far outwards, towards the sea, for Elaine on the terrace to hear.

He had no alternative but to shout repeatedly. This he did, at regular intervals, all the time striving to eliminate the slightest accent that would rouse her sense of fear. It seemed, however, as if no sort of cry could bring a response from the top. He moved to another position at last and tried with a longer, shriller tone.

"Yes! Yes!" came a bright, clear call, at last. "Can you hear me now any better?"

She had answered before, as he instantly knew, but her voice had been snatched afar from the cliff by a circular current of wind.

"All right!" shouted Grenville, enormously relieved. "I'm down here below and I'd rather return by the ladder. Can you hear me quite distinctly?"

"Oh, yes!" cried Elaine, whose fears were vast, though she would not betray them in her voice. "Do you want me to change it—or something?"

"A trifle, yes—as I'll direct you." He paused for a moment to make his directions as clear and concise as possible. Then he shouted:

"First move a few of the rocks to a point as near the edge as possible and about ten feet to the left of the present position…. Is that clear?"

"Yes—very clear—quite clear—— And then?"

"Then lift off the others and remove the ladder—carefully. Mind it's just a bit heavy."

He paused, and she cried: "Yes! I hear you!"

"Take the ladder at once to the rocks already placed and roll them on its end, to hold it down."

"Then heap all the others upon it?" Her question came ringing down the cliff.

"Yes—and as promptly—— But don't overtax your strength."

There was no reply to this final instruction. That the quickest of action was highly essential, she had felt in the very air. She was hotly, valiantly tugging at the rocks before his last words had died upon the breeze.

He presently saw the ladder-end jerk about spasmodically and ascend for perhaps a foot. Elaine had the weight of it in her hands—and her strength was equal to the task!

He watched it, his heart wildly thrilling at the thought of her ready wit and courage—her certain, sturdy helpfulness in every trying crisis.

With more wild gyrations about the ledge, the ladder-end now disappeared. It was gone for a moment only, to return at a point more directly above his head. Here it halted, moved about uncertainly, then lowered jerkily downward, to dangle at last with its last rung all but on the water, some eight or ten feet away. He knew that its upper end was lightly anchored and would soon be firmly held in place.

He caught up his pole, with the hook at its end, to fish the ladder inward. But, fearing that any untimely tug might fetch it all doubling down the cliff, he instantly halted the maneuver and compelled himself to wait.

Five minutes went by—five ages for slowness of movement. He was certain by then Elaine had made the end too secure to be readily dislodged. He stepped to the outermost edge of the shelf, with the pole horizontally extended.

It was short by perhaps six inches. Strain as he would, he could not reach either one of the rungs or supports. A light puff of wind then bent it slightly inward, and he fished out wildly, in the hope the discrepancy thus amended might be wholly overcome.

But his hook still prodded the empty air, while the zephyrs that played with the dangling thing seemed solely bent on his torture. The sweat oozed out on his temples, for the straining made him warm. A sense of disappointment amounting almost to despair attacked him for a moment.

"I shall leap out and swim!" he told himself, at last. "I'll not remain here for the night!"

He returned to the point from which Elaine had finally been heard.

She did not immediately answer when he called as he had before. When her voice came down, he was certain her breath was broken.

"I've—carried the last rock—over—and one or two—extra, besides."

"Right ho!" responded Grenville, cheerfully. "You might stand away while I test it."

He knew that a sudden throwing of his weight upon the ladder might suffice to fetch it down. He could not be sure that, with all her ready helpfulness and promptness, Elaine had so heaped the rocks above as to make the thing secure.

"I can always get back here for the night," he murmured to himself, as he scanned the swirl below. "And when it calms down from that bally twist——"

The whirlpool was even then subsiding, in its intermittent way. He quickly ascended the sloping ledge, the better to run and leap far outward. His pole he dropped upon the rocks as he hung there poised for his plunge. His eyes were keenly fixed on the tide.

The waters became quiescent. Swiftly Grenville darted down the ledge, leaping well out, towards the end of the ladder. He was fairly in midair when his gaze was directed to a dark form loafing in the depths.

Before he struck, by some quick flirt the huge form rose, coming inward, and a black fin cut through the waves.

CHAPTER XXIV

A DREADED VISITOR

What it was that happened when he felt the waters swiftly rising all about him Grenville could never have told. He was almost certain his foot had come in contact with a heavy, pulpy surface, like a wet thing made of rubber, as he did his utmost to strike his assailant with his heel.

He could only be certain that he seemed to plunge downward interminably, and that afterwards a horrible rush of waters, lashed to violence, was sounding wildly in his ears and confusing his staring eyes.

Then he came to the top with a sickening conviction, that one of his legs would be gone almost before he could feel the incisions of the teeth where the shark was closing upon it. He lurched tremendously forward in the water, to close the short but vital gap between himself and the ladder.

It seemed to him then a nightmare must be binding his limbs to inaction— that incredible time was elapsing while he still remained in the tide. As a matter of fact, he had moved with prodigious energy, his strokes and velocity through the water phenomenally swift. And, when he caught at the lowermost rung, he shot from the depths like some weirdly living projectile, doubled up in a knot by its speed.

For his knees were drawn sharply upward, and hand over hand he scaled up his swaying support. But his ears heard the hiss where that terrible fin was cutting the waves beneath him. One quick glance he sped to the place comprehended the turning monster's belly, the open mouth, and even the hideous nose that shot beneath his very foot like the point of a speeding torpedo.

To the round above he scrambled no less galvanically—only to feel a sudden giving of the ladder. A wild conviction of the structure's insecurity above—its giving way beneath the incautious strain he had unavoidably put upon it—scorched its way into his brain, while he still looked down upon the shark.

But that one slip ended as abruptly as it had come. It was all in the rung he had clutched in desperate violence, and not in the ladder itself. Elaine's rock anchorage was firm!

A swift and weakening reaction now ensued in all his being, as he clung there, dripping but safe. He leaned on the ladder-rung heavily, to regain his breath and strength. He was panting and all but exhausted for the moment. When at length he resumed the upward climb, the shark was no longer to be seen.

He paused a bit longer on the shelving ledge above to gather his wits in proper order.

"Sidney!" he heard. "Are you coming? Are you there?"

"Well, rather!" he called out, cheerily. "Stopped like a kid to—examine the geological formation." He started upward promptly, whistling as he went.

It was not, however, without a tremendous effort that he finally pulled himself over the brink, in all the weight of his soaking garments, and struggled to his feet.

"Why—you're wet!" said Elaine, concealing her hands, which were cut and bruised from the heavy stones she had carried. "Did you have to swim to get the ladder?"

He knew her hands were hurt, but maintained his usual manner.

"I did. But the water is warm—in fact, it was very warm, indeed."

"But couldn't you use the raft?"

"I couldn't," he answered, candidly. "The raft got away while I was pothering about, and, unless it faithfully floats ashore, we may never see its

124

honest face again."

Elaine's expression brightened.

"I'm perfectly delighted to hear it! Now you never can go there again!"

Grenville was amused at the turn of her reflections.

"But what about the treasure in the crypt?"

"I don't believe there's any treasure in the crypt. There never is, except in wonderful stories. And, if there was, what good could it be to us?"

Grenville met her magnetic gaze, now brightened by her challenge. It was not a time to excite new alarms in her heart by divulging the facts he had discovered. For she would be alarmed were she once informed of the wealth concealed beneath their feet. She would instantly understand the dangers to them both from the men who had hidden the treasure.

"Well," he said, with an air of lightness he was very far from feeling, "I confess I'd rather have a good pot of steaming black coffee at this particular juncture than all the gold and jewels of the land."

"Oh, please don't mention it!" said Elaine. "Haven't I tried every leaf I could find, to make you something to drink?" And a wistful pucker came to her brow that made her more than ever enchanting. "You've no idea," she added, "what horrid messes this island foliage can make."

"Wouldn't wonder," said Grenville, calmly. But, having come to the shaded cave, he was grateful for a drink of cool, sweet water and glad to sit down for a rest.

The subject of the cave was dropped, but his thoughts could not fade in Grenville's mind. They lay in substrata, beneath more homely plans for resuming his interrupted labors. But, beyond going down to dig some yams to roast with a pheasant killed the previous day, he returned to no toils that afternoon. He paused to examine the shell of his boat, which fire, plus his chisel, was finally evolving from the log, and, finding unusual quantities of blackly charred stuff to be gouged away in the morning, determined to be early at the task.

This plan was one of the sort that "gang aglee." He fished, with Elaine, till nine o'clock the following day, to provide a needful change of their diet; then placed some fresh signals on their flagpole. At eleven, however, he was once more at his boat, with his fires freshly blazing. He was working gayly, aroused to a new enthusiasm over final results to be achieved by the excellent progress his former fires had made upon the log. A few more days of work like that—and he would have to be thinking of the launching.

This was not a thought he had neglected. In a vague sort of way the problem of moving his boat to the water's edge had bothered him from the first. It would have to be run on rollers, he admitted. Doubtless a way would have to be cleared through some of the undergrowth.

Reflecting that this was a task to be performed while the fires were doing their daily stint, he made a preliminary survey of the jungle to select the most practical route. The way across the grassy clearing was not only long, but in places inclined to be rough. Fortunately, in either direction the way was all down-grade.

He had never yet forced a way to the shore through the jungle beyond his tree-trunk smelter. Thither he wended his way to note what this route might offer.

Breaking the branches from before his path, and rather inclined to believe a trail might once have been forced through the thicket, he was penetrating deeper and deeper into the moist and thickly shaded region when he presently halted, almost certain he had heard someone calling his name.

"Sidney! Sidney!" came the cry again, from Elaine up above him on the cliff. "Sidney! Where are you? A boat! I've seen a sail! There's someone coming at last!"

He had smashed his way out while she was calling.

"A sail!" she repeated, excitedly, the moment he appeared. "Oh, come!—please come at once!"

She disappeared swiftly from the edge, running back, lest the sight be lost forever.

Actively, Grenville went bounding across the clearing and up their narrow trail. He was panting and eager when Elaine ran forward to meet him, and clutched him by the arm.

"I knew it would come!—I knew it!" she cried, as she hastened hotly forward at his side. "We must wave things as hard as we can!"

She had guided him swiftly to the great lone tree that stood like the island's landmark, to be seen for many a mile. She pointed in triumph afar across the sea—and Grenville beheld a tiny sail, like the merest white notch in the sky.

"Can they see us yet? Shall we wave?" said Elaine. "They couldn't go by and miss us now?"

She was still clinging fast to Grenville's arm, and tears had sprung to her eyes. What long, long hours of torture, anxiety, and hope she had expended, uttering no complaint as the days went by, the man abruptly knew. Then something indescribably poignant shot boltlike through his heart.

Elaine felt him harden, grow rigid, as his gaze narrowed down on the distant thing she had found in their purple sea. The note that broke from his lips at last made a shiver go down her spine.

He suddenly turned, and his arm was wrenched from her clasp. He sped like a madman back to their mast and heaved all his weight against it. He threw back the rocks that held it in place in the crevice to which it had been fitted.

Before she could follow, to question what he did, Elaine saw him drop the pole over.

"Sidney!" she said, but the face that he turned wore a look that was new to her ken.

"Pull up the ladder from the rocks!" he called. "Then go to the shelter and stay!"

He himself ran to the cavern, to take up their largest jug of water. With this in his arms, he hastened down the trail to quench the flames beneath his boat.

And when, with more water, hurried from the spring, he had drowned the last blue wisp of smoke, he brought the full jug to the cave again and tore down the improvised awning.

"We had better hail death than that craft!" he said, "unless I am very much mistaken!"

CHAPTER XXV

AN IRREPARABLE LOSS

Elaine was dumbly appalled for a moment by the words that Grenville had uttered. She finally found her voice.

"But—why? I don't believe I understand. It isn't someone—some horrible men who hunt human heads for trophies?"

Grenville was glad she knew what a head-hunter means. He loathed the necessity of making revolting explanations. He vainly wished he might spare her now—that his judgment might be in error. But the rakish angle of that sail, though so far away on the water, had left him no room to doubt that natives were manning the craft.

"They may be friendly visitors, after all," he answered. "And then again they may not. It may be as wise for us to see them first, and determine our conduct later."

"You do fear them, then? But how can we hide—if they land and come up on the hill?"

"They shall never come up—if I can help it! If I only had a few more bombs!" He had gone to his cave and was dragging forth his little cannon. "I haven't even a hatful of slugs with which to charge this plaything!"

Elaine had remained obediently at her shelter, in the door of which she stood.

"Won't they see you?" she said, her voice already lowered, as if in fear its accents might be overheard where the distant boat was approaching. "Have you more old pieces of brass?"

"Some," said Grenville, reluctant to use his remaining metal in such an extravagant manner. "I have nothing else that will answer, hang the luck! ... They can't see us yet, but we'll move about with caution.... I wish I had made more powder! I have only a few feet of fuse. I must get some additional creepers at once and let them dry out in the sun."

He went down to the jungle immediately for a fresh supply of this highly essential growth, leaving Elaine at the shelter, a prey to dread that had utterly obliterated her bitter disappointment. She stooped, to steal forward on the rocks and look for the sail again. It was still so far on the sun-lit surface of the ocean that it seemed no nearer than before. She returned once more to the cave.

Grenville came up, fairly laden with freshly severed creepers.

"I've thought of a means for making bombs!" he told her, triumphantly. "Perhaps you can split these creepers and take out the cores while I go to fetch some bamboo poles."

"Couldn't I fill them with powder?" Elaine inquired, anxiously. "I watched you before. I am sure I would make no great mistakes."

He knew she was nervous, eager to be employed.

"Sure shot you could," he answered, briskly, and, going to the cave employed as his "powder magazine," he brought her a jar of explosive. "Don't be afraid to put in all that the creeper tube will carry," he instructed.

"And tie it with fibers here and there, to keep the edges together."

With his heaviest tools he descended at once to the bamboo growth, where he was presently toiling hard. Elaine, no less industriously, was hotly assailing the creepers, held firmly down with heavy rocks, to make their manipulation easy.

She had filled and bound a considerable length of this simply manufactured fuse when Grenville returned to the terrace. For his part, he bore across his shoulder three great long steins of green bamboo that were three inches through at the base.

"I can cut this stuff at its divisions," he explained, "fill the smaller sections with powder, and fit the larger ones over them, like a shell within a shell. A natural growth plugs each one up at the end, and I'll also cap each end with a rock, and wrap the whole contraption about with creepers. Of course, the fuse will go in first. I wish the stuff were dry!"

The spirit of battle was no less aroused in Elaine, whose mood was the equal of his own.

"Couldn't we use the cannon first—keep them off with that while the fuses and things are drying?"

"It's our only chance, if they raid us by the trail. They can scarcely arrive for two or three hours more. The tide will be against them—— If we keep out of sight, they may not detect our presence."

"Anyway," added Elaine, sagely, "they needn't know how few we are in numbers."

"Right ho!" he answered, cheerily. "The trail is steep and narrow. We can train the gun to rake its entire width. For the second shot, and any succeeding charges, we can load the piece with stones—— I'm in hopes our visitors may not land, but we'll keep our fire smoldering, making no smoke; and I'll fetch all the fruit and water we may need for a couple of days."

Elaine looked up at him quickly.

"A couple of days? We may have to fight two days?"

Grenville smiled, suggestively.

"Not if they come within range of the cannon or linger about a bomb. In time of peace prepare for the worst—and then a little extra."

He moved out cautiously, as Elaine had done, to scan the distant sail. He could see that it was steadily approaching. With eager impatience he hastened below to lay in needful provisions.

Luncheon was forgotten. When a large supply of fruits and water, with fuel sufficient for perhaps a week of flameless fire, had been stored in the coolness and protection of the caves, Grenville immediately set to work constructing the shells to fill with powder.

This was a task involving much difficult cutting. For this employment his tools were not encouragingly suited. Of fuse, Elaine had finally produced as much as all his bombs would require, with lengths for the cannon as well.

The gun was finally charged and primed, after Grenville had rebound it to its "carriage." It was lodged in the rocks, where it covered the trail, and stones were piled abundantly about it. A fuse was laid to the vent.

From time to time both the exiles had crept towards the one lone tree on the wall, to observe the on-coming boat. By three o'clock of the afternoon the wind had practically failed, but the craft drifted slowly forward. It was plainly in sight by then—a fair-sized affair with a singular out-rigger and a queer, unmistakable sail. So far as Grenville could determine at the distance, there were three or four natives aboard.

"If none of them ever go back to tell the tale," he announced, a bit grimly to Elaine, "we may be all right for quite a time."

She understood at once.

"You think, if they leave, they may return here later—with a larger force— if they find we are ready for a fight?"

"If they do, we'll not be at home—provided the boat can be finished."

Elaine was evidently thinking much—of the battle that might presently ensue, with all its unknown results.

"They'd kill us if they could, I suppose, if only to cut—— They are not human beings, really—the kind we ought not to shoot?"

Grenville could hardly repress a smile.

"If they try to steal the gun, I think we'd be justified in firing. At any rate, I shall fire first and debate the question later."

Elaine was growing nervous, now that all they could do was practically accomplished.

"Oh, I wish it was over!" she declared. "Do you think they'll attack us soon after landing?"

"They may not land this evening."

Grenville was thinking of the tidal sounds that haunted the island's wall.

These were still of considerable volume every day, and, according to his theory, frightened the ignorant natives away. He added, presently: "You see, they may be aware the tiger was living here before we disturbed his possession. In that event they might be cautious of landing after dark. They rarely take chances, I believe, by attacking in the night."

"But suppose they arrive an hour or two before sunset?"

"They might, if the breeze should freshen.... We can only wait and see."

But this waiting was an irritating business, so slowly did the craft appear to move against the tide and so fraught with possibilities was its visit to the place.

Sitting or stooping behind the rocks, Elaine and Grenville kept a constant watchfulness on the boat, now less than half a mile away. It was apparently becalmed. The day grew old and still it came no nearer.

The sun at length departed from the scene, with the riddle still unsolved. It appeared to Grenville the day-end breath would have wafted the stranger to the shore. He thought perhaps it did approach considerably closer, but of this he was not at all certain.

The brief, soft twilight soon began to wane. At Sidney's suggestion, their simple repast of island fruits was eaten. The fish they had captured in the morning was not cooked, in the absence of the customary fire. The calm that settled on the "Isle of Shalimar" was far from being reassuring. It seemed fraught with silent agencies of fate, moving noiselessly about the shadowed jungle.

When the darkness came down, the mysterious craft was no longer to be seen. Grenville had fancied it drifting rapidly in when he last discerned its form. No lights were displayed upon its mast or deck to indicate its presence off the headland.

Elaine was persuaded at last to retire, though she knew she should not sleep. Grenville remained on guard alone, pacing back and forth from the head of the trail to the lone tree reared above the cliff. His senses were strained to catch the slightest sound, but none came upward from the sea. From time to time he halted by their smoldering bit of coals to assure himself the last of the sparks had not been permitted to die.

At length, far in the silent night, the tidal wailing began, its weirdness increased an hundredfold by the tension of the hours. It seemed to Grenville unusually loud, so acute had the darkness made his hearing.

No sooner had the final note died out on the gently stirring air than answering cries, no less weird and shrill, arose from out upon the water. The visiting craft had drifted past the headland and was somewhere off on Grenville's right. The cries from its deck were like a response to some spirit of the island. They were rather more awed than exultant, Grenville felt, and he fancied some chanting, that came to him brokenly out of the heavy shades of night, was possibly a prayer.

When he came before her shelter again, Elaine was standing in the door. She had heard the cries from the boat.

"They haven't landed yet?" she said, in a whisper.

"They won't land now till daybreak, and perhaps not then," he answered. "Go back—and go to sleep."

"I'll try," said Elaine, and disappeared.

For Grenville, however, there could be no sleep, though the darkness rendered up no further sound. Like the outer sentry of a picket-line, with the enemy close, and his whereabouts unknown, he glided silently from one dark edge of the terrace to another, as the hours wore on, alert for the slightest alarm.

He finally sat by the head of the trail, convinced that the visitors would give him no trouble till morning, yet guarding the only way by which they could gain the summit of the hill.

He was weary and doubtless he nodded, lulled by the softness of the breeze that came up at last, burdened with its ozone from the sea. And, despite the fact he was afterwards positive the nod was the briefest in the world, full daylight was spread to the ends of the world, and the sun was gilding the island's tufa walls, when at length he started to his feet.

It seemed to him then some sound from below had played through the fabric of his dream. But nothing disturbed the usual calm, save the morning cry of distant parrots. Stooping, he moved through the scattered rocks, to survey the waters far and wide.

There was nothing to be seen, in all that expanse, of the craft that had ridden near at midnight. All the round of the wall he made in this manner of caution. When he came at length above the blackened clearing, where for day after day he had toiled with fire and chisel, he gazed about the open space bewildered and incredulous.

His half-finished boat was gone!

CHAPTER XXVI

AFTER TO-MORROW——

The truth of his loss was hardly to be credited as Grenville continued to stare below where the hollowed log had been.

There was not a sign of a living thing in the clearing or near-by jungle. There had been no sounds of unusual movement in the thicket, he was sure, or otherwise he must have wakened. No voices had spoken, since his ears had all but ached to catch the slightest disturbance.

On the blue of the sea, so tremendously expanded from this particular point of vantage, there was not a hint of a sail. But the fact remained his boat was gone, with all the work it represented, and all the hope their situation had centered upon it for them both.

An utter sinking of the heart assailed him. His moment of sleep, he told himself, could have been no more treacherous had it been planned by a scheming enemy to complete their abandonment to some rapidly impending fate. And yet had he waked in the gray of the dawn, with his bombs and fuses still too damp for employment, and his cannon planted only to guard the trail, the boat could hardly have been saved. At most, his protest would merely have betrayed the fact he was camped there on the terrace.

A new line of thought sprang into his brain, as one suggestion after another was swiftly deduced from his loss. The natives who had landed and carried off his precious craft must certainly have found the wall with which he had barred the trail. He could hardly doubt they knew of his presence on the hill. They might even now be lying in wait to get him the moment he appeared.

His preconceived theory, that they dared not land while those tidal sounds still haunted this end of the island, received a shattering blow. Their craft was doubtless hidden now behind either one of the other lofty walls comprised by the neighboring hills. The thieves had cut off all possible hope of his escape with Elaine by means of his solid, if crude, canoe, and could finally starve them on the hill, if they had no courage for a battle.

Yet how had they happened on his boat and why had they removed it? That they must have carried it bodily down to the shore, through the jungle, was absolutely certain. And this, he thought, argued a half-dozen men, though it might have been done by four.

He remained there, stunned by this utterly defeating discovery, watching the thicket for the slightest sign that might betray the presence of the enemy and revolving the proposition over and over in his mind. When at last he admitted that the natives might have known the log was lying there, if they had not indeed prepared it with fire for some of their uses the previous year, he was more than verging on the facts. They had felled it solely for a boat—and much of their work he had completed.

This line of reasoning did not, however, serve to quiet further questions. The visitors must certainly have wondered how it came about that the log was so nearly hollowed. The clay, still plastered upon it, must have suggested to their minds the work of a craftsman minus tools. That the workman must be present on the island would be more than suspected, since his boat was not even launched.

They might suppose the tiger had captured and devoured him—always admitting they knew of the brute's former presence on the place. It seemed far more likely to Grenville they had found his tracks about the spring, his gate on the trail, and the signs of his recent fires and general activity about the region of his smelter, and would therefore conclude he was still encamped on the hill.

He could fancy a half-dozen pairs of maliciously glittering eyes fastened even now upon the crest and edges of the terrace, all hidden by the thickets. Had the poisoned dart from a blowpipe come winging swiftly up from the shadows of the foliage, he should not have been surprised.

But not a leaf below him was disturbed. Not a sound arose to warn his eager ears. With a sense of bitter rage and humiliation in all his system, he finally crept once more to the trail, and beyond it to the cliff's final shelving.

From this extremity of the heights new aspects of the island were in view, as well as different expanses of the sea. His keen eyes searched the jungle and the clearings first, with no more results than before.

It was not until he gazed afar, on the darkening silver of the waters, that his search was at all rewarded. Even then, for a moment he was not wholly convinced that what he saw was not a spearlike leaf of foliage projected beyond the clean-cut edge of the farthest of the island's tufa towers.

But the angle of color detached itself and receded in far perspective. It was plainly the sail of the visiting craft, previously hidden from his sight by the hill at the island's end. It was already far on a northern course, where he should not have thought to find it. The freshening breeze was heeling it over gracefully; it would vanish in less than half an hour.

He wondered instantly—had they towed away his boat? Or might they have left it moored in some inlet of the island, to be taken upon some future visit?

Stifling an impulse to hasten down the trail, and aware that one, or even more, of the natives might have been left concealed upon the place, to ambush himself and Elaine, or anyone else suspected of being present on the rock, he remained behind his barrier of stones, no less cautious than before.

The fact that the entire morning passed in apparent security, with never the flicker of a leaf below to advertise a lurking menace, could not suffice to render Grenville careless or overconfident. He had told Elaine of their loss—which worried her less than himself. Together they maintained an all-day vigilance, half expectant of the sailing-craft's return and keyed to the highest tension of expectancy at every stirring of a shrub below them in the jungle.

Grenville finally armed himself with his bow and straightest arrow, to descend the trail, go quietly over to the spring, and then to the spot from which his boat had vanished. About the pool of crystal water there was not so much as a track of human boots or feet, other than his own. There were none to be seen about the foot of the trail, where there was ample dust in which they might have been recorded.

Where his boat had lain, with its end on a rock, there were far fewer footprints in the ash and soil than Sidney could have believed possible, judging the visitors at only four in number and their task not particularly light. Apparently, however, they had landed down beyond the jungle, proceeded straight to the log, and, wasting no time in wondering how it chanced to be covered with clay or hollowed to a shell, had taken it up, to depart with it as swiftly and directly as possible.

Even his tools still lay beside the hollow tree utilized for a smelter. The one explanation that addressed itself to his mind as being plausible was that the visitors, knowing of the log and having planned to secure it, perhaps in merely passing by the island, had come ashore so soon as the first faint gray of dawn broke the shadows of the jungle, when they had taken their prize and halted for nothing, not even a search for whatsoever tools they must have seen had been employed.

Once more his original theory of their superstitious fright of the island's "haunt" seemed to Grenville to be confirmed. He felt the natives had sneaked ashore—not in fear of himself, since they could not have foreknown his presence on the hill, but in possible fear of some spirit of the place whose wailing filled them with dread.

Barely less cautiously than heretofore, he followed the faintly imprinted trail of the boat's mysterious abductors, where it led across the clearing. He was certain now that a cleared path did exist where he had partially explored the previous morning. But branches and shrubbery had been freshly cut, as if to insure the silent passage of the log.

The lane thus created through the thicket led directly down an easy slope to a broken bit of seawall at the bottom. This, at high tide, would be scarcely a foot above the water. Here the log had undoubtedly been rested. Both broken clay and a charcoal smudge recorded the unseen fact.

The entire inlet was no more than twenty feet across. It was bounded on either side by pitted walls that permitted no access to the jungle. The last faint hope of again beholding his precious boat now vanished from Grenville's mind. It had not been moored, nor probably even towed, but doubtless loaded bodily on the visitor's deck, to be taken to parts unknown.

But, if this heavy fact sunk home in his breast, the man was somewhat relieved, at least, concerning a probable native left behind. He felt practically certain that none of the crew of the native craft had stepped beyond his clearing. How much they might guess as to who had hollowed the heavy log was another matter altogether. He knew that their tale would be widely told— and felt that developments would follow.

He went to Elaine, to whom he owed a report.

"I think we're alone on the place," he said, and related all he had discovered. "We may as well re-light our fires," he added, in conclusion, "and eat the best our sunny possessions afford."

Elaine could not so promptly recover from all she had undergone. She still sat staring at his face, a prey to confused emotions.

"Suppose they had really been friendly, after all—and we let them go and leave us here like that?"

"In that event they may return, since the boat will excite a bit of wonder."

"You mean they will know, of course, that someone must be here who made it?"

"It certainly tells that story rather plainly."

She was thinking rapidly.

"Then—if they shouldn't happen to be friendly, they would know it all just the same—and may still come back to—look us up?"

Grenville nodded.

"I shall certainly go to work with that chance in view."

"Yes," she agreed, "we'll certainly do all we can. But another boat would take you weeks! After all your patient, tedious work—to have it stolen like that! Oh, I could cry, if I weren't so vexed and sorry!"

Grenville smiled despite his sense of loss.

"Perhaps I can rig some sort of a catamaran," he answered. "But for day and night sailing, such as we would doubtless have before us, the best of boats would be none too comfortable."

"And we don't know where to sail."

"Well—not precisely."

"Then—what is the first thing to do?"

"Cook and devour a hearty dinner."

"But after that—to-morrow?"

"Thank God for peace—and prepare for war, meanwhile praying it may not come."

Elaine was grave, but her voice was clear and steady.

"You think it will—that a fight will come? ... I'd much rather know the worst."

"So would I!" said Grenville, cheerfully. "We can't. We can only get ready to acquit ourselves like—well, like gentlemen, and keep out an eye for a steamer.... Would you mind retreating to the cave I found, if dire necessity arose?"

"I'll go wherever you tell me," she answered, with a smile that went to his heart. "But of course I can't help wishing that a steamer would really come."

CHAPTER XXVII

A FATEFUL EXPLOSION

With feverish energy Grenville was at work, attempting to achieve a dozen ends at once.

Nearly a week of high-pressure application appeared to have accomplished so little. Yet a hundred pounds at least of his liveliest powder had been mixed and stored away, either loosely or packed in the bamboo bombs, of which he had a dozen; much extra bamboo had been cut and brought to the terrace; a new lot of jugs had been molded of clay and were finally being fired in his former smelter; baskets were made and ready for fruits, should retreat to the cave be rendered expedient, and his first small raft, or catamaran, for gaining the exit to the cavern, was all but ready to launch.

He had taken the bowsprit of the barque and three large stems from the bamboo growth as a basis for this craft. The bamboo stems were firmly lashed together, to act as a mate for the bowsprit. They were held away from the latter at a distance of about three feet by some of the few unrotted bits of board he had torn from the old vessel's cabin, plus more bamboo, split and employed for his platform.

Two half-cylindrical sections of this useful plant he had lashed to eight-foot poles of considerable stiffness to complete a pair of oars. His rowlocks, saved from the smelting processes, he finally tested in their sockets, where a rigid bridge had been stoutly secured across his raftlike contrivance, and found them all he could desire. The seat he had planned to occupy in rowing he abandoned now as quite superfluous.

He felt he must lose no time in draining the cave, for possible use in a siege. There was no other task that had been altogether neglected. The flagpole was once more standing on the terrace; abundant fuse was made, dried, coiled, and safely stored from damp or accident, and a mold was hardening in the fire for running lead slugs that would make the cannon effective.

For this latter need he meant to sacrifice his hammer. It, with the lead he had saved before, would supply some six or seven pounds of this needful ammunition. Now, as he swiftly braided three slender creepers in a "painter" for his crudely fashioned catamaran, he glanced at the tide inquiringly, and likewise up at the sun. There was over an hour in which to get to the cave, lodge a bomb in the ledge, and blow out the dam that held back the water, but the tide was still running against him.

With ten feet only of his mooring-line completed, he abandoned the braiding impatiently, secured one end to his raft at the estuary's entrance, and, wading in behind the clumsy structure, launched it with one impetuous heave across the sandbar to the sea. Boarding immediately with his oars, he rowed it far enough only to prove he could drive it against the tide, and then brought it back to the shore.

"One bomb and a torch," he meditated, aloud. "I can hang the bomb across my shoulder to keep it out of the wet."

The catamaran having been made thoroughly secure, he hastened away to the terrace. He missed Elaine. She was down at the "smelter," attending the fire that was roasting the new clay vessels.

With a bomb and his lighted torch in hand—held well apart and not for a moment handled carelessly—he hailed Elaine from the edge of the thicket by the wall.

"Just thought I'd drop around and drain out that water from the cave," he announced. "Everything's ready—and I've nothing else to do. When you hear the salute, you'll know it's a commonplace affair."

"Oh!" said Elaine, who had her doubts concerning his various explosions. "I'll watch to see you from the cliff."

"Well—er—I wouldn't stand just at the edge, you know—not till you know it's all over."

"You're not going to blow down the hill?"

"Hope not, I've taken a baby bomb, but I didn't wish to let it off till I'd told you what to expect. I'd keep away, in case of flying pieces."

"I will," said Elaine. "But I'll go up now, and perhaps you can call to let me know how well you have succeeded."

"I'll send you a wireless."

Grenville hastened to his raft. "Please God she may never have to hear me fire another!" he thought, as he went, reflecting on things that might happen. He could not have known that only a mild beginning had been made on their programme as scheduled by the Fates.

He was soon rowing eagerly and vigorously against the current of the tide, which would run with lessening velocity for perhaps another hour. When he came to the cave, he promptly discovered why the injunction to enter its mouth at high water only had been made a point in the mystic directions found with the map in the tube.

The ledge whereon he had landed before was deeply undercut. During a tide no more than two or three feet lower than this that would serve him to-day, the place could scarcely be approached, and could never be entered at all. The swirl, which was rarely ever absent from the place, increased in violence steadily with the lowering levels of the water.

It was not without some chance of catastrophe that he presently landed on the shelf. He lost little time in securing his painter to the rocks, the line so adjusted he could readily slip it from the crevice should a hasty retreat seem wise.

The task of blasting out the ledge was not a simple matter. To lodge the bomb where its energy would be directed almost wholly against the dam, or rock, and yet protect it from the trickling stream that could readily render it useless, involved an extra toil of piling rocks, on which he had not reckoned.

Fortunately, much of the thickest wall was opposed to the pot-hole in the dam, while one or two extra-heavy fragments from the cliff were so lightly poised he could drop them in the breach. Despite these natural advantages, however, he labored hotly for fully half an hour before he could even lay his fuse.

Meantime, his torch was blazing smokily, against his final need of igniting the match and later exploring for results. At length he looped the fuse along a ragged line of broken honeycomb, where pits had been eaten in the tufa, and trailed it well down to the brink of the ledge, with its end propped high between two bowlders.

With one last look at all his careful arrangements, he slipped off his raft-line, caught up his torch, and was stepping down to board his float when a sharp piece of rock broke away beneath his foot and dropped him forward on his hand.

The torch was flung against the fuse, where it lay along the slope. He heard it hiss, where the powder had caught, and aware that, by three or four feet, it was shorter now than he had ever intended to light it, he lurched full-length upon his raft and fumbled to clutch up the oars.

But the swirl was on, and the catamaran seemed possessed to bump against the ledge.

In a final desperate outburst of strength, he sent the thing shooting outward. Its bow would have turned in the whirlpool then, but he drove it clear of the point.

Like a madman he pulled at the clumsy oars, to reach the protection where the wall all but folded the basin from the sea.

His raft was around it—half of the raft—and another good foot would have covered himself, when the blast abruptly boomed.

Even out of the tail of his eye he saw the dull-red flare behind a blot that represented ragged rock in motion.

A fragment no larger than a man's two fists came as straight as a cannon projectile and struck the pitted wall beside his head.

He had ducked instinctively forward, which doubtless saved his life. But dozens of smaller and barely less violent fragments were broken away from the edge of the wall by the piece with the meteoric speed. One of these struck him above the ear—and down he went, face forward, on the platform, to hang with arms and shoulders loosely supported on the bridge that was used for the sockets of his rowlocks.

A rain of loose pieces hissed about in the sea. The cave belched smoke like a suddenly active volcano. The tide took the raft, with its motionless burden, and floated it back whence the man had come, but not so close in the shore.

Then up on the cliff, when the shock and hail had subsided from all the air about her, Elaine came inquiringly over to the brink, to receive some word that all was well.

The smoke still rose from down below and obscured the face of the waters. There was nothing Elaine could discover. She waited a time that seemed very long, in her usual determination not to seem unduly alarmed or importunate concerning Sidney's safety.

But at last she called his name.

There was no response. Her uneasiness increased. She called again, and moved along the brink, staring eagerly down at the sea.

Then at last a sound like a stifled moan escaped her whitened lips. She had seen that prostrate, helpless figure drifting down by the shore on his raft.

CHAPTER XXVIII

WHAT THE BLAST DISCOVERED

Grenville revived, with his characteristic pertinacity. An impulse to save himself was still alive in his brain. Actuated by its survival, he struggled galvanically to rise.

"Oh, please!" said a voice, that sounded remarkably familiar. "Please try to keep quiet for a little!"

Yet he had to sit up, with one hand to support him, if nothing more.

He was still on the raft, and there was Elaine, on her knees, pulling hard at his oars to drive the float ashore. She was dripping wet from head to foot.

For a moment Grenville regarded her blankly, while the situation cleared in his brain.

"What ho, skipper!" he said, a bit faintly. "You didn't swim out to this contraption?"

"You are bleeding," she answered, tugging no less stoutly at the oars. "I thought you might be dead. The tide was floating you away—and I don't see why—— Won't you please sit still and behave?"

Grenville had felt of his head, then arisen to take the sweeps from her hands, though the catamaran was about to ground on the beach.

"You did swim!" he said. "I should have warned you of the sh—— I'm an idiot!—trying to blow my head off!" He knelt on the edge of the platform and began to bathe his scalp.

"I hate that cave!" Elaine declared, with emphasis. "And I hate those awful bombs! I sha'n't have any clothing left, if you go on killing yourself like this every day!" She was tearing another bandage from her petticoat and felt obliged to scold.

Grenville was not at all certain it would not be decidedly pleasant to be wounded constantly. It was perilously joyous to be scolded and bandaged by Elaine. He certainly submitted most meekly as she now tied up his head. He was not deeply cut, and felt considerably aggrieved that the blow had rendered him unconscious.

"You'll find the skull isn't dented," he observed, "unless it's from the inside out."

"There's a great big swelling," said Elaine. "And suppose you had been killed?"

Grenville made no immediate reply. He was gazing abstractedly out across the water. His inner vision conjured up the picture of a brave, unselfish little comrade, swimming fearlessly out to board a raft whereon a helpless figure was lying—a pale-faced girl who would doubtless have had no hesitation had she known of all the sharks in the world. He could see her scramble on the float to ease him where he lay. And then her hot tussle with the clumsy oars, as she knelt on the wave-slopped platform, to urge it and him to the shore!

"I'm a thoughtless brute," he told her, finally. "But I felt the work was important."

"It is important! I'm sure of that," she answered, at once all contrition. "But perhaps next time—you might take me along—— If anything should kill us both—why, that would be simple and easy."

He understood her thoroughly.

"Quite an idea," he answered, briefly. "I was sure you understood the situation—— To-morrow I'll go and see what the blast accomplished. I shall have no more explosions, however—so I may not need a chaperon."

She was slightly hurt. His offhand speeches were not always absolutely welcome, despite her former attitude and declarations. After all, it was God, she told herself, who had brought this partnership into being. It was He who had cast her into exile with the bravest man she had ever known.

"You mean," she said, "you do not want me along."

"It's the tide that's ungallant," he said. "It objects to anyone's landing on the ledge."

"But you said I might be obliged to hide there later."

"I did, and till then—let's enjoy the sunshine—while it lasts."

Elaine said no more. The hint of inimical things to come sufficed once more to carry her thoughts away from all personal emotions.

They returned in silence to the terrace, Grenville first having urged his catamaran within the estuary, to secure it with the line. The commonplace duties of their daily existence were promptly resumed, and the cave as a topic was forgotten.

The following day, while he waited for the tide to rise to its highest level, Grenville completed the labor at the furnace, where additional vessels for water were being permitted to cool. The importance of being enabled to store an unusual quantity of water, should the need arise for such a storage, had early been presented to his mind. He was therefore particularly gratified to find this present firing of jugs considerably more successful than the first.

Elaine was engaged in weaving two nets, in which these clay vessels could be carried. With a yoke for Grenville's shoulders, or even for her own, a pair of the jugs could thus be fetched at once and the labor thereby materially hastened, should a moment arrive in which such haste would be wise.

It was ever disturbing to her mind to reflect on this possible need. The thought was never wholly absent from her as she watched the horizon, far and near, for the steamer that did not come. Not even in her happiest moments— and many were happy, she confessed, despite all the hardships of their daily life, as they two toiled together, an exiled pair alone in this tropical garden— not even in these was that sinister, underlying *motif* too indistinct to be acknowledged. It hung like a thing in vague suspense above their every occupation, throughout the day and night.

A tremor more tangible played through her breast as Elaine watched Grenville take a torch as before and depart for the third of his visits to the cave.

Without consulting the lord and master of the island, she moved her work from the shelter of her "house" to the cliff-edge, from which she could watch him a time before he should come to the cavern itself and so be lost to sight.

She was thus enabled, unobserved, to inspect him, to her heart's content, as Grenville came rowing his raft along the tide, far down below her rocky aerie.

The man was absorbed in the task thus set to be accomplished. He did not look up, as Elaine thought he might, as he skimmed along under the wall.

When he came to the cave he was somewhat surprised at the wreckage his blast had accomplished. Not only was the former ledge completely shattered, but much had fallen below in the sea, while the wall to the right, where the bomb had expended its energy, was agape with new-formed fissures.

Chiefly concerned with the dam of rock, Grenville secured his raft with boyish impatience and carried his torch ashore. A moment afterwards he walked through the breach in the erstwhile solid ledge, and could readily imagine the roar with which the water, formerly behind the barrier, had tumbled torrentially into the swirling tide.

There was still a tiny trickle flowing down the channel made by the bomb. The basin formed by the bottom of the cavern was still exceedingly damp, and here and there it retained a shallow pool of water too low for the gateway to drain. He walked about freely, pausing here and there to hold his torch aloft and measure the cave's dimensions by means of the light from both the open entrance and his blazing, yellow flame.

He was struck, in gazing at the wall he had broken near the cavern's mouth, with the size of one of the fissures there, where the blast had wrought its havoc. So black and significant appeared this new-formed aperture that, although a certain eagerness to proceed forthwith to the treasure niche was upon him, he returned at once to investigate the hole.

What he found upon his first superficial examination was merely a crevice, half as wide as his body, where a plinth of rock had been split from the mass and dropped towards the breach in the dam. Into this crevice he thrust his torch, and was instantly interested to note that its flame blew decidedly from him, in a draught of air that was flowing unmistakably upward. Moreover, on lifting himself sufficiently high to look about in the dimly lighted space, he became convinced that either a second chamber or a passage like a hall existed just back of the principal cavern, from which it was partitioned by the wall.

He planted his torch between some loosened fragments and shook at the piece that blocked this auxiliary cave. He thought he could topple the slab out forwards on the ledge. But, when he rocked it with his customary vigor, it fell abruptly backwards and disappeared in the gloom.

The hole he had thus created was quite large enough to admit him, squeezing in sideways. He promptly entered with his torch, finding the foothold rough and insecure. The chamber itself was small and low. He could readily touch the ceiling.

Ahead it apparently ended in a wall, with a gaping crack. On moving there, however, he found, to his surprise, an angular turn, still wide enough to admit of easy passage. The way under foot was slightly upward. It was pitted rock, but surprisingly free from broken fragments.

Persuaded at once that no other man had ever discovered this channel-like chamber in the tufa, and that therefore no treasure would be found concealed in its depths, Grenville continued onward with unabated interest, curious to see how far the passage might extend.

It narrowed again, and pierced decidedly upward through the bulk of the huge rock mass. Obliged at last to stoop too low for comfort, Grenville began to wonder if the thing would never end. It appeared to be exceptionally straight for a natural tunnel in volcanic rock, but Sidney began to realize its upward incline had rapidly increased.

When he presently found himself enabled to stand once more erect, he paused to cast a light on the walls to confirm a new thought in his mind. He had finally remembered a feature long before noted on top of the terrace itself —the long straight crack through the massive tower of tufa and the "slip" that had once formed a shelf.

Not without a certain sort of excited hope did he now discover unmistakable signs that some convulsion of the island had at one time actually parted the right-hand mass of rock from the larger portion on the left and permitted the former to drop. If this channel could only continue——

He went upward again, more swiftly, wondering thus belatedly how far he might have come and regretting he had not thought to pace the distance. Through a place ahead he was barely able to force his supple body. Then came another passageway that was not only narrow but low. Fragments of stone were likewise under foot, and the passage formed another angle.

Beyond this turn he found himself confronted by more broken stone and a difficult ascent. But, toiling up there eagerly, he presently raised his eyes and beheld a bright white line, as narrow as a streak of lightning.

It was simply a crack through a shattered bit of wall that closed up the end of the passage. It was daylight—sky—that he saw thus slenderly defined, and the man could have shouted in joy!

He could not, however, escape to the outside world when he presently came to the wall. For all the fragments he loosened and threw back behind him, he could not open the exit, or even determine where it was. Only work outside could accomplish this end, and this he was wild to begin.

About to turn back and hasten to the terrace, he realized instantly how utterly impossible might be the task of finding the place from without. But Elaine was doubtless on the terrace. If only his voice could be carried to her ears, she could mark the spot at once.

But, although he called with all his lusty might, there was no response from the camp where Elaine was doubtless working. His torch was burning low, with the draught fanning constantly past him through the channel. It occurred to his mind to go back to Elaine and instruct her how she could assist him. He also thought to place his torch against the crack and permit its smoke to filter through and perhaps thereby blacken the fissure.

Until he felt he must save what remained, to illumine his way downward, he burned the torch close to the rocks. And thus, when he came to the larger cave again, he was once more obliged to depart with not even a sight of the treasure.

CHAPTER XXIX

AN INTERRUPTED DIVERSION

Not only had Grenville to a small extent succeeded in smudging the outside terminal of the passage discovered through the rock, but also Elaine had discovered the smoke so strangely ascending in the air.

She had been thoroughly mystified by the singular sight, but had crept about the place inquiringly, expecting perhaps a volcano to begin some destructive demonstration. She had likewise fancied that rumbling sounds proceeded from somewhere in the "mountain." The entire phenomenon had finally ceased, however, greatly to her relief.

On a narrow ledge, some four feet down from the terrace-level, and directly beneath the extensive crack that had once been formed in the massive upheaval of tufa, the broken fragments that blocked the subterranean hallway were wedged to their places in the wall. The place was sunk in a shallow niche that was screened by the trees of the jungle.

This ledge Grenville not only promptly rendered accessible, but, after the opening had once been cleared, he fashioned a door of the lightest construction, that still resembled solid rock, with which to conceal it again.

His door was of wattle, plastered with clay, which he then thrust full of tufa fragments. These, when the substance presently hardened, were found to be substantially cemented to the framework. The clay itself dried yellowish gray and could hardly be distinguished from the rock. He was thus enabled to plaster over all the chinks and other ragged openings which the door could not completely cover. When the job was done, not the faintest suspicion of anything unusual about the niche could the keenest eye have discovered. Grenville was none the less glad, however, that the tallest foliage of the near-by growth still further concealed the spot.

He was toiling no less feverishly than before, thankful each day that the tidal wailing still continued and anxiously watching the round of the purple horizon for the cut of a rakish sail.

Despite the fact that several days had passed since the passage was discovered, he had made no effort to return to the treasure crypt below. The communicating gallery was too important to be neglected. He had spent long hours in its upper reaches, clearing the rock from underfoot, to make its use entirely practical for Elaine and himself in all conditions, either with or without some needed burden.

He had managed to widen the narrowest squeeze by chipping the rock with his chisel. He had carefully rearranged the broken fragments down where the corridor entered, or branched from, the cavern, and there provided a second of his wattle doors, considerably heavier than the first and more artfully studded with stone. This he had made to be adjusted from without or within the passage it concealed. From within it could also be barred in place with a heavy billet of the toughest wood his brazen tools would shape.

This late afternoon, when the last of his jugs had been taken down and concealed by the spring, all ready for filling and carrying back the moment occasion should arise, Grenville felt that, save for a meat supply, he had made nearly every possible provision against attack and siege.

The day was practically spent. He glanced at the sun. Undecided between an hour of hunting with his bow and a quick excursion down to the crypt of treasure, he remembered certain ornaments Elaine might wear and decided to go for the gold and gleaming jewels. They had meat for dinner, already being roasted in a sandpit with several newly gathered yams.

Elaine, with a basket of tempting fruits, returned to the terrace from the thicket before he was ready for his trip. The fact that he bore a torch and basket aroused no query in her mind, so frequently had he made his underground excursions.

He left the door at the gallery entrance open and made an easy descent. Glad to be independent of both the tide and his raft, he paused when he came to the main cave's ragged opening, for a moment thoroughly startled.

The weird tidal wail had just commenced, so close at hand it echoed all through the place. It had never before occurred while he was actually in the cavern. Immediately rendered curious to see whence and how it was produced, he hastened down the outside ledge, completely baffled by the intermingled reverberations.

He had barely concentrated his attention on a certain hole in the rock, below the tidal level, when the last uncanny moan seemed choked to a horrible gurgle which could not be renewed.

The thing had never before been so brief or so abruptly ended. Its brevity jarred upon him no less unpleasantly than its prolongation had done when he and Elaine first arrived upon the island. As if the occurrence sounded a warning not to be mistaken, he proceeded at once within the cave.

His mind was filled with thoughts of native visitors, who might only be waiting for this natural phenomenon to cease before they came swarming across the sea, perhaps to search and loot this very cavern. He reflected they might have searched it before, and had either been baffled by the water it formerly contained or had missed the niche his accidental interest had discovered.

Though he thought that less than half the wall he had previously assaulted could now remain in the arch of the treasure cavern, yet fully a half-hour's labor was essential before he could worm his way inside where the gold and the stones dully glittered. He cleared out a few more stones to admit his carrying basket.

A thrill went through him as he laid his hands upon the priceless treasures disposed in the tomblike place. Notwithstanding the fact the cave had been scaled, almost hermetically, a coating of thin, impalpable dust veiled everything he touched. The things had undoubtedly been here years on years, till perhaps tradition only still affirmed their existence, while old fanatics might, for generations, have persisted in tattooing that "map" on some victim's breast for the cavern's living concealment and the faithful preservation of its contents.

The gold was all wrought in ornaments—like anklets, bracelets, amulets, and girdles. It had all been crudely pounded into shape from virgin metal. There were pieces of odd, unfamiliar shape, the uses for which could hardly be conjectured. It was all of it heavy and massive, many pieces crudely resembling cumbrous seals with mystic devices stamped on either side.

Of the stones—comprising principally diamonds, rubies, and sapphires—many were still uncut, while others, by the handful, were crudely mounted in hammered gold to form girdle after girdle. A crown, exhibiting nothing of the jeweler's modern or even ancient craft, was none the less of extraordinary intrinsic value for the heft of gold that formed its band and the huge stones thrust rudely through its substance.

Despite his impatience to collect the lot in his basket and depart the place, Grenville remained there inactively, absorbed in a study of this piece or that, to identify, if possible, the curious workmanship. That much, if not all, the gold work argued craftsmen of the African wilds he felt convinced. But the stones could have come from India only, he was sure, either through tribute or plundering, and the latter was by far the more likely method.

He had heard from one of his oldest friends, who was likewise the best informed of all his military acquaintances, that the West Coast Africans still conceal vast treasures of kings or chiefs deceased, such buried wealth to be utilized by former possessors in some life beyond the grave. That this hoard, by some strange and unusual chance, had resulted from that barbaric practice he felt there could be no doubt. The fact it was hundreds of miles from Africa argued nothing against the theory, since either by imitation or as a result of far excursions over sea the present collection could have landed here in this remarkably hidden and "spirit"-guarded cave, where even the hardiest, cleverest seeker of fortune would never be likely to search.

He was still engaged, like some merely scientific archeologist, in examining piece after piece of the metal, or one after another of the stones, which were cut as never he had seen them before, when he fancied some weird, faint echo called his name.

With pounds of the trinkets in his hands, he returned to the broken heap of stones he had lately overthrown. Out of the ringing silence of the larger cave came a distant wisp of sound——

He knew that Elaine was calling from somewhere in the passage.

It was only the work of a moment to catch up his basket and place in its hold the small stone sarcophagi of jewels. Carelessly then, on top of these, he swept in the ornaments of gold. They fell, dully ringing, from the shelves, where perhaps they had lain for above a century—a heterogeneous collection which he was sorry to disturb till the various positions in which they had been disposed could be noted and remembered.

He was certain no less than a hundredweight of the treasure taxed his strength when he presently lifted his burden from the place and bore it across the larger chamber.

Elaine was calling again. Her voice was clearer in the passage. Grenville came there, panting from his effort, with his dusty and useless riches. He answered at once on entering the gallery, where he paused to close and secure his concealing door.

"Please come!" was the cry, in response to his shout, like an unreal voice from the blackness of a tomb. "They're here! They're close to the island!"

With a short but inarticulate ejaculation, Grenville once more took up his basket, blundered forward with it a few feet only, and set it down against the wall. Why he had paused to bother with it, for a moment he did not understand. With his torch flaring back, in his greater speed, he plunged along and up the passage.

Around the first of the sharper angles he came upon Elaine. She had brought no torch, in her hurry to sound the alarm, but had groped her way downward through the Stygian blackness of the gallery, calling time after time as the gloom rendered up no reply.

Her eyes were dilated wildly, from her efforts to see in the dark. Her face seemed intensely white against the impenetrable ebon.

"Oh, I thought you'd never come!" she said, as Sidney approached with his light. "They were almost up to the island before I dreamed such a thing could be! The tree must have hidden the sail!"

Grenville placed the torch in her hand and urged her upward before him. They presently emerged on the ledge.

He had no more than crept to the terrace-edge and studied the craft below on the sea than he came once more to Elaine.

"No use in striking our flag," he said. "They've seen it. We'll fly it till the end."

CHAPTER XXX

REVEALING AN INTENT

The native ship, that had sailed unobserved within almost hailing distance of the headland, was not the one that had come to the island before. It was larger. Six men at least comprised its crew, a villainous-looking collection.

Grenville had seen them close at hand, as they passed by the entrance to the cave. That they contemplated an immediate landing seemed probable, making as they were towards the crescent indentation along by the estuary's mouth.

Sidney had lost little time in vain regrets for the hour spent uselessly below. He had gone at once to the gallery and hidden its entrance with the door. He had caught up Elaine's well-finished nets and the pole for a yoke she had been working to complete when the visitors' sail was discovered and, only pausing to make certain he could not be seen, went at once to the spring for extra jugs of water.

The sun was already dipping redly in its bath when he brought his first burden to the terrace. He paused to observe the maneuvers of the ship, now coming about in the sunset breeze, just off the tiny inlet where his catamaran was moored.

The queer sharp sail was reefed while he was watching. He saw three men heave overboard an anchor, which promptly sounded the shallow depths where the strange craft presently swung.

Considerably to Elaine's discomfort of mind, he hastened once more down the trail. She was certain the Dyaks would go to the spring before Sidney could got away. However, he brought another pair of jugs, an armful of fuel, and a basket of fruit with the greatest possible expedition.

The boatmen made no movement to come ashore as long as the twilight revealed them. The highest notes of their voices floated indistinctly to the terrace, towards which the men were frequently seen to gesture, but even these sounds were finally lost as darkness enwrapped the island.

Despite the fact that four of his water-jugs still remained in the thicket near the spring, Grenville made no more trips for water that evening, since Elaine was obviously distressed by the thought of the risk he might incur.

He was awake all night, maintaining the life of their smoldering fire, and alert for any signs or sounds of movement in the clearing by the trail. In one of the darkest hours before the dawn he heard the familiar wails and moans of the headland cave rise briefly on the wind.

From the anchored ship the cry was returned, as on the former occasion. After that a droning chant came fitfully up from the darkness of the waters, to die at last in the silence. Later he heard a shout, and then vague accents of speech. But, when daylight arrived, the craft had disappeared.

Elaine had not yet risen. Grenville quietly moved from one extremity of the headland to the other, searching the sea in all directions. He was soon convinced the visitor had not decamped, but had moved the vessel to one or another of the island's hidden inlets, that its movements, as well as those of its crew, should be no longer observed.

One lingering hope, which he had fostered in his breast, that the natives might not prove a bloodthirsty lot of head-hunters after all, he felt he must definitely abandon. This furtive move under cover of the dark was not the sort of maneuver to excite one's trust or confidence.

Elaine was standing in her shelter door when at length he came once more to his place by the top of the trail. She, too, had discovered the absence of the native vessel.

"I think another one came in the night," she said, when Sidney explained his belief that the boat was in hiding behind the farther walls. "I am sure I heard another voice."

Grenville recalled the shout that had followed the chanting and felt that this accounted for Elaine's conviction that more of the Dyaks had arrived.

"We have not been actually seen as yet," he assured her. "Our flag of distress is not a positive sign of anyone's presence on the island. We shall soon determine by their movements whether these chaps intend to be friendly or not."

"Would they hide if they meant to be friendly?"

"It isn't a friendly sign—— You see, I'm still of opinion the island's wail is a sound they rather dread. Have you noticed it's rapidly failing?"

"I've been ever so glad it seems so short and growing fainter."

"Yes," he drawled. "I'm afraid it will soon cease altogether, when our friends may buck up their courage and—show us their state of mind."

"What can we do in the meantime?"

"Sit tight and watch for developments."

But all that day there was never so much as a sound or a sign of the crew they had seen arrive. At one time, just before noon, Grenville fancied some movement occurred in the rocks that crowned the second hill. But he detected no further indication that someone might have scaled the cliff to spy on himself and Elaine.

He had never in his island rambles discovered a place by which that hill could be surmounted. That easy access might be obtained on the seaward side he readily understood. He fretted under the long suspense—the uncertainty brooding over the island. He much preferred that the visitors exhibit a downright hostile intent than to feel that beneath the sinister calm of thicket and jungle might lurk insidious death.

He felt that Elaine and himself would lack for nothing, except fresh meat, for at least a couple of days, yet he knew that even their fruit supply was wholly inadequate for a siege, should the new arrivals make up their minds to starve them on the terrace. Rather than weakly submit to any such abominable tactics, he was fully determined to bring about an attack. But how was an open question.

When once again the night drew on the man was impatient and weary. He had taken no rest after all his long previous day of toil, yet to sleep and invite disaster up the trail was quite impossible.

"We shall have to divide the night," said Elaine, with her customary practical courage. "We have simply got to be sensible to preserve our strength in case we have to fight."

Grenville consented to give her the watch till midnight. The island's wail in the late afternoon had seemed no fainter than that of the previous day. He was quite convinced there would be no night attack. Yet he stretched a cord across the trail that must pull at his arm and so give an alarm should anyone enter at his gate.

Doubtless in this confidence he fell asleep with more than usual promptness. He was far more weary than he knew, and Nature demanded her dues.

Elaine was glad he could slumber so profoundly. The night was barely cool; she was not in the least uncomfortable as she sat at Grenville's side. She knew he would waken at the slightest tug on the cord so quickly contrived to warn of an enemy's approach, and therefore felt a decided sense of security, despite the living silence of the night.

Long before midnight she was tense with nervous apprehension. Sounds from the jungle arose from time to time where some animal prowled for its prey. A whisper came up from the waves that lapped the cliff, and haunted the air as if with spirits. She had steeled her heart, however, and would not weaken by a jot. The hours would wear away somehow, and meantime— Sidney was resting.

She did not arise to walk about as Grenville would have done. Instead she sat there, stiffly alert, turning her head from side to side, as the minutes dragged heavily by, listening, staring through the darkness, fancying shapes had begun to move in the shadows of the rocks.

It was finally late in the dead of night when a sound of unusual heaviness arose from the brink of the cliff. Had someone dropped a rock in the sea, the disturbance could scarcely have been clearer.

It had come, she thought, from over beyond the great black tree that loomed against the sky. She wondered if perhaps she ought to speak to Sidney. She put out her hand to touch him lightly on the shoulder, but withdrew it again with a smile. He was sleeping so like a tired boy!

The sound had doubtless been nothing to rouse the slightest alarm. If it came again——

It did come again, less loud and distinct, but none the less unmistakable. Her heart responded immediately with a quicker, heavier beat. Perhaps she should try to ascertain the source or the cause of the noise. She should feel so ashamed, so weak and burdensome, to Grenville if she woke him for nothing at all. To look about was assuredly part of her duty while on guard. It was only a step to the edge of the terrace, across familiar ground.

Chiding herself for unwarranted timidity and lack of courage, she silently left her seat at last and stepped from Grenville's side. One of his sticks was lying near. She took it in her hand. Then over through the shadows she glided as noiselessly as a spirit, goading herself to the ordeal with thoughts of the bold and fearless manner the man would show were he in her place on this safe and childish excursion.

She had heard nothing more, though she frequently paused to hold her breath and await a further sound. It was wholly absurd, she told herself, for her heart to pound so madly. Just there to the brink, past those few large stones and shadows, and she would probably hear some slopping of the waves that would quiet her liveliest suspicion.

Despite her utmost efforts, however, she could not stand upright as she went, and she could not continue quite to the edge without one or two more pauses to catch her breath that would not come calmly to her lips. But she forced herself all the way—save just the final cautious edging to the scarp, where she suddenly knelt and leaned a little forward.

She was still a bit short of the brink, but remained where she was to calm her heart and listen. She could hear the water plainly. She felt entitled to arise and hasten back to Sidney—since of course there was nothing further to be heard.

But, before she could gather the strength to rise, a series of short, percussive sounds all but froze the core of her heart—so much did it seem like someone heavily panting.

Then, as she sat there staring helplessly at the jagged edge, four dark things—four fingers—crept actively over the lip of the wall—and a face abruptly followed, with a knife between its teeth!

"Sidney!" she cried, and, madly thrusting the stick she had brought against the dark and hideous countenance, she arose and fled wildly from the place.

CHAPTER XXXI

THE SILENT VISITORS

Grenville came running across the rock-strewn terrace as if guided by superinstinct. He fancied a sound like a heavy splash arose from the base of the shadowy wall, and momentarily sickened to the bottom of his soul with the thought that Elaine had fallen over.

He saw her darting towards him a moment later, however, and caught her protectingly in his arms as she stumbled on a rock and plunged headlong against his breast.

She instantly regained her foothold and clung to his arm, brokenly stammering her story and facing back the way she had come to show where the loathsome apparition had appeared above the brink.

Sidney hastened there at once, armed only with a stone. Elaine, in a violent tremble, stood a few feet only away, having followed in unabated dread.

Not another sound could Grenville detect as he leaned above the precipitous plunge attempting to pierce through the shadows and gloom, as he watched for some movement below. Whether the man had fallen backward from the lip, to go hurtling down through the darkness, or whether he had accomplished some swift and silent retreat, Sidney had no means of ascertaining. Only the ceaseless lap of the tide made a whisper in the air.

He arose and returned to Elaine.

"I had no idea the cliff was scalable," he told her, quietly. "I doubt if that means of spying will be attempted again—— It was a beastly way of showing their intentions towards us, but I'm glad to know what to expect."

"Where has he gone?" Elaine faintly chattered. "If he should only be waiting to come again—— Such a horrible fright—— I don't know why I didn't faint, or what I did. I'm so weak I can hardly walk."

"Oh, you're as right a trivet!" said Grenville, with a ready comprehension of the need of keeping up her courage. "You can now retire with a comforting sense of having saved the night."

But Elaine's sense of comfort was a woefully negative quantity. She was shaken to the center of her nerves. She dreaded to be left for a moment.

Grenville, however, sent her off to bed in the most peremptory manner. A realizing sense that their trials had only well begun was his one deeply settled conviction.

"Cheer up!" he said to her, finally, "the worst is still to come."

"I'll try," she answered, courageously. "But please don't let it come to-night."

For more than two hours she did not sleep, or even close her eyes. Then she dragged her couch to a space outside her door. Every movement made by Grenville, as he watchfully policed the edge of the terrace, she thus followed for a time, half rising beneath her tiger-skin rug in her dread to hear him go.

When she finally slept she dreamed once more of the murderous eyes, the clenched white teeth, and the flame-shaped blade she had seen at the brink of the cliff. Grenville heard her laboredly call his name as in her dreams she once more underwent her disturbing ordeal, but he did not move from his seat.

At dawn she was slumbering more peacefully, a smile on her lips as she lay there facing his position. What a royal little princess of the island she appeared with her colorful robe lying out upon the rocks, her hair so much more golden than the tawny hide, and the warm, healthy glow restored once more to her cheeks!

Grenville was sure he had never half appreciated the wonder and abundance of her hair, the darker penciling of her arching brows, the delicate beauty of her features.

He presently once more bent his attention on the island that rendered up never a sign.

Neither the jungle, the summits of the further hills, nor the sea that stretched interminably about them enlightened his searching eyes. Save for that night experience, it might have seemed preposterous that enemies existed in the miniature world by which they were surrounded.

He crept in his cautious manner to the crumbling edge where Elaine had seen the face. There was nothing below in the water. He could readily follow the bits of shelf and succession of pits in the wall, however, whereby a daring, barefooted native might grope his way to the summit, even in the dark. It would doubtless be possible here, he reflected, to explode a bomb against the pitted surface and break away so large a cavity as to render all future ascents impossible. But this was a task to be deferred for a time, since he had no wish to acquaint the visitors oversoon with the fact that he possessed an explosive.

When he returned to the shelter again, Elaine had waked and carried her couch to the cave. Despite the fact the hour was early and the sun only well above the ocean's rim, she declared she had rested much longer than was either wise or essential.

Yet there was nothing to do for either, now that the day was begun. Their breakfast of fruits was soon concluded, then of occupation there was none. Grenville felt it inadvisable to move about too freely on the terrace, and thereby risk betraying the fact they were only two in number. A watcher stationed on the second hill could not, as a matter of fact, examine the entire top of the terrace, or even discern its principal features, but he might ascertain decidedly too much, should they carelessly expose themselves to view.

The morning proved for Grenville another exasperation. He thought of nothing by way of labor he could advantageously perform. Their defense, though crude, was fairly complete, and could scarcely be improved. To watch the edge of the jungle, hour after hour, where never a sign was vouchsafed his vigilance, was a dulling inactivity, yet a highly essential precaution that was not to be neglected.

By noon he was fairly in a mood to seek out the island's invaders alone, to hasten some definite action. That the natives intended to starve them into a visit to the spring seemed all too obvious. Grenville felt assured, however, the water down in the cavern would suffice for their needs, if no better could be relied upon, when once their jars were empty, while gathering fruit would not be wholly impossible under cover of the night.

With the thought in mind that only the trail would be kept under watch by the Dyaks, he made up his mind he could readily contrive a ladder-like platform to extend from the brink, whereby the distance to the nearest tree might be conveniently bridged to permit easy access to the jungle. Of creepers and extra bamboo poles he had laid in ample stock. For the lack of better employment, he began the construction of his bridge when their meager luncheon had been finished.

His mind, as he worked, spun schemes innumerable for the daily defeat of the natives. Aware that as long as the terrace could be held starvation and thirst would be their only unconquerable enemies, he entertained no end of plans for catching fish without bait and even trapping or fishing up small animals that might rove at night below the cliff. From these reflections he returned to the men who prowled about them after dark.

To secure his cord across the trail and thereby provide an alarm, or notice of the enemy's approach, from that direction, was a very simple matter. When he finally invented, in his mind, a singular "rattle" to guard the approach by the cliff, he dropped all employment on the bridge at once and began forthwith on the other.

What he made was a series of bamboo buckets, or cuplike sections of the hollow tube, with stones suspended inside to knock against the walls when the things were lightly shaken. These he intended to hang, one beside another, in a line from the brink of the wall, where a climber must strike them unawares and sound a resonant warning.

But he found, on hanging a pair some ten feet down along the face, where the man had climbed in the night, that the wind would sway them to and fro against the rock and constantly ring their hollow tones.

This defect he presently remedied by forming a frame, some ten feet long and one foot wide, in which all his cups were suspended, or moored, both top and bottom. They were thus so lightly hung that the smallest jar against the frame would joggle them all to musical utterance, while the wind could have no effect on any single one.

The entire frame was lowered down till it rested a bit unevenly on two projecting shelves of rock, where it leaned a trifle outward like a picture on a wall, as the creepers that held it from falling were finally made secure. When

Grenville, by way of a trial, nudged it once with a pole thrust down against it for the purpose, it rattled out a decisive alarm that one could have heard from the trail.

Grenville thereupon brought out a bomb from his store and lowered it down below the frame, and six or eight feet to the side. This was secured not only by the fuse, but likewise by more of the creeper.

Elaine, who during his absence had maintained the watch of the trail, now ran to the place, at Grenville's signal, for a moment's inspection of the whole arrangement and instruction concerning its use.

It was while they were there that the haunting wail arose for a gasping spasm. It had practically failed. Sidney doubted if its loudest note could have been heard as far as the spring. But still the end of the tiresome day developed no attack.

Grenville was completely puzzled by the tactics the boatmen had adopted. That they knew Elaine was present on the terrace there could be not a shadow of doubt. Even if the man she had thrust away from the cliff-edge fell to the sea and was dashed to pieces, or drowned, his friends who had brought him around to the place must have heard her voice and recognized its feminine quality.

They would likewise know she could hardly be alone, and would guess her companions were not numerous or likely to be armed. No plundered wreckage lay about the shore from which castaways could have drawn ammunition or rifles. It was utterly impossible for any ignorant natives to imagine the loading of a cannon or the making of bombs from materials on the place.

What, then, was the reason of their long delay? They could scarcely be waiting for reinforcements. They would hardly be dreading the island's "spirit" now, since the sounds had practically ceased, and one man had dared ascend the cliff with a knife between his teeth. That they feared an open attack by day and dreaded the tiger by night was the only tenable theory that Grenville could devise.

Yet the fact of the matter was that, until the cavern "spirit" should be absolutely silenced, the superstitious Dyaks could only be forced by the bulldozing threats and ferocity of their fiendish leader to set foot upon the land. It was he who had sent the climber up the wall, having thrust a pistol behind the fellow's ear. A certain tragic outcome of this premature adventure had been wholly attributed by the victim's companions to the anger of the wailing soul who inhabited the headland.

The bridge, constructed of bamboo supports, was a simple affair, completed and ready by sunset. Before the darkness was absolute, Grenville conveyed it along to the eastern jutting of the cliff, slid it down to a ledge below the level of the terrace, and easily thrust the end across to the nearest tree, where it rested securely on the branches.

He found that it bore his weight remarkably well. With an ordinary length of pliable ladder he could reach the ground beneath the tree without the slightest difficulty, thereby escaping all the undergrowth and broken rock that would render a straight descent from the brink not only a noisy piece of business, but likewise one of considerable hazard and discomfort. And descending thus, instead of employing the trail, he could certainly expect to escape the shrewdest observation on the part of any native set to watch for some night adventure.

Indeed, so alluring became the prospect of leaving the hill, to conduct some helpful and informing explorations, that he could scarcely wait for the shadows of night to settle on the island before he should test his apparatus.

Elaine was frankly and confessedly alarmed when at length he could resist the temptation no longer and announced his intentions for expending a portion of the evening.

He set an alarm at the gate on the trail, however, and, arming himself with his heavy, cleaver-like implement for chopping, instructed his worried companion to fire the cannon without delay should attack develop in his absence.

"I am sure you will have no visitors, but, in case you do, don't wait to see who it is, or how many," he said; "let the little gun count the numbers."

"But suppose—it might be you!"

"I shall not return that way. You may look for me back in fifteen or twenty minutes at the most. I feel it's important to know what is going on, as well as to gather a bit of fruit, and see what I may be enabled to do by way of setting some traps for game. If one of my snares could be brought a trifle closer, it might provide us with the meat we certainly ought to have."

Without another word, she watched him depart for his bridge and ladder to the jungle.

CHAPTER XXXII

DEATH AS A BROTHER

Despite the ease with which, in theory, he expected to descend to the ground, Grenville was fully ten minutes escaping from the tree.

A number of twigs that he could not have passed without creating a disturbance he cut away with his knife. His ladder was also badly caught and stubbornly refused to be adjusted. One violent rustling of a heavy limb he caused when it finally slipped straight down, with his feet all but striking on the ground.

He remained perfectly silent, ready for immediate retreat, regaining his breath and straining his ears for the slightest sound, for a long, uneventful minute. When he finally drew his sharp brass cleaver from his pocket and started through the thicket, there was not the slightest sound in all the region about him, either of animals or men.

Into one of the numerous wild creatures' trails he found his way with greater ease because of his thorough familiarity with all that end of the island.

The trail, as he knew, led down by the spring, where a branch wound first towards the estuary and then across the bed of the rill, where it cut the path through the axis of the island.

Almost as noiselessly as one of the creatures hunted or hunting in the hours of blackest shadow, he made his way down to the rear of the pool, where he paused as before to listen. The squeal of some little nocturnal beast and the patter of something paddling about in the water convinced him at once the Dyaks were certainly not there, or else were most skillfully hidden.

With a steadily increasing conviction that the boatmen would stick to their craft at night, he felt his boldness strengthen. The importance of discovering the enemy's position was duly impressed on his mind. He felt that once he could gain the principal pathway down the island's length he could follow the edge of a narrow bit of clearing, off to the left of the rotting old barque, and thus arrive above the inlet, where he was certain their vessel was concealed.

No less quietly than before he continued out around the spring, then turned to the left, in the narrow runway of the animals, and emerged behind the estuary, where absolute stillness prevailed.

He presently fancied, as he slowly continued towards the old-time wreck, that a murmur of distant voices arose from off at the left. This became a certainty when he reached his irregular clearing. Moreover, he was halfway only down this slope of rock and thicket when simultaneously, out on the tide, some eighty or ninety feet apart, two matches were lighted, as he could see, for pipes or cigarettes.

Elaine had been right! There were two of the boats that were anchored here together!

But, although more murmurs continued to arise, where a desultory conversation was from time to time renewed on either craft, he could by no means ascertain either the number of the Dyaks or what it was of which they talked. Satisfied with what he had discovered, and certain now the fellows were afraid to remain on the island after dark, he returned up the slope with an easier stride, determined to see what might be done by way of collecting some fruit.

He came once more to the main trail through the island, pausing to hearken once again as a sound of splashing in the inlet came uncertainly on the breeze. Doubtless the crew had dipped a pail of water, he thought, or thrown overboard some refuse from their dinner.

He had no more than headed again towards the hill where Elaine was waiting, and swung about from the branch to the principal trail, when, without the slightest warning sound, he suddenly and heavily collided with someone moving as noiselessly as himself in the opposite direction.

He only saw that the man thus encountered was bare of shoulders and taller than himself as he thrust out to fend the fellow off. He knew on the instant it was one of the boldest of the head-hunters, if not indeed their chief.

The fellow had grunted at the impact, and, quick to discover it was not a member of the vessels' crews, abruptly sounded one triumphant yell as he reached for his knife and lunged forward.

There were answering cries from a few feet only behind him—which Grenville heard as he crashed precipitately through the near-by thicket and made for the trail to the barque.

The hue and cry was instantly raised as the fellow pursuing came wildly through the jungle on his track. Shouting instructions to his following, this obvious leader of the prowling band continued as closely as possible on Grenville's heels, while the others headed swiftly towards the estuary, convinced that their man would dart around and make for his camp on the hill.

The chief of the natives entertained the same belief, as Grenville immediately comprehended. Having planned exactly as they had supposed he would, Sidney altered his course on the instant, dived down on all-fours in an animal path he had frequently followed before, and thus crept noiselessly off to the left, once more towards the plundered wreck.

Almost at once an ominous silence reigned as before in the place. The natives, having soon missed their quarry, stood perfectly still, at command of their chief, to listen and gain a new guidance.

Tempted to put all possible distance between himself and his pursuers, Grenville continued on, a bit incautiously. A branch he had thrust from before his face slipped back before he had intended its release. At once the listening head-hunters plunged forward again in his direction.

Fortunately, Sidney retained his presence of mind and continued to crawl on hands and knees, instead of attempting swifter flight through the branches that closed above the trail. With the sounds of his eager enemy approaching to a sweat-starting proximity, he dared lie perfectly motionless on the earth, till he heard them quietly exploring as before on the lines he must take to regain the terrace at the rear.

As silently now as a shadow, he wormed his way forward as before. He had gained perhaps a matter of twenty or thirty feet in this manner when, on coming at last to the edge of the clearing where the old barque lay, he heard the natives beating back, convinced that he had not passed.

For one moment only was he seized by indecision. Then he darted across the clearing unobserved and, slipping between the ribs of the wreck, as he had on a previous occasion, went rapidly groping to the cabin, where sat the mummy-skeleton in chains.

He had not achieved this maneuver in absolute silence, having sacrificed something to speed. Two of the head-hunters broke through the fringe of the thicket with furtive swiftness, as he noted through a hole in the planks. They were followed, a little further on, by the tall man first encountered, and later by a small but constantly moving companion, who disappeared again.

At a given signal two of the creatures ran swiftly about the barque, one going in either direction. They had evidently expected to corner their intended victim crouching behind the empty shell. When they presently returned to their leader, a brief consultation was held.

Grenville watched them breathlessly, aware that Elaine's position, alone on the hill, was tremendously jeopardized every moment he now remained away. Should more of the Dyaks be summoned from the boats—the time would be short for prayers.

Considerably to his relief, the three dark figures resumed the search along the edge of the clearing.

They were gone from sight for several minutes, and again returned, apparently persuaded their quarry had not escaped them back to the camp.

One even ventured to approach the barque and peer through its rotted ribs.

Grenville had quietly moved aside, though the darkness would have shielded him completely. When the fellow rejoined his companions again, the chief issued new commands. A brief expostulation followed. Sidney was certain that one of two things portended. Either the leader had ordered his man to go down to the boats and compel a force to land and storm the now half-guarded hill, which the fellow argued was more than he could do with Dyaks afraid of the darkness as well as the island's spirit, or the order was— to board and search the wreck.

Either was sufficiently disquieting, as Grenville controlled his breathing and watched for the next development to follow. He presently saw the tall, bare-shouldered native strike his protesting follower a savage blow across the face, thrusting something that gleamed against the shaken creature's ear so soon as he had righted.

The craven was then ready to obey. He accepted something that Grenville could not see, doubtless another revolver, and came forward as if to enter the old ship's hull—but not through the hole in her side. Meantime, the fourth of the party had once more appeared from the growth. He apparently suggested that crews from the vessels be summoned, doubtless to attack the hill. Also he presumably volunteered to go and compel their attendance on their chief. His gestures and those of the leader, as they thus conversed in murmurs, were all towards the inlet where the boats were anchored or towards the distant hill.

He who had plainly been commanded to enter and search the wreck took advantage of the colloquy to linger with the group. It was not until the small and active demon of the lot had darted away to land more men that the chief once more turned his attention to the coward.

Whining his impotent excuses and expostulations, the fellow affrightedly climbed upon the deck and was ordered to explore the cabin. That he might be killed by the desperate white man possibly hiding in the vessel's hold, the chief was well aware. The sacrifice of a man more or less was unimportant— provided the quarry was thereby discovered in a hole where he could not escape.

This fact was fully appreciated by two other persons concerned. One of these persons was Grenville, the second the terrified native. This shivering wretch, who had known for years of the terrible guardian sitting in iron chains within, blundered noisily about in the upper quarters, so afraid he could have offered no defense to a child's attack.

Grenville was undecided as to what he were wiser to do. To sink his cleaver through the Dyak's skull would presently be comparatively simple.

And, should absolutely silent death overtake this miserable slave of the man outside, the moral effect might be of value. It might be supposed by his companions he had died of fright alone. Yet Sidney argued that any fate whatsoever silencing the fellow now might be construed as proof of his own presence in the wreck.

Instantly deciding that, once they concluded he was not here, the Dyaks would leave and permit his escape, Grenville silently crept to the open door beside the dead man held in chains, slipped behind the rotted old partition, and, without a sound, replaced the door almost as he had originally found it.

The chief had meantime approached the barque, to order his man to the hold. To the musty cabin where "Buli" sat, the fellow was forced to stumble. Some report he quavered in accents of terror was not received with favor, and a new command was issued.

Grenville made ready to drop the man, should he dare push open the door. He was certain the craven had been ordered to this fatal exploration. But, instead, the whining demon lighted a match, to reveal all the contents of the place.

By the yellow light both this fellow and the leader, peering through the side, met the vacant stare of "Buli's" eyes—and both were frightened to utterance. The chief's brief note was a rigmarole of charm, to avert the evil eye. His slave's shrill performance was a scream, as the fellow reeled back, stumbling blindly away and falling as he went.

The pistol he carried was discharged. The fellow was wounded in the hip. His groans, as he dragged himself out on the deck, were drowned by the curses of the leader.

This dominant brute, having noticed the door where Sidney stood concealed, now ordered the second of his men to explore where the first had failed. As Grenville once more looked out through a ragged hole to observe the proceedings, this second fellow began a somewhat stouter objection than his predecessor had done, but was even more promptly cowed or persuaded to submission.

Meanwhile, the cries of a horde of Dyaks from the boats arose from the jungle below. They had evidently landed with considerable willingness of spirit, as Grenville was thoroughly aware. He thought of Elaine with a sudden sinking of the vitals. No sooner had the second of the natives started to mount to the deck, where number one still lay groaning, than a wild idea shot into Sidney's mind. At any cost, he must make one dash for the hill.

He quietly slipped to the cabin again, where "Buli" had long been captain and crew of the barque. The one brief glance he bestowed, through the hole, on the leader of the murderous demons, now hastening to the place, showed that ingenious savage standing perhaps a rod away and calling to the on-coming crews.

The fellow on deck was making sufficient noise to mask a fair disturbance in the cabin. Taking instant advantage of this fact, Grenville groped downward with his hands—and encountered "Buli" promptly.

"I need your services, brother," he murmured, grimly, and, finding the chain that shackled the sitting skeleton, he placed one foot upon its upper end and tore the staple entirely out of the rotten wood it pierced.

Bodily lifting the mummified thing in his arms, he hastened forward, to the hole that he alone had dared to utilize, broken through the decaying hulk, where he passed first his burden and then himself between the ancient ribs.

A cry had been sounded from within the barque. The chief of the Dyaks suddenly turned and rushed, knife in hand, upon the man he beheld escaping from the hold.

Grenville waited for him, deliberately. Just as the fellow lunged actively forward, Sidney thrust the hideous effigy of a human being into the arms and against the face of his wildly stabbing assailant and nimbly leaped towards the trail.

A sound of horror broke from the Dyak's lips as he rolled on the earth with the skeleton rattling down upon him. But a brief time only was he prostrate there with his terror. Uttering screams as shrill as a woman's and darting swiftly to meet his crew of men, who suddenly swarmed from the thicket, he headed a wild, fanatic pursuit where Grenville was speeding for the terrace.

CHAPTER XXXIII

THE GIRL BEHIND THE GUN

Alone on the hill, and already strung to the highest tension of dread by Grenville's long absence, after what he had said of a prompt return, Elaine had been struck with alarm to the core of her being, as the various sounds came clearly up from the jungle about the disintegrated wreck.

It was fears for Sidney, not for herself, that had finally possessed her fluttering heart as the muffled shot and subsequent cries floated uncertainly from down there in the darkness. She knew that Grenville had no gun, and was, therefore, certain it was he who must have suffered a wound.

With a blazing torch she had run to the edge of the terrace, to light Sidney home, if, by any bare chance, he had escaped. She was there, transfixed by apprehension, when at length, with cries like a pack of wolves, the Dyaks came racing towards the clearing.

Meantime Grenville had gained a considerable lead of the devils on his heels, and, on passing the spring, had caught a glimpse of Elaine with her brand of fire. He paused for a second to shout essential directions, lest she might have forgotten in her plight.

"Don't fire, Elaine, till you see them on the trail!"

With that he darted abruptly to the left, for the animal trail that would lead him to his ladder. He had no more than gained it when, with a chorus of demoniac yells and screams of triumph, the straggling pursuers broke madly into the clearing and darted across it for the trail.

Even then, afraid that Elaine might fail to perform her allotted task, Grenville sped up his ladder like a creature of the wild, and came to the end of his platform.

The Dyaks were immediately storming the barrier, the breach of which was promptly discovered, and Sidney's alarm was jerkily resounding.

Like a spirit of maternity, nerved to any ordeal by the sense of protecting one she loved, Elaine crouched low beside the cannon, her dilated eyes intent upon the trail. She had clung to a hope that Grenville might yet appear in time to take charge of the gun. But suddenly now, to her terror, four or more figures darkly appeared on the ledge above the gate, coming swiftly towards her position.

She thrust the torch desperately down upon the fuse, saw the powder spew out a shower of sparks, and rolled and tumbled hotly from the place.

She was suddenly agonized by the thought that the thing would fail, but Grenville had barely reached the solid rock when the cannon abruptly thundered.

A wide-spreading cataract of fire was projected in a red-and-yellow cone across the space between the brink and the wall behind the trail, as the powder poured its punishment into the ranks of the creatures leaping upward to destruction. The detonation, sharp, crisp, appallingly loud in the stillness of the island, fairly stunned Elaine, now kneeling helplessly among the rocks.

Shrieks of dismay and sudden agony immediately succeeded the explosion, while its echoes still rattled wildly back from the distant hills of rock. In the utter darkness, by contrast following the one brief glare, there was nothing to be seen along the path. But wounded men were staggering downward, in blind retreat, already abandoned by their unscathed companions, in flight below the gate.

Grenville had run to his store of bombs, instead of coming straight to the gun. He meant to be prepared against a second attack. As his active figure now appeared where he hastened brinkward, watching both trail and clearing, Elaine beheld him at last. She arose and stumbled towards him, her feet still heavy with her dread, her heart wildly leaping in joy.

"Were you shot?" she cried. "Are you hurt?"

"No, right as a fiddler!" he assured her, quickly, glancing down at the shadowy path. "I only wish I could bait them again and lead the remainder to the gun!"

He charged the piece at once, having brought for the purpose a bamboo canister of powder, open and heaping at the end. This he thrust complete down the muzzle of the cannon, to be rammed home with dozens of his slugs.

Cries still arose from the jungle, more faintly, now, as the Dyaks retreated down the island. Excitement still rang in the air. Neither Grenville nor Elaine felt certain the attack would not be renewed. There was something dark that Sidney could see, crawling painfully down the incline of the trail, assisting something more inert. He purposely shielded Elaine from the sight, lest she understand too well. He much preferred that the Dyaks recover their possible slain from about the place.

Elaine was still too tensely wrought for reaction. She could hardly understand how the situation had been changed so abruptly from attack into utter rout. Her ears were still ringing from the cannon's deafening roar. She had taken no time to comprehend the results of what she had accomplished.

"How shall we know if they do come back?" she questioned, excitedly. "They probably broke the alarm."

"I'll repair it soon. Did it ring? But, of course, you couldn't have taken time to hear. Did you understand me when I shouted?"

"I heard it, horribly shaken," said Elaine. "I heard so many awful noises. I heard you call, of course. But, perhaps, I didn't wait long enough, after all. I don't seem to remember. I waited as long as I could. I hope I only frightened them away!" She sat down, overtaken at last by weakness in her limbs.

The torch she had used had fallen from her hand. It barely smoldered on the rocks. Grenville extinguished it completely, then continued to prime the cannon as before, with powder sprinkled on the vent, and a fuse laid for several feet along the ledge. He was glad to note the little piece had been securely held in place upon its log by its wrappings and the weight of heavy stones.

"I'll go down and examine the gate," he said, aware that, though the Dyaks had undoubtedly suffered severely, a still attack might yet be attempted in the dark. Therefore, leaving Elaine to recover as best she might, he was soon moving cautiously along the narrow ledge.

The night had precipitated war. That he and Elaine would be called upon to endure war's customary hazards, hardships, and horrors he was grimly ready to concede. She had made an amazingly fine beginning. It was certainly not the time for him to weaken her now by misplaced tenderness, vastly as he wished to spare her shock and trial.

The crawling objects he had seen from above had vanished beyond the solid wall he had built to shut out the tiger. All the way down to this barrier he made his way, Elaine meanwhile watching from the cliff. There were dark, irregular blotches here and there along the rocks, and on these he scraped a hiding film of dust. How much of the contents of the gun had been expended uselessly against the wall could not be determined in the dark. He felt assured a heavy toll had been collected on the trail, if not in killed, at least in wounded and, doubtless, disabled men.

The cord arranged to sound his alarm had been broken in the charge. He found the ends, repaired the damage, crept further along to scan the silent and deserted clearing, then promptly returned to secure a basket, and boldly went down to gather extra fruit.

"I wish I knew where to get some meat," he told Elaine, as he came with his plunder to the terrace. "I don't know when I shall have another hour so absolutely safe."

But beyond removing his ladder and bridge, he performed no more labor that night. It was not yet late. Elaine was too excited to retire. She sat with him, nervously listening to all the far sounds of the jungle, as he kindled their fire to a blaze.

"I wonder how long we can keep it up—go on as we are going now," she reflected aloud at last. "Mustn't they get us in the end?"

"Well—not till we've made it a fair exchange, at least."

"There must be a dozen of them about us, six or more to our one."

"There were, perhaps, an hour ago, but hardly so many now. One shot himself, down in the jungle, gunning for me, while the cannon—— But your intuition was accurate—a second boatload did arrive to join the first." He added a brief recital of what he had seen and what had taken place at the rotted barque, sparing the details which, he felt, would more alarm than assure her, respecting "Buli" and the drama played at the clearing.

"Two boatloads!" she repeated. "What reason could they possibly have for coming at last to this island? They couldn't have known we were here—at least not the first who came."

"No," said Grenville, slowly, reflecting that the time for his revelation was, perhaps, a trifle overdue, "they came, I believe, to secure the treasure in the cave."

Elaine glanced up at him quickly.

"The treasure you have joked about before?"

"It was not altogether a joke. The treasure is there—or, at least, it was, before I removed it to the passage."

"Not something actually valuable? What sort of things do you mean?"

"Gold and precious stones—a lot of heavy plunder—enough of the jewels alone to fill a hat."

Elaine slightly gasped. "And they came for that? And you have taken it out —have hidden it, rather—and you think, perhaps, they have missed it?"

"No, I hardly believe they have been to the cave as yet. It isn't theirs, the beggars! Not that it's of any account to us, but I don't feel sure if I gave it up they'd depart and leave us in peace. At any rate, I don't propose they shall have it."

Elaine was silent for a moment, and filled with wonder.

"How did you manage to find it?"

"Entirely by accident. I pulled down a stone that concealed a secret chamber, where someone had walled it in. It has doubtless been there for many generations—as these fellows have probably known."

"And suppose they find the chamber looted—may they not be all the more savage and eager to tear us to pieces?"

"Well—I should say their ambition in that respect has already about reached its limit."

Elaine could still feel her heart pounding heavily in her bosom. She returned to her original query.

"If we go on like this for a week, what then? Is there anything in the world to prevent them from waiting and waiting and waiting, till——" She did not finish her sentence, but the slightest shudder shook her frame.

"They were goaded to action to-night," said Grenville, hopefully. "They may feel sufficiently aggrieved to return for more. If not—they must be invited."

"But surely you'll not attempt such a venture as this again?"

Grenville rubbed at his jaw. "I wish it might be duplicated! No such luck is likely. But I feel very certain we'd both rather cash in fighting than to starve like rats in a trap."

"Yes," Elaine faltered, in her quiet way of courage, "but—if it has to come —let's try to—receive it here together."

CHAPTER XXXIV

DYAK DARTS AND METHODS

Long-distance fighting began an hour after sunrise in the morning. It was rather a long-distance attack, since Grenville, armed only with the cannon, was powerless to retaliate, except at great expense of ammunition, and with questionable results.

One of the Dyaks had stationed himself on the central hill of the island with some sort of ancient rifle. He took a deliberate shot at Sidney the moment that unsuspecting thorn in their sides chanced to make an appearance on the western section of the terrace. The bullet went wide, having struck among the rocks some fifteen feet away, arousing Grenville's contempt.

Not even Elaine was greatly frightened by this overture from the enemy, whose marksman could have but a limited view of that unused section of the headland.

But the first small dart that sped lightly up from the jungle, to drop almost at Grenville's feet, was another affair altogether. He knew the thing was not only sharp, but literally soaked with poison. It had only to prick through the skin of one's hand, or even, perhaps, through the thinness of their garments, to perform its deadly function. The merest chance shot was thus extremely likely to achieve what the rifleman could not.

These hideous little messengers of agony and death were rained all morning on the terrace. They fell near the furnace for keeping fire; they dropped by the door of the shelter. A few even sped as far as the powder magazine, where Grenville found them on the rock and gravel roof.

Ample protection was afforded by remaining under cover, but this was not altogether wise or safe, except, perhaps, for Elaine. Grenville felt he must constantly watch the clearing. In the light of day his alarm could be discovered and removed, to permit an attack too sudden to be opposed.

He, therefore, constructed a bamboo shield, with which to protect his head and a part of his body, as he moved about among the rocks, or concealed himself near the cannon.

Not more than twice in all the morning did he see so much as one of the tubes—the long, slender blowguns of the hidden foe—while this silent bombardment continued. It was useless to think of slewing about his little brass piece for a shot at mere motionless jungle. It was equally impossible, he confessed, to excite the Dyaks to another charge until they should finally make up their minds a sudden assault would succeed.

He was rather surprised they had made no attempt to rush him at earliest dawn. The ledge was, however, very narrow. It afforded the one and only approach, and the dire disaster of the night before had rendered far more cowardly the set of treacherous and utterly craven murderers these boatmen undoubtedly were.

All afternoon the darts continued falling, intermittently—and Grenville made no response. His silence, indeed, was a mystery which the Dyaks not only failed to understand, but, likewise, a little dreaded. That he had no rifle they were thoroughly convinced. But that roar of his cannon they had understood, and to hear it again they had no appetite. Moreover, its deadly hail and detonation had come so unexpectedly, from the erstwhile silent terrace, that they knew not what to expect concerning the future.

Not without hopes of actually slaying some of the unknown forces on the crest of the hill, they shot an exceptional number of their darts from the nearby thicket as the sun at last declined. Grenville, having at length established what he thought to be a line of the little missiles' flight, hastily made and bound up a bomb of no more than two pounds' weight.

This, with a fuse too short for ordinary safety, he finally carried to the westward brink with one of his glowing coals of fire.

The patient rifleman, waiting on his hill, immediately blazed away, as before—and missed the entire bulk of rock. Grenville paid not even the tribute of a glance at the opposite summit, as he thrust his fuse down upon his coal.

The hiss of the powder gave him a start, so swiftly did it travel towards the bomb. With all his might he threw the thing outward at the shadowed spot whence he thought the darts were flying.

The quick, sharp bark and the patch of flame behind the design of a palm leaf, came like a clap of thunder, just before the second when the bomb would have struck on the earth.

A yell of dismay, or anguish, or both, and a scattering shower of shredded greenery supplied the only report of results that Grenville was destined to receive. The flight of darts was ended. A few hurried movements in the thicket, and a groan that Sidney felt was smothered, were the only signs vouchsafed him that the powder had not been cheaply wasted.

"It's a poor way to fight the hidden devils," he told Elaine, as he came once more to the shelter, "but it may possibly serve to keep them further away, and force them to different tactics."

It certainly had this latter effect, but not immediately.

There was no attack that night, and no disturbance in the jungle, though Sidney descended to the thicket and returned, not only with more fresh fruit he had located during the day, but also with a small wild hog he had captured in one of the older traps which the Dyaks had failed to discover.

The morning developed nothing aggressive, save the presence of the marksman on hill number two with the rifle that Grenville said would only be deadly around a corner. Some plan of patient waiting appeared to have been matured in the Dyaks' mind, since one of their boats issued forth at last from its place, to circle about the headland like a vulture atilt for prey, while down in the cover of the greenery other natives undoubtedly lurked.

They affrighted a flock of parrots here and there, from time to time, or set the timid monkeys to chattering and leaping through the upper foliage, apprising Grenville thus that the thickets were haunted below. No darts sped upward from the jungle edge, however, which, Sidney argued, might signify that the men with the deadly blow-guns possibly hoped to excite over-confidence in the keepers of the terrace, who might finally expose themselves to fewer, but more accurate, shots.

In his forced inactivity, Grenville once more waxed impatient. He felt the heat of the blazing sun, which was daily growing more intense. He chafed at the thought of doing nothing while their water supply was steadily diminishing, and the Dyaks apparently planned to subdue him by thirst or famine. He dared not risk an exposure of the door to the secret passage by going for water to the cave below, especially as all his jugs were porous and permitted the water's escape by percolation, whereas the supply in the basins below might be better preserved where it was.

A hundred useless plans for taking the war to the enemy's camp were presented to his mind, always to be promptly abandoned. He could only utilize his artillery for defense, and could not even hasten an attack. He could devise no means of ascertaining how many of the natives had either been killed or disabled. That fully ten survived, however, he felt was probable. One or two at the most was all the little cannon would be likely to rake in a charge.

Early in the afternoon there was ample evidence of exceptional activity down in the heavy jungle growth, though none of the Dyaks was seen. The movements of birds and animals, as well as the swaying of branches or trees in various thickets under the cliff, sufficiently advertised the facts.

Grenville was puzzled to understand what might be occurring, till, at length, he discovered that some of the fruit-bearing trees, on which he had counted for supplies, had been quietly denuded of their burdens, or even altogether destroyed. One large banana palm with fruit of exceptional quality, he even beheld as it toppled to the earth, where some fiendish head-hunter hacked through its fibrous trunk.

Something sank in his breast as he witnessed this atrocious vandalism, and realized his helplessness to avert the oncoming famine of himself and the girl in his charge. That the spring would be guarded, night and day, was, of course, a foregone conclusion. And not even a plan for goading the Dyaks to another attack came in working order to his brain.

That was a thoroughly disheartening day, sultry, and fraught with menace from all directions, as the Dyak craft continued to hover about upon the sea, and the pillaging continued in the thickets. All the work was, moreover, silent, grim, and ominous, with once in a while a dart spinning swiftly up from the tangle below, or, from time to time, an echoing shot coming from the opposite height with a bullet singing crazily by, or ripping along the rocks.

Sidney made no attempt to descend that night, aware of the folly of an exploration into the enemy's lines, and the utter impossibility of discovering fruit in a nearer portion of the jungle. His entire wild hog had been roasted. For, perhaps, two days the meat might keep, in the coolness of the passage to the cave.

Once more the night was uneventful, and silent. Once more came the day, and a blazing hot sun poured unveiled caloric on the summit of the terrace, where sultriness drank up the water that oozed through the substance of the jugs.

"I've got to do something," Sidney declared. "We can't go on like this." Elaine was already denying herself the food and water she required. "I shall try to invent some means of enticing the creatures to the cave below—and, perhaps, explode a mine. If the watchers on that hovering ship saw me disappear in the hole, it is rather more than likely they would follow, thinking they had me bottled."

Elaine always manifested interest, no matter what his scheme.

"But how could that possibly be managed, now that you haven't your raft?"

"I think by a ladder and platform, the ladder anchored as we had it the day I came up with your assistance, and the platform arranged of bamboo poles, which I can carry down through the passage. It will take me some time to get it ready—but something has got to be done."

Elaine's eyes brightened with hope.

"Please say there is something I can do to help," she begged. "You work so hard and constantly."

"There will be rather warm employment for us both," he assured her, in his former way of cheer, "particularly towards the end."

He brought his neglected ladder to the shelter, where Elaine was presently as busy as himself, rewinding the rungs in the creepers, and testing it all for strength. Just what his final plan would be she did not understand, but her confidence in his ability and resourcefulness was almost wholly without bounds.

The usual vigilance was not for a moment neglected, but nothing occurred in the world below, save a repetition of the former day's activity on the part of the unseen natives. It was not until well in the afternoon that the Dyaks' plan developed.

A breeze had sprung up from the north, bringing gushes of heat and jungle fragrance across the summit of the hill. Then, at length, as if this steadying wind was the final agency for which they had waited, the Dyaks set up a queer, wild chant from various places in the thicket.

A few minutes later a cloud of smoke arose from one of their centers. This was followed by several more. A huge, thick smudge was soon rising upward from the earth, and rolling on the breeze to envelop all the headland.

The Dyaks had gathered enormous quantities of resinous wood, and had deliberately fired the jungle!

CHAPTER XXXV

A BATTLE IN THE SMOKE

No doubts could be for long entertained as to what the smudge was expected to accomplish. Its dense and suffocating fumes not only rendered a further watch upon the clearing or the trail practically useless, but it seemed to Grenville highly improbable that he or Elaine could for long survive the pungent reek they were soon obliged to breathe.

There were two slight elements only in their favor. One was the passageway, through the rock, where clean fresh air was constantly flowing upward; the other was the very breeze itself that swept the smoke upon them. It frequently split the cloud of black and gray upon two juttings of the headland, or even beat it down and mingled its own overheated but acceptable ozone with the otherwise stifling fume.

Anger and horror together had lodged in Grenville's being. That the Dyaks would soon attempt a sneak upon them, under cover of the cloud, he felt was as certain as that hideous death must be their portion, were this business sufficiently prolonged. Even retirement to the cavern could avail them nothing but a short delay of the fate they must finally face when their food and water should be presently exhausted.

Under cover of the drifting smudge, he sent Elaine to the passage. As long as a breath remained in his lungs he resolved he would not desert his post, where he waited for attack by the trail. To permit the fiends to swarm upon the terrace, destroy or capture his powder and the gun, and prison himself and Elaine in the narrow gallery, was a thought that aroused him through and through.

All further contemplation of his scheme for alluring the Dyaks to the cavern was necessarily abandoned. The most he could do was to watch as before, and, perhaps, convey his bombs and stores to the passage, as time and his highly essential vigilance permitted.

Back and forth through the smoke he moved upon the hill, seeking the better air that came occasionally through the billows, and listening intently for the faintest sound from the always ready alarm. When an hour had gone and no attack had developed, his heart underwent a new despair. He began to doubt that the Fates would supply him an opportunity for further retaliation on the fiends below, who could finally overcome him with the fumes.

The drift of smoke was intermittently broken, near the trail, where apparently a current of wind that assumed a rotation as it rose through a half-round niche of considerable dimensions in the wall, swept vertically upward to lift the billowing cloud. Thus for at least a portion of the time Grenville could glimpse the ledge behind the trail where besiegers must finally pass.

So dense became the reek, however, that he feared his post must soon become insupportable. There was neither time nor air in which to arrange a longer fuse, which, as a matter of fact, would be too long for accurate work with the gun.

He knew at last the hour was nearing sunset, and silence still seemed to roll with the smoke across the enveloped terrace. His eyes were burningly filled with water; his head had begun to ache. He went weakly over towards the gallery, intent upon breathing a little fresher air before resuming his duties.

Suddenly, above the ringing in his ears, came a sound from his gate alarm. Its deep hollow tone was strangely resonant in all that blanket of smoke. He darted back, where lay his bombs and the short fuse laid to the cannon.

The smudge had, unfortunately, fallen like a pall, concealing all the trail. It lifted slightly, however, as a fog may lift over waters, revealing one half-seen form upon the ledge.

Then, in the second that Grenville laid his fire to the powder, his second alarm, from the frame of bamboo buckets, hung behind him on the wall, rattled out its xylophonic warning. The head-hunting demons, front and rear, were practically upon him!

He fired the gun. Its orange flame shot out through the smoke in ragged spears, mingling the fume of imperfect powder with all that reek from the jungle.

A gap was apparently torn in the rolling cloud, to be filled with a denser substance. Nothing could possibly be discerned where the charge must have splattered on the wall. There were cries in the air, but whether from pain, or the Dyaks' exultation, Grenville could never have told.

Aware that the demons were capable of sacrificing some of their number to the gun, to beget its discharge, and thus clear the way for concerted attack by greater numbers, Grenville promptly lighted the fuse of a bomb and hurled it from him down the trail.

It burst in the smoke, its red blot of fire a lurid illumination in the black and gray billows from the smudge. Again a cry succeeded, this one unquestionably voicing some wretch's mortal agony in the all-concealing fume.

Without for a moment pausing, Grenville plunged swiftly through the drifting envelope, to gain the brink at the rear. He caught up a rock as he stumbled half blindly onward, and blew on the fire of his brand.

A thicker shroud of the reek revolved about him, halting him there to gasp for breath, which he stooped in the hope of finding. He dropped the stone as a useless burden. Once more he staggered onward—and blundered against a Dyak, more blinded than himself!

The creature had scaled the wall despite the bamboo framework and its cups, or wooden bells! He and Sidney were instantly locked in a fierce and deadly embrace!

A battle as silent as it was swift and ferocious was curtained there in the smoke.

That the edge was near was a knowledge equally shared, as each man wrestled in desperate violence to overcome his antagonist and hurl him down to the sea.

More by instinct than design, Grenville had paused to grip his firebrand hotly between his teeth. He had seen that the head-hunter held a knife, which was instantly turned, as the boatman writhed in Sidney's arms, in an effort to sink it to the hilt.

Grenville, however, clutched the wiry wrist with all his might, and tried to fetch it upward for a quickly planned maneuver. It slipped from his grip, and together he and the native froze more savage than before. The Dyak once more attempted a stabbing pass, and Sidney again caught the sinewy hand, in a clutch that he knew must fail.

The wrist left his impotent fingers like a snake. The whole arm writhed backward for the stroke. Sidney abruptly leaned forward, turning his head, and jabbed the red-hot firebrand against the Dyak's eye.

With a shriek of pain the fellow lurched galvanically, to stab with demoniacal might. But the blow went wide, in his agony, and when Grenville had caught the wrist in a grip that a serpent could scarcely have broken, he instantly laid hold of it with his second hand, with a motion incredibly swift. Then turning his back with the skinny brown arm across his shoulder, and abruptly stooping forward, Sidney hoisted the scoundrel free from the rocks, on his shoulders, and, moving quickly towards the cliff, ended the fight then and there.

He broke the arm thus used as a leverage against the Dyak's weight, and literally slammed the shuddering creature down on the rocks, at the brink of the wall, where he poised but a moment over death.

If he tried to writhe backward to the solid ledge, the effort was belated. With a piercing scream he toppled over, flinging out his broken arm in a gesture grotesque and disordered. Then he suddenly grayed, in the limbo of smoke, and shot swiftly downward to his doom.

Grenville still bit upon the branch that glowed with fire. He searched about pantingly, found his end of fuse, and saw the powder sputter with ignition. He had barely stepped back when, from over at the trail, came a sudden and tremendous detonation.

That the Dyaks were there on the terrace, after all, destroying his bombs, was the one thought that flashed through the smoke in his brain, as his own sharp explosion shook the air and hollowed huge masses from the cliff.

He stumbled and groped laboriously across the uneven heaps of stone to reach the secret passage, where Elaine must be crouching in fear. In his ears rang her words "If it has to come, let's receive it here together."

Already he feared her one grim wish had been brutally denied her in this hideous pall of smoke. He saw a figure, dimly, through the reek, and crouched to take revenge.

CHAPTER XXXVI

THE LAST CUP OF WATER

The figure was Elaine's. Grenville was almost upon her, prepared for some swift and terrible deed of retaliation, when a swirl in the shroud that enveloped them both revealed her standing near the edge.

She still held a glowing fire-stick in her hand, as she peered through the billowing cloud of smoke where she had flung an ignited bomb. She had fled from her shelter, in desperate dread, lest a murderous fate overtake her companion, battling alone with the fiends. She had found his post deserted, and, having discerned two figures on the trail, had instantly obeyed an impulse to protect the hill with the only means provided.

She uttered a cry as she saw Grenville crouching behind her, raising her brand like a weapon, then sinking in relief.

"You!" he said. "Elaine! I might have known!"

"I am sure they are coming up behind us there!" she answered. "I know I heard the bamboo buckets jangling! Have you been across to see?"

"I fired the bomb," he answered. "Didn't you know?"

She shook her head. Her ears, that had been so finely attuned to catch the warning from the rearward cliff, had received or recorded no impression whatsoever of the huger disturbance, while her own bomb's colossal thunder and shock engrossed her eager attention.

"Was anyone there?" she asked, half choking with the reek. "I suppose you couldn't see."

"I saw no one when lighting the fuse," he answered. "What was happening here?"

She related what she had seen and what she had done.

"I hope I killed them!" she added, weak and dizzy from the smoke. "But they probably ran away!"

It was the first time she had entertained such a feeling.

He urged her again to the shelter, where he coaxed her to drink, and bathe her face, for the freshening and soothing influence of which she was sadly in need. Returning, then, to the shelter for some of their fruit, he groped his way down along the trail—and found that one or the other of the bombs had so shattered the ledge, as to render it useless for passing till the gap could in some way be bridged.

They were safe from invasion in the night—but they were, likewise, marooned on the hill! It was hardly likely the Dyaks would attempt to construct a platform across the yawning cavity, under the shadow of the gun, while, as for themselves, descent at present was entirely out of the question.

Meantime the smoke was unabated, if it was not, indeed, more dense and choking than before. All the man's characteristic doggedness of purpose was required in preparations for the night. The sun was down; the brief and usually comforting twilight seemed entirely absent, as darkness was hastened by the fumes.

Back and forth from the now deserted shelter to the passage Sidney groped time after time, fetching her couch and robe for Elaine, and their meager supplies for dinner. The gallery then became her boudoir, sanctified to her uses. Outside on the ledge, where at least a breath of air trailed upward from the cave beneath, to escape at the door and a little dilute the stifling smoke, he finally made his sentinel post to pass the long session of darkness.

He was roused repeatedly in the night by the sheer discomfort of his resting-place, and the smoke that smarted his nostrils. All the long hours through the dull red flames glowed fitfully, down through the jungle. He was tempted, times without number, to throw out his platform to the tree and descend with a bomb, to hurl at some group of the demons, there in the nether gloom of the Hades they created. He curbed his impatience rigidly, however, and crowded the impulse back. That one or two natives at the most maintained the fires was a supposition not to be ignored. The possible results of such an enterprise were incommensurate with the risk that must be incurred.

Despite his uneasiness of mind and body he slept for a time between midnight and dawn as the mere result of overstrain and the weariness accumulated for several days.

For a brief time after sunrise the northerly breeze abated, permitting the smoke to ascend more nearly straight. The headland was thereby freed and sweetened, only, however, to be re-enveloped later, and, veiled from the other features of the island.

Grenville took advantage of the respite to make an examination of the cliff at the rear of the camp. It had been so shattered, where the bomb shook down the disintegrated tufa, that its ascent would never again be attempted. The framework of bamboo cups was gone. There was nothing below to indicate whether or not a Dyak boat might have been swamped by falling rock.

The cavity torn in the regular trail was rather more exaggerated than diminished by the morning's revelations. Grenville was certain the enemy would hardly hazard bridging the gap while they thought a single ounce of punishment remained upon the terrace. He was not altogether certain he should not construct a bridge himself, since only when they charged upon his position could he hope to decimate the blood-desiring savages, who must still remain in menacing numbers on the island.

The little brass cannon was once more charged, though its use was hardly likely. The wind and the smoke resumed their steady flow across and about the hill before Elaine appeared.

She was pale and plainly weary, when at length she emerged from the passage. Her sleep had been broken, and haunted by dreams of countless new atrocities committed by the demons below. Her courage was phenomenal. She made no complaint, but attempted a smile and a cheery outlook on the day.

Grenville was wrung, more than comforted, at the wistful effort she was making to sustain her slender hope and encourage his own flagging spirit. When he found that hardly a pint of water remained in the jugs he had thought would supply them at least for a couple of days, his despair for Elaine became intensely acute, and his heart began dully to ache. Two of the clay receptacles had developed tiny cracks, perhaps from the jarring of explosions, while a third had toppled over and spilled its precious contents after having been placed in the passage. Percolation and usage had drained the others inevitably —and the day was beginning with heat and stifling reek.

Much of the fruit that Sidney had gathered was now unfit for use, and was, therefore, thrown away. By way of conserving the water supply, they made a breakfast of paw-paws and bananas only, though the meat remaining from the previous day was still acceptable.

Grenville descended to the cavern as soon as this scant and oversweet meal was concluded. He bore two jugs, to be filled from the basins in the rock. When the light from the blazing torch he held above his head dimly outlined but one of the pools he had seen on a former occasion, he realized that some insignificant fissure must have resulted from his blast, and permitted the other pools to trickle to the sea.

He filled his jugs with the utmost care, scooping up the water at the deepest hole to leave all unclean sediment undisturbed. That the pool must soon succumb to evaporation was obvious. Vaguely he wondered which might last the longer, this underground well, or the breath in his body and Elaine's.

Even the sight and touch of the precious water excited his mouth to thirst. With the jugs both full and set carefully aside, he sprawled out eagerly, flat on the rocks, for a deep and satisfying draught.

Hardly had the water reached his palate, however, when he lifted his head with a sound like a stifled groan. The pool was connected with the tides—*the liquid there was brine!*

He rose to his knees, with his fist before his eyes, his whole body tense and rigid with his soul's recoil from the visions abruptly shadowed in his mind. The cordon about the helpless girl was so hideously complete! It seemed like the bitterness of her doom that he tasted on his tongue.

It appeared so useless now to struggle. How he should take this latest news to the uncomplaining comrade of his destiny was more than he could determine. Wild thoughts of offering all the treasure he had found, as ransom for Elaine at least, possessed his mind, as he conjured up the final, triumphant approach of the Dyaks, whom the two famished keepers of the terrace would at length be no longer able successfully to resist.

He likewise thought of offering himself, could Elaine be finally spared. But through it all he was sickeningly conscious that neither course could avail with these treacherous fiends. A human head was more to them than treasures of earth or heaven. Moreover, the murderous savages had already paid a heavy toll, and would smart in their blood for revenge.

There could be no bargain made with such an enemy, all but victorious already, and certain of final success. They should never find that treasure, however, Grenville swore, if he had to sink it in the sea! And as for a final triumph—there were many ways, in a last extremity, whereby at least the unspeakable horrors, certain to follow their capture alive, could be escaped by both himself and Elaine.

Wild rage possessed him, kneeling there, as he thought of the merciless head-hunters smoking them out on the hill, and waiting as loathsomely as vultures for the slowly approaching end. Mad plans for sinking their anchored boats, for loading himself with torch and bombs, to charge like a Nemesis through their ranks, or for luring them up to some deadly mine, ranged erratically through his brain.

He thought of attempting a condensation of sea water to provide Elaine with drink. He was swiftly possessed by a plan, even more absurd, of making a float with his bamboo stems, and sailing away with Elaine on board, under cover of the darkness.

He arose at last, dizzy, with the vortex of impractical suggestions revolving in his mind. He emptied his jugs and strode to the mouth of the cavern, looking out on smoke and sea. The tide was low. Whole colonies of mussels clung there below him on the rocks. They were food! The thought came home to him swiftly—only to be immediately succeeded by the realization they were salt, and would make for greater thirst. He thought of the wail that had formerly haunted the island—a friendly, invaluable phenomenon that had not been repeated for days. He thought of the raft he had rowed with such ease when he came here to blow out the ledge. Was it floating still in the estuary's mouth, or had some of the Dyaks destroyed it?

The estuary!—could he only reach its tepid pool, creep towards its source, fill one of his jugs, and return to gladden Elaine! His busy mind was instantly working on the various steps by which he might succeed in lashing together some sort of raft, for a night excursion to the tiny rill that fed the vine-surrounded inlet where the water was not brine.

CHAPTER XXXVII

A BREATHLESS MARGIN

Grenville returned for his jugs and the torch, impatient to be employed. The clay receptacles were useless on the hill, but he carried them back to the gallery, to leave them on the floor. The lower rock-and-wattle barrier he carefully readjusted to its place, and secured with the bar of wood.

"The water below is rather poor," he informed Elaine, when he once more rejoined her above. "I believe I can reach a supply considerably better by building a bamboo platform that will give me access to a larger and fresher pool."

laine was thinking of another, more personal danger.

"Do you think these creatures have visited the cave?"

"If they have, they left no signs."

"You are not afraid they may go there soon—and discover the end of this passage?"

Grenville shook his head. "I only wish they would try—every man Jack of them hunting there at once! If it weren't for this smoke, I should try to lure them in!"

Glad of an occupation, no matter how forlorn the hope it afforded, he went promptly to work fetching all of the largest bamboo stems from his generous supply, together with wood for fuel and many lengths of creeper. By the time these various transfers were complete, he had left but little of their meager possessions in or about the former camp.

Bombs, fuses, torch-wood, and much of his extra powder he now proceeded to store along the wall, and in a niche of the gallery, where they should neither obstruct the passage under foot, nor yet be exposed to possible accident from necessary fire. The terrace continued to be wrapped in smoke, as on the previous day. Instructing Elaine to call him instantly, should any attempt be made by the Dyaks to bridge the gap on the trail, he now began the laborious task of carrying one after another of the bamboo stems down the passage to the cave.

The stems were large, some of them fully six inches through at the butt, and while they were never heavy, yet the twelve or more feet of length to which he had reduced them made their transfer through the narrow and angular gallery an awkward and troublesome maneuver, with only a torch for light.

He had made up his mind that six of these stems, lashed together in pairs, or even laid side by side, and slightly separated, would complete a float on which he could readily find sufficient buoyancy for himself and a couple of water jugs, more especially as he thoroughly intended to stretch himself out flat, full length, upon it while moving about the shore. He felt, moreover, it must be so light he could not only launch it from the cave, but even withdraw it inside again, should danger so require.

Fortunately, he reflected, none of the stems was split. Each comprised a set of water-tight compartments that a load of double his avoirdupois could hardly sink beneath the surface. If he found that four of the lengths would answer as well as six, he would certainly use no more.

As he stumbled and edged his way downward once again, with the last of his load colliding here and there along the wall, he thought, perhaps, it might be possible to test the float in the salty pool that remained in the basin of the cavern. Could this be done, much time would be saved, and no risk of being discovered at his work need be incurred.

For his greater convenience in assembling materials and tools, he placed both his torch and final burden for a moment within the passage, when he came once more to the cave. Three of the bamboo stems were then in the cavern proper, while all of the creeper and the other essentials remained on the gallery floor. He paused to wipe his brow, for he was sweating. His mouth was dry with a growing thirst that refused to be forgotten.

He had barely stepped out to survey the space for the likeliest site convenient to his needs, when, abruptly, a human voice sent a murmurous echo through the hollow tomb. A sharp command immediately followed—all in some barbaric tongue. But before the noise of something dully scraping on the outside ledge could add its confirmation to the somewhat belated alarm, Grenville was certain that a Dyak boat had come to the cavern, and its crew were about to land.

Instantly pouncing upon the nearest length of his precious bamboo, he darted with it to the passage. The second stem struck on the inner wall, not only delaying his movements, but sounding a thud that he felt must be heard through all the vast bulk of the hill.

Yet he dared not either betray the fact he had been in the cave, or lose that final pole. Once more, as he heard the Dyaks coming, and even beheld a shadow, preceding its owner to the place, he darted silently out at his door to lay hold of the last remaining stem.

He was certain its end must be plainly seen, as the Dyaks now rose above the ledge. A sound that he made seemed incredibly loud—and his door was out where the boatmen's torch must play a red light upon it!

He stumbled across his materials, now congesting his narrow space. He thrust out an arm, laid hold of his door, and had barely drawn it across the opening when the glare of the torch the Dyaks held sent red rays in upon him.

Not another move could he make without betraying his presence near at hand. To adjust the barrier solidly in place might readily prove fatal. To leave it loose, a palpable sham where all should appear as solid wall, was scarcely less of a risk.

Holding it firmly, lest it slip, and peering breathlessly out through the chink which it failed by an inch to cover, Grenville beheld three half-naked forms, incredibly magnified and diabolized not only by the torch they held, but also by the shadows they cast upon the rocks, and the general aspect of the region, black as Inferno. Three thinner, more furtive fiends of the nether abyss would have been hard, indeed, to imagine. In the tallest Sidney recognized the chief.

As they turned about to scan the wall, and the breach he had made with his explosion, the whites of their eyes and the gleam of their teeth rendered all of their faces strangely hideous, with the yellowish glare projecting them indistinctly against the ebon of the tomb.

That their keen, malicious eyes must instantly discover the wall's decided imperfection, where the gallery door was askew, seemed to Grenville inescapable. They motioned towards him, and down at the floor, in manifest wonder that the place was no longer filled with water. Their voices were low. They spoke as if with a certain awe in which the place was held.

It seemed to Grenville they would never go about their business. His muscles ached with the unaccustomed strain put upon them to support the heavy door. How long he could stand there, making no sound, and permitting no movement of the barrier, was a question he could not answer. If only his cleaver had not been dropped around the bend, beside his torch, he would almost have dared spring out on the unsuspecting Dyaks to brain them where they stood!

At thought of his torch, redly glowing, in beyond, he sweated anew, convinced that as soon as the boatmen grew accustomed to the darkness of the cavern, these torch rays must impinge upon their vision, and instantly divulge the secret of the passage to the top.

One of the Dyaks now approached even closer than before. Savagely determined he would slay the man, should he raise a hand, or otherwise give the slightest intimation that the door was seen at last, Sidney grew hot in his farthest pulse, and became as tense as a tight-coiled spring as he steadied to leap from the place.

But the man in command now grumbled another of his orders. The fellow so near discovery and death turned slowly about, made one more gesture towards the shattered ledge, and followed the other where they made their way across the uneven floor.

Until they had passed to a second ridge, where their feet disturbed a few loose fragments that rattled down towards the base, Grenville made not the slightest move to alter his position. Then cautiously, without a sound, he adjusted the door to its proper place and secured it with the bar.

He still had a chink through which to peer, but he first moved back to his blazing torch and smothered its light on the rocks. When he once more groped his way to the tiny opening, the Dyaks had come to the rifled chamber. He could hear their exclamations of disgust and anger, but only their torch could be seen.

Aware they might still return to his wall and discover the one remaining retreat where Elaine was even remotely secure, Grenville was seized with an irresistible impulse to destroy the fiends on the instant, if such a denouement could be rendered possible.

He turned about to grope his way upward and secure a bomb as swiftly as the darkness would permit. Over the basket of treasure, some time since deposited there by the wall, he blundered, and fell to his knees. The thing was in the way. He took it up impatiently and carried it well up the passage to one of the broadest galleries, where he placed it again on the floor.

With one of the smallest of his bombs, and carrying one of his firebrands only for a torch, he once more descended, feeling his way along the wall, eager to regain the lower entrance, lest it might be already discovered. He had been delayed in securing the brand, without which his bomb was useless. He had told Elaine his measures were only of defense.

They were hardly even that. When he came to the door he could see no torch, for the Dyaks had gone, in new exasperation, and their voices echoed back from the ledge. The impulse to rush out thus belatedly, ignite his fuse, and hurl his engine of destruction upon them, or their boat, was one he curbed with difficulty, at the dictates of sober sense. For a dozen reasons the maneuver might fail to destroy the murderous trio. And should one escape to advertise the fact he was somehow concealed in the cavern, no possible cleverness could avail to protect Elaine or himself.

Should a larger number come to the cave—— But he knew it was hardly likely, now, that even a few would return. If the Dyaks had, as he felt convinced, concluded that the open niche meant that the tomb had been pillaged, that the treasure was gone, either taken by himself or another, they would have no conceivable reason left for courting disaster here again. For unless they should dare approach the place by night, it was only under cover of the rolling smoke they would risk attack from above.

He even thought of hastening back to the terrace now to drop a bomb upon them. It was only a recollection of the all-engulfing smoke that halted this intent. Instead he dislodged the wooden bar, removed the door to his secret gallery, and crept out to glide to the breach in the ledge for a possible view of the boatmen.

Only the disappearing end of their craft was shown through the fumes that veiled the tide. It was Grenville's useful catamaran, as he instantly discerned. A new resentment burned in his blood, but left him as helpless as before.

CHAPTER XXXVIII

GRENVILLE'S DESPERATE CHANCE

At noon Elaine reluctantly consumed the last remaining drop of water. Grenville had taken a sip, and pretended to take a swallow. To refuse it longer, Elaine quite clearly comprehended, would be but to see it ooze away through the jar, to be drunk by the merciless heat.

"I shall get a new supply," said Sidney, attempting an accent of cheer, "but I'd rather avoid using that of the cavern, for fear it may not be wholesome."

Elaine, in her way of divining the truth, was only partially deceived. She felt that the water below in the cave was wholly unfit for consumption. She knew that if anything even remotely possible could be done to refill their vessels, Sidney would have filled them long before.

She made no discouraging comments, however, despite the fact her hope was succumbing to despair. The smoke continued to roll in sullen clouds across and about the terrace; the sun beat down through it redly, soaking the rock in caloric, that sank to the gallery itself.

The noonday meal had been slight and unrefreshing—a bit of fruit, too warm and too ripe for relish on the palate, and a few odd scraps of the meat. It was water that both insistently craved, and for which they grew fevered and distressed.

The smoldering brands in the furnace of rocks could not be permitted to die away in ash. Elaine had undertaken the maintenance of this, their altar spark, which rarely rose to a flame. She was safe enough to come and go from the passage entrance to the nearby furnace Grenville had moved to facilitate her duties, but the smoke seemed far more stifling and hot than it had the previous day, while, with headache, thirst, and a heaviness in all her weary being, the endlessly cheerful and courageous little companion of Grenville's maddening ordeal felt ready to drop and rise no more.

Again at his task of constructing a float that should bear him from the cavern to the inlet formed by the spring, Sidney toiled with no mercy to himself in the workshop far down in the rocks. He felt at times he must gulp down even the water of the sea, so parched was his throat, and so craving was his system.

At five o'clock his bamboo raft was completed, even with braces for his jugs. It had also been tried in the basin of the cave, and made finally ready for launching. But the tide would be low till eight. His blast had made the water more approachable than formerly, yet to fight his way against a powerful current would over-tax his strength. In any event he must wait for the darkness of night.

He returned to Elaine, and although he, too, was weary to the bone, her patient endurance of suspense and suffering aroused him to a state of anguish in which no exhausting task would have seemed too great for him to undertake. He was wrung by her wistful attempt at a smile.

"The day is nearly done," she said. "The night is sure to be cooler."

It was considerably cooler, but scarcely more fresh, since the smoke appeared to pour in even vaster volumes from the greenery below. That the Dyaks were keeping strict watch on the water supply there could be no reason to doubt. From time to time a weird bit of chanting arose from that fume-creating garden that had once been so fair as to win from Elaine the prettiest name she knew.

Grenville felt certain, in fact, the boatmen's camp had been made about the inlet or the spring. The short stretch of beach where he and Elaine had landed, and where he had later made a bower of the trees, would be certain to attract these half-amphibious savages, though their boats were moored behind the opposite hill.

For a time he wondered if he might not be more wise to pass entirely around the island, to approach the pool of fresh water from below. But reflecting that various currents of the tide would buffet and beset him, in addition to which he must run the gauntlet past the Dyak boats, he surrendered the suggestion without delay, and impatiently awaited the tide.

Three times he went down the passage, torch in hand, to examine the stages of the water. At length he bethought him of two short scoop-like paddles, to assist in propelling his craft, and feverishly set about their construction.

They were done in less than half an hour, since they consisted merely of two half-sections of bamboo cylinder, lashed to a pair of handles.

Elaine was aware he was making ready for more than an ordinary adventure, as she watched him with her wide and lustrous eyes.

"Perhaps relief may come to-morrow," she finally observed. "You are quite exhausted. Might you not be wiser to rest to-night? We can get along, I am sure."

But even her voice made a rasp in her throat, so distressed was her system for water.

"I need a bit of change," he said. "It is certain to do me good."

With a touch of his former brusqueness, he presently bade her seek her couch, during the time he expected to be gone, and vanished once more down the dark, steep passageway, with his paddles and torch in hand.

The torch was left in the gallery, extinguished. The concealing door was adjusted to its place. These were mere precautions against the cave's discovery, yet Grenville was certain no Dyaks would approach the place that night. His two best jugs were placed on the ledge; his cleaver was hung at his belt. He could take no bombs or lighted brands on such an expedition.

The task of launching his raft on the tide involved unexpected labor. Its lightness made it an easy prey to the swirl that always filled the cavern's walled approach. It was sucked once nearly under, its farther end disappearing entirely from view—and Granville withdrew it, desperately glad the jugs had not been placed upon it.

Awaiting a quieter mood of the whirlpool, half seen in the darkness, he launched the float again, and beheld it rest there, quietly, nosing against the ledge. He turned for the jugs, but, casting a quick glance backward, at the slightest of scraping sounds, saw the raft swinging outward from his reach.

His arm was too short for its recovery. Leaping wildly out in the water, he caught it again, and was washed against the jagged wall before he once more returned it to the landing. He was soaked to the skin, but his pulses throbbed with heat and dogged energy that would think of no defeat.

With his jugs finally laid flat between the bamboo supporters, front and rear, and with paddles in hand, as he lay at full length on the light but half-submerged platform, he rowed the raft out with a motion as if he were swimming.

Indeed, like a giant oar-bug, more or less helplessly carried by the current that it rides, he spun slowly about in the maelstrom of the gathering tide before he could escape past the portal and head for the inlet below.

He soon discovered that to continue far in this fatiguing attitude would abominably strain his neck, if not his entire body. Not without considerable difficulty, in balancing the craft, he effected a change of position, and knelt upon the supports.

The waves washed up about his knees and feet, but of this he was practically oblivious. Assisted now by the current, and with eyes intent on the darkened shore, beyond the uprise of the cliff, he propelled himself much farther out than formerly, with the purpose of avoiding the possible vigilance of Dyaks on the beach.

The night was not exceedingly dark, so brilliant was the light from the stars. Once the region of smoke was left behind, the blurred and blended features of the island were sufficiently well revealed for his purposes, since he knew its every silhouette as well as the contours of the coast.

He had rowed and drifted, perhaps, half the distance essential to land at the estuary mouth, when the sound of voices, floated out from the shore, abruptly halted his movements. The Dyaks were there. Either motion or any unusual disturbance would suffice to betray his presence off the land.

And now, as if every fate had become malignant, the current drifted him inward, where he knew he should keep well away. At the risk of exciting curiosity, if nothing more, he dipped his paddles, with a slow and silent expenditure of strength, and swept the float powerfully outward again, till the shore seemed a part with the sea.

For a time that seemed interminable he hung about that outer stretch, awaiting a further sound of the voices. They did not come. Once more at last he paddled silently inward, finally worming, as before, to a prostrate position on the raft. The chant of the head-hunters came again, as if from the depths of the jungle.

"Now, if ever!" muttered Grenville, half aloud, and impelled by a new and reckless desperation, increased by his thirst and his impotent rage at the creatures still feeding the fumes that Elaine could not avoid, he sent his craft swiftly landward, thankful, at least, for the mild disturbance of breaking ripples on the shore that would drown what slight noises he might make.

Tempted to moor his float outside the estuary, he readily agreed it might thereby lead to his discovery, and must, as a matter of fact, be completely concealed in the shadows of the pool. Excited now by the possibility that his catamaran, with the oars and rowlocks, might still remain in its former harbor, he was doomed to prompt disappointment on gaining the estuary basin. There was nothing whatsoever in the place.

His jugs and paddles he had placed upon the sand. It was only the work of a moment to draw his float across the bar and gently thrust it away from sight beneath the overhanging verdure. Then he stood there, knee-deep in the water, straining his ears for the slightest sound of the Dyaks stirring in the thicket.

Only the drone of a halting voice was wafted to the place. In silence he concealed his paddles, and took up his jugs, to wade with the utmost caution up the pool, towards the spring that formed its source. The water about him was brackish, from its mixture with the tide.

Deeper and deeper grew the basin. The water had risen to his waist. He sank in steadily with every step, despairing now with the sickening thought he might be compelled to swim. Such a task, with two filled jugs, would be impossible, as he bitterly realized. But on he went, as noiselessly as before.

The water was now about his breast, and he held his jugs above it. Something gently nosed against him—and gave him a start. Thoughts of the tropic serpents so frequently inhabiting the water, chilled a thin channel down his spine. Then he saw that the thing which might have been a reptile head was the cork and neck of a bottle. He dipped down and caught it between his teeth, more gratified in all his being than if it had been a thing of gold.

It almost seemed to the man like a sign that the tide of ill-fortune had turned—the tide of luck. He had certainly passed the deepest section of the estuary; he was rising on higher ground.

To avoid the soundings of dripping water, ready to fall from his clothing, he proceeded more slowly than before. When at length he came to a strip of barren sand, he rested his jugs, withdrew the cork from his bottle, and was gratified to detect the odor of stale beer, or stout, which the thing had formerly contained. He rinsed it then and there, to make it sweet, and crowded it into his pocket.

When he once more took up his jugs, to resume his quest of drinkable fluid, he was presently confronted by an exceptional tangle of the shrubbery, arching the tortuous windings of the estuary's head. Here he found himself obliged to pause and noiselessly bend back or break a number of the slender branches before he could wade as before.

He started some small nocturnal animal out through the growth, and the rustling disturbance made by the beast was heard by the Dyaks beyond. One of them called out sharply. To Grenville's complete astonishment and dismay another man, barely a few yards off, replied with a species of grunt. The fellow had come there, either to visit or to set a snare, and must have believed he had frightened the animal himself.

Sidney could hear him working now, as he leaned a bit closer to the foliage, incapable of moving further while the hunter delayed in the thicket. The fellow presently arose, as if to go. Instead, however, he approached even closer to Grenville's place of concealment, and Sidney oozed cold perspiration, helplessly occupied, as he was, with a jug in either hand, and his cleaver still swung at his waist.

To have moved, or attempted to place either jug in the water at his feet, must have been fatal to his mission. Yet he felt convinced the Dyak must fairly run against him, unless he could move to the side. One of his shoes, moreover, was sinking deeply in slimy mire.

That his balance must be overcome seemed well-nigh inevitable. A branch from one of the larger trees that grew above him on the bank now swept so forcibly against the other foliage as the Dyak hauled it downward, to sever a twig for his trap, that Grenville's face was lightly brushed. When the limb sprang upward a moment later, he pulled his foot from the hole.

It seemed to the man a quarter of an hour at least that the trapper remained there, a few feet away, making one more sound, from time to time, when it seemed at last he must have departed. When he finally went, there could be no assurance he would not return again. Notwithstanding this possibility, Grenville slipped furtively along once more, disturbed to find how far towards the spring this narrowing, sea-level neck of the inlet continued through the growth.

When he came at length to a rise of the island, down which the trickle from the spring had made its course, he found himself at the edge of a small, grass-grown clearing, that could hardly be more than a stone's toss away from the Dyaks' temporary camp. A small, deep basin, filled with the precious water he sought, reflected a star at the zenith of the heavens. It some way gave him hope. Of courage he had no lack.

Noiselessly, but without hesitation, he crept forward to the place and bent to drink, then to fill his bottle and jugs. At a snap that came from the shadows beyond he looked up alertly, beholding through the leaves a bright bit of fire upon the earth, with two of the Dyaks at its side. Every accent of their halting conversation came clearly to his ears.

With his three receptacles filled at last, he began his retreat from the place. He had barely vanished from the clearing, and come to the cover of the growth once more, when the man who was laying the snare in some pathway of the small jungle animals came back to complete his work.

Grenville thought his arms must relinquish the holds in their sockets before the unsuspecting hunter was content to leave the neighborhood. The jugs, so long and silently held, were rested a moment on the bank, when, at last, the moment did arrive when Sidney could dare retreat. Then down through the stubborn tangle, once more, he moved like a silent shade. With every yard thus placed between himself and the natives by the spring, the hope in his breast increased.

He came once more to the deeper estuary pool and, lifting his jugs to his shoulders, waded cautiously forward, nearly up to his throat in the tepid brine that smelled too rank for anything but swamp. He paused by his raft, for a moment undecided as to whether he should place his jugs in the braces lashed upon it, before he pushed it past the bar, or after it should float on the tides.

While he stood there, with a sense of exultation daring to warm in his soul —an exultation centered on Elaine and the joy it must presently be to see her thirst allayed—he suddenly stiffened at the sound of Dyak voices, alarmingly near at hand.

Retreating instantly, under the shadow of the foliage and against the end of his raft, he placed one jug upon it, noiselessly, and put out his hand to grasp at a branch to draw himself further from sight.

But the branch on which he laid his grip was suddenly alive. It writhed and lashed sharply at his knuckles until, with a shudder of comprehension that he had clutched the tail of a snake, he flung it off and knew it had glided away.

He had no choice but to try again, and this time met with better fortune. Out through the foliage, arranged thus hurriedly about him, he peered towards the low bit of beach. There was no one in sight, but beyond, on the sea, suddenly looming before him, and coming about to face the protected inlet, a third of the Dyak sailing-boats, a new arrival, manned by an additional group of head-hunters, nosed gracefully up against the tide.

Her anchor was cast, and there she rode, not twenty yards out from the shore.

Like shadowy demons from some world beyond, arrived on some mission mysterious and tragic—some service of the foulest fiend in Hades—four half-seen figures moved along the railing of the craft, destroying the hope in Grenville's bosom.

CHAPTER XXXIX

ADDITIONAL HEAD-HUNTERS

The boatmen thus newly arrived off the estuary's mouth were proceeding in a leisurely and confident manner to make themselves and their vessel snug for the night, and Grenville had placed his second jug upon his raft when, without a sound having come to announce their movements, two or three Dyaks from the camp in the growth called some greeting or challenge from the shore.

That their words were interpreted in a friendly spirit by the shadowy natives on the anchored boat seemed to Grenville entirely obvious. There was something akin to cheer in the voices that replied across the water. Every man was seen to halt at his work and come to the shoreward side of the craft, to peer through the darkness towards the beach.

Three of the fiends with whom he had waged unequal battle now appeared on the sand strip a rod from where Sidney was standing. Their backs were presented as they called and gestured to the men beyond, and Grenville identified the chief once more by the fellow's unusual height.

Apparently an argument ensued, conducted, as to the shoreward end, by the tall and dominant leader. He waved quick, eloquent gestures, frequently towards the headland whence Grenville had come. That some report of recent proceedings was being thus delivered there could be no reasonable doubt. Expressions of astonishment, satisfaction, and a diabolical glee came back in guttural staccatos from the blood-loving creatures on the vessel.

Grenville almost forgot where he was, and why, such indignation burned in his breast as he grasped at the substance of the conference thus held across the tide. Four more head-hunters, come to swell the already heavily outnumbering forces of the island, was too much for Heaven to permit!

Against such odds and such diabolism, what possible chance——

He smiled in a grim, sardonic manner at the thought that a fight between himself and the now augmented Dyaks would ever again be likely, with this boat anchored here before him, Dyaks camping in the jungle, and no trail left by which he could reach the terrace and Elaine, even could he creep away in the shadows and silence of the thicket.

It appeared to him now that the chief on shore was becoming impatient, or angry. He shouted orders and waved his hand down the length of the island in a style growing rapidly more and more imperative, while the new arrivals answered back in a stubborn and sullen dissatisfaction that Sidney began to hope might lead to open rupture. Should one of the factions war against the other, he would think these four boatmen a Godsend.

Even then, he reflected, the situation, as bearing on himself, might present no altered aspect till all was decidedly too late. Should he fail to return to Elaine with water to-night—she would doubtless never see his face again. Should morning still find him hiding here—their fates would have a sudden termination. And now, with this craft at anchor in the current, so close inshore, there could be no chance to escape around it unobserved, what possible alternative was offered but to stand here, nearly to his waist in the water, aware that the deadliest sort of snakes might be coiled within a foot of his hand?

One of the Dyaks a rod away now sat upon the sand. The colloquy continued. The domineering leader, waxing more and more imperious, made gestures now in both directions. That what he imparted and declared was again concerned with himself and Elaine, Grenville could not fail to understand. He was puzzled, however, to determine the reason for this lengthy contest of words.

It occurred to his mind the dispute might have sprung from rival claims as to sharing the trophies, when, at last, the defenders of the terrace should no longer require their heads. The ghastliness of the suggestion did not greatly disturb him; he was too far dulled and wearied by things already undergone.

When it seemed at last as if the verbal combat might result in a deadlier feud, the matter between the land and water factions was suddenly adjusted with accents amazingly mild from either side. Considerably to Grenville's astonishment, the boatmen heaved up their anchor, eased off their sail, and put about towards the farther end of the island.

The three men ashore called out additional instructions, presumably, and followed for a distance down the shore. The boat was presently gone from Sidney's view. He did not stir, though he ached in every bone and muscle, from his long, hard session of suffering and toil, and this cramp and strain of hiding. He was well aware that even the Dyaks would soon be obliged, either to retrace their steps and return as they had come, or force a way up through the jungle to cross to the island's farther side.

That the vessel would join the others, already at anchor behind the second hill, he had finally comprehended with a wildness of hope his heart could scarcely contain. The chief had undoubtedly ordered the craft away from this particular anchorage lest it be too readily seen.

With barely a grunt or two of conversation between them, the trio seen before him on the sand now presently returned. They stood about the estuary inlet for a moment, as if debating some second affair of importance, then finally glided away.

Even then Grenville stirred with silent caution, waiting with heartbeats once more quickened lest he move too soon, and be discovered after all. The place, however, was deserted. Stiffly, but none the less eagerly, and alert for the slightest alarm, he coaxed his raft from the overhanging shrubbery, urged it gently out across the bar, and, hurriedly lashing his jugs to the braces provided, pushed away and headed far out in the tide.

The current had turned. It was flowing strongly towards the cliff, in a certain impetuous manner that was far from being assuring. For while, in a measure, it assisted Grenville's float, it swirled and battled with other counter currents, into which he was helplessly carried. His frail, narrow raft was not infrequently threatened with disaster.

Twice, for a second, he well-nigh despaired of righting before he should sink or plunge end downward, capsizing himself and his jugs. He was shot far outward from his course by one of the treacherous torrents of tide, then rocketed straight for the rocks of the cliff by another. His paddles were wholly inadequate for such a struggle; his arms refused the demands that his will insistently made upon them. It seemed as if he must break at some vital center of his being before he at length was enabled to avoid a collision with the cliff. Then he sank exhausted, obliged for a moment to pause and rest, when the tide once more drifted him outward.

Before he could rouse his flagging sinews to another effort, he had floated by the cave. He was prodded to new desperation. The struggle he waged to regain that rocky niche—only to have the whirlpool cast him to the outside current as before, with his raft entirely submerged—-was enough to break his heart.

Nothing save the thought of Elaine could have availed to spur him yet once more to fighting vigor. He did fight again, till it seemed he must topple like a man of lead, and sink almost gladly in the sea, with a sense of welcome to its endless peace.

A weak and staggering figure he presented when the landing was finally achieved. He barely pulled his raft within the cavern. He had no strength left to conceal it in the passage.

Hugging his two heavy jugs of precious liquid, and also with the bottle weighing down his pocket, he groped and stumbled slowly up the gallery, pausing with ever increasing frequency to lean against the walls and recuperate his strength.

Elaine was aroused from a state of lethargy, where she watched and listened at the upper door, by sounds that for a moment filled her with alarm. That some noisily breathing animal was making its way up the passage from the sea was her first half-waking impression.

With a cry of relief and worry blended, she immediately understood. It was Grenville's labored panting she had heard, where he would not call for assistance for fear she should be alarmed. She caught up the torch she had kept so faithfully alight for his guidance, and ran hastily down to give him welcome.

He was leaning against the wall once more, his mouth a little open for the air his lungs demanded, his face drawn and white with his utter weakness and exhaustion. In one keen glance Elaine comprehended his condition.

"Sidney!" she cried. "Oh! but why did you go? Why would you work so hard to-night?"

He could conjure no smile to his lips. "I love you, Elaine," he answered. "It kills me to see you suffer."

"Oh please—please don't," she begged him. Her eyes were brimming with tears.

He sank on the floor of the passage as he tried once more to raise the jugs. And yet, when Elaine pounced eagerly upon the bottle full of water, and pressed it to his lips, his stubborn resistance was once more reasserted. He accepted a few sips only, then thrust it firmly away.

"That last little pull was steeper than I thought," he admitted, as he forced himself to rise and set his jugs more carefully in the rocks against the wall. "If you will oblige me by taking a drink of water——"

"Not now," Elaine interrupted, as self-denying as before. "I am not the least bit thirsty. If you'll only rest—if you'll go to sleep——"

"I shall go to no rest till you have taken a cup of water."

She knew he would not. She drank from the bottle, perhaps three ordinary swallows of the liquid, like nectar to her palate.

"Good-night," he said, with a touch of his old-time brusqueness, and, adding nothing more, he continued on to the barrier and out to his post of duty. There he sank on a rock before the door to guard Elaine from harm.

Elaine, softly crying, went back at last to her couch. And some time, deep in the silence of the night, she awoke sufficiently to creep to the door, where she listened to Grenville, deeply sleeping.

CHAPTER XL

PLOT AND COUNTER PLOT

The smoke that for two forbidding days had veiled and grayed the headland, continued to drift from the jungle, when Grenville roused from his slumber.

He was much refreshed, yet had not entirely recuperated the strength so drained in the night. The aspect of the barren rock, engulfed in the fumes, was only what he had expected. He felt convinced that, like the mistral of the Riviera, this wind would continue for three full days at least. And the Dyaks were hardly likely to permit an abatement of the smoke while it brought no discomfort to themselves.

Apparently they had made no effort to bridge the gap that rendered the trail completely useless. It was clear to Sidney's mind, however, that so soon as they believed the adventure safe, they would swarm upon the terrace, if for nothing else, then in search of heads and the treasure.

With the possible development of an earlier plan in his mind, he crossed at once to his cannon, loaded and primed in its bed, and began to adjust a lot of loose stones above and upon it, to hide it completely from view. The fuse he drew, meantime, aside, where he meant to splice another length to its end.

Elaine came out from the narrow confines of her gallery in the hope of lending assistance. She was wearing the tiger's jeweled collar about her slender waist.

"I'm hiding the gun—masking our battery," Sidney informed her, quietly.

"Its muzzle is still unobstructed and pointed as before. In case it seems wise to permit the Dyaks to climb up at last and look about, I prefer they shouldn't steal our thunder." If he noted the golden girdle, he made no unusual sign.

Elaine was considerably puzzled.

"But—why should we let them come?"

"To convince them their prisoners have flown. It may give us a chance to punish them harder, later on."

"If a steamer would only come!" she said, turning vainly to the sea, still shrouded from view. "Even a Chinese junk! Anything, almost, but more of these horrible fiends!"

"You see," continued Grenville, "I can make an imitation cannon, from one of my bamboo lengths, and leave it here to fool them. They may be led to think it the only gun we've had, and search no farther for our ordnance. The smoke is likely to lift, I think, which is why I'm at work before breakfast."

He did not complete the arrangements of his ruse before they broke their fast, however, since the making of an imitation cannon required at least an hour. The last of their meat, save a little intended for fishing-bait, was consumed with the insignificant remnants of their fruit supply, and Grenville took time to catch one silvery fish from the ledge in front of the cavern, as well as to gather a lot of the mussels, for luncheon and dinner, before he returned to the terrace.

Already the breeze was failing. There were streaks of highly acceptable air interspersed with the billows of smoke. Not without a certain impatience to have this business concluded before the veiling fumes should leave the terrace entirely exposed to the penetrative sight of the Dyaks, Grenville hastened the construction of his imitation gun, to be left by the heap of stones.

That a more convincing appearance of over-use might assist in creating the desired impression, he selected one of the bamboo sections already badly split. This he readily blackened by burning a handful of powder, loosely, inside its muzzle. With a rude vent cut and similarly treated, the affair was ready to be bound with discarded creepers, then lodged in the rocks above the genuine bit of artillery still ready for grim engagements.

All that remained of the powder in his cave was carefully moved to the passage, there to be most cautiously deposited, away from all possible fire, along with his coils of fuse. Somewhat to his disappointment, the northerly breeze seemed once more freshening as the morning hours advanced. He had hoped not only for a lifting of the smoke, but likewise to find the Dyaks' boat once more encircling the headland.

Beyond transferring his water supply from the jugs to a number of bamboo buckets, which permitted no waste by percolation, he had nothing further to employ his time as the day wore slowly on. The heat in the meantime was intolerable. The fish was roasted in an "oven" he fashioned of the heat-retaining tufa. The mussels were likewise "steamed" in their own exuding juices, occupying the large and basin-like sea-shell for the purpose.

It was not until nearly four in the afternoon that the wind definitely veered. Grenville had noted the coming alteration that would clear the hill of fumes in time to make all essential preparations for the Dyak watchfulness. His furnace of fire was duly banked, to continue a smoldering glow among the ashes without producing smoke. Elaine had retired within the passage, and the entrance door to this secret hiding-place was adjusted against the rock.

Grenville remained upon the terrace. No less a degree of vigilance than that previously exercised was, he felt, highly essential. Concealed in the caves or rocks comprised by the former camp he could not only guard against surprise by a bridging of the ruined trail, but his view of the sea, that might once more be haunted by the Dyak craft, was practicably without limit.

Apparently the Dyaks, too, had been aware the breeze would serve them no longer. The smudges in the jungle were extinguished. In a time comparatively brief, after the shifting of the wind, no smoke at all was visible. But during the final hour preceding sunset another phase of fiendish ingenuity developed.

The Dyaks began shooting arrows of fire all about on the summit of the terrace. They were shafts made highly inflammable by means of resin and pitch. Their flight through the air was not sufficiently violent to extinguish their glowing ends. If they did not blaze upon alighting on the rocks, they still retained sufficient heat and redness to ignite a pan of powder.

It was this that occurred to Grenville as he made up his mind that some genius of diabolism among the new arrivals was doubtless responsible for this effort to explode his magazine. His satisfaction with himself for his foresight in storing his powder anew was his one real joy of the day. He wondered how long this business might continue, and how many of the enemy must now be reckoned with.

As a matter of fact, with the four who had come under cover of the night, there were nine unscathed by previous engagements. Also, it was, as Grenville had suspected, one of the latest comers who had counseled the use of burning arrows. Since the terrace defenders were employing some dreaded explosive, the one course readily suggested was to reach his supply with a brand of fire—and, perhaps, thereby destroy its maker. In any event, deprived of this one deadly means of defense, the whites could be readily slaughtered.

Already the Dyaks had built a bridge, to be used, when the time should at last arrive, for spanning that gap on the trail. It was not impossible, many had urged, that the prisoners lodged on the headland's summit were already either dead or dying. How they had managed to survive so long, with no supply of water, was sufficiently mysterious. Should they still be found alive another day—all the greater the joy of bringing about the end!

The Dyak plan for reaching the magazine had been too hastily concocted. The supply of tarred and resined arrows was decidedly insufficient. Less than a score had been sent to the top of the terrace when the last was speeded on its way. But during the short remaining hour of daylight, and even by firelight, after dark, the shafts accumulated swiftly, against the coming of the dawn.

Meantime to Grenville had come an inspiration. His one clear hope for the morning was that more of the arrows might be shot from below to make his plans complete. If the Dyaks were busy after dark, they could scarcely have matched the fever with which he likewise toiled.

Down to the cool, dry chamber of the cavern he had carried no less than eight of his largest bombs, with coil upon coil of his fuse. Two mines of four bombs each he planted, concealing all with rocks. From each of the mines one fuse only was laid, to the inner angle of the passage. Each bomb had a shorter bit of fuse thrust in a handful of powder, to which the two main fuses led. The lines were carefully protected, not only against discovery, but as well against himself, or his boots, as he tramped back and forth from the cave. When this arrangement had been made complete, he could do no more in that direction till his favorable hour should arrive.

His next attention was directed to his bamboo float, which had been practically dismembered. He had utilized the heavy stems to construct a long and narrow platform, with two rude hooks lashed on the end to engage a rung of his ladder. This ladder he not only lowered down from the wall to a position in front of the cavern's opening, securing its end with more than ordinary caution among the rocks he piled upon it, but also he had tested the length, and every rung, by extending his platform across from the ledge and climbing from the sea to the terrace.

It was midnight before his final preparation was complete. This had been simply arranged. He had carried a canister of powder to the outside rocks, considerably back of Elaine's former shelter, together with two small bombs. The powder he laid in a six-foot ring, or spiral, that narrowed towards the center, merely to provide a lasting and widespread flash when at length it should be ignited.

The bombs were placed near by, simply laid in a cave of no considerable dimensions. Their fuses were trailed across the rocks to a place of observation, and were opened out in such a manner as to fire both the spiral and the noisy but harmless explosives.

Despite his nervous tension and the worry occasioned in his mind, lest, the Dyaks fail of their allotted part, Grenville finally slept as soundly as a boy, when at length he could work no more. But Elaine, strangely tingling with apprehension, concerned with the part that she must likewise play to render his plans effective, had not Sidney's weariness to overcome her nerves, and therefore rested badly.

For long she lay there, listening, as always, to the silence enfolding the island, thinking how fair it had really been when the wail alone had been with them, and wondering, eagerly wondering, if by chance her companion of the hours both bright and dark had noticed the girdle she was wearing.

CHAPTER XLI

A LIVING BAIT

The morning dawned in beauty, a few clouds riding with thistle-down lightness athwart the illimitable dome of blue, as intense as that of the sea. A light breeze stirred in the jungle, to wander aimlessly from one deep chalice of fragrance to another, before it trailed across the hill. Sea tang arose from the restless tide, that washed at the cliff incessantly.

As far as sight could pursue the richness of its causeway, the sun laid gold in glittering mosaic across the tropic ocean. Never had the sparkling waves seemed brighter, the world more promising, as Elaine peered forth through her chink in the door, awaiting—God only knew what.

She had never been more excited, and rarely more alarmed. The unknown element in Grenville's plans kept her nerves at the highest tension. They had eaten a breakfast solely of fish before the light of daybreak. Grenville had carefully closed the passage barrier, and crept out upon the terrace. On no account must she open the door, or call him, to her side. She must wait, and not even expect to hear a report of what was occurring.

The longest cord she had ever helped to braid was lightly secured to her arm. Its farther end was tied in the rocks at the lower exit of the passage. Until she should feel his tug upon this signal line, she could only imagine that Sidney was near, or, perhaps, was climbing down his ladder.

She dreaded the thought of that ladder, so frailly depending above the rocks and water, not to mention all its use might mean when the time for the signal should arrive. And she might be obliged to wait all day, as Sidney had warned her, duly—all day, while the wildest, the most tormenting of conjectures would leisurely elaborate themselves in her brain to convince her that Sidney was no more.

Should he fall from the cliff, should he chance to underestimate the Dyaks' treacherous activities—should any one of a dozen possible calamities occur—how long must she wait till she knew?

Meantime Grenville was barely less keyed to excited expectancy than Elaine in her prison-like retreat. Times without number he goaded his mind to review once more the inventory of his scheme, where the lack of one small detail might prove his entire undoing. Yet, after all, there were a few links only in the chain, though each was vitally important.

He counted them over carefully—the signs or proof of calamity, here on the hill, to convince the head-hunting demons his magazine was gone, and with it all possible defense; the ladder and platform down below, whereby he could reach the cave; the bombs for the climax, should his hope succeed; and fire for their certain ignition.

He had taken a double precaution to provide himself with fire. Down in the passage several brands were smoldering slowly in their ashes, while others did the same on the hill. He could think of nothing lacking—not even the cord to warn Elaine to open her door and flee outside when at length he should give her the signal!

But as if in mockery of all this careful business, the day began with never a sign from the jungle. The Dyaks, he feared, had altered their plan, and might shoot no more of their arrows. He could not have known they were waiting for the breeze to freshen and fill a certain sail. One of their boats had been prepared and manned to police the headland as before.

When Grenville at length beheld it, gracefully sharp and picturesque, as it rounded towards the master cliff, he was filled with conflicting emotions. He had wished for this, precisely, but not without the rest. The arrows first, had been his hope, and then this silent vulture, atilt in the purple tides.

The arrows presently arrived. He was still engaged in watching the movements of the boat, in an effort to count the crew, when the first of the flaming messengers struck dully against a bowlder and lay there, fiercely blazing.

Then the sudden flight, which, against an inky background, must have presented an extraordinary spectacle, afforded a sight strange enough, as Grenville presently conceded. The pitch and resin with which the shafts were tipped, burned with a black and heavy smoke, that trailed in their wakes like nebulous tails of cloud-producing comets. There were some of the flames that the flight only served to fan to fiercer heat and color. Like a candle sputtering in a draught they sounded as they flew.

Others that lost their yellow blaze smoked the more blackly in the air. In half a dozen different spots the hotly burning lengths of wood were soon consuming bits of scattered leaves and grass, one almost at Grenville's feet.

He was soon convinced that, should this rain of fire be long continued, he should have no need to fire his bombs and spiral. The arrows would actually accomplish the mission for which they were intended. He had no wish for a premature climax to the singular attack, but rather hoped to create the impression he was fighting desperately to protect his magazine.

When a heap of waste and useless creepers was presently ignited, he ran from his place and promptly beat it out. He wished he might be seen. He was gratified without delay. The rifleman, posted, as on previous occasions, in the rocks that crowned the second hill, promptly discharged his erratic weapon, and nearly killed one of his kind.

Grenville ran as if to cover. A shout of exultation came from below. A larger and swifter flight of the blazing shafts immediately ensued.

Sidney now cast a glance about for the ship that was cruising by the headland. Somewhat to his disappointment it had gone about as if to return to the west, from which the cave, his platform, and ladder could not, of course, be seen. He fancied, however, it had come up in stays at the sound of the shot on the hill. It certainly appeared to be paying off to continue about the headland. He dared not longer delay.

The arrows were blazing all about him. He feared at last that one lucky shot might even fire his cannon. Almost amused by the irony of the situation, he caught up the nearest blazing shaft of fire, and used it to light his fuse.

In the briefest time the serpent of fire sped down through the hollowed creeper to the spiral, where, also, lay the bombs. Of a sudden the powder was ignited.

With a flash of quickly leaping flames and a grayish geyser of fume, the destruction began. Then, as a cry of glee arose from the clearing below, the bombs went off in quick succession.

They made a splendid noise and smoke, scattering fragments of the tufa far and wide, till a rain of the smaller pieces spattered thickly down in the jungle. Grenville arose from his hiding-place, quite unharmed, and ran about on the terrace crazily, holding his head between his hands for the distant rifleman to witness his discomfort.

The Dyak was overjoyed. He shouted in reckless delight to his kind, who howled like a pack of wolves now certain of feasting. Yet they did not emerge from their places of concealment, nor undertake to bridge the trail, and immediately ascend the hill, as Grenville had somewhat feared.

He crept to a point of vantage, watching the clearing for a demonstration which, much to his gratification, did not arrive. Back once more towards the cliff at the rear he scuttled, beholding the Dyak craft at last heading well around towards the cave. The moment was ripe for his scheme!

Hurriedly creeping to the eastern brink, with one of his firebrands gripped between his teeth, he began a descent of the ladder. Halfway down he paused for breath, and furtively watched, from the tail of his eye, for the boat that should presently appear.

It came within range of his vision silently, and down he continued as before. He could only hope that he might have been seen, for never a sound arose from the crew to make the matter certain. For, perhaps, a distance of twenty feet he must have been plainly in view. The last fleeting sight he caught of the boat, she was putting about with a suddenness enormously exciting to his blood.

That the Dyaks had seen him, and were now intent upon turning away before he should turn and see their boat, and know himself discovered, was an inescapable conclusion. A moment later he was hidden by the ledge, and descended more at leisure, climbing inside the ladder presently, where it hung well out from the overhanging shelf, and so coming down upon his platform, with little or no exertion.

Immediately on landing under the mouth of the cavern, he lifted the platform bodily, disengaged the hooks from the ladder's lower rung, and drew it behind him to the cave. The ladder itself he could not remove without climbing up to the terrace and issuing forth at the hidden door, which would doubtless prove fatal to his plans.

He proceeded at once to his supplementary firebrands, in the larger spread of the gallery. Here all was going well. He extinguished one or two branches of the smoldering wood, to conserve the limited supply. After that it was simply a matter of waiting.

How long it would take for the boat crew to land, inform their fellow head-hunters of what they had seen, and fetch the entire company to capture him, here in the chamber, was not a matter for easy estimation. He hoped it might happen soon.

In this he was doomed to disappointment. The Dyak sailors had seen him, clearly enough. They had hastened back to report this eminently satisfying outcome of their tactics, and the nine eager fiends had then and there commenced their counter scheming. But they meant to commit no errors, assume no unnecessary risks.

For, notwithstanding the fact they were fully convinced the white man's explosives had been reached by their arrows and destroyed, they retained a vivid memory of punishments inflicted by the gun, where one more deadly hail of slugs might lurk to find them again. It was, however, important that one or more men should mount the terrace, to watch at the head of the white man's ladder, and even render its use a fatal experiment, should the climber attempt to regain the summit by its means.

They began investigations cautiously—all noted by Elaine. Peering breathlessly out at her narrow chink, her heart consumed with haunting worries, lest Grenville had met with some accident when the bombs were finally exploded, she now beheld a pair of the Dyaks in the clearing, apparently exposing themselves as if to draw any latent fire from the hill.

As the minutes went by and trouble failed to come, their boldness plainly increased. They were not particularly hurried, however, in producing their bridge for the trail. When at length four natives brought it from the jungle, Elaine's heart pounded in her breast like a hammer forging at her soul.

She had instantly recognized the bamboo platform. She thought that Sidney ought to come—to know of what was occurring. But he did not come, and could not leave his post below, where one of his fuses, he had found, had opened and spilt out its powder. This he was feverishly and gingerly working to repair, by the light of a glowing brand.

Not for a moment daring to abandon her place by the door, Elaine felt a horrible sense of weakness attack her entire system as the Dyaks cautiously adjusted their bridge, while watching against a new surprise.

That the four men now constantly visible must presently succeed in placing the slender platform from one broken ledge to the other, to mount in full possession of the terrace, Elaine could not fail to comprehend. The impulse to creep from her hiding-place and once more fire the cannon was fairly overwhelming. She was certain that Sidney, with all his wonderful scheming, had never contemplated this!

He had simply instructed her to wait—to remain in the passage, behind the concealing barrier, no matter what occurred, till she felt at last the tug of the cord on her arm. She felt she must obey, that even to desert her post for the little time required to hasten down the gallery and let him know of the dangers now about her might cost them everything!

Never had she in her life been subjected to such a trial as that which presently developed.

The Dyaks had spanned the gap where the ledge was broken. Two of them crept a little forward on the bridge. It was now or never to fire the gun, while the four were still in range. She dared not disobey the order given by her chief. Suddenly darting past the spot where the cannon had taken its toll before, the Dyaks gained the summit—and were finally in possession of the camp!

CHAPTER XLII

LONG HOURS OF DOUBT

Grenville had hoped to be able to hasten for a moment up the gallery and assure Elaine that all was well, and the matter now merely one of patience.

His belated discovery that one of his fuses was deficient had somewhat shaken his nerves. Except for this timely restoration, his whole project must have been weakened, perhaps to absolute failure. His line of fuse was necessarily long, to assure essential safety for himself. He was obsessed with a fear that countless defects might have developed in the long line of powder-loaded creeper since the day it was made and laid away.

In a fever of anxious searching, he examined practically every inch of both the lines, meantime returning frequently to the cavern's mouth, to guard against surprise. Before he felt certain the fuse could all be relied upon to perform its part in the business, he finally detected a Dyak boat attempting to go about and escape his possible observation from the dark retreat, while obviously hovering near, to watch that he did not escape.

After that he dared not for a moment desert his post. And the longer the expected Dyaks remained away, the more imperative became his watchfulness and constant attendance at the cave.

Meanwhile, up at her flimsy door, Elaine leaned affrightedly against the chilling wall, no longer peering forth at the chink, but tensely listening— listening for the sounds of feet above her head. All four of the Dyaks were there on the terrace, and, therefore, a few rods only from the passage in which she crouched, alone.

There was nothing to see, save the platform and part of the trail, and she dared not stand so close to the door, lest her very breathing, or the beat of her heart, betray her presence at her post.

When at length the unmistakable sound of beings on the rocks directly overhead came dully down through the roof of pitted stone, she shrank entirely down to the floor, her heart in a sickening flutter. Just to have cried out Sidney's name and to run like a child down the passage to his arms, would have been a relief so incredibly vast its comfort could not have been measured.

But she did not move. She still obeyed, like the faithful comrade in arms she was, awaiting her portion, allotted by the Fates, though it might be death in its most revolting form.

What sounds were made by the Dyaks, in retreat from that particular position, failed to come down through the rock. She was, therefore, denied the abatement of her apprehension which she might otherwise have known. She was thoroughly convinced that one of the fiends had been posted above the passage opening to remain indefinitely on guard.

The Dyaks had, however, concluded their examination of the terrace rather promptly. There was almost nothing worth investigation. Grenville's imitation cannon had served its purpose to perfection. The head-hunters marveled that a gun so simply and readily constructed could have wrought such havoc in their ranks. But they found no reason to doubt it had been used, and they readily overlooked the small brass piece so artfully hidden by the stones.

They had lost no time in removing the bowlders that supported Sidney's ladder. One or two only they suffered to remain—sufficient to anchor the affair in place, yet permit their man to drop back in the tide, should he intrust his weight to it.

That the white man's powder magazine had been greatly diminished before their flaming arrows completed its destruction seemed indisputable. The bombs had torn out and blackened so much of a cavity that the Dyaks' gratification was complete. It was scarcely possible, they argued, that the man seen running crazily about had escaped a mortal hurt. He had certainly summoned the strength to escape to the cave, but there he might have died.

All the waste sections of Sidney's bamboo were thrown with his cannon and his flag-pole in the sea. A thorough search was made of Elaine's former shelter, as well as of all the rock heaps on the place, for the treasure the man might have taken from the cave and concealed about his camp.

Not until some time after noon did the visitors finally leave the hill and disappear in the jungle growth to mature their further plans. Elaine knew nothing of their departure. She still remained back in the darkness of the gallery, and, therefore, neither heard nor saw the movements made on the ledge. She was hardly less prepared than before to see the door of the gallery rudely torn away at any moment, and the hideous head-hunters confidently pouncing in upon her.

Grenville, down in the blackness of the cavern, was hardly more easy in his mind. The Dyaks had failed to appear before the cave. He realized they might conclude to starve him to death in the tomb-like place, rather than risk another of his traps. To return to the terrace was out of the question. Not only might the natives be present, but, if once he were seen, they must immediately realize he had some unknown means of passage from the cave to the summit.

That the ladder would be watched he was certain. It was also more than likely, he was sure, the Dyaks would either cut through the strands to weaken it, near the top, or displace the rocks he had heaped upon its end. Reflecting that to pull it down while one of their craft was cruising about the headland might convince them he had fallen in the sea, he laid his platform out on the ledge for the purpose before the terrace had been deserted. But the boat was not to be seen.

At noon the sun beat down on the rocks about the cave with a hot, intolerable glare. Grenville was weary, as well as thirsty once more, and faint from lack of food. He dared not abandon the cavern now, however, since any moment might find the Dyaks slipping to the open niche to complete the deed they had vainly attempted before.

Never had the long, sultry hours of afternoon dragged by more tediously. Never had the man so vividly realized how much it meant to be near Elaine, to hear her voice, to gaze in the depths of her eyes.

It was not till the sun was about to set that his long, impatient vigil was somewhat rewarded at last. The Dyak boat drifted barely in sight, as he crouched there on the shattered ledge.

Without a moment's hesitation, even as he saw that the craft was beating back, as before, to the shelter behind the cliff, he ran out his platform, dropped its end across a rung of the ladder, and cast a heavy stone as far out upon it as possible.

It hung there, solidly enough, for a moment, then slipped a foot—and abruptly the whole writhing length came down, to land in the whirlpool and sink. The platform, however, was recovered. Returning at once to his place behind the wall, Sidney waited in new expectancy for the Dyaks to appear.

They did not come. The sun went down—and with it Grenville's hope. The head-hunters feared him still! They must have determined some trick was prepared against their invasion of the cave! He was utterly sick with discouragement. His long, hard day, to say nothing of Elaine's, had been spent like this, in vain. He felt he had merely lost ground. The Dyaks were doubtless already in possession of the terrace, where he could not attack them to advantage, since precisely as soon as he made his appearance on the hill-top the passage must be revealed.

He clung to the hope that dusk would bring the murderous pack to his stand—that they might have waited for darkness to sneak upon him unawares. But the twilight faded into blackest night, with clouds obscuring the friendly stars, and still no head-hunters came.

When at length he was certain no native would dare intrust himself or his boat to the treacherous maelstrom of the niche, he abandoned hope for the night. Returning to the passageway, he closed its door behind him, secured it with the bar, and groped his way upward through the velvet gloom for a word of cheer with Elaine.

He called to her softly as he came towards the top, and she hastened down to meet him. She was certain something had gone amiss, but her courage was sufficient to sustain almost anything, so long as she knew he was safe.

"Got a bit hungry," he told her, off-handedly. "Those chaps do keep one waiting!"

"Sh-s-s-sh!" she said, in a warning whisper; "I think they're just outside."

"You saw them come up?" he asked her, eagerly.

"Four of them—after you fired the bombs. They put a bridge across the hole, as you thought, perhaps, they might."

"H'm," said Sidney, quietly, going to the door and peering forth on the jungle. "They haven't gone down since?"

"Not that I saw. I wasn't watching all the while."

"You haven't heard them talking, near the door?"

"No, oh no! I haven't heard a thing! I haven't known what to do—or whether you were alive or dead. I didn't know what my duty was when I saw them come up, and wanted to fire the cannon! I thought the day would never end! Have you had to give up at last?"

"Certainly not!" he assured her, cheerfully, aware from every accent of her voice what tortures she had suffered there alone. "I must soon return—and you must go to bed. I haven't the slightest idea they will come before next high tide, about eight, or later, in the morning. Meantime you did exactly right. They haven't the slightest notion of this secret passage, you may be sure, or nothing on earth could have kept them out. And they long since returned to their boats.... I suppose you have had neither food nor water. A little hurried supper for us both, and I must go down to the basement for the night."

Elaine had removed the cord from her arm, and secured it by the door. Sidney ignited a slender piece of torch-wood, by the smoldering brands maintained in the upper passage. He carried it promptly around the angle of the gallery, however, as an added precaution against the escape of one revealing beam through the chink that pierced the barrier facing the jungle world.

The dinner they ate was neither warm nor comforting. Cold fish is barely sustaining, while the tonic properties of water are scarcely worth describing. Elaine, however, was enormously reheartened, thus to have Sidney there again, and know he had suffered no hurt. She bade him good-night when their meager repast was finished, with the bravest cheer that Grenville had taken to heart for many a weary day. Then, with the cord once more on her arm, she resumed her place by the door.

CHAPTER XLIII

THE HOUR OF CLIMAX

Grenville made no attempt to sleep as the long night went laggardly by. He dozed, from sheer weariness, now and again, with his back against the rocks, but two or three times in every hour he rose from his place to go out on the ledge, where he listened to catch the slightest sound that might be made above the ceaseless lapping of the water. He would then return to the gallery, assure himself the smoldering brands were ready for use at any moment, and once more sit down to wait and nod.

Elaine was equally sleepless. Far more than Grenville she feared night treacheries on the part of the Dyaks from the jungle. The state of her nerves, since the terrace was so readily accessible to the head-hunting butchers, permitted no thought of sleep. Moreover, never since their arrival on the island had Grenville so far exiled himself from her side throughout a night. She had always felt protected heretofore, and upon that protection had relied.

As restlessly as the man below she came to the door, times without number, to listen for sounds the jungle might surrender, as well as to watch through the darkness for the slightest inimical sign. Not a sound, however, did the night vouchsafe her straining senses; not the slightest movement in all the world of shadows, life, and tragedy about and below her position could her blazing eyes detect.

She had never known a night so long, or one so haunted with fears. Her imagination played cruelly upon her heart, picturing one dread scene of butchery after another, with Sidney completely overwhelmed and finally slain, while she, no longer desirous of life, awaited her fate in a dumb and dulled indifference. She was certain the morning would never dawn again, or, if it did, the one man pitted against these savages might not even have time for one faint tug on the cord about her arm, more like a farewell than a signal.

It was a red and troubled break of day that finally reddened the eastern sky, where clouds were banked above the sea. Grenville had dozed for perhaps as much as twenty minutes. He awoke with a start from lurid dreams in which he had fancied himself awake after criminally oversleeping, only to find himself and Elaine pinned down by a horde of the merciless brutes to whom human heads are trophies.

The red of the sky for a moment confirmed some remaining disorder of his thoughts. He had stumbled quickly to the cavern's mouth, from which the sanguinary streaks and blotches, now painting the far horizon and dully reflected in the sea, were confusedly presented.

The coolness of the haunting breeze, that crept like a presence about the silent island, restored him soon and cleared the mists from his brain. He stood for several minutes, gazing listlessly forth, disgusted with the outcome of the night.

Once more he returned to the gallery to inspect his brands of fire. And once again, on returning to the chamber, his inclination was to prop his back against the wall and let himself sink in slumber.

The dawn-light was slowly increasing. He watched it dully for a moment more, and yawned as he stumbled heavily towards the utter discomfort of his resting-place.

Once more he adjusted his weary limbs upon the ledge, reflecting on what expedient he must now adopt, since this, his *coup-de-main*, had so egregiously failed. He thought he was planning brilliantly when he once more fell asleep. The slightest of sounds that was foreign alike to tide or breeze now failed to arouse his senses as his head came forward on his breast.

Not another sound was made where that one had strangely risen from the front of the shattered ledge. Even the sharpest eyes would have been for a moment tricked by the shadows of the rocky niche, where the tide was darkly swirling. A fragment of the lower cliff then appeared to be detached.

It was simply Grenville's catamaran, with two or three natives upon its deck, silently maneuvering to land. Back of it, just well off the frowning headland wall, the bow of a larger Dyak craft appeared for the fraction of a minute.

The head-hunting fiends had arrived! They had chosen the hour when exhaustion finally culminates and claims the helpless sentinel, heavily dreaming that all is well!

Aware that the slightest disturbance might warn their intended victims in the cave, the Dyaks labored with the utmost caution to fetch the float to the ledge. This they presently accomplished, fending it off at a vital moment lest it scrape against the rock.

Two of the half-clad demons now landed, their movements as sinuous and silent as a serpent's. Instantly flattening down upon the tide-lapped shelf, while the third of their party skillfully guided the catamaran once more to the larger craft without, they waited as patiently as the shadows, of which they seemed a part.

The plans of the crew on the boat without had been matured with much sagacity. The transfer of two more men to the raft was quickly and noiselessly accomplished, and once again the catamaran was permitted to swing on the tide's rotation into the open entrance of the inlet.

This second pair, with knives between their teeth and hands therefore unencumbered, were a trifle overeager to gain the mouth of the cave. One of them caught at the fissured edge of tufa with avid fingers, while the float was responding to the force of the whirl. His hold was rudely broken, yet so sharply had he dug in his nails that a fragment of rock was broken away. It plumped with a gurgle in the water.

Grenville was suddenly awakened—not so much by the sound the bit of rock had made as by something more subtle in the very air—a something only to be interpreted by that instinct surviving from ages dark and old.

He was suddenly alive to a sense of imminent danger lurking fearfully close at hand. None too soon and none too silently he rose to his feet, for there at the ledge the catamaran was halted and, even as the two impatient Dyaks landed, their companions came worming up the shelf.

A moment more and all must have been too late, as Grenville clearly realized. Indeed, with the utmost caution only could retreat to his gallery be effected without a betrayal of his presence. He dared not move swiftly from his post—and yet he must be quick!

Slowly and noiselessly withdrawing from his place beside the wall, he took one long step inwards, towards the door he must place against the open gallery entrance.

The dawn-light, redder and more intense, now cast an intangible shadow in the chamber as a Dyak's head appeared above the ledge. The fiends were all but on his heels!

He slipped within the passage, without creating the slightest sound, save the loud, tumultuous pounding of his heart. Lifting the door no less cautiously into its proper position, he left a crack, that was barely a half-inch wide, through which to watch his visitors, writhing like so many pythons over the shelf and into the ebon well of gloom.

Their plan was to crawl to the confines of the cave—unless they should creep by chance upon their sleeping victims sooner, leaving a couple crouched outside to prevent the quarry's escape. Torches were not to be lighted until every man was posted, and then would be thrown to the center of the cavern where their light would reveal the chamber's occupants, while the outer rim of darkness still concealed the gleaming knives. A counter attack would be rendered out of the question. The cordon would be complete.

Three of those strangely-moving shadows Grenville plainly discerned. There was nothing more to be seen—and nothing to be heard. That several Dyaks were almost at his feet he felt, but could not have proved. He had hoped for half a dozen at the least. He hoped for them still, and deliberately waited, trusting they might arrive.

It seemed such a pity to waste his mines and not obliterate the lot! He wondered if more of them might not come—then how he should know, if they did.

Meanwhile, the three not included here in the cave-attacking party were equally active above. The red of the dawn had seen them advancing through the jungle where they meant to take the hill and block the retreat of the victims to that eminence by any chance of extra ladders or white man's baffling magic.

Elaine beheld them, through the strengthening light, so soon as they crossed the clearing. They paused there as if for a signal, which they may or may not have received. It gave the girl, who had watched with an ever-increasing fever through the night and that blood-red dawn, a long wild moment in which to imagine fates untold that must have overtaken Sidney.

She was certain at last he was murdered in the cave, and that now, with the passageway finally known, the fiends, whose passion was taking human life, had come to complete their tale of butchery and plunder. Why else should they once more visit the hill at such an hour of the morning? They had barely waited for the dawn to make certain of their work!

She saw them coming furtively up the trail, aware, she was sure, that by means of the hidden gallery their movements might be seen. She had held a wasting firebrand in her tense little fist for the past two hours. And now—if only Sidney had told her what to do in such an extremity as this! If only it might be her duty to fire the cannon!

It seemed as if she must obey the impulse—and perhaps save both of their lives! The Dyaks were almost at the bridge. They must soon come fairly in range of the gun! After that—it would be too late!

Below, in the cavern, during this time, Grenville was haunted with doubts. He had waited in hopes other Dyaks would come, and not a sound had rewarded his straining senses. He began to fear he had waited too long—that the creatures whose shadows had crept within had searched all the place and departed.

Yet he knew that they could not have passed him and left him unaware. The light was now all in his favor, and steadily increasing. With a sudden determination to take what toll the Fates had offered, he groped his way back to his brands of fire, and then to the ends of his fuse.

Elaine, with her heart all but bursting, with excitement for which she had no vent, saw the head-hunters pause on the slender bridge before they crept upward as before. Her weight was leaned against the door till it moved a little from its bearings.

She was sure it had made some far-reaching sound that the Dyaks could not fail to hear. They had paused again—and again moved up the trail—and found her helpless. The cord on her arm!—if Sidney would only pull the cord

————

The sharp little tug that suddenly came now startled a cry from her lips. Instantly thrusting away the door and bounding from the narrow ledge to the upper level of the terrace, she ran towards the fuse with her cone of fire, just as Grenville, down in the gallery of rock, came madly plunging upward.

He had lighted the fuse, and was groping towards the top, a fear that he might be buried pursuing at his heels. He stumbled across the heavy load of treasure, left in its basket by the wall.

As one in an earthquake or fire clutches up something to save it, instinctively, so he laid hold of this useless dross and tugged it hotly up the passage. He reached the upper angle thus before he realized the folly of his action. He was certain then, as he dropped the load, that something had happened to his mines.

Before this time——

With the thought half finished in his swiftly-working brain came the thud and shock of his explosion—a tangible movement in the bulk of rock—and then the cataclysm.

Almost as one with Elaine's small detonation, the mighty jar, the air-confounding concussion, the smothered boom, and the dizzying tremor that swayed the hill, shook down the girl's bewildered senses. She saw the red leap from the cannon's mouth—and saw three men, surprised to inaction on the deadly angle of the trail—then down she went, her mind convinced she had rended the island asunder.

Sounds of colossal destruction stormed through the air for a time that seemed to have no end. The roar of a cataract of broken stone, confusedly toppling from estates erected by the ages, was lost in a tumult of other sounds where the headland seemed to fill the sea.

Dust of the rock and smoke of the rock ascended with fumes of the powder. Tidal disturbances splashed and seethed where the sea, having split to receive those tons of chaos, surged back with augmented violence at this displacement of its waters.

The cave had been blotted from existence! Its walls and its ceiling had crashed from their several places. to leave only an ugly scar. Whole towers of rocks, cleaved from the hill's main mass in sudden violence, had hung in disordered ruin against the quaking air for a second, then rioted downward on the Dyak boat to plunge it, rent and shivered, to the bottom.

Not a man of that murderous group below had survived the climax of that second. The place that had once been a treasure tomb, with a wailing "spirit" at its portals, was at last a very tomb indeed; but nevermore would its tidal wail arise on the air to render the cavern sacred.

Like a veritable spirit of underground destruction, Grenville emerged from the passage, unaware of all he had done. His thought was only of Elaine. He called, as he climbed to the terrace, but no glad little cry made response.

Then, abruptly, he saw her prostrate figure on the rocks—and beyond her two men, with one limberly inert, limping blindly down the trail. To dart to his store, snatch the last of his bombs, and pursue these three who had threatened Elaine was the first wild impulse of his being. Just one such blow, to follow up his victory, and perhaps they should need no more!

But he ran instead to the helpless figure near the cannon. He knew what she had done. He took her up swiftly, calling on her name, and carried her back to the former cave, where a rosy light from the risen sun made it seem like a haven of promise.

CHAPTER XLIV

A LOTUS BLOSSOM

It was still very early in the morning when Grenville finally discovered, afar out northward on the sea, two Dyak boats making swiftly away from the island.

He feared for a moment, when the sails were first discerned, they were new craft about to arrive. He could not have known that his mines sunk the third of the boats formerly at anchor in the inlet, and was in no way enabled to determine how many of the enemy had perished at the cave.

It was almost too much to credit, this apparent retreat of the fiends so bent upon his capture. He made no positive report to Elaine of the fact he felt he must verify, lest he find himself obliged to retract it later.

She had quickly responded to his ministrations, having fainted as much from lack of food and rest as from shock in that final moment. Concerning the final effect of her shot, she was destined never to know. Grenville was far too wise to let her believe she had taken the life even of a fiend in human semblance.

He told her the Dyaks had fled from the place, which flight he had personally witnessed. He was certain, moreover, they would hardly return again that day, if they did not quit the island. Assured of the safety of the adventure, he descended to the jungle and returned with an armful of fruit. He proceeded later to the spring for a fresh supply of water.

Estimating the final fighting force of the Dyaks at ten, and conceding that five, at the least, must have perished at the cave, since one or two must have guarded the boats while three were searching the chamber, he concluded that no more than four at the most could still remain uninjured.

He had gone to the edge of the ruin, above the obliterated cave, and, having discovered no boat either near or far, had arrived at a fairly accurate conjecture respecting the fate of the craft the Dyaks had employed. One more calculation, respecting the number of able seamen required to navigate the retreating vessels, convinced him the island was deserted to the uses of Elaine and himself.

It was not, however, till that afternoon that he cautiously explored their former possessions and confirmed the hope in his breast. There was ample evidence about the spring, and in the jungle, of the methods of living the Dyaks had employed, but neither at the western inlet, back of the central hill of rock, nor at the friendly estuary, was anything boatlike to be found. His catamaran had vanished, along with the larger craft, and its fate he could readily surmise.

He lost no time in arranging a number of his snares and traps for the meat of which they were in need. Their camp was made as before on the terrace proper, despite the heat of the sun.

It was not until many of these essential comforts had been once more established that Sidney explored the gallery to determine what destruction had been wrought by his double mine.

Everything stored in the lower depths had been hopelessly buried by the rock. The passage was open for no more than half its former length. His bamboo raft was among the possessions sacrificed to the ruse that had finally succeeded beyond even his wildest dreams. Not ten feet back of his basket-load of treasure the last of the caving had been halted.

When Elaine's robe and couch, their water-jugs, and his last remaining bomb had been once more returned to the earlier camp, practically nothing but the gold and precious stones remained in the gallery. Elaine was aware the trinkets were lying there on view, but so vast was her relief at the vanishment of danger—though it might be temporarily only—she had no desire for gauds and baubles, and no particular curiosity respecting their worth or appearance.

Indeed, these two had endured too much to dwell upon jewels and gold. They were free from menace for a time, but—the future still loomed before them, inimical and obscure. Their life in this tropic exile was still to be faced, day after day.

That morning and long sweet afternoon, however, they passed in restful inactivity, possessed by ineffable thankfulness and a sense of relief that was utterly relaxing to their racked and exhausted nerves. It seemed a strange, impossible state, this peacefulness, security, and freedom to move about once more, alone in their Shalimar. And Grenville knew it was far too good to last.

Yet for several days it seemed as if the propitiating Fates made every possible endeavor to erase from the tablets of their memory all records of the agonies and apprehensions they had recently undergone.

They were wonderful days, for sheer inspiriting beauty. A cool, spicy breeze was wafted, with the sunshine, across the smiling ocean. The jungle was redolent of fragrances of intoxicating sweetness. Down on the beach her leafy bower once more found Elaine idly resting in her hammock, or busily preparing a tempting repast from the once more generous larder.

The girdle of gold she continued to wear in happiness that stole unbidden to her heart—a happiness as subtle and welcome as the perfumes that stole to her senses on the breeze. And when she finally found and plucked a solitary lotus blossom, floating near the estuary's edge, it seemed as if the ecstasy possessing all her nature must bring about some miracle of untold joy and bliss.

Grenville was hardly less transported by the hourly pleasures that day and night alike seemed bearing to this island world, like argosies from Eden. Subconsciously, beneath it all, he knew the boats that had sailed away would one day return, perhaps with more of their species, and better prepared for a swift and merciless revenge. Yet even then he was slow to employ his wits and energies to prepare for another siege, his disinclination for more revolting ordeals casting a lethargy on all his fighting attributes, while days like these, voluptuously serene and toxicant, suggested vast contentment to his spirit.

Indeed, his spirit as well as his body needed rest. To this he was constantly urged by Elaine, who understood, far better than himself, how unsparingly he had drained the vital essences of his being through all these uncounted weeks.

She, too, was aware they were only secure for a moment, that untold dangers must be lurking just beyond the rim of their purple horizon. She had finally learned from Sidney's lips how the vessels had sailed away. She had, however, seen this sign of security previously fail—and felt it would fail again.

The future her soul avoided. Darkness and tragedy were only too readily imagined. At best it was all uncertain, rife with shadows, peopled with ghosts of doubt and haunting dreads. Meantime, their own green Shalimar was once more fresh with sunny smiles that enticed her spirit to song.

She sang to herself through many hours of joyous "household" duties. The songs she chose were happy little fragments wherein she imagined Grenville set, with herself always traipsing at his side. She sang her songs to and of him, watching him shyly when he was near, and sending her thoughts to seek him out when he hunted or wandered in the jungle.

It was not until one of those incomparable mornings, with the tropic greenery fresh as a breath over clover, that he finally heard the notes she had prisoned in her bosom break forth in clear, sweet utterance, as crystal bright as the sun.

He paused in the screen of ferns and palms to partake of her wild, sweet rapture. And how lightly and gladly she sang!

> *"Come out, come out, my dearestdear,*
> *Come out and greet the sun!*
> *The birds awake on tree and brake,*
> *The merry May's begun!*
>
> *"Come out and drink the diamond dew,*
> *Come out and tread the lea!*
> *The world is all awake, and you*
> *Are all the world to me!"*

All that was starved in his nature stirred in response to the song. His blood leaped faster, its glow like that of rich and sense-delighting wine. A vivid memory of the one lawless kiss he had dared to snatch from Elaine's red lips inflamed a sweet desire.

He had called her his sweetheart, called her his mate, for the frenzy of joy, the ecstasy, her nature had wrought upon his own. He felt to-day his claim had been proved, by their life alone with God. They had worked and fought and planned the days away together, like a mated pair fresh created and cast to an Eden of the sea. They belonged to one another.

Love had come at last to Elaine—a love to match the strength and purpose of his own—a love overwhelming, natural, unabashed—was their rightful heritage. Its holiness gave it sanction; its rightness made it as pure as fire that makes hard metal molten.

He started slowly towards the hill whereon Elaine was busied. He halted, however, hidden from view by a new banana foliage, wondrously unrolling. Another song was floating on the air.

> *"Pale hands I loved, upon the Shalimar,*
> *Where are you now? Who lies beneath thy spell?*
> *Whom do you lead on rapture's roadway jar*
> *Before you agonize them, in farewell?*

> *"Pale hands I loved, upon the Shalimar,*
> *Where are you now? Where are you now?"*

The mad intoxication of his senses rocked him strangely, there in the thicket. He saw the gleam of the jeweled girdle that spanned Elaine's lithe figure, as she moved about on the brink of the terrace above. Once again his heart struck mightily against its walls, as it had the first day she had worn this gold, by way of a maid's confession.

He knew at last her Shalimar was a wild little garden of love, to be sacredly shared between them. Excited to trembling he started again to join her at the cavern. Before he could come to the foot of the trail she suddenly ran to the terrace-edge, looking down like a vision of despair.

"Sidney!" she cried, "another Dyak boat! I've just this minute seen the sail!"

Ready to curse the merciless Fates, as well as his own recent laziness, which had made calamity possible, Grenville ran swiftly up the mended trail and followed Elaine to the tree.

The sail was certainly plain enough to see, far out in the purple waters. It was, to all appearances, bearing directly down upon the island. But, as Grenville watched, it altered shape. His face showed a sign of relaxing.

"I don't believe it's a Dyak craft," he told her, hoarsely. "It looks like—— I think it's a yacht."

CHAPTER XLV

THE LAST BOMB

It certainly was a modern yacht that the two of them saw, straining their eyes to identify the stranger roving afar in their waters.

A trick of the sun, or perhaps her paint, had concealed both masts and funnel for a time, presenting only a rakish angle of her prow and quarter, incredibly like a sail of the shape the Dyaks employ.

But, if eager excitement surged uninterruptedly through the pulses of the two ragged exiles, there on the barren headland, the bitterness of vain disappointments promptly began their inroads to its centers. The yacht was not only in great apparent haste, but was heading far off to the eastward, with not the slightest curiosity respecting the tiny island of whom no one could give a good report.

The flagpole was gone—and a new one had been neglected. There was no time now to erect another, as Grenville realized. He stood with Elaine on the brink of the rock, frantically waving his arms and cap, and even a large banana leaf, while the slender distant visitor came abreast them and continued straight ahead.

"They've got to see! They've got to!" he cried, in the desperate plight of mind begotten by this promise thus mercilessly snatched away.

Suddenly abandoning all other possible devices, he ran to his powder "magazine," where the last of the bombs was stored. He came with it hugged against his breast, in thoughtless and dangerous proximity to the firebrand clutched in his fist.

"Run back!" he said. "I haven't time to make it thoroughly safe!"

But Elaine remained to see him lower it down on the broken rocks, where the cave had formerly existed. She waited, indeed, till he lighted the fuse and drew her away towards the shelter.

His eyes were on the distant yacht, fast fading once more from their vision. The bomb must have failed. The fuse was deficient, he was sure. He started back to recover the thing and make it certain of explosion.

Then it burst, and flung shattered fragments along all the face of the wall.

Grenville was watching the distant yacht with fixed, almost frenzied, expression.

"They haven't heard!" he groaned, despairingly. "They're going faster than before!"

It certainly seemed as if the hurried stranger would no more halt than would a fiery meteor overdue at some cosmic appointment.

Then of a sudden, from its bow, broke a pure-white cloud of smoke. She had answered with the small brass piece employed to fire a salute. Her prow was turned before the sound came dully across the waters. Sobbing and laughing together, in sudden relief, Elaine sank down on her knees, among the bowlders, to watch this deliverance come.

CHAPTER XLVI

A GIFT REFUSED

The yacht was the "Petrel," luxurious hobby of Sir Myles Kemp, diverted from her homeward course by the merest whim of her owner to run up northward for a day while Sir Myles should inspect the rubber plantation and estate of his old fellow-officer, Captain Williams, who was not even present at the place.

The inspection was never made. The utter amazement occasioned by the chance discovery of the exiles of Three-Hill Island, plus their story of its fateful occupation, completely overshadowed all else in the minds of the "Petrel's" commander and crew, whose one idea was to assist the castaways home with the greatest speed of which steel and steam were capable. The picture the pair presented as they came aboard—Elaine amazingly tattered, a supple, tanned, incredibly sweet and womanly little figure—Grenville, a bearded, active master of the wild, clad in the skin of a cheeta for a coat, and bearing a richly colored tiger-skin, rolled up to contain a hundredweight of treasure—was one that Sir Myles was destined never to forget. He was likewise always destined to misunderstand the emotions with which, as they steamed away at last, Elaine looked back, with tears in her eyes, at the unpeopled Isle of Shalimar, so green in its purple setting, presenting its headland to the sea with that lone tree reared above its summit.

Grenville, too, had seen her eyes—and he more nearly comprehended.

By great good-fortune much of Lady Kemp's wardrobe had been left aboard the yacht. She and Elaine must have been of a size, to judge from the manner in which her yachting apparel and her dainty boudoir adjusted themselves to the form of the girl whom Sir Myles began forthwith to treat as he might a daughter.

The "Petrel" was put about and headed for Colombo—the nearest port at which an Orient steamer would be likely to be encountered. It was not until after dinner had been served and his guests had been made as thoroughly comfortable as warm-hearted hospitality, admiration for the two of them, and exceptional thoughtfulness could compass that Sir Myles related the accepted fate of the "Inca," from the wreck of which they escaped.

The news had gone forth that she foundered, and not a soul was saved. A few insignificant pieces of wreckage had been found afloat, far from the unknown ledge of rock the earthquake had lifted in the sea, but no one till now had heard so much as a theory as to what had been her fate.

That some such intelligence must have been sent to the worried and waiting relatives and friends beyond the seas, both Grenville and Elaine had long before comprehended, despite the preoccupation engrossing their minds all these many age-long weeks. But now, when at length they were homeward bound, the facts presented an aspect which there had been no occasion to prepare against while struggling for existence on the island.

There was one thought only in their minds. It was Fenton, and what he might have done when that news had expended its shock. And what would be the outcome of the story, now that the home-coming journey was resumed— now that he, Sidney Grenville, could at last complete and discharge his original commission?

He faced the business hardly more calmly than did Elaine. No argument possible to him now, respecting the warning Fenton had received, availed to allay and satisfy his haunting sense of honor. The man had matured on Shalimar, and his soul had been refined.

But what strange days those were that now succeeded! How they robbed him of his happiness, as they brought him nearer home! His spirits sank and would not rise, the nearer Colombo was approached. He told himself then, once he could wire, acquaint Gerald Fenton with the fact they were safe, and would soon be with him, he would come to some peace of mind.

But, when at length the wire was sent, he experienced no such relief. Relief, indeed, had failed to come when for three days and nights the Orient boat had been plowing across the Indian Ocean, rushing headlong from the tropic heat to the distant ports beyond.

He thought, perhaps, if he informed Elaine, the business would be settled.

He attempted that day to introduce the subject, but in vain. Elaine was so sparklingly happy! He postponed the ordeal for the night.

The moon had returned to the skies again, bringing to the wanderers ineffable memories of other nights, when peace lay tranquilly fragrant on the world of their Shalimar. He detected its subtle influence on the ever-vivacious little woman who had shared his perils and his joys.

Elaine was softly thrilling to the spell of it all as she halted beside him, finally, on a strip of the deck abandoned to their uses. She felt that the atmosphere was overcharged, and wondered what might be impending. To still the pounding of her heart she leaned on the taffrail, ecstatically in touch with Grenville's arm. She spoke of the wonder of the night.

"Yes," drawled Grenville, in his old dry way, "great facilities here for manufacturing nights—— I wired Gerald from Colombo."

For a moment Elaine was puzzled by this wholly irrelevant remark. Then her heart began to rock uneasily.

"You—wired we were coming home?"

"Wired I was fetching you home, after unavoidable delay."

She recognized the difference between the way that she and he had expressed the principal fact. She felt herself, as it were, already surrendered to a man grown singularly foreign to her nature. It seemed to her incredible that Sidney and she should ever again be parted, or work out their several destinies in any manner save together—especially after all he had said and even done.

"Was that—all you said?" she asked him, faintly.

"No. I said I'd be best man—or something of the sort."

Elaine felt something leaden go down to the point of her heart.

"You wanted him to know that you had no idea—— You wanted Gerald to understand——" She could not finish her sentence. Her face was hotly flaming, but at least she could turn it away.

Grenville's voice was hard and strange.

"It was barely his right to know that we were coming. I could do no less, as you'll certainly agree."

His speeches were constrained, unnatural, as Elaine had instantly felt. Her own were scarcely less embarrassed—after all these months when their entire world had comprised themselves alone. It seemed a monstrous error that anything but free, unfettered companionship and candor should exist between them now.

"I know," she said. "Of course." She added, after a moment, "It seems so peculiar, that's all—to—resume as we were before."

He was looking at his fist, for no good reason in the world.

"It is what you have hoped for every day."

"To get away from the Dyaks—why, of course."

Another silence supervened. After three unsuccessful efforts at speech, Elaine at last found the voice and the courage for a question:

"Do you wish to be—best man?"

Grenville spread out his fingers, for further inspection.

"I probably shouldn't have suggested it otherwise."

She turned upon him impulsively. "Sidney, are you absolutely honest?"

"Oh, I wouldn't trouble old Diogenes to get out of his grave and look me up," he answered, in his customary spirit, "but I've got a faint idea what honor means."

How well she knew his various manners of evasion! Her heart was pounding furiously. She leaned with all her weight against the rail, as if for fear he must hear its clamorous confessions.

She had never been so excited in her life—or more courageous. Likewise she felt she possessed certain God-given rights that were poised at the brink of disaster. For a love like hers comes never lightly and is not to be lightly dismissed. Her utterance was difficult, but mastered.

"One night—in the smoke—on the island—when we might have died of thirst—and you came with water—— You remember what you said?"

"Concerning what?"

"Concerning—love."

He was gripping a stanchion fiercely; his fingers were white with the strain.

"Vaguely—— I think I was exhausted."

"Oh! you're not—you're not honest at all!" she suddenly exploded. "That day of the wreck—on the steamer—you know what you said to me then! And any man who has acted so nobly, so thoughtfully——"

He turned and gripped the small, soft hand by his coat-sleeve on the rail.

"Don't do it, little woman—don't do it!" he said, in a low voice, charged with passion. "You told me some stinging truths that day, and now—they're truer than ever!"

"I didn't!" she said, no longer master of her feelings. "I didn't tell the truth! I said I hated—said I loathed—— And you *said* I'd throw his ring in the sea—and you said you'd make me—like you—some—and you know that I couldn't help liking you now—when you've treated me so horribly all the time! And after everything we've done together——"

"Elaine!" he interrupted, hoarsely, "when did you throw away his ring?"

"After the tiger—the night I gave you the cap, and you acted so hatefully and mean! It bounced and went into the water."

He was white, and tremendously shaken, while gleams of incandescence burned deeply in his eyes. How he stayed the lawless impulse to take her to his arms he never knew. He dropped her hand and turned away, with a savage note of pain upon his lips.

"Good Heavens!" he said, "why don't you help me a little? I had no right then! I have no right now! ... I'm going to take you home to Fenton, if it's the very last act of my life!"

She, too, was white and trembling.

"I know what you mean—you *never* loved! You don't know the meaning of the word!"

"All right," he said. "We'll let it go at that."

"Oh, you're perfectly horrid!" she suddenly cried, the hot tears springing to her eyes. "I refuse to be taken back to Gerald! I refuse to have anything more to do with any selfish man in the world!"

She retreated a little towards the saloon, her two hands going swiftly to a gleaming band that all but spanned her waist.

"And there's your old girdle, with Gerald's ring, that you made me throw away!" she added, flinging the tiger's collar towards the sea.

It struck on a stanchion, bounded to the deck, and settled against a near-by chair. She waited a second, instantly ashamed, and longing to beg his forgiveness. But he leaned as before against the rail, his eyes still bent upon the water.

Weakly, with drooping spirits, Elaine retreated through an open door, still watching, in hopes he would turn and call her back. Then, stoutly suppressing her choking and pent emotions, she fled to the dismal comfort of her stateroom, and, falling face downward in her narrow berth, surrendered to the vast relief of sobbing.

CHAPTER XLVII

A FRIEND IN NEED

That one more shock of surprise could overtake the returning castaways before the final landing could be accomplished would have seemed incredible to either Grenville or Elaine—and yet it came.

They had spent a number of wretched days—days far more miserable and hope-destroying than any their dire experience had brought into being, as the mere result of that final scene enacted in the moonlight by the rail.

The steamer had touched in the night at some unimportant, outlying port of call to which no one had paid the tribute of interest usual on the sea. A single male passenger had boarded.

The man was Gerald Fenton. The message dispatched from Colombo had fetched him, post haste, to this midway ground for the meeting. But the meeting occurred in a manner wholly unexpected.

Like the wholly considerate gentleman he was, Fenton had made all preparations for removing the startling elements from the fact of his presence on the boat. Like so many of life's little schemings, however, the plans went all "aglee."

Elaine not only did not linger in her stateroom in the morning late enough to receive his note from the stewardess, but, when she hastened up to the topmost deck for her early morning exercise before the more lazy should appear, she literally ran into Fenton's arms at the head of the narrow stairs.

Her surprise could hardly have been greater. She recoiled from the contact automatically, before she had time to see who it was with whom she had collided. Then a note of astonishment broke from her lips as she halted, leadenly.

"Why—Gerald!" she managed to stammer, without the slightest hint of gladness in her tone. "Here?"

"Well, little girl!" he answered, smilingly; and, coming to her in his quiet way, he took her hands to greet her with a kiss.

A note of uncertainty forced itself to audible expression as she slightly retreated from his proffered caress and received it on her cheek.

"Well! well!" Fenton continued, "you're certainly fit—and brown! You couldn't have had the note I sent to break the news. I tried to give you warning."

"No," she said, constrainedly, "I've had no word. How did you get here—come aboard? I don't see how——— It took me so by surprise."

"I'm sorry," he said, his smile losing something of its brightness. "I boarded at midnight, when the steamer touched at Fargo. When I got Sid's wholly incredible wire that you were both safe and well and coming home ——— But how is the good old rascal?"

Elaine's constraint increased.

"Quite well, I believe—as far as I know."

"Isn't he with you, here on the boat, going home?"

"Oh, yes, he's on the steamer."

Fenton was groping, without a woman's intuitions, through the something he felt in the air.

"Don't you like him, Elaine?" he asked her, bluntly. "What's wrong?"

"Why—nothing's wrong," she answered, unconvincingly. "It's just the surprise of meeting you like this."

"I'm sorry," he said, as he had before, his eyes now entirely smileless. "I might have managed it better, I suppose——— Aren't you a little bit glad to see me?"

Elaine attempted a smile and a manner more cordial. "Of course—I'm delighted! But it takes me just a minute or so to realize it's really you."

"Never mind. Take your time," he told her, indulgently. "Perfect miracle, you know, that you and old Sid should have come through the wreck of the 'Inca'—the sole survivors of the accident—and lived out there—somewhere —on an island, I hear—and now be nearing home. I'm eager to hear the story."

"Yes," she agreed, "it doesn't seem real to me, now. It's more like a long, strange dream."

"I have only heard a little from the captain," he continued, forcing a conversation which he felt was wholly unspontaneous and hardly even

231

congenial.

"Naturally, all his information——"

She saw his eyes quickly brighten as his gaze went past her to the stairs.

"Sid!" he cried, moving swiftly forward; and Grenville appeared on the deck.

His face was suddenly reddened, beneath the veneer of tan. But the boyish joy with which he rushed for Fenton was a heartening thing to see.

The two simply gripped, with might and main, and hammered each other with one free hand apiece, and laughed, and called one another astonishing names till it seemed they might explode.

"You savage! You tough old Redskin!" Fenton finally managed to articulate, distinctly. "If it isn't yourself as big as life! And I want you to know I haven't made your fortune—not exactly—yet—but it's certain at last. And how about your winning my little girl? Speak up, you caveman of the —— Oh, Elaine!"

But Elaine had fled the scene.

That moment began the tug at the ties of friendship and the test of the souls of the three. It was not a time of happiness that thereupon ensued. Elaine avoided both the men as far as possible. Grenville alone seemed natural, and yet even his smiles were tinged with the artificial.

He was glad to relate their varied adventures—the tale of the perils through which they had finally won. But how much of it all Gerald Fenton really heard no man could with certainty tell.

Fenton was neither a self-conceited person nor a blind man, groping through life. Through the stem of his finely colored calabash he puffed many a thought, along with his fragrant tobacco fume, and revolved it in his brain.

Between certain lines of Grenville's story he read deep happenings. That Sidney had saved and preserved Elaine, and battled for her comfort and her very life, against all but overwhelming odds, was a fact that required no rehearsal.

Mere propinquity, as Fenton knew, has always been the match-maker incomparable, throughout the habited world. Add to the quite exceptional propinquity of a tropic-island existence a splendid and unfaltering heroism in Grenville, together with a mastery of every situation, months of daily service and devotion, and the rare good looks that Sidney had certainly developed— and what wonder Elaine should be changed?

The change in her bearing had struck him at once at the moment of their meeting by the stairs. He had never got past that since. When at length his course was clearly defined and his resolution firmly fixed, it still required skillful maneuvering on Fenton's part to manage the one little climax on which he finally determined.

But night, with her shadows, her softening moods, and her veiling ways of comfort, was an ally worthy of his trust. When he finally engineered the unsuspicious Grenville to the upper deck, where Elaine had already been enticed, evasion of the issue was done.

"It's amazing," said Fenton, in a pleasant, easy manner, "how I am becoming the talker of the crowd, when both you fond adventurers should be spilling out lectures by the mile. However, such is life." He paused for a moment, but the others did not speak.

"The genuine wonder of it all," he presently continued, "is seeing you both come back thus, safe and sound. I underwent my bit of grief when the news of the monstrous disaster finally arrived, as, of course, did many another. I thought I had lost the dearest friend and the—well, the dearest two friends—the dearest two beings in the world to me, in one huge cataclysm."

He paused once more and relighted his pipe. The flame of his match threw a rosy glow on the two set faces on either side of his position, as well as on his own. No one looked at anyone else, and the two still failed to answer.

"Well—here you both are!" the smoker resumed, crushing the match and throwing it away. "If I were to lose your love and friendship now—— But never mind that—I sha'n't! You were dead to me, both of you, all those months, and mourned rather poignantly. That's the point I want you both to understand—that I had accepted the fact of losing you both, forever."

Grenville slightly stirred, but did not speak. Elaine was clasping her hands in her lap and locking her fingers till they ached.

"Naturally," Fenton told them, quietly, "I conformed my thoughts to your demise, at last, as we all must do in actual cases. I adjusted my heart-strings, when I could, anew. Nobody else came into my life, to occupy your places, for nobody could. Yet I did adjust things as I've said. Well—now that brings us up to the point."

Grenville sank back against his seat, but restlessly leaned forward as before. Elaine alone remained absolutely motionless, rigid with attention, if not also with suppressed excitement at something she felt impending. Fenton thumbed at the glowing tobacco in his pipe.

"It appears to me," he continued, "all the circumstances I have mentioned being taken into consideration, that you two friends that I love so well have so many times saved one another's lives that no one living has the slightest right to think or to act as might have been the case if you had not passed so entirely from his ken, and his plans, and daily existence. His claims to your resurrected selves are—different, let us say, or secondary."

The silence that fell for a moment became acutely painful.

"That's all I'm really driving at, after all my long and labored preamble," Fenton concluded, deliberately rising and facing about to confront the pair on the bench. "I recognize certain inevitable things—and I know they're right—and the way the Almighty intended.... Don't let me lose my friends again.... Let's all be sensible.... I don't ask or expect to be loved the way you love one another—but I'd like to be old Gerald to you both."

He turned and went slowly down the narrow stairs, and his pipe trailed a spark behind him.

*   *   *   *   *

After a time, when Grenville moved over and placed his arm about Elaine, she struggled for a moment, feebly.

"I don't—I don't love you in the least!" she protested. "I hate you—as I always have—and the way I always shall!"

Her arms went swiftly about his neck, however, in a passionate, fierce little hug. She was laughing and crying together.

"All right," said Grenville, calmly. "That's the kind of hate I want."

He kissed her once on her upturned lips for every hour they had suffered.

THE END

Lightning Source UK Ltd.
Milton Keynes UK
UKHW010633240820
368739UK00001B/308